Trickle-Down Grace

A Short Story Collection

by
RICHARD P. PRINCE

Published by Author Academy Elite
PO Box 43, Powell, OH 43035
www.AuthorAcademyElite.com

Edited by Abigail Young Stressless Edits

Identifiers:
LCCN: 2019914940
ISBN: 978-1-64085-957-9 (paperback)
ISBN: 978-1-64085-958-6 (hardback)
ISBN: 978-1-64085-959-3 (ebook)

Available in paperback, hardback, e-book, and audiobook

Book design by JETLAUNCH. Cover design by Debbie O'Byrne.

**THIS WRITING IS DEDICATED
TO MY LOVING WIFE,
HELPMATE AND BEST FRIEND.**

TABLE OF CONTENTS

ECHOES FROM THE SHOUT-OUT

CHAPTER ONE

Troy Beckham got out of his truck, grabbed his toolbox, and headed toward his largest account. Cross Creek Assisted Living and Nursing Care facility was in a quiet part of town. There was the usual background noise of a peaceful morning—the drone of traffic and competing chirps from the birds. As he walked toward the south side of the building, mentally tallying the number of HVAC units he'd need to service before his next stop, another sound jumped into the mix—a raspy voice.

"Vince! Vince, come over here."

Troy was unsure where the voice was coming from. He was guessing a Vince must be in the area. He walked on, but again heard, "Vince, can't you hear me? Come on over here."

Vince, you better wake up and pay attention. He picked up his pace, and the call came again. Troy stopped and looked at a first-floor window about 75 feet away. It was the only open window in view, and an elderly man was leaning out of it.

"Son, come over here."

"Sir, are you trying to get my attention?"

"Yes, come around to my door."

"Let me drop these tools off in the back, and I will be right over."

"Fine," the man behind the window replied. "We have a lot to catch up on."

"Sure thing." The old guy was clearly confused. Troy thought perhaps he should chat with him and see what was on his mind, but he didn't want to get overinvolved. He moved on to the business at hand. He continued to the south end of the complex and dropped his tools in front of the compressor.

Troy then noticed Bart Collins, the administrative manager for Cross Creek, apparently heading for his office. "Bart, I have a question."

Bart turned and began walking toward him. "What's up, Troy?"

"I was walking on the north end and heard an older fellow holler out for a 'Vince,' but he was definitely referring to me."

"About the fifth window down?"

"Yeah, that's right."

"That would be Lester Corning, one of the residents. Extremely easygoing and loves to chat. He's actually related to my wife."

"Who's Vince?"

"Why don't you go ask him?"

That wasn't the response Troy was looking for. "Let me think about that. Right now, I need to complete this service call and keep you people content."

"We appreciate that. Stop by my office when you finish."

Troy recharged the unit, replaced a relay, and completed his inspection of the other air conditioners throughout the complex before taking his tools back to his vehicle, an old Honda Ridgeline that had seen better days. He started the pickup and had almost backed out when he remembered the elderly stranger and his appointment with Bart. This account was critical to his business, and if talking about an old man was part of it, well, so be it. He headed for Bart's office.

The door was ajar, but he tapped on it. Bart invited him in. He gave Troy a big smile. "Well, if it isn't Vince! Good to see you. Come on in."

"Please…" Troy sat on one of the leather office chairs, self-consciously dusting off his work pants. "Soon I won't even know my own name."

"I have some info for you. Vince was Lester's son."

"Was?"

"Yes. He was killed in Vietnam. 1967."

"Wow," Troy whispered. "Vietnam. How old is Mr. Corning?"

"That's confidential." Bart smiled. "Let's just say he's in his nineties."

Troy was thinking that Bart's family should be the ones indulging Lester Corning, yet he had been tagged by the old man as his long-lost son. "What do you know about Vince?"

"West Point graduate with an engineering degree. Commissioned into the infantry and served with the 173rd Airborne Brigade. He was killed in action—some place called Dak To—in 1967."

"Four years at West Point, busting his butt, all that education and training—wiped out just like that," Troy said.

"Well, do you want to meet Lester?"

"I'm not sure. If he thinks I'm his son, it seems deceptive, maybe even cruel, to string him along."

"Perhaps. However, I think it's OK to play along casually. Sometimes it's good just to listen. Give him a little encouragement and hang out for a while."

"Hang out" with a man in his nineties? Troy was struggling with the whole scenario. Was it right or disrespectful to Lester Corning? He had little free time as it was, and zero social life. Business came first, and he embraced that. Maybe he should just walk away and not get involved. Simply leave things alone. It was sad about Vince's death and the old man's situation, but it was not his concern. Could this somehow become a conflict of interest with the Cross Creek account? *What a mess.*

Bart made one more overture. "Cut him some slack. A quick visit and you may be all done. It's possible he may forget he ever met you and move on to other things. Anyway, I have two meetings this afternoon, and I'm not prepared."

Troy sensed the ball was back in his court. "I understand."

"Let me know, and thanks for even considering it."

Troy left the office and deliberately exited on the opposite side of the building to avoid the old man's location. He walked past the open veranda on the front of the complex and suddenly realized that Lester Corning wasn't going away. He was rocking in one of the big chairs on the porch.

"Vince, come over here." *Is this old guy stalking me?* Troy turned around and began walking toward Lester Corning.

"Good morning," he said.

"Good morning to you, son. Come on over and have a seat."

This was a slippery slope, but he recalled Bart's challenge "just to listen."

CHAPTER TWO

Troy shook hands with the old man. Lester, in spite of his age, clasped Troy's hand firmly and pulled him close for an embrace.

"Sit down and tell me about the army. Are they making any progress on your promotion?"

Just listen, my butt. This old guy is going to engage in conversation and want some feedback. Troy thought that his feedback could be labeled as fraud. He could be accused of being deceitful, have the Cross Creek administration call him out, and be removed from their service account. A lot of was flowing through his head, but he fabricated an answer to Lester's question that surprised himself: "My promotion is hung up in channels. My time will be up soon, and I may just get out of the army."

"Get out? You West Point ring knockers have the inside track for advancements." Lester was proving to be very perceptive. "If you leave the army, what will you do?"

"Well, I have been giving a lot of thought to starting a business."

"What sort of business? Hope it's something I can help out in. Do you need a loan?"

"I want to get into the heating and cooling business. I have enough money to get started." The puzzled look on Lester's face indicated he had no clue what he meant by heating and cooling. *How do I break it down for him, and how much detail is appropriate?*

"Oh, you mean HVAC." Troy was impressed. "Well, son, I have to get ready for our evening meal. They serve it at four o'clock, but we line up at three. I would have you stay and eat, but the meals are similar to army chow. Come back tomorrow, and let's discuss your business plans."

That was too easy. Hopefully this bridge has been crossed, and now I can burn it.

* * *

Troy headed to his truck as he checked his phone for messages. A text from Lisa. "Can't make dinner tonight, working late." Another vivid sign they were drifting apart. He and Lisa had been dating since high school, but their eight-year relationship was fading. He was OK with that.

The only time his blue-collar background fit in with Lisa and her pack of friends was when it came time to pick up the check for an evening outing. Their chatter about income and ladder-climbing always faded, and the elbows that bent easily enough while eating and drinking became rigid and unable to reach into wallets when it was time pay up. Troy knew some of them had maxed out their credit cards and were probably struggling to make minimum payments, yet they continued bantering about their professional achievements. Supposedly, no company could exist without their contributions, and their personal market demand continued to soar. But they still were caged in their cubicles, and most would never get out.

Troy had considered college—mechanical engineering—but hesitated at the last minute when the reality of the expense hit home. Accumulated debt was not how he planned to begin a career. Had he chosen the college route, maybe he would have fit in with Lisa's group, but … he didn't dwell on it. He and Lisa had taken different paths.

At 18, Troy had been offered a journeyman position with Clark and Black Heating and Cooling, in part thanks to Lisa's connections with Tommy Black. Troy learned quickly and was praised for his work. He acquired all the necessary certifications related to HVAC operations, but he soon realized he would not progress far above his tech status in that organization.

Tommy's son, Adam, had the Black surname, and that meant more than all of Troy's hard work. When he bothered to show up at Clark and Black headquarters, Adam drove a Torch Red Corvette and parked it in a prominent place for all to see. He was always rattled when Troy parked his battered Ridgeline right next to him. The inevitable memo would be generated, reminding employees to park in the rear of the building. But Troy's rebellion was always short-lived. He had a career trajectory and stuck to it. His tenure at Clark and Black lasted four years. Then, at age 22, Troy opened the doors of his own business.

In the beginning months, a storage unit functioned as his warehouse, the kitchen table as his office, and the Ridgeline as his commercial fleet. Troy was determined not to poach any of Clark and Black's customers. He decided to let the quality of his work decide his worth in marketplace. His plan succeeded.

As Troy's business grew, Lisa's career also advanced. Her trajectory was one of corporate success. Her goals came with a price—long hours, title flashing, butt smooching, and personal sacrifices. Striving for the next rung produced more competition within the confines of the organization than with her competitors on the street.

Troy was making his own sacrifices. He knew he generated his own paychecks, and no appointments on any given day meant he was unemployed with no income. He and Lisa were serving different tyrants. He had an advantage since his playing field was limited to the town of Decatur and the surrounding areas. He was aware of his competition and their tactics. Lisa faced a vast array of internal corporate challenges combined with the opposition of like corporations striving for supremacy in the marketplace. Taking no prisoners, they all clawed for dominance. Even though each day took its toll, Lisa's perseverance propelled her on. She was a trench fighter.

Four successive quarters of budget and quota bullseyes got the attention of the home office, and six months ago, the invitation had come. She interviewed well and received an offer from the home office. The package offered more authority, responsibilities, a corner office, and a slight boost in pay. It was adios to Decatur and Troy. He would never fit into the Chicago scene, so there was no use in discussing him moving with her. They had a short meeting. An embrace and a peck on the cheek was the culmination of growing up together and a multi-year link as a couple.

Now, Lisa was living four hours away with a new title and office. Troy had no desire to navigate the roads to Chicago and had yet to visit Lisa, although he knew Adam Black often made the trip in his Corvette. Photos of him and Lisa at exclusive dinners showed up on social media from time to time, and Troy knew that there was more than a professional relationship there.

Troy focused on his business and his new acquaintance, Lester Corning. The challenge to Troy became distinguish which entity was part-time. Which deserved all in?

CHAPTER THREE

Cross Creek was on Troy's radar again the next morning as he worked on a new proposal for Bart. He went to one of the file cabinets in his bedroom and pulled out the proposal, then sat down at the kitchen table to make some modifications. As he read it over, he was reminded of Lisa badgering him to go paperless with his business. She'd always rolled her eyes at the disorganized piles of receipts and invoices scattered around the house. But he didn't have time for scanning and uploading and organizing—there was real work to do out in the field.

He left for Cross Creek. After dropping the proposal off at Bart's office, he half-heartedly went to Lester's apartment. He didn't owe the old man anything, but here he was tapping on his door. He waited for a response. Nothing. He was about to leave when he heard, "Come on in!"

Troy entered the apartment and saw Lester sitting in a rocker, gazing out the window. "Good morning."

"Vince!" Lester turned around at the sound of his voice. "Wow, I thought you were coming this evening."

Troy didn't comment on the confusion. "I was in the area and wanted to check on you."

"That's great, son. Want some breakfast?"

Troy glanced at the tray of partially eaten food and declined. Lester seemed a little crestfallen. Troy was uncomfortable posing as Vince, but his heart was moved by the frail old man with the raspy voice. He felt sorry for Lester, and the issue of being proper and strictly honest seemed to pale in comparison to Lester's need for a son.

"Um, Dad, how are you feeling this morning?"

"Well, Vince, I was a little down this morning, but seeing you has been marvelous." *Marvelous.* He hadn't heard that term since grade school when he'd turned in his leaf collection to Mr. Snell, the science teacher.

They spent the next twenty minutes chatting, and then Troy's phone began lighting up with texts. He had service calls that couldn't wait.

"Dad, I got to be going."

"OK." Lester's eyes dropped, and he shuffled his feet. Troy patted him on the shoulder and Lester smiled, but Troy could see tears in his eyes.

The remainder of his workday was productive. Eight service calls, a new installation started, and an email from Lisa. She had found an apartment in downtown Chicago. She complained about the high rent but bragged that it was nearly six hundred square feet. It gave Troy a new perspective on his apartment.

That evening, he tolerated a frozen dinner, caught up on paperwork, took a stroll, and returned to collapse on his bed next to the file cabinets. Before he passed out, Troy mulled over a way to fit in a visit with Lester the next day. He felt compelled to see him again. Time spent with Lester seemed like time well spent.

Troy's visits to Cross Creek became more frequent. Occasionally, he would sign Lester out of the facility and they would take a ride in the country or a walk around a park, always culminating in a meal of hot dogs, milkshakes, or pizza. Lester never bothered about dietary restrictions. He usually ate about half his meal and packed the leftovers for later, but he polished off the milkshakes. The bond between the two men became stronger each time they met.

Lester had become Troy's social life. He didn't miss Lisa or the friends she had provided. Lester demanded less time and was more entertaining.

During their visits, Troy and Lester talked about nearly everything under the sun, but one area that was still untapped was Lester's occupational background. The real Vince would have known his father's profession, but Troy was in the dark and couldn't find a creative way to ask.

CHAPTER FOUR

Troy had taken a rare day off to take Lester to a local park. However, as they drove, Lester changed their plans.

"Let's stop by the high school and get in before the crowd," Lester said.

Troy was unprepared. "What school?"

"Don't be coy with me, son. You know perfectly well which school. If it helps, the one your mother and I retired from. All those years there, and you ask me what school. I worry about you at times. What is the army doing to you?"

"Sure thing, Dad. Which way do you want to go?"

"Where are we now?"

"Just outside Clanton."

Like a typical father addressing his son, Lester started giving directions. "Pick up 83 and head on down south to County Road 125, then turn left. Westbury is about 15 minutes from there." With that, Lester dozed off.

Perfect. He's asleep, and I'm headed for a school in Westbury. Troy was vaguely familiar with the route, and Westbury wasn't so large that he couldn't find a high school. He recalled seeing a school building on the south end of town. No need to search it.

They arrived at the outskirts of Westbury, and Troy kept going south. He found the school, and it was obvious the building was vacant. He nudged Lester. "We're here." *Hopefully, this is the right location.*

Lester awoke from his little snooze and looked at the building. "Westbury Consolidated Schools," he exclaimed. "Let's go in." He struggled with his seatbelt.

"It's summer break. No one's in there, and I'm sure it's locked up."

"Nonsense. Dan Proctor never locked the doors. If we have to, we can crawl in through a window." Lester couldn't even unbuckle the seatbelt, and here he was ready to pop in through a window and wander the school halls.

As they approached the main doors, Troy thought about the possibility of a security guard patrolling the property. However, the lobby windows were dark, and they couldn't see any movement inside. Troy gently tried the doors, walked down the front of the school, and attempted to enter through a service door. It was locked too. His elderly companion followed directly behind him.

"Let's try a window," Lester said.

"No, Dad. No windows. The building is secured." Troy hoped that would be the end of this escapade.

"Not if Dan Proctor's in charge. He always left the rear doors open. Follow me." Troy had a bad feeling about this. He followed Lester to the back of the school where they found a small overhead door.

"Reach down and try the handle. This was always our way in and out if we forgot our keys, which happened many times." Troy was sure it wouldn't work, but he reached down and feigned an attempt to lift the door. Even with his half-hearted tug, the door moved and got Lester's attention.

"Good. Now shove it all the way." Apprehensive, Troy lifted the door, and up it went. *Why is it unlocked? Is this a security oversight or a coincidence?* The door was open, and Lester calmly stepped inside. Troy took a deep breath.

Breaking news from local media. HVAC contractor and old man guilty of breaking and entering closed school facility. Perpetrator dupes old man to be his shill in crime. Posing as his son to gain his confidence. Nefarious young punk takes advantage of senior citizen. Mastermind loses all his business contracts as punishment.

Lester seemed to treat this as just another day at the office. The light from all the windows provided visibility as they walked the halls of the old school. As they moved down a long corridor, Troy glanced into each room, expecting confrontation at any moment. Lester also glanced around quite a bit, but he seemed to be looking for something. He was humming as they went along.

Then an interesting sign appeared on the dark wall. It read "Corning Coliseum" with an arrow pointing straight ahead. Troy forgot his apprehension, intrigued by the familiar name.

They walked to a staircase leading down into a huge lower area. Fortunately, there was enough natural light for them to descend the steps to the coliseum entrance. As they reached a large passageway, Troy saw a marker over the entrance. Its message sunk into the pit of his stomach.

You are entering the Vincent L. Corning Coliseum, dedicated to the memory of Vince Corning, Class of 1962. United States Military Academy, Class of 1966. Killed in action in Đắk Tô, South Vietnam, November 1967.

Troy went numb, but Lester was oblivious to it all and made no reference to the large plaque. "Son, remember your high school games here? Mom and I sat right over there." He pointed to a court-level section that appeared to be right behind where the teams would have been seated. Troy felt too awkward to even mention the commemoration sign just above them.

Lester continued to stare at the empty gymnasium. He was lost in memories only known to him. Troy saw the look in Lester's eyes and felt a surge of pity. The old man had lost so much, and the pain showed in every line of his wrinkled face. Tears pricked the corners of Troy's eyes, threatening to spill over. Fortunately, Lester broke the silence.

"Let's get going." He turned toward the steps and began the climb back to the main level. Troy walked behind him, one hand gripping Lester's arm and the other at the small of his back to steady him. When they reached the top of the stairwell, a voice challenged them.

"What are you people doing here?" Troy was blinded by the glare of a Tac light in his face. They were busted.

Lester spoke up. "I'm Mr. Corning, and this is my son. We are just arriving for the game."

"Sir, say that again?" The light dropped, and Troy could see a uniformed policeman.

Lester continued. "We're here for the game. We came early—wanted to get seated before that mob from Jackson arrived. Me and my boy. He used to play here before his army tour." Troy was trying to flash some signs at the deputy by waving his hand under his chin back and forth. The officer acknowledged it.

"You two are trespassing and have to leave immediately."

Lester, with the authoritative voice of a teacher confronting a student, said, "Son, what's your name?" Troy rolled his eyes. *I can't believe this is happening.*

"Deputy Arthur Watkins."

"Watkins. Is your daddy Benjamin Watkins?"

"No, sir, he was my grandfather. My father is Bernie Watkins. Let me ask the questions. Do you fellows have any ID on you?"

Troy reached for his wallet to pull out his driver's license, but Lester said, "Bennie was your grandfather? I had him in my biology class. Don't recall a Bernie Watkins."

"Officer, I can explain." Troy motioned for the officer to step aside with him and began speaking in a hushed tone. "I am Troy Beckham, and I live in Decatur. This gentleman is Lester Corning, also from Decatur. Lester is a resident at the Cross Creek care facility. It's all sort of jumbled up, but he thinks I am his son, Vince Corning, who was killed in Vietnam. I try to oblige him and do the roleplay of being his son. Nothing underhanded, just being a friend to him. I do have a signed day pass from Cross Creek giving me custody of Lester for the day. I just learned today that he is from Westbury and taught school in this building. That's why we are here, just a trot down memory lane for him and a look into his past for me. We never intended to be any trouble, and we will gladly vacate."

"How did you get in the building?"

Their quiet conversation wasn't unnoticed by Lester. "The usual way."

The officer scowled. "Excuse me, 'the usual way'? And what is the usual way?"

Troy intervened. "Lester, uh Dad, let me handle this." Troy again motioned for the deputy to step back a little from Lester. "There's an overhead door in the rear that wasn't secured. Evidently, it's been that way for years."

"Ok, we'll exit that way. You can show me the door, and then you two can be on your way off the premises. I am going to let this slide and give you a verbal warning. Do not ever break and enter this building again. You understand me?"

"Perfectly." Troy breathed a sigh of relief.

"So, you are posing as Vince Corning, the same Vince Corning the gymnasium is named after? Are you taking advantage of this man?"

"No sir, not in the least." The deputy looked at him with a hint of possibly believing him.

"And this fellow is Vince's father?"

"Yes."

They returned to the door where they had gained their unlawful entry, the deputy raised it up, bid them goodbye, and slammed the door down behind them. They could hear him attempting to lock it from the inside. Troy escorted Lester back to the truck and helped him with his seatbelt.

"That was fun, Vince. Good to take it all in again. Let's come back soon. I want to explore the whole building." Troy rolled his eyes, thinking *That's not going to happen!*

They drove back to Decatur, and Lester slept the entire trip. Troy stopped on the outskirts of town at the Dairy Palace. He entered the drive-through and ordered two milkshakes. He woke Lester when they arrived at Cross Creek. Lester beamed when he saw the shake. Troy escorted him back to his apartment and gave him a hug before Lester collapsed in his recliner. Now familiar with the routine, Troy removed Lester's shoes, tilted him back in the chair, and put the remainder of the shake in his refrigerator. *What a day. We're lucky that deputy was understanding. What a day.*

Troy returned home, reviewed some pending contracts, foraged some leftovers, and headed for the twin bed behind the file cabinets where he soon fell asleep. The gymnasium and the deputy lurked in his dreams.

CHAPTER FIVE

Troy's first appointment the next morning wasn't until ten, so he had time to drive to Cross Creek and check on Lester. As he approached Lester's apartment door, he noticed it was ajar. *The maid must be servicing the room.* He tapped on the door. "Dad, it's me."

"Please come in." The voice clearly wasn't Lester's. *Must be a maid or a nurse. Whoever it is, she has a sweet voice.* He pushed open the door.

"Son, look who just dropped by!" Troy looked across the room and became putty. Staring directly at him was the most compelling girl he had ever seen. Her green eyes penetrated his.

"Good morning, Vince." She winked at him with one of those emerald eyes. Troy muttered a faint acknowledgment and was lost for words. Then Lester informed them he was meeting his friend Carl for breakfast and would leave them alone to catch up. Troy wanted to keep him there, but Lester urged Troy to greet his wife and pick up his son. After Lester left, Troy stood still, gazing across the room. The more he looked at the girl, the more he was enthralled by her.

The young lady took control of the situation. "I am Leah, and this is Titus." Defying true motherly instincts, she got up and extended the child in her arms to the stranger in front of her. "Let's oblige Lester, and you can hold 'your son.' It's only to accommodate him short-term, nothing else." Leah offered Titus to him.

Troy accepted the child automatically. He had never held a baby, so he braced himself for the experience. As his mother released him, Titus reached out with his tiny hand and grasped Troy's index finger. Troy's knees felt rubbery, but he gained confidence as he cradled the child. He drew him up close for a gentle embrace and whispered, "Hey there, little guy." It didn't occur to him that he had yet to introduce himself to the child's mother. Her eyes were fixed on him, vigilant. Troy saw the look and handed the baby back to his mother. Transfer completed, he sat down in Lester's recliner.

He posed a question. "This is awkward, and please don't misunderstand me, but who are you?" Again, never introducing himself.

"I was wondering the same thing about you." Her look reminded Troy of the officer they'd encountered the day before. Piercing. But she was smiling at the same time. "Do you want the whole story or just the last chapter?" She didn't wait for a response. "I am the granddaughter of your alias, Vince Corning."

"No way."

"It's true. My mother was born to Grandma Cindy Crenshaw about ninety days after Grandpa Vince was killed in Vietnam. Grandpa's first assignment after West Point was Fort Benning, Georgia. My Grandma Cindy worked in one of the procurement centers at the post. She and Grandpa were involved right up to when he shipped out to Vietnam. They were in love, and even though there was no formal engagement, they planned to marry after his tour. Few knew of the depth of their relationship. They wrote each other every day while he was over there. Grandpa got a five-day leave, and they met in Hawaii, June 1967. My mom was conceived during their time there. Want to hear more?"

"Absolutely." Troy was hooked, and he hoped his interest would help shed his appearance of a con man targeting Lester. He was waiting for an opening to introduce himself.

"Grandpa Vince was aware that she was pregnant. Their correspondence indicated they would get married when he returned stateside. Then he was killed. Vince's side of the family wasn't informed of the baby. It was a disgrace, and my grandma's family covered it up."

"Did Lester and his wife ever learn of your mother's birth?"

"One of Grandpa's army friends contacted Lester. He wasn't aware of any secrecy in the matter and asked about the baby. This was about a year after Grandpa Vince was killed. Lester reacted quickly and traced his granddaughter and her mother back to Fort Benning, where she still worked. He reached out to her, but Vince's family was not welcomed by her parents. Her father was a local judge, the honorable Stanley Crenshaw; he had influence and knew how to use it. Eventually, resentment cooled down, and arrangements were made for the two families to meet."

Troy was amazed that Lester had never shared any of this with him. Had he forgotten it as he had forgotten his son's tragic death? "I can't imagine all the frustration and heartache for them. A lost son, a discovered granddaughter, and a maze of barriers constricting them."

"I try to stay neutral in matters of the past. I'm sure it was burdensome for them. It was compounded when my grandma got married."

"Whoa, a whole new set of family involvements."

"Yes. Grandma met an army officer at Benning. They got married right after my mom's fourth birthday. Brian was his name. Brian Hopkins, a career army officer."

"Where do your folks live now?"

"Mom still lives in the Benning area, across the border in Alabama. I lost my father two years ago to cancer."

"I am sorry to hear that." An alert popped up on Troy's phone, and he realized how long he'd stayed listening to Leah's story. He needed to hurry if he was going to make it to his appointment.

Leah said, "I must be keeping you from your busy day."

Troy went red in the face at her look of disapproval. He slipped his phone into his pocket and made an attempt to recover from his blunder.

"Not at all. It's been interesting." The morning had been full of bold moves, and he made one more. "Do you have any plans this evening? Maybe we can get together for a bite to eat?" Suddenly, it dawned on him that she was probably a married woman. He tried to recover. "I apologize. It never occurred to me that you might be married."

The green eyes cast a different glow. "No, I am not married and never have been. I've only known you for a few minutes, and you're asking me out?" Then she gave him her radiant smile again. "Give me your number, and we'll see if we can fit dinner into your busy schedule." Troy watched as the woman picked up her son, cradled him to her face, and whispered something in his ear. True, he had only known her for a few minutes, but he couldn't help thinking that those green eyes were windows into her soul, and he liked what he'd seen.

"I am staying with my Aunt Jodie and her husband, Bart. He works here at Cross Creek. I'll send you their address."

Troy fidgeted in the recliner. *Everyone is related to Bart and Jodie. Was this meeting all their idea? I wouldn't put it past them—not that I mind the results.* "Not necessary to send it; I know them. So, Jodie is your aunt?"

"Yes, she's my mom's younger sister. Well, half-sister, but we won't go into all of that." She steered the conversation to meeting later that evening.

"We can meet at seven o'clock. Then it will be your turn for the life narrative."

Troy knew his account would pale beside hers. He excused himself and headed to the lobby. As he walked, he tried to unravel all the twists and turns of Leah's lineage—a family tree that he had been artificially grafted into. He was fascinated with Leah. He realized he didn't even know her last name. He liked her air of confidence. He liked everything about her. She was quite a package.

CHAPTER SIX

The promised texts were exchanged, and Troy picked Leah up to take her to a family-style diner on the west edge of town. It was the local go-to for good food and a relaxed atmosphere. Good for talking. Jodie was watching Titus, so their conversation was uninterrupted.

It was Troy's turn to share his background. He got through it quickly, explaining that he was committed to his business, terrible at organization, and at the end of a long and unfulfilling relationship with Lisa. He elaborated on his time spent with Lester and the respect he had for him. He was deliberately fast-forwarding through most of his story—he wanted to know more about Leah.

Once they received their food, Leah was ready to open up. "I met this guy in my junior year in college. Initially he was respectful, considerate, and we really hit it off. I got caught up in all his hyperbole and believed his lies. We toyed with the idea of getting married. He painted a grand future for us as a couple. He convinced me that we would spend a lot of time near the ocean at his parents' summer home. We would have a condo in New Orleans while he went to law school and joined his father's law firm. Success and bliss—that's what we'd have."

Troy hated this guy already. He couldn't help asking his name.

Lisa grinned. "Hunter Smith-Spangler III."

Troy couldn't avoid a smug smile. Spangler would have dovetailed with Lisa's crowd very well.

"One morning, I informed him that I was pregnant, and that jump-started his transformation. The pompous ass shed his sheep garb, and his true inner self came out." Troy knew the next step with Spangler's kind. *He probably denied the pregnancy and questioned her fidelity.*

"He accused me of seeing others, and he said the child couldn't be his. Naturally, I was hurt, but his true character had surfaced. Mistakes had been made, and I took ownership. I vowed not to pursue any of it and distance myself from him. Hunter bolted to his parents' summer home. There was no more communication between us. Titus was born, and I never informed his father. Watch it—your food's getting cold."

Troy realized he hadn't taken a single bite of his dinner. He had a heart for this girl—and a sudden urge for a smackdown with Hunter III. He managed to take a few bites of his burger as he listened.

"True relational people, including my mother, encouraged me to remain in school. I completed my degree in software engineering. I was fortunate to get some attractive career offers, but I accepted the one here in Decatur with Bricker and Kulina. They're developing a startup, and the sky's the limit for growth." Troy knew the firm and had applied for their service contract. "My mother liked the fact that Bart and Jodie were here, and then there was Great-Grandpa Lester. Incidentally, we share the same last name. Grandma gave my mother the Corning name, and it was passed on."

Troy was full of questions, but he knew they could be clarified at another time. It was a convenient excuse for more outings with Leah.

*　*　*

The months passed, and Troy and Leah became a couple. The two workaholics made time for each other. Troy dreamed of a possible future with her, but he kept quiet for the time being. Troy never mentioned Hunter Smith-Spangler III's name, but he still thought about smacking him. Leah was curious about Lisa and asked about her from time to time in subtle ways, but Troy was casual in his responses. Titus became a part of Troy's life. He never forgot the baby reaching for his finger when they first met. Then there was Lester, isolated from all social entanglements, who was content to have them in his life. He wasn't concerned about the fractured genealogy—he was just glad to see Vince and his family. They kept going for regular outings, and they always ordered three milkshakes.

The situation at the software startup was a perfect fit for Leah. Modern technology combined with contemporary management. There were few walls in the building—it was a place of open communication, and all were committed for achievements. Leah stood out in a good way. She shared in the forward progression of the company. She also had time for an HVAC contractor who had never gotten around to digitizing his paperwork. They spent many evenings sorting through stacks of documents, taking breaks now and then to sit out on the balcony and admire a sunset or prepare a meal in the tiny kitchen.

Leah signed a lease on an apartment near Cross Creek, across town from Troy's place. She and her mother, Rebecca, worked out the details of getting her things up to Decatur. Rebecca secured a box truck, got it packed, and navigated up north to Leah's new residence. Leah warned Troy that her mother would be shaking him down, military style. Ever since Leah's disastrous relationship with Spangler, Rebecca had disliked any man who had an interest in her daughter. She was fiercely protective and had her daughter's back.

CHAPTER SEVEN

Leah's mother arrived on a Saturday afternoon. Troy and Leah met her at the apartment complex, and quick introductions were made. Rebecca eyed Troy up and down, and he was aware of the scrutiny. He, in turn, saw Leah's looks and traits in her mother. She was all business and had no time for idle chatter. Troy knew he'd have to wait for an opening to share about his feelings for Leah.

The mother-daughter kinship was confirmed when Rebecca deftly backed the 15-foot box van into a single parking place between two parked cars, perfectly aligned for unloading. He thanked himself for not offering to back the truck in for her—that would have been a huge mistake. She was in control. When the truck door was rolled up, he saw that it was packed perfectly, like interlocking bricks.

He started the process of unloading, with both women giving him frequent reminders to be careful with each box. Troy smiled and nodded at each remark. Mother and daughter were definitely linked. He knew he had to build his own link to Rebecca.

The truck's contents began moving toward Leah's second-floor unit. Bart and Jodie arrived 45 minutes later with Titus. Rebecca relinquished her supervisory role to cuddle her grandson. The momentum continued. Leah's stuff kept making its way up the steps. Fortunately for Troy, Bart was in reasonable shape. He helped with the heavy lifting of the sofa, loveseat, and other bulky pieces. The empty two-bedroom apartment had seemed cavernous when they started but quickly filled up. Troy appreciated bedrooms without file cabinets cluttering the pathways.

When the truck was empty and ready to be returned to the local rental center, Troy offered to follow Rebecca over and bring her back. On the way back, Troy drove her past Cross Creek, indicating that this was where Lester lived and pointing out Bart's office.

When they arrived back at the apartment, they saw pizzas had been delivered and a trail cleared through the apartment. The pizzas were devoured amid scattered conversation.

Leah opted to stay in her place that night, despite the mess, and Rebecca went home with Bart and Jodie. Before leaving, she thanked Troy for his help, but she kept looking him straight in the eye with the same piercing stare her daughter often pinned him with. It was clearly implied that he should be leaving as well. Leah saw the exchange and intervened, explaining that Troy would stay behind to help with a few things, but he would leave at an appropriate time. Rebecca, partially satisfied, left the apartment.

Troy helped Leah assemble her bed, program the TV sets, and clear an area in the family room. When they were finished, he dropped onto the couch next to her.

"Girl, am I tired. But it's a good tired."

"I feel the same." She leaned over and kissed him on the cheek. "What do you think of my mother?"

"She can handle a truck. She's pretty cool, and a lot like you."

"Good answer." Leah's green eyes said the rest. She drew closer to him, and Troy put his arm around her. It was perfect—until Titus interrupted the blissful moment, disturbed by his unfamiliar surroundings. He needed his mother. Leah knew it and didn't hesitate. She urged Troy out the door, thanked him for his help, and gave him a parting kiss. As she closed the door, she whispered, "I love you." Long after the door shut, Troy stood in the hallway staring at it, repeating the same words under his breath.

As Troy drove back to his apartment, he pumped his fist in the air at least a dozen times. He was tired and full of pizza—but smitten. Restlessness kicked in, and he couldn't relax. He read briefly, scanned some paperwork, and lay in bed staring at the file cabinets. Finally, at 2:30 a.m., he gave into his impulse and called Leah.

It only rang once. She picked up and whispered, "Hi, Troy."

"Leah, sorry to call so late, but I need to talk to you."

"What's up? Is something wrong?"

"This is awkward, but it's coming from the heart. I love you, and I want you to be my wife."

"Oh, is that all? You want to get married?" There was a pause, and then she whispered, "Yes, I accept. But it's late. Let's talk more in the morning. Good night, Troy."

He couldn't believe it. She had accepted. He jumped from the chair and fist-pumped the ceiling. "Yes, Yes, *Yes!*" He fell back onto the bed and closed his eyes. He prayed and then reflected on the six months he had known Leah. Some might perceive they were rushing into a possible storm. He saw it differently.

The next day was Sunday. No work schedule—a time for rest. Troy always made it a point to pick Lester up for church since he preferred a real church service over the groups that visited Cross Creek, and Leah had been coming with them. Lester went to the senior adult Sunday school while Troy and Leah dropped Titus off at the nursery and headed for their young adult fellowship class. They kept their late-night conversation to themselves, but Troy suspected their frequent glances at each other drew some attention from observers.

After the service, they took Lester to his favorite pancake spot and then dropped him off at Cross Creek. Titus was left with Grandma Rebecca. Troy and Leah drove to their favorite getaway, the echoes of their 2:30 a.m. chat ringing in their ears.

CHAPTER EIGHT

Troy drove to the entrance of Rocky Bottom State Park. They parked and walked along one of the trails for over half a mile and climbed the bank of a knoll to a grassy crest that overlooked Rocky Bottom River. They knew the exact spot they wanted and claimed it. They sat down very close to each other, and for a long while, no words were spoken.

Troy broke the silence. "There are two things I need to do."

"And what are those two things?"

"I need to buy you a ring and then have a nice talk with your mother."

"Maybe you should reverse the order and talk to my mother first. If she objects, you can put the ring money toward a newer truck." Leah gave him a playful poke in the ribs.

"The way I feel about you—I can overcome any of her objections. And since I do drive the Ridgeline, I'll have money for a ring." He returned the poke in the ribs. It was quiet again, and they spent the rest of their time watching and listening to the gentle flow of the river.

Fifteen minutes later, they left to pick Titus up. As they drove, Troy mulled over his words for Leah's mother. He was exhausted from yesterday's moving and lack of sleep, but he was determined in his mission. He would attain Rebecca's blessing.

They pulled up in front of Bart and Jodie's house. Leah got out, but Troy remained in the car.

"Are you coming?"

"Sure, give me a second."

"Are you OK?"

"I need some time to think." Leah gave him a look, got out of the car, and went into the house. Troy got his thinking programmed and joined the others. He found them all in the family room. He went for it.

"Ms. Rebecca, can I speak to you in private?" All eyes fixed on him, then on Rebecca.

"Right now?"

"Yes, ma'am, if you please."

"Certainly. Excuse me, folks." She gave Leah a look but walked out to the front porch with Troy.

Troy kept up his momentum. "I've asked your daughter to marry me. She has agreed, and we both want your blessing." Fortunately, Rebecca had her iced tea in a paper cup, because it dropped to the floor. She stumbled backward and managed to sit down on a chair.

Rebecca looked over the young man she had met only yesterday. "Troy, I recently lost my husband, then embraced and encouraged my daughter through her unwanted pregnancy. Grief for my husband turned to anger toward that scum that deserted Leah. I silently watched as Leah relocated up here. Now you tell me you want to marry her." She looked directly at Troy.

He answered her as best he knew how. "I am sorry for all you have been through. Your resilience is impressive. I can only say that I will be the husband Leah is entitled to have and be the father Titus deserves."

Rebecca was silent for several long moments, and Troy saw tears gathering in her eyes. "For some reason, I believe you. Yes, I approve of you marrying Leah." She got up and walked toward Troy, extending her hands to him. He tenderly held her hands in his. After a minute of silence, they walked back into the house.

Rebecca's voice was choked. "Leah, Leah, Leah. I am so happy for all three of you."

Bart and Jodie were quick on the uptake. Jodie began tearing up like the others. "Oh, my goodness, this is so unbelievable." The three ladies came together and embraced. Bart stood up and approached Troy to shake his hand. Titus was fast asleep on the couch, but there was a little smile on his face.

* * *

Troy and Leah picked out a ring, and the old pickup survived. Their next step was to contact Troy's pastor, inform him of their plans, and arrange premarital counseling.

Pastor Jim obliged them, and his minimum of six 90-minute sessions were scheduled. He always reserved the right to extend the number of meetings or cancel them altogether. If he thought a couple was on the wrong track, he would tell them to reconsider the entire arrangement. His method was based on the ordinance of marriage and biblical teachings. He supported all the Bible's ground rules. The sessions went well, and the pastor was impressed with their maturity. The wedding plans went forward.

Troy's parents were surprised at their son's engagement. They'd anticipated that he would remain a bachelor for some time, and the breakup with Lisa had seemed to guarantee it. Both of them figured his business would continue to be his primary ambition, and his home would forever be in chaos. Now they were gaining a daughter-in-law and a grandson.

The wedding date drew near. Plans and more plans were reviewed; those that passed muster were put into place. The ladies knew what they wanted and kept moving forward. Leah chose her maid of honor and bridesmaids, and then it was up to Troy to decide who would be his best man.

CHAPTER NINE

Troy pondered the choice of best man, but he eventually surrendered to his gut feeling. He wanted Lester Corning. *Perhaps it's slightly unconventional, but who cares about conventional anyway?* Lester had been the reason he and Leah met in the first place. Troy knew Lester might question the arrangement, as he considered them already married, but he took a gamble and asked Lester to be his best man. Lester's immediate acceptance said it all—he didn't ask any questions. Troy was satisfied, and the deal was done.

Troy upheld his vow of never inquiring about Leah's past and Titus's father. He loved both of them, and that abolished any judgment. Leah, however, made a pointed comment about Lisa and the fact that she was coming to the wedding. Troy explained that Lisa had invited herself. She had implied she had to be present, and she was bringing another uninvited guest. Troy expected that she would be bringing Adam Black in his newest Corvette. He chose to downplay the whole thing. It would be an excuse to showcase his future wife.

The wedding day arrived, and the ceremony was smooth—with one happy distraction. A lot of focus was on the best man. Lester Corning was dignified in his attire, and he broadcast a huge smile as he escorted the maid of honor up the aisle. Lester was a little fragile, but his escort had a firm grip on him. She was tactful about it, and few people noticed.

Jim Cowan performed the ceremony and introduced Mr. and Mrs. Troy Beckham to the assembled guests. As the guests filed through the receiving line and into the reception venue, Troy noticed Lisa had not been present. Perhaps it was for the best that she and her escort were no-shows. Adam had always been a bit snarky.

Then the best man made his center-court appearance. Once the band got jumping, Lester got jumping. He headed for the center of the dance floor. He was slow, but moved to the rhythm. The bride and groom got behind him just in case he began to wobble.

The whirling dance of a man born before Prohibition was new to most of the group, but soon everyone was clapping in unison. Leah joined him, and her mother and grandmother were right behind her—three generations of ladies clapping and circling a man that they all loved.

They were amazed at Lester's endurance, but after a while he tired, and they escorted him back to his table. Lester indicated he was a little warm, so Troy loosened his bow tie and shirt collar and walked him to an open window.

As they got closer to the window, Troy heard the unmistakable roar of a pair of Harley motorcycles throttling down and circling the parking lot. *Cool rides.* His wife joined him at the window.

He watched as the two riders, both decked out in leathers, dismounted the bikes and came toward the reception hall entrance. It was a big man and a petite lady.

"They must be lost," he said to Leah. They got closer, and the lady rider removed her helmet. "Uh-oh."

"What's that mean?"

"Nothing much. It's just Lisa and, I guess, some biker dude." Not Adam. The guests watched as the Harley couple came in and approached Troy and Leah.

"Hi, I'm Lisa, and this is my fiancé, Ansel," she said, extending a hand to Leah. "Congratulations to both of you." She turned and winked at Troy.

"Thank you." Leah was surveying Ansel closely. He was a big man, heavily bearded, with some interesting tattoos that were crowding each other for territorial rights on his skin.

Troy stepped up to them. "Ansel, I am Troy Beckham. This is my wife, Leah. Thanks for coming." *So, this is Adam's successor. Not what I would have expected, to say the least.*

"Sorry we missed the ceremony," Lisa said. "Ansel had an emergency appointment with one of his patients. His brother's mare delivered a foal late last night and needed Ansel's help. The little guy was born around four o'clock this morning." She glanced around at her listeners' confused faces and laughed. "Ansel is a veterinarian. Works with everything from kittens to horses."

"Well, I wouldn't have guessed it. Here—sit down and get some food." Troy turned around and looked at his bride, shrugging his shoulders. *This is unreal.*

The day's festivities drew to a close, and the guests began leaving. Troy declined Lisa's invitation to ride on the back of her Harley; Ansel made the same suggestion to Leah, who likewise refused. Goodbyes were spoken, and the two bikers roared off into the evening. Troy looked at his wife.

"Lisa hasn't changed one bit—still unpredictable—but she looked happy with that Ansel. Let's get out of here."

"I'm ready, but let's drop off your best man first." They took Lester back to Cross Creek. The drained dancing machine slept all the way back to his place. Troy helped him to his room, plopped him down, patted his head, removed his dancing shoes, and left.

*   *   *

Work commitments for both of the newlyweds dictated a brief honeymoon. Troy promised Leah an extended trip in the fall, this time with Titus.

They arrived back in Decatur late Sunday evening, picked Titus up from Rebecca, and went to their apartment. Troy checked his calendar on his laptop (something else Leah had helped him with) and saw he had an opening early in the morning. He would use that time to drop in on Lester. Leah suggested they take him out for supper that evening. The newlyweds put their son to bed and headed for their bedroom.

Troy stopped by Cross Creek the next morning to see his best man and they made plans for that evening. Lester remained in his recliner and didn't see Troy to the door. He seemed unusually quiet. *I'll have to ask him about that tonight.*

CHAPTER TEN

Lester remained in his chair for some time after Troy took his leave. The old man felt extremely tired, but he had two tasks to complete. He knew that tonight was the final home game of the season over in Corning Coliseum. It would be a classic.

Lester forced himself to get up from the recliner. He then pulled two pieces of paper from his kitchen drawer, sat down at his breakfast nook, and began writing. When he finished, he put the notes in an envelope and placed it on top of his recliner. It was the most conspicuous place in the room. Next, he contacted Mercury Cab Company and ordered a ride to Westbury.

The cab arrived on schedule. Lester discreetly left the complex, climbed into the backseat and asked to be taken to the high school building in Westbury. The driver plugged the location into his GPS, and they were on their way. They chatted the whole trip, and the driver had plenty of questions. When they arrived, the building was obviously vacant.

"Sir, are you sure this is the correct location?"

"Yes, this is it. I'm meeting some friends here for the basketball game." Lester viewed the meter and handed the driver the fare, complete with a generous tip. He thanked the driver and exited the cab, hardly listening to the man's well wishes before shutting the door and letting the taxi drive away.

Lester plodded along the side of the building back to the familiar overhead door. He gripped it with both hands and lifted it up. Deputy Watkins had neglected to secure it. The natural light gave Lester enough visibility to navigate the halls and make his way to the Vincent L. Corning Coliseum. He pushed open the main door and shuffled across the gym floor to the familiar seats two rows up from the home team bench. Climbing the short incline to the seats, he looked up at the rafters of the gym and became absorbed in memories. As he got closer to his personal seats, he felt weak and dizzy. Lester caught his breath, turned to face the court, and slowly lowered himself onto the old wooden bleacher, seat 16 C.

He heard the cheering of the crowd and the foot stomping after a game-winning basket. The chant of *Vince, Vince, Vince* echoed in his ears. His son had once again led them to victory. He closed his eyes and leaned back against the bleacher behind him. He trembled slightly and then was still. The final home game was over. God had called him home. The perfect victory was now in place. The echoes in the coliseum had ended, but the cheering resonated far beyond the rafters, reaching up to the heavens.

* * *

Deputy Watkins was sitting in his patrol car watching an unusually boring Westbury intersection when a cab pulled up alongside him. The driver was uneasy about a passenger he'd just dropped off at the old high school. Watkins showed no surprise. He'd expected Lester Corning would come back. He obtained some further information from the driver and thanked him before heading for the vacant school building.

He knew how the slick old trespasser had gained access. He was cursing himself for his oversight. He arrived at the rear of the building, called for backup, and advised them he was going into the old school. He was concerned for the old man, who might get into any amount of trouble inside. He went down the main hall, picked up his pace, and called out for the perpetrator. No response. Never mind—he knew where the old man would be.

Watkins went through the main door of the coliseum and shined his light up into the bleachers. He saw Lester slumped backward in a seat behind the home team bench. When the officer reached Lester, he knew it was too late to help him. He was surprised at how peaceful he looked.

He called the squad and instructed them to come into the Corning Coliseum. He found some ID on Lester and the main contact number for Cross Creek. Deputy Watkins made the call.

* * *

Troy heard the news from Bart. Lester Corning had passed away. They had all known he was old and could die at any time, but the news staggered them, nonetheless. Troy took it the hardest. Leah was affected too, but she did her best to console her husband.

Troy and Leah tried to finish their interrupted lunch, but neither had any appetite. Troy got up from the table and said he was going over to Cross Creek to check on Lester's apartment. Titus was asleep, so Leah stayed behind. Troy was relieved. He needed to be alone.

He walked slowly through the halls of Cross Creek. He thought of the countless trips he had made to Lester's apartment, and this might be the last. He came to the familiar door, unlocked it, flipped on the lights, and immediately saw the envelope lying on top of the recliner. Walking over to the chair, he saw that the envelope was addressed in Lester's distinctive handwriting. It read,

"Troy Beckham." Troy sat down in the recliner and held the letter in his hands for a few minutes, thoughts racing, before tearing it open.

> Troy or Vince—either way, you are a son to me. I am going to the old school today. I feel very tired; who knows, I may never make it back. If I do get back here, I will tear this note up, and it will be forgotten.

Troy squinted at the scribbled writing, affected by Lester's quivering hands.

> Thank you for befriending this old man. You have always been very kind. Sorry we got busted in Westbury at the school. Maybe someday you will look back and laugh about it.

> I have updated my will. Jeff Schneider is my attorney. He has all my paperwork; you can trust him. It all goes to you and Leah. Start in my underwear drawer. Once you get over the informality of it, root around. There's some cash in there.

Troy leaned farther back in the old recliner. He missed his friend. He grabbed a tissue from the box that was always on the side table and wiped his eyes. He continued reading.

> Do me a favor: Always cherish your wife and be a real dad to Titus. Comfort him in the recliner that you are probably sitting in. Keep the memory of us and your response to my shout-out from my window. Your best man, Lester.

Troy sat there for a few minutes, prayed, and reminisced about their time together. Then he went over to the underwear drawer and looked for the cash supposedly hidden in there. Wrapped in Lester's boxer shorts was an envelope full of hundred-dollar bills. Troy quickly counted out over $16,000. All that cash left unsecured. Open access to rooms, the envelope and note in full sight—it was unbelievable that all this was still there. Someone had kept watch.

He fell back into the old recliner and smiled as a thought hit him. He stuffed the cash into his pants pockets. It was somewhat conspicuous, so he readjusted it. *Good problem to have.* Then he began scooting the recliner out of the room, down the hall, and out to the truck. They would make the recliner fit in their apartment somehow. He drove back to his wife and son.

He doggedly pushed the recliner up the steps and down the corridor to their apartment, every now and then stopping to make sure the cash was still in his pocket. He got the chair inside and was proud he hadn't scratched or torn the leather upholstery. It was just the way Lester had left it. Leah watched in silence as he manhandled the old chair into the family room. He caught his breath and then went to their bedroom and stuck the envelope in his underwear drawer. The precedent had been established. He went to the other bedroom, picked Titus up, and carried him back to the recliner. As he plopped down, Leah joined him on the arm of the chair.

"What's going on? What did you hide in your underwear drawer?" Those pretty green eyes had caught it all.

Troy looked up at her, recalling one of her first comments to him. He whispered back, "Do you want the whole story or just the last chapter?"

LOOKING BACK BY
HEADING WEST

CHAPTER ONE

It was Saturday morning, early, and Seth Marin was fully awake. He had been lying there for about two hours dwelling on thoughts of his wife. He wanted to reach over and feel her lying beside him, but Sherri, his helpmate of fifty-three years, had been buried four days ago.

It had been fifty-nine days since she had suffered her first stroke, and thirty-six days since her second stroke. In that time, he had acquired a new vocabulary: medical terms like *hemorrhagic* and *bleeding in the brain.* He could identify malignant middle cerebral artery syndrome. He knew that was what had killed her.

He had some peace in the knowledge that recovery would have been agonizing for his bride. Possibly prolonged for months or even years. He thanked God for sparing her from prolonged suffering.

Seth's eyes were closed, but sleep eluded him. He glanced at the clock—6:15 a.m. *What's the point? Time for coffee.*

Coffee prep in the morning had been his task all of their married life. It was his choice to let Sherri sleep in and have the coffee waiting for her. He knew it was a small token compared to all the meals she had made for him day after day. This morning, he got up and inadvertently made a full pot. The habit would be hard to break. He chided himself for the error, but it was quite early; maybe he would finish all of it.

He went out to their Florida room, opened the windows, felt the cool morning breeze, and drank the first cup from the full pot. In the solitude, his emotions kicked in. Seth sat back a little lower in his chair and meditated.

Coffee pot empty, Seth went upstairs and into the master bedroom. Memories flowed as he looked around the room at the king-size bed and the huge closet that held Sherri's wardrobe. Seth forced himself to walk inside the master closet. All of her clothes were neatly aligned. He felt a twinge of sorrow looking at her things, but he knew there was a task at hand. The clothes had to go. He didn't know lady's styles, but someone could get some use from them. He hoped Alexis would claim the majority of them.

His attention wavered, and he walked over to pick up a hairbrush on the dresser. He examined it, touching the strands of Sherri's hair caught in the bristles. He quickly pitched it in the trash can. He walked back to the closet, but then came back and retrieved the brush. How many times had he seen his wife use that brush before they retired for the evening? When their goddaughter was young and had come over to spend the night, Sherri had used it to brush her silky brown hair.

Alexis was really their granddaughter, for all intents and purposes. She came from a broken home, but the term "broken home" did little justice to her plight. It was never a real home. The slippery father had abandoned his girlfriend, Rita, and their one-year-old daughter. Gone in the night and never heard from again. Many saw his departure as a blessing. He was devoid of ambition and character and never grasped the reality that he was the stupidest poker player in the county. Some said his debt-welching prompted his flight. Whatever the motive, he was missed only by those holding his markers. Rumors circulated he was cornered up in Joliet and met with street justice for his gambling debts. Nothing was ever confirmed, and most people didn't even care. They were concerned for the mother and daughter, both of whom benefited from an outpouring of love they had never experienced. As for Seth and Sherri, they became Alexis's godparents and nurtured her like the child they'd never had.

CHAPTER TWO

Seth again went to the clothes closet and steeled himself for the task. He was convinced there were some things that a young professional could use, although a few were definitely dated. He started pulling out the pieces one by one and laying them on the bed. He smiled as he pulled out a color-block power suit that Sherri had bought back in the Eighties. He found a few strands of cat hair caught on the collar that must have come from Boswell, a cat he and Sherri had owned for years.

Alexis was always drawn to the fat and lazy cat. Boswell had never caught a mouse, chased a squirrel, or laid a trophy catch on the doorstep. Boswell's lethargic lifestyle made him the perfect target for Alexis, a wannabe veterinarian. The child had an in-home practice in the Marin house. Seth often found her toting around her toy doctor kit under one arm and Boswell under the other—the patient always wrapped in makeshift bandages. Perhaps it was this TLC that enabled the cat to live to the age of twenty.

By the time Boswell passed, Alexis had completed her veterinarian studies, and Seth and Sherri presented her with an oil painting of the cat for display in her office. It was an excellent rendering of the cat staring off into nowhere, possibly awaiting his next examination by the child veterinarian. The painting attracted considerable attention from Alexis's clients.

Seth turned from his thoughts about the painting and finished laying out all of Sherri's clothing. Suddenly overcome with weariness, he fell back on top of the pile and closed his eyes, trying desperately to free his mind from the barrage of memories. Despite the stress and all the coffee he had consumed that morning, he fell back asleep.

Later, when he opened his eyes and glanced at the clock, he couldn't believe how long he had been out. The rest had invigorated him. He completed his morning routine, even shaving, regardless of the fact it was Saturday. He felt a little better and decided to go over to Alexis's clinic. He needed to get out of the house.

Seth pulled up in front of the clinic. It was a busy Saturday. Local parents who had been working all week usually left pet care until Saturday, sandwiched between kids' sporting events.

"Hello, Mr. Marin," said Minnie, the receptionist. "Do you want to see Dr. Alexis?"

"If she is available," he replied.

She announced over the intercom, "Dr. Alexis, front lobby, please. Dr. Alexis, front lobby."

"Thanks. And how is Minnie today?"

"I'm fine. We are busy today! Alexis's husband is out in Croton, at Sanders Dairy Farm, delivering calves and keeping up on all the inoculations for the herd. He'll be gone all day."

Alexis came into the reception area, glanced toward Minnie, and then saw Seth. She said softly, "Hi, Grandpa." She paused, "Been thinking about you. Are you doing OK?"

Seth knew he was being a burden, showing up at the clinic at such a busy time, but he was grateful for Alexis's attention. "I am doing better. I took a nap this morning. I wanted to let you know I have most of Grandma's belongings laid out. Anytime you want to come by is fine with me."

"Let me stop over later this week."

"That works for me. You're welcome anytime." Alexis gave him a kiss on the cheek and headed back to her exam room. As Seth turned to leave, he noticed a young man bringing in a huge cat. The man approached Minnie and asked to see a vet.

"Do you have an appointment?" Minnie asked him.

"No, I don't. Is anyone available to see me?" the man said curtly.

"Please have a seat, and I will check their schedules. It has been a very busy day for us," she said, rolling her eyes toward the ceiling as the walk-in moved away to take a seat near the in the reception area. Seth had no desire to go back to his empty house and decided to chat with the young man instead.

"Hi there, my name is Seth Marin. Excuse me, but that is such a beautiful cat. It reminds me of a cat my wife and I had many years ago. Is the big fellow sick?"

"No, he's not sick. I have to give him up, either to a new home or to have him put down."

"You can't care for him anymore?"

"My work schedule doesn't allow any time for pets, and he belonged to my wife."

Seth figured it was a divorce situation. "Your wife doesn't want him anymore."

"It's more than that if you don't mind."

Seth sensed the young man's irritation, but he probed another question. "Why does she want to give up the cat?"

The young man seemed to break then. His face crumpled, and his voice broke as he said, "It's nothing to you, but I buried Natalie last week."

"Oh, I'm so sorry to hear that. I apologize if I pushed too much."

"You are fine, sir." The man told a deep breath while rubbing the big cat's head. "A lot of the facts are still incomplete, but she was hit by a drunk driver. She was killed instantly a mile from our home. A man ran straight through a red light and t-boned her car. The other driver survived, just a little banged up, but I lost my wife. Our first anniversary would have been this Friday." Seth was moved by the young man's account of all the events.

At that moment, Alexis came back into the lobby. "Hi, I am Dr. Sizemore. How can I help?"

"I'm Jack Jillian. I have to give up this cat. I can't care for him, so it's either find a new home or do what you vets do to unwanted animals.

"Nonsense," said a smiling Alexis. "He looks healthy. There's no reason to have him euthanized. What do you suggest, Grandpa?"

"I suggest a new home."

Alexis said, "Very well, Mr. Jillian. if you are convinced that you can't care for him, we will relieve you of the cat, keep him here temporarily, find him a new home, and confirm it back to you."

Jack gave a weak smile. "Thank you. Truthfully, I couldn't bear to have him put down. I admit that I was playing on your sympathies."

"Well, you succeeded. Minnie will make the arrangements; we'll need his records. And now, please excuse me. I have to get back to work. Nice meeting you. Bye, Grandpa!" Alexis went back to business, and Jack delivered his cat into Minnie's hands, where it received plenty of attention.

Seth spoke up. "Do you have time for a cup of coffee?"

"How about a beer instead," Jack responded.

"No, I prefer coffee."

Jack shrugged. "Sure, why not?"

*   *   *

Jack tapped the address of the coffee place into his phone. *Andy's Diner. Sounds old-fashioned.* With one backward glance at Natalie's cat, he walked out of the clinic and made the short trip to the south end of town.

His first impression of the place was that this was a classic diner—good food, huge quantities, value pricing, and small-town friendliness, and a lot of old people. He joined his new acquaintance, and a waitress led them to Seth's "usual table." He remarked, "You've been here before?"

"I have. I've known the owners for forty years, and we all attend the same church. My wife and I were passionate about helping with children's summer camps. Andy, the guy who owns this place, did the grilling. His wife, Lorna, and my wife, Sherri, counseled many kids over the years. Those youngsters never forgot Andy's massive cheeseburgers and the caring discipleship of their teachers. All of us had a heart for the kids."

Jack settled into his chair, feeling a bit more at ease with this stranger. "What was your function?"

"I did many tasks. Playground and lake supervision and general oversight, mainly."

A man in a white apron brought coffee to their table and greeted Seth like an old friend.

"It's good to see you!" The two men embraced, then Seth excused himself to go to the restroom. The other man turned to Jack and introduced himself.

"Hi there, I'm Andy, the guy who runs this joint." As he poured Jack's coffee, he leaned in and said quietly, "Say, how's Seth doing?"

Jack was taken aback by the question. "I'm sorry, but I don't follow you."

"I guess you don't know about his wife's death. Her funeral was just a few days ago."

Jack felt the equivalent of a sucker punch in the gut. "I had no idea. I just met him at Sizemore's Vet Clinic earlier this morning. He's masking his grief well."

"He's hurting, but I know Seth. He's trusting in God's amazing grace."

The mention of "grace" perplexed him. Seth returned to the table and took a seat just as Jack said, "I have to be honest. I don't know what you mean by amazing grace. To me, it's nothing more than part of a hackneyed song played on bagpipes at burials. Where was 'grace' when that drunken S.O.B. ran a red light, slammed into my wife's car, and killed her? He survived, and I'm left to bury her. Can you two explain that?"

Seth and Andy were quiet, but another voice was heard just then. "Jack, please forgive me for butting in. I'm Lorna Richards, Andy's wife." The older lady who'd come up to their table was pleasantly plump and wore a bright, sweet smile. "I couldn't help overhearing about the accident. I am truly sorry for your loss. Neither we nor anyone else can explain why it happened. Frankly, I wouldn't trust anyone who attempted to provide answers."

In spite of his overwhelming grief, Jack was warmed by the woman's gentle words. He pulled out a chair from their table and encouraged Lorna to join them. She sat down and reached out to clasp his hand. "We would be privileged to pray for you."

Jack felt a cold wave rush over him. "Isn't it a little late for that?" As soon as he spoke, he regretted it. "I need to get going." He abruptly stood up. He needed a beer. Without any explanation, Jack left the table and headed out the diner door. The others watched as he left. Each of them had compassion for the young man. Lorna wanted to go after him, but Andy asked her to refrain.

Jack didn't even think about paying for his coffee until he'd pulled into the parking lot of his apartment. Someone had taken his assigned spot, so he moved down the front of the building to the guest spaces. The inconvenience added to his frustration, and he was tempted to leave a nasty note on the intruding car but decided it wasn't worth the effort. *The dolt probably can't read anyway.*

Jack went upstairs to his apartment, dreading the empty flat. Natalie's absence tore at him. He wanted to placate the feeling with a cold beer, and then, more. He had no appetite but realized he had to eat something. That desire was offset by a frozen meatloaf economy dinner from the freezer. Chopped, formed, and shrink-wrapped for dining delight.

As he waited for the microwave, Jack rummaged in the fridge for his beer and came up empty. The only cans were the diet sodas Natalie had thrived on. He decided on a glass of milk, hoping it would neutralize the taste of his upcoming dinner. The milk was a week out of date. *Perfect. First coffee and no beer, and now old milk and still no beer.* The microwave chimed, telling him to come and get it. After he removed the top wrapper, the smell completely turned him off going any further. *Cat food*, he thought, but then remembered the cat was history—and probably eating better than him. He plopped down on the couch.

Then an uncanny feeling hit him. Jack decided to go back to Andy's Diner. He couldn't explain it, but he felt he had to go back there. If nothing else, anything on the menu had to be better than this. He went back to the visitor's parking space where he had been forced to park and thought about facing the diner group he'd just left without any explanation. Possibly even apologizing. That was not his thing, but he would give it a try. It certainly couldn't be any more awkward than when he'd walked out.

Jack was surprised when his return to the diner was graciously received. Lorna was the first to greet him. She walked him back to the table where Seth and Andy were still talking.

"Look who's back!" Lorna said. Seth and Andy both greeted him as an old friend.

Jack was relieved that they weren't making a big deal about his disappearance but attempted to explain himself. "I guess I overreacted when I was here before—"

Andy didn't let him finish. "Jack, we know that you are under tremendous stress. We understand. No further explanation is needed. Now, how about a late lunch?"

"I thought I smelled meatloaf earlier. Any left?"

"Absolutely. The two sides are mashed potatoes and green beans. Does that sound appetizing?"

Jack only gave it a quick thought. "It does."

Andy took the order back to the kitchen and Lorna followed him. Seth and Jack were temporarily alone.

Jack buried his head in his hands and muttered, "This is a rhetorical question, but is there any chance of getting a beer around here?"

"None," Seth said.

"I thought so."

"Andy and Lorna have always kept a family atmosphere at this diner. They're even closed every Sunday. Their business model has worked for them. They have done very well, but that's a professional secret. I was their accountant from day one."

Jack raised his head. "An accountant, eh? Are you still practicing?"

"No, I sold the business, but I do some consulting with a few folks. Sort of help them stay abreast of all the tax changes. I also help people in our church and a couple of non-profit groups. Anyway, enough about me. What is it that you do?"

A waitress delivered Jack's meatloaf, and he began to eat, speaking between bites. "I'm an electrical engineer, and I work at Spencer Electronics over in Springfield. I've been there a couple of years. I met my wife, Natalie, there. She worked in human resources. Sort of amusing—I was their third choice for the opening I interviewed for. The first two declined the company's offer. They went on down the line to me. Natalie interviewed me; she let me know I was their third choice, so I didn't have a lot of negotiating leverage. Not that it mattered to me—I was more attracted to her than the job. I asked her out even before getting the job offer. She declined for obvious professional reasons, but I was determined. After landing the job, I kept after her, and we started dating. I bought her a ring six months later. We married one year ago this coming Friday." Jack choked up, threw down his fork, and blurted out, "Damn, all this is gut-wrenching."

Seth reached over and put a hand on his shoulder.

"I understand. I *really* understand."

"Thanks." Now Jack felt awkward, knowing what he knew. "Andy shared your loss with me."

Seth just smiled grimly. "One year for you and fifty-three for me. Both too short. Do you want some coffee now?" Jack shoved his empty plate aside, and Seth poured a cup for him. Both men sipped their coffee without speaking, looking past each other at the diner's eclectic décor, lost in thought.

Jack finally broke the silence, "Let me ask you something. I hate to bring it up again, but Andy mentioned God's grace, and I can't stop thinking about it. Frankly, it's just fancy religious blather to me."

Seth seized the opening. "God's grace is simply unmerited favor—something we are not worthy to receive, but He extends it to us regardless. We have the option of accepting or passing. As you know, I'm a CPA, so I tend to think of things in terms of finance. Think of sin as a debt we owe to God. Our sin debt was paid in full when Christ died on the cross for us. I use a fancy word, *propitiation*, to describe the exchange. That five-syllable word simply means 'paid in full.' It's all wiped clean, with no penalty. The sins are eradicated. Can you imagine people today with all their accrued debt—credit cards, mortgages, college loans—having it all paid in full? Euphoric would be an understatement.

But that's how Christ works. My wife, who believed, is now in heaven. That same grace will prevail when God calls me home. I will see her again."

Jack threw Seth a bold question. "Do you think my wife is in heaven?"

Seth took a long sip of coffee, then said, "I can't answer that. But you can be confident of your home in heaven by simply trusting in Christ."

"So, if Natalie's not in heaven, she's in hell?'

"Unfortunately, I can't answer that one either. I can only ask you about your personal acceptance of Christ as your Savior."

Jack had reached his tipping point. He stood up and tossed a twenty on the table.

"Thanks for the sermon. I'm out of here."

"Jack, I apologize if I threw too much at you all at once, but my comments about Christ are true."

"True, as a convenient courtesy to you. I need to go." All this talk about his wife's existence in either heaven or hell was giving Jack chills. Seth reached into his jacket pocket and pulled out a thin booklet.

"Here, please take this with you."

More propaganda, Jack thought, but he accepted the little pamphlet with a picture of Kiser Bible Church on the cover. "Thanks. Very nice meeting you, Seth." Jack walked out the door, almost running over other customers coming into the diner.

CHAPTER THREE

Jack entered the silent apartment, headed for the bedroom, and collapsed on the bed. He was exhausted, but his mind was racing. The tract that Seth had given him was prodding him from his hip pocket. He pulled it out and rolled his eyes at the title: "Propitiation Made Clear." *Why won't that word go away?* He threw it on the floor.

Although it was still early, Jack crawled under the covers. It felt almost safe there, as if he were hidden from the world. But he couldn't hide from his thoughts. He kept picturing his beloved Natalie in heaven and then in hell—the scenes were colorful and distorted pictures from a childhood Bible. He struggled with all the thoughts the entire night.

Finally, at seven o'clock, Jack gave up and went to the kitchen to make coffee. He had a lot of questions that needed answering. He then decided to visit Kiser Bible, the church pictured on the tract he'd received from Seth. Looking it up online, he saw there were two service times, and he opted for the earlier one. He wanted to get in and out fast with the answers he needed. Perhaps he could talk to someone his own age and get the answers he was seeking.

Jack arrived at the church and was amazed at the full parking lot. After parking in a visitor spot and entering the building, he went with the flow of the crowd through the lobby toward the sanctuary area. It was there he found Seth.

"Good morning, Jack! It's good to see you."

"Good morning. Do you have a moment?" Seth asked him. "I need to talk to you."

"Sure." Seth directed Jack on down the hallway. A few minutes later, Seth was introducing Jack to the leader of Kiser Bible's grief share group: Jonathan Kramer. Jonathan was a young pastor, the same age as Jack, and newly married. He reached out to shake Jack's hand. "How long have you known Seth?"

"All of twenty-four hours."

"Hopefully, you can spend more time with him. Seth is worth knowing," Jonathan, in his typical caring mode, popped an invitation to Jack. "How about joining my wife and me for dinner tonight? She makes a world-class meatloaf."

Jack was taken by surprise. "Do you want to check with her first?" he asked.

"Normally, I would, but I know her well enough that I'm sure she will be glad to have you over."

Meatloaf, Jack thought. *Why not?* "Thank you, I accept."

"Perfect. How about five thirty? Seth, would you like to join us?"

"I'm going to pass. You young folks spend time getting to know each other. I have some things at home to attend to." The clothes piles were still awaiting him.

*   *   *

Jack, the engineer, arrived promptly at five thirty. Jonathan and his wife, Camille, greeted him at the door. He was warmed by Camille's hospitality, the quaintness of their small home, and the now-familiar smell of baking meatloaf. It was all good. Jack learned that the couple had met at college and later married while Jonathan took his seminary training. They leased their home from Andy, the owner of the diner. *It's a small world.*

The meatloaf dinner was served, and the talk was open. Jack started the conversation with a blunt question. "Now, I have no biblical background, but I want to know what you think." He looked directly at Jonathan. "My wife was innocently killed by a drunk driver. Is she in heaven?"

Jonathan and Camille exchanged glances, and Jonathan quietly stirred his coffee.

"Jack, that is a tough question. Let me begin by saying that the Bible doesn't provide philosophical answers. However, it does establish biblical truths. I would be remiss if I gave you a rosy response just to appease you."

"I understand. I don't want to be placated; I'm seeking answers."

"Well then, first of all, the only way anyone can get to heaven is to know Christ personally as Lord and Savior. Did your wife ever mention her spiritual background during your time together?"

"No, we never discussed any of that. She knew I had no use for religion."

"Would her parents know if she was ever involved in a church?"

"Hard to say. Her mother died when she was a young teen, and her father is an alcoholic. He never attended our wedding or her funeral. I am sure he was blitzed both times. Not drunk from sorrow—just a worthless boozer." The thought of that man passed out in some godforsaken hole while his beloved Natalie was being buried brought tears to Jack's eyes. Tears of anger or sorrow, he wasn't sure which.

"We are for you," Camille whispered.

He looked up. "What's with all you people? Seth, Andy, Lorna, and now you two. You don't know me, yet all of you are treating me as if I was family. I don't get it."

"Jack, it's just the love of Christ. In a way, you are family," Camille told him.

"Thank you." There was silence, and then Jack said, "Maybe a grandparent or an old family friend would have the key to Natalie's church background. Is it possible to search for someone's spiritual genealogy?"

"Where did she grow up?" Jonathan asked.

"Billings, Montana."

"Of course, it couldn't have been around here. I was hoping that she was from this area because I know exactly what you're thinking."

Jack smiled. "What am I thinking?"

"I see you trekking out to Billings—2,000 miles or however far it is—and doing some fact-finding. There's a lot of bluegrass between here and there. I suggest that you do some internet research on her family and seek out relatives."

Jonathan had read his mind. Jack realized that an internet search would usually be far easier than going to Montana to search for records of his wife, but Natalie's family wasn't normal, far from it. "It pains me to bring her worthless father up again, but you see, he deserted Natalie's mother even before my wife was born, and she never took his surname. Natalie's mother was born in Eastern Europe, one of the Slavic countries, and she dropped her name after arriving in America. Natalie told me it was too long and joked that it had no vowels; very difficult to pronounce. Her mother chose a new name from the Billings phonebook, Gilarski, and had her name legally changed to that. So, the family's original surname is a dead-end to research, and the Gilarskis in Billings are no relation to Natalie. I can't come up with any other possibility other than starting at ground zero and moving forward."

A sudden thought came to Jack, and he jumped at it. "Hey, do you two want to come with me?"

Camille looked shocked. "Oh my! No, I don't think so. Out of the question."

"Didn't you two do any road trips in college?"

"Sure, but nothing transcontinental," Camille said. "I'm sure it would be fascinating, but I have too many commitments. I'll have to pass."

Jack turned to Jonathan, who seemed to be absorbed in his thoughts. Perhaps he agreed with his wife. Maybe he thought the venture was crazy and pointless.

"Jack, have you given any consideration to your own personal salvation and the resulting heavenly home that comes with it?"

Jack hadn't expected that. "You mean propitiation?"

Jonathan laughed. "I can tell you've been talking to Seth Marin. That is part of it." He got up and went to fetch a thick, well-worn Bible.

Over the next half hour, Jonathan shared verses regarding salvation and then challenged Jack about his personal salvation. Jack shifted from speculation about Natalie to the reality of his own spiritual situation. He and Jonathan prayed together through tears. Jack made a note on his phone with the date of his acceptance of the rule of propitiation. The engineer was leaving no doubt for any future discussion or speculation.

Later that evening, Jack excused himself. He thanked the Kramer's for their hospitality and their concerns for him, then he walked out to his car and Jonathan walked with him.

Once outside, Jonathan asked, "Are you really kicking around the idea of a trip out to Billings?"

"I am, but there is a lot to consider. There may be some litigation regarding the driver that hit Natalie, and the attorneys want to meet ASAP. I'm backed up at work, and…I'm tired." He paused and reflected on the time they had just spent together. "You have been very kind to me. I feel some relief. I have been living a nightmare, but your support is appreciated."

"When you get home, pray about all of this, and get some rest. Let's talk tomorrow."

"I will take you up on that." They shook hands, and Jack returned to his apartment. He was beginning to make progress in his desire to solve the mystery of his wife's salvation. Now that he knew he had a heavenly home, he wanted more than ever to be sure that he'd be seeing Natalie there.

CHAPTER FOUR

Jack researched the distance from Bradford, Ohio to Billings, Montana: 1,542 miles. He felt good. He'd already shaved about 450 miles off Jonathan's speculation. His mind was in a flurry, but he lay down on the couch and exercised his new option of praying. He had a feeling of peace now, and he wanted to keep pursuing it. Later, he fell into a tranquil sleep.

He woke up Monday morning close to his usual time of six o'clock. It was a weekday, but his boss had exempted him from work and ordered him to take a few days off. He'd also accrued some vacation time, enough to make the Billings trip. Jack pondered it all as he left home and drove toward Andy's Diner. Was there anything keeping him from making this trip?

As soon as he entered the diner, he spotted a familiar group in the back. Seth, Andy, and Jonathan were gathered at Seth's usual booth. They appeared to be bowing their heads in prayer. Jack heard a joint "amen," and Andy got up and headed for the kitchen. He caught Jack's eye as he passed him.

"Hey, Jack! Are you hungry? What will it be for you?"

"Since you asked, two eggs over easy, hash browns, and ham."

"Another Jonathan order up." Jonathan looked up at him. "Are you still musing over the road trip?"

"It's on my dashboard," Jack said.

"Billings is 458 miles closer than I estimated," Jonathan informed him.

"Yeah, I checked it last night."

Andy brought their food and refilled the coffee cups as Jack informed him and Seth of his quest into Natalie's past. He mentioned he knew little of her family and even less of her background, but Billings seemed to be a natural starting point.

"Jack, that is a big step and the trip could prove to be a huge vacuum." Seth said.

"I know. Trust me, I know."

The four of them finished their breakfast and chatted a while, but they were interrupted by Lorna tapping on a plate back int the kitchen, indicating it was time for Andy to get back to work. She threw them all a kiss and waved goodbye to them. Jack attempted to pay the tab, but Andy put it on the house.

"This one is on me. Save your money for your trip."

* * *

Jonathan went to his office at Kiser to attend the usual Monday staff meetings. He passed by the office of Ed Dalton, senior teaching pastor. Jonathan had a deep respect for the minister of eighty-seven and decided that he could use some of his insight and advice. The younger pastor shared Jack's whole story and the proposed trip, and Pastor Ed began to share his insights.

"If that trip does occur, the young man you are discussing will need some guidance. He's a new follower and is vulnerable."

"Are you suggesting that I should go to Billings with him?"

"I think it would be appropriate."

The lead pastor, Dan Fenton, popped his head in the door. "Good morning, fellows. I need to discuss something with you. Seth and Andy both called me this morning regarding a guy named Jack Jillian and a proposed trip to Billings, Montana. Jonathan, can you enlighten me about that? I would love to hear some details."

"I'd be happy to."

The three discussed Jack's trip. Was it feasible? Should he go it alone or have a companion? While their conversation was at a lull, the receptionist buzzed in and asked for Jonathan.

"I'm here."

"There is a gentleman here to see you, a Mr. Jillian."

"Please have him come on back to Ed's office, thanks." They knew this was not a coincidence. They heard a tap on the door and invited Jack in.

"Sorry, am I busting in on your meeting?"

"Not at all. It's not our meeting—possibly it's your meeting," Dan said.

"I don't get it."

"I can clarify. First of all, I'm Dan, the lead pastor here, and this is Ed Dalton, one of our pastors, and you have met Jonathan." Dan informed Jack of their conversation. He emphasized that they were not trying to micromanage his personal life but wanted him to know they had concern for him.

"Frankly, gentlemen, a couple of days ago, I would have told you all to butt out, keep your piety, and take a hike. Maybe I'm mellowing, or growing, in your terms. I welcome your input. In fact, why don't we all pray about it and meet back here later this afternoon and discuss it?"

"I'm OK with that," Dan said. The agenda was set for four o'clock. Jack excused himself, and the trio of pastors prayed. Jack headed to the attorney's office.

* * *

Jack arrived at Smith and Baron law offices ten minutes early for his appointment. While waiting in the lobby, he tilted back in the chair, memories of his wife flowing in his mind. He was summoned to come back to the conference room. They had their meeting, and Jack tried to concentrate on the details, but mentally, he was driving westward on I-70. At the conclusion, he mentioned he was going to be away for a while, and could they please update him via his cell phone.

*   *   *

Jack was on time for his afternoon meeting at Kiser and was greeted by the friendly receptionist. "They're waiting for you back in Ed's office, Mr. Jillian. Please go on back." Then she whispered, "I've been praying too."

"Thank you, and please call me Jack." He tapped on the door and was greeted by the three pastors.

"Jack, have a seat. We've concluded that you should make the trip, but the decision rests with you. If your goal is to discover whether or not your wife is in heaven, here are a couple of things you should know. First, there is only one way to God. If you find out she was baptized as an infant or she went through confirmation classes or just led a good clean life, that wouldn't get her into heaven. None of those qualify for eternal life in heaven. Remember what Jesus said: He's the only way, not just one of the options. Only through Him. If you are interested, Jonathan has volunteered to accompany you. I honestly believe that you will need a spiritual mentor in your search. He can also be a good backup driver."

Jack didn't hesitate. "I would enjoy Jonathan's company. I thought about inviting Seth also."

Ed spoke up. "He needs to stay home. You would be stopping at every rest stop to accommodate him. Need I say more?" The point was respectfully taken.

Jack wanted to leave the next morning, and Jonathan was good enough to agree. Jack knew he probably sounded obsessed, but he wouldn't be able to concentrate on anything else while he was thinking about the possibilities of the coming trip.

CHAPTER FIVE

At a quarter to six the next morning, Jack heard a knock on his door. He was already up and topping off his bag. Opening the door, he saw Seth, Andy, and Lorna. Lorna handed him a small cooler of meatloaf sandwiches and thick wedges of pie as well as a thermos full of coffee. *How did they even find me?* he asked himself.

"Here, sweetie, something for you two to munch on and reduce your exposure to fast food."

He didn't know what to say, except, "You three are more than friends, I consider you family." Lorna smiled and wiped away a tear. "Well, Jonathan is waiting, and he wants to make Omaha by nightfall."

The four of them prayed, and Jack left to pick up his traveling buddy. Jonathan and Camille were waiting for him in the driveway. Jonathan threw his bags into the trunk, kissed his wife, and they were off.

Seconds later, Jonathan asked a question.

"Just how old is this car?"

"It's only ten years old and barely broke in with 220,000 miles."

Jonathan whistled and leaned back in the seat that was to be his home for at least 3,000 miles, if they stayed on course. "You must have a lot of faith in this vehicle."

"I do have a lot of faith in my car. Isn't this entire trip based on faith, Preacher?"

"Touché."

They made Omaha by seven that evening. No reservations had been made; they'd decided to wing it for a room. Jonathan got on his phone and found a bargain rate at a chain hotel. After getting their rooms, they ordered pizza, and both were sound asleep by nine thirty.

Jack awoke at midnight, and his thoughts were on his wife. He prayed for direction and wisdom as they continued their journey.

*   *   *

Both men were awake at six. After their morning preparations were completed, they headed out to the parking lot to get back on the road. Jack noticed Jonathan walking around the Toyota and examining the tires. He just smiled and got in the driver's seat. He was tempted to bring up faith again, but he passed. They were on the road by a quarter past seven, and the goal was to reach Billings that evening.

After an hour on the road, Jonathan asked him, "What's the first step when we get there?"

"I hope to find some school or church records that may give me a clue. It's a stretch, but hopefully a starting point."

"Do you know where she used to live? Who her neighbors or friends might have been?"

"I have an obscure old address from her college records, but it appears the neighborhood was bulldozed and rebuilt years ago. Maybe we can kick around in that area of town. It's weak, but it can be the first step."

In the late afternoon, they crossed from South Dakota into Wyoming. Jack had just completed his 250-mile shift when he spotted a giant arrow on a sign reading "Josie's Haven: Home-Cooked Food."

"Do you want to take a risk on this place for a meal?"

Jonathan had just woken from a quick snooze and didn't catch the big sign, but complied. "Why not?" They exited the interstate and traveled down a mountain road. The scenery was spectacular, and they found Josie's at the end of the road. The parking lot was empty, but the sign on the door said it was open. They got out of the Toyota, stretched their legs, and ventured into Josie's Haven. Immediately, they realized that "Josie's Biker Haven" would have been a more appropriate name for the place. The rustic interior, completely devoid of customers, was covered in motorcycle memorabilia. Jack and Jonathan stood staring for a few minutes.

"Big mistake," Jack whispered.

"In a word, yes." They were about to exit when a captivating voice stopped them short of the front door. Josie had come out of the kitchen.

"Hi, fellas, I'm Josie. Welcome to my haven!" Josie was a middle-aged woman with long curly hair and the fashion sense of a Sixties flower child. She could have been the poster child for a carefree spirit. "We offer the best Tex-Mex in all of Wyoming and Montana."

Jack thought the absence of customers didn't support her claim but said nothing.

"What a wonderful day God has made! Don't you think sunshiny afternoons like this are just the closest thing to heaven?" Jack almost expected her to break into song, but she kept talking. "Where you boys from, and where are you headed?"

"We're from Ohio, and we're headed to Billings."

"Well, I hope you're having a safe and blessed trip, and It's good you stopped by when you did!" She picked up two menus, and it was apparent that she expected them to stay. Jack looked at Jonathan, shrugged, and allowed Josie to take them to a table.

She poured two tall glasses of water and kept talking. "Before you choose your meals, I want you to meet my husband, Dexter. He's in the kitchen. We settled here from Vegas, you know. I was a prostitute, and Dexter was my pimp." Jack nearly spewed the first drink of water out of his mouth but just managed to keep it in. "Jesus changed us! We migrated here, got married, and started this eatery. We are simply blessed to be here. What a great day."

Jack and Jonathan remained silent, but Josie kept the one-sided conversation flowing. "Dexter, come on out here. I want you to meet our guests." When Dexter appeared, it seemed the room went dark. Jack pegged him as at least six foot six and weighing in at about three hundred pounds. His massive upper torso was covered in a plethora of tattoos, and he carried a meat cleaver, wiping it on his apron as he approached. Jack silently gave thanks that this man was on God's team and presumably meant them no harm. He kept looking at him.

"I'm Dexter, you boys going to try my enchilada surprise special?"

Jonathan spoke up in a halfhearted voice, "Nothing compares to a good enchilada."

"Perfect. You better move to one of the tables in the back, one with the view, before we get real busy."

"Thank you," Jack said. He leaned over toward Jonathan and whispered, "If this busy, what's it like on a slow day?"

"Quiet, he may hear you."

Dexter smiled at them.

They moved tables as requested, and as soon as they sat down again, they heard a deafening roar from the once-empty parking lot. Looking out the window, they saw at least a dozen Harleys circling around and navigating for side by side parking. Behind them were as many pickup trucks.

CHAPTER SIX

The riders dismounted from their bikes and the pickup trucks emptied out. Some of the arriving group removed musical instruments from their trucks. Then forty people paraded through the front door of Josie's Haven. Once inside, the instruments were placed adjacent to Jack and Jonathan's table, and other tables were moved aside to make more room.

"Is this what they mean by sitting near the view?" Jack asked.

Dexter's voice boomed out again. "Hey, everyone, come on over and meet Jack and Jonathan. These gents are from Ohio." The friendly but curious crowd surrounded the two travelers from the Buckeye state. Jack and Jonathan noticed that pretty much everyone was covered in tattoo art. Jack deduced the local tattoo artist must be doing well.

"Which one is Jack, and which is Jonathan?" a beefy man asked.

"I'm Jack," he said, extending his hand to the man.

"Good to meet you. I'm Earl, but my friends call me Clinch." He gave Jack a smothering bear hug. "Then you must be Jonathan." He "clinched" him the same way an opposing lineman would throttle a quarterback. "What part of Ohio you boys from?"

"Town called Bradford. Western part of the state," Jonathan said.

"Know exactly where it is. I drive a truck and go back east quite a bit. How do you like this country, and what brings you out here?"

"We came out here to find out some information about my wife." The group went silent.

Jonathan spoke up. "Jack recently lost his wife in an accident. We're trying to find out whether or not she's in heaven." The blank stares showed that this explanation hadn't clarified things. "I am a pastor, and Jack is a new Christian. He's assured of his home in heaven, but he's seeking the assurance that Natalie, his wife, is with Christ now. She was from Billings, so we're heading there to find out what we can."

"I know this trip sounds bizarre," Jack said. "I have no idea how all of this will end, but good things keep happening." He smiled at the group.

Josie stepped in. "Well, we're so glad you stopped here on your way. Jack, Jonathan, this is our mid-week praise and worship gathering. In fact, this is our church, and we're the gathering. We will have a meal and then follow it with the service."

Dexter stepped forward, dodging a hanging light fixture, and bowed his head to ask God's blessing on the enchilada feast. The food was brought out from the kitchen and two lines formed. The two guests stepped back, but they were motioned to the head of one of the lines by a young man on a pair of prosthetic legs.

"Hi there! I'm Leon Albert. Go to the head of the line." He whispered to them, "Enchilada surprise is aptly named. Only Dexter knows the ingredients in his creation. Rumor has it the stray dog and cat population drops big-time the night before he prepares this delicacy. Even the night creatures won't go near any of the scraps, but go ahead and load up your plates."

"You are kidding, aren't you?" Jack whispered back.

Leon grinned. "Bone appetite—or however you say it."

Jack hesitated but followed Jonathan's lead and bit into his portion. It was excellent. *Maybe Andy could use this recipe*, he thought.

During the meal, Leon shared that he was an army veteran of the Afghanistan campaign and had lost his legs from an explosive device. He offered them some advice for their Billings visit. "When you get there, seek out Refuge Home on South Cody Street. They've served the area for over sixty years and ministered to hundreds of people. They will be a good place to start searching for some details." Jack, between bites, gave him a thumbs up.

The praise and worship began right after dinner, and the unique fellowship lasted for over two hours. The Bible leader did an adequate job. Jonathan caught some minor flaws but respected the layman's approach and sincerity.

After the meeting ended, the food, fellowship, and fatigue took their toll on the two travelers. They sought out Josie and Dexter, thanked them for everything, and explained that they really needed to get on the road to Billings. Dexter reminded them that Billings was still a long way off. Maybe too long for weary folks. He made an offer to them.

"We have a couple of cabins out back. Stay there tonight. Get rested up, have breakfast with us, and then you can be on your way." The offer appealed to them and was accepted.

"Thank you, but please let us pay for the night's stay."

"Never think of it. God has blessed us with all this, and we want to share it with you." Jonathan stepped forward and attempted to hug him but was as successful as a chipmunk trying to hug an elephant. Nevertheless, the gesture was well received.

"Let me show you to the cabin." Just then, the night air came alive with the sound of motorcycles and trucks firing up and departing. The roar seemed more mellow than before as the pack disappeared into the light of the full moon overlooking Josie's Haven.

The cabin was perfectly suited to its mountain locale. The bunk beds reminded Jack of boyhood camping outings. He claimed the bottom bunk and then walked over to the back door, stepping out on the deck adjoining the rear of the cabin. "Jonathan, come out here." They both gazed out at the valley before them. The full moon glowed amber in the sky. They sat down on two rustic rockers and drank in the stillness.

Jack whispered, "I've done a lot of travel, but I never saw anything like this."

"I haven't traveled much. I always dreamed of going to the mountains, but never imagined it would be this beautiful," Jonathan said. The fresh cool air was soothing. Then the tranquility was shattered by Dexter's voice hollering from across the parking lot.

"Don't be concerned by any noises you hear during the night. It's only the wolves, grizzlies, coyotes, and mountain lions. They've formed a little choir and like to harmonize."

They couldn't hear Josie admonishing her husband. "Did you really have to tell them that? Those poor city boys need a good rest." Dexter laughed and then a door closed, and everything was quiet again.

"Seth and Andy would love this guy," Jonathan said. They went to their bunk beds, climbed in, and laid there with their eyes wide open. The more he thought about the creatures of the night, the more Jack regretted his choice of the bottom bunk.

Early that morning, both men were awakened by gastronomic rumblings—the enchilada surprise had its own wake-up call. In mountain cabin vernacular, the dwelling had a one-holer. Jonathan sprang from the top bunk and claimed it. Jack had two choices: wait or head down the mountain path. He chose the latter, hoping the mountain wildlife was now snoozing and he wouldn't be caught in any comprising situation. Both survived the experience and fell back asleep.

Later, they tidied up the cabin and found their hosts out behind the restaurant. Dexter was splitting wood and Josie was in her garden.

"Good morning," Jonathan greeted them.

"Morning to you two," Dexter said. "Did you sleep well?" He had a sly smile.

"We were just fine," Jack told him.

"Would you like to have breakfast with us?" Josie asked. They respectfully passed on the offer. Jack explained their need to get on the road but failed to mention the fact that he was still nursing his early morning stomach challenges.

"How long do you plan on staying up in Billings?" Dexter asked them.

"I have no idea. No idea at all."

"Please stop by here on your way back. The cabin is yours. No more enchiladas on the menu for the rest of the month," Josie said, and she winked at them. Both men blushed.

"I think we will. Thank you for all your hospitality." Embraces and handshakes were exchanged, and Jack and Jonathan took off in the Toyota.

Jack was hoping that Refuge Home would prove helpful. Hopefully, they kept good records.

*   *   *

They reached Billings, and Jonathan found the Cody Street exit on his phone. He located Refuge Home's address, and as they pulled into the parking lot, they admired the old building. It had a brick exterior, high arched windows, and mint green trim. A faded awning shaded the front door. Jack felt a little edgy as they entered the building. He couldn't help feeling that he was possibly on a fool's errand. They walked down a dimly lit hallway to a reception desk where an elderly lady was sweeping the area.

Jack coughed. "Excuse me."

The woman was startled by his voice but apologized for not seeing them come in. "Yes, gentlemen, how can I help you?"

Jack explained the reason for their visit and shared everything he knew about Natalie's time in Billings.

The lady gave them a knowing look. "Let me see if Ruben is available." She hobbled down the hall and turned a corner. Shortly, she reappeared and introduced them to Ruben Hanawalt, a skinny man with large spectacles.

"Good morning, fellows. I see you met my wife, Elsie. She mentioned you're interested in the Gilarski family."

"Yes sir, a woman named Natalie in particular. She was my wife, and she's recently passed away. I was referred to this place and told you could possibly give us some information about her. Natalie and her mom might have come through here about twenty years ago."

"Interesting. And who referred you to us?"

"Leon Albert."

"Ah, Leon and Andrea. Wonderful young couple, I performed their wedding. How do you know him?"

"We just met last night."

Ruben started moving away. "Gilarski...let's search our system. Please, follow me downstairs."

Jack anticipated a computer room, but instead, they climbed down a set of stairs to a room full of file cabinets and dusty storage boxes. Jack's heart sank, and he whispered to Jonathan, "Can you believe this? At least he doesn't need to be concerned about any data bugs—but real insects could be a problem."

"Just be cool, and we'll see what he can uncover," Jonathan whispered back at him.

Ruben looked around at the files and the boxes stacked six high on each cabinet. "Let's begin in the late nineties." He opened a file drawer labeled "Jan–June 1997." He fished around and poked through the files. "Nothing here." He continued thumbing through all of 1997.

"You know, a lot of the people coming in here deliberately provide false information. Some are dodging the law or just want to stay under the radar. Our mission isn't to do fact-checking but simply to minister." He pulled a cardboard box of files from the 1999 stack, July–Dec, and went through them. "Here we go! Ludmilla Gilarski, daughter Natalie, 12-24-99. Looks like they came in on Christmas Eve."

Jack felt numb. "Any notes or comments in their file?"

"Only a note indicating their arrival, and it looks like they stayed through Christmas. Ah—we provided them bus tickets to Ohio, and they departed on December 26. Nothing else here."

Jack sat down hard on a box. They'd come all the way to Billings only to discover that Natalie and her mother had left here for Ohio. Jonathan put his arm around Jack.

Ruben blinked at them and adjusted his spectacles. "Boys, please forgive me, but what are your names, one more time?"

"It's Jack, sir. Jack Jillian. And he's Jonathan Kramer."

"What were you hoping to discover about your wife, Jack?"

He explained their intentions.

"Did you think to pray about making this trip?" Ruben asked.

Jonathan answered, "Yes, sir, we did, and others joined us. We all concluded it was God's will to proceed."

Ruben nodded sagely. "God is not an author of confusion. Maybe you won't find what you are seeking, but there is a purpose for this trip. Keep an open mind and look for wisdom. Don't give in to defeat. Discern between direction and destination."

"Thank you. Mr. Hanawalt, may I make a suggestion?"

"Certainly, by all means."

"You really should get all those files organized and download them on a computer system."

Ruben smiled at him. "Well, I did find what you were looking for, correct?"

"Yes, sir, you did." Ruben gave them a big grin.

"We have a computer room upstairs. There's a young fellow about your age that comes in twice a week and takes care of all that stuff for us. I don't trust all that tech junk. Does that answer your suggestion?"

"Yes, sir, it does." He thanked Ruben for his time and sage advice. On their way out, he and Jonathan discreetly dropped some money into one of the donation boxes in the reception area.

Once outside the building, Jack stood still on the sidewalk and took a moment to clear his mind. "Jonathan, we have hit a wall. Maybe we can check out the neighborhood of the old address I have, but if that's inconclusive, I'm pulling the plug, and we're heading back home."

"Think it through carefully, but I support any decision you make."

Driving through the area that could have once been Natalie's home provided no clues. It had all been revitalized. Jonathan said, "Remember Ruben's comment about continuing to seek wisdom. That will be our focus."

Jack looked at him. "Agreed. Let's head back. I want to stop at Josie's, pay them for a cabin, and get up early to make Omaha by tomorrow evening. But I need to do one more thing."

Jack went back to Refuge Home and placed an additional $200 in the donation box. Ruben's input was invaluable. He returned to the car, reset the odometer, and they headed east. Jack now had no qualms about the trip. Even if he hadn't found what he was looking for, it was all good.

*   *   *

They arrived at Josie's Haven in time for dinner. Josie and Dexter were sorry that they hadn't found more answers, but they were enthusiastic about having them join in their Bible study. They asked Jonathan if he would be willing to lead the service. He enthusiastically agreed and asked which passages they were studying.

After some prep time, Jonathan took a break and wandered down a trail behind the cabin. It ended at a huge precipice overlooking the valley and river below. Two Adirondack chairs were conveniently placed there. Sinking into one, he wished that Camille could be next to him. He took a photo of the view with his phone and sent it to Camille. He closed his eyes and drifted off, only to be awakened by his ringing phone.

"Some view! Where are you?"

"A small town in Wyoming, just south of the Montana border. By the way, we're heading home in the morning. Should be back late Saturday evening."

"So soon? Did Jack accomplish anything?"

"Not much, but he's OK to return. If nothing else, the trip has taken his mind off Natalie's death. He's doing pretty well."

"I'm happy for him, and I miss you."

"I miss you too. The sunsets out here are fabulous, and the full moon is unbelievable. I need to bring you out here one day."

"OK, dear. Don't get any grandiose ideas. Call me back tonight."

Later that evening, the Bible study ran over its normal thirty-minute session time. The lesson lasted ninety minutes, and no one objected; they all enjoyed Jonathan's teaching. Jonathan knew they would benefit from an experienced leader, and he would keep that need in his prayers. God would provide the right person.

CHAPTER SEVEN

It was after midnight when an old pickup with a faulty muffler entered the city of Bradford, Ohio, and pulled into the parking lot of the Sizemore Vet Clinic. The truck circled the lot twice before finally parking in the shadows of the west end of the building, away from the security lights. The driver killed the engine, reached for the six-pack next to him, and popped the top of a cold beer. He chugged it and then went on chugging others. Lawrence Chandler was back in town.

*   *   *

The next morning, Alexis parked in the rear of the building and saw that the clinic lights were off. Strange. Minnie always arrived before her and had the place up and running by the time she arrived. She checked Minnie's parking spot and found her car there as usual. Feeling uneasy, Alexis got out of the car and hurried to the back door. The alarm had been reactivated. She called out, "Minnie, are you here?"

"I'm up front in the lobby. Get up here!" She sounded panicked.

Alexis moved quickly up the steps to the main floor.

"Minnie, are you alright?"

The receptionist was crouching in the dark behind her desk. "Please come over here. Look across the parking lot at that old truck."

A battered pickup was parked across two parking spaces with a pile of empty beer cans scattered around it. "Do you have any idea who it belongs to?" Alexis asked her.

"No, it was just sitting there when I got here. Oh no, there's someone in there!" Minnie shrieked. A scruffy man had just sat up in the driver's seat.

"Alexis, let's call the police."

"Just wait. Maybe he's a vagrant and took advantage of the lighted parking lot. Hopefully, he will go away." She was trying to be calm, and she didn't want to alarm Minnie, but she was clutching the can of Mace in her purse. Her husband was out at Swanson's Dairy for most of the day, and no customers would show up for at least another half hour.

The truck door popped open, and the man got out. He went to the rear of the pickup and gathered up a large box, then he began staggering toward the front door.

Minnie whimpered, "Let's hide!"

"No. Stay down and out of sight. Let's see what he wants, but stand by the phone." The stranger approached the door, then attempted to lay the box on the ground but wound up dropping it. Shoving it aside, he tried the locked door. After jerking it a couple of times, he started knocking very aggressively. Alexis, clutching her purse, spoke loudly through the glass door but refused to open it. "Sir, we are closed."

He responded in a loud but slurred voice. "I'm looking for…Alexis."

"I am Dr. Sizemore. How can I help you?"

"You don't know me, do ya?"

"Should I know you, sir?"

"Come on, girl. I'm your father."

Minnie shrieked from her crouched position behind the desk. Alexis tried to remain cool. "What do you want?"

"I just want to talk, and then I'll get the hell out of here. I have some things for you." He shuffled the box toward the door with his foot. Alexis didn't answer. She continued to stare at the man on the other side of the door, the menacing stranger claiming to be her father. She now had both hands on her handbag, grasping it even tighter.

"Alexis, please don't let him in. He scares me."

Alexis kept looking at Lawrence in disbelief. She was about to call the police when she heard the slamming of car doors and saw her grandfather and Andy walking across the parking lot carrying cups of coffee and a bag of pastries. She'd never been so grateful to see them.

Seth walked up to the man on the doorstep with Andy standing alongside him. "What's going on here?"

The man opened his mouth, and his alcoholic breath was toxic. "Why don't you two just butt out and let me talk to my daughter."

Seth examined the seedy-looking stranger. "Lawrence Chandler. Is it possible?"

"That's me. Do I know you?"

"I am Seth Marin."

"Never heard of you," he mumbled.

"What do you want with my granddaughter?" Seth seemed to have grown several inches in height, and his hands were curled into fists, and his stare was fixed on Lawrence. He decided that the bum in front of him didn't look to be in a condition to challenge anyone, and Andy was right behind him.

"I just want to talk to her and give her a few things, that's all. Give me a few moments, and I'll leave." He picked up the box and clutched it to his chest.

Seth looked at Andy, who nodded in agreement, and told Alexis to open the door. Still clutching the Mace in her handbag, she let them in. Minnie stayed behind the desk as the three men entered the clinic. The odors of alcohol and poor hygiene permeated the empty lobby.

Alexis kept her distance. Then she noticed that everyone was looking at her. She stepped back to the desk, placed her purse on it, and moved toward Lawrence.

"Please have a seat. Would you like some coffee?"

"Yeah." Seth still looked defensive but handed over one of the coffee's he'd brought. Lawrence was eyeing the pastries.

"Why have you come here?" Alexis asked.

"I'm not here for a handout if that's what you're thinking. My life is wrecked. I'm not very well, and I just wanted to see you." He put a hand up to his eyes. "I just lost my other daughter. I need someone to talk to."

Alexis reached over and gently grasped his hand. His stench was formidable, but she hung in there. Until this moment she'd had no idea that there was another daughter, a sister to her, if she could believe this man. "Tell me about your daughter. How did she die?"

"All I know is what her husband told me. She was killed in a car wreck." Alexis found it hard to believe that this reprobate was showing compassion for his children for the first time.

"Can you give me some details of my sister's death?" She was testing him.

"Jack, her husband, told me she was coming home from work and was killed by a drunk driver."

Seth looked at Andy and spoke up then. "Lawrence, was your daughter's name Natalie?"

Lawrence's shoulders shook, and he took a moment to collect himself. "Yes, her name was Natalie. Why are you asking?" The coffee was shaking in his jittery hands.

"None of us knew her, but we all know Jack, her husband." Seth placed his hand on Alexis's shoulder and began telling Lawrence the details. The man listened, hung his head, and began to weep in earnest. For once, the crowd around him was not threatening.

Despite her inner turmoil, Alexis noticed Minnie eyeing the parking lot and knew what she was thinking. Clients would be arriving soon. Seth picked up on it also and made a bold suggestion.

"Lawrence, these folks have to prepare for business. Let's go to my house and get you cleaned up, and then we will join Andy at his diner for breakfast."

Lawrence shook his head and got to his unsteady feet. Alexis thought he looked upset and possibly afraid. "Why are you hesitating, Dad?"

Her words seemed to melt him. He looked at Seth. "You would take me into your home and then go out in public with me?"

"Absolutely."

"Thank you," he said. He then held out the box he had brought in and said, "Alexis, this is for you."

She opened it and looked at the moldy contents. It was just a bunch of junk, and she had no interest in any of it. What could her father have to offer her after all these years of desertion? She asked Seth to take the box home with him.

"Do you want some help with him?" Andy asked.

"I can handle it. Go on back to the diner, and we'll be there soon."

* * *

Seth took Lawrence to his home and helped him get settled in the guest bedroom. He then got some of his old clothes out for him. *Ironic,* he thought. He was now giving his clothes away rather than disposing of Sherri's.

Lawrence emerged from the bathroom looking much cleaner and better groomed. His speech was steady and calm. Seth had brewed his usual full pot of coffee and handed him a cup.

Lawrence stared at him as he sipped. "I remember you now. Ain't you the tax and accounting guy? I heard you and your wife helped out Rita and Alexis."

"I am the tax guy, and yes, we did help them out."

"Where's your wife?" Lawrence asked, looking around the downstairs area.

"I lost her about the same as Natalie's death."

"That's too bad. What was her name?"

"Sherri."

"Man, that sounds familiar. I've seen that name somewhere recently. Hey, where's that box I have for Alexis?"

"It's still in the trunk of my car, why?"

"Let's go look at it."

Seth had no desire to rummage through the box, and secretly wished he could purge the filthy thing. He changed the course of the conversation.

"Lawrence, let's head over to Andy's place first and get some breakfast. Then we'll deal with the box."

"Breakfast sounds good."

They made the short trip to the diner and parked in front. Andy had apparently been waiting for them and met them in the parking lot. Lorna had intuitively followed her husband outside.

As soon as Lawrence got out of the car, he went to the rear and tapped on the trunk. "Seth, open the trunk."

Seth hedged—*not this box again*—but he did pop the trunk. "Lawrence, this can wait. Let's go on in and get something to eat."

Lorna intervened. "What's in the trunk?"

"An old box full of junk, that's all I know. It reeks," he whispered.

"Just give me a couple of seconds," Lawrence said. He rummaged through the moldy box. Everyone but Lorna stepped back as he picked through the contents. She watched as he kept flipping through the stuff in the box.

"Here it is," he said proudly. He pulled a dusty book from the box and banged the dust off on his pant leg, forgetting he was wearing someone else's clean clothes.

Lorna gasped. "It's—it's one of the children's Bibles that we handed out at our church camps! Mr. Chandler, can I look through this?" Lawrence eagerly handed it to her, and Seth and Andy came closer to look over her shoulder.

After she had the Bible in her grasp, Lorna opened it to a page where an old envelope had been shoved between the pages. It bore a distinct heading on the front: "TO MISS SHERRI." The envelope had the Kiser Camp Logo.

Lorna carefully extracted the letter, and the brittle paper rattled as she opened it up. She began reading the contents:

Miss Sherri,

Thank you for telling me about Jesus this afternoon and how he died on the cross for my sins. Thank you for sharing how he could be my savior. I went back to cabin four and asked him to come into my heart and forgive me of my sins. I want to be with him in heaven someday. Please say thanks to Miss Lorna too. I love you both, but not as much as I love Jesus.

—Natalie Gilarski

"There you have it!" Lorna said. "Proof of an innocent child coming to faith in Jesus. Where did you get this Bible?"

"I've had it for about twenty years. I stopped to see Natalie and her mother one time looking for money. I got none, but Natalie gave me that Bible and told me Jesus loved me. At that time I was running for my life and, well...never got around to reading it."

Suddenly, a memory blossomed in Seth's mind. "This is uncanny, but I think I remember Sherri talking about a little girl she mentored in one of those weeklong camps—her name might have been Natalie. Sherri wanted to stay in contact with her, and the girl said she'd written her a letter, but she got picked up early that week. Sherri was really disappointed that she never heard from her again. Until now. Lawrence, this Bible and letter are the answer to a lot of prayers."

"Well, I knew I saw that name 'Sherri' somewhere." Lawrence turned and shook Seth's hand. "Now we can get that breakfast." Andy led the way. He mentioned to Seth that he should contact Jack.

Jack was relieved when his phone rang, it gave him a respite from Jonathan's forty-five-minute spiel regarding Josie and Dexter and the need for a pastor at their place.

"Hi, Seth, what's up?"

TAKE IT TO THE HOUSE

CHAPTER ONE

Olivia Hood slumped low in her office chair, staring around her former office. Her dismissal had been quick, execution-style. She had been summarily fired from Shannon Mergers and Acquisitions Corporation. She would receive no severance pay. She was gone. Her key role in the merger of Murphy Auto Supply and Blanton Automotive meant nothing. Another casualty meant to serve as a reminder to others.

Her head hurt from the excesses of the night before. It dulled her thinking. She wasn't a drinker, but the exuberance of success had gotten the best of her. Olivia sank even lower, itemizing the details of the merger. She had pioneered and facilitated every move. She was the one who'd mollified John Murphy when Aaron Blanton suddenly bolted and attempted to kill the proposal. She'd worked for days to placate both parties and bring them back to the table. Her boss, Rory Shannon, had been pleased. He'd promised her the role of vice president. The newly decorated corner office was all but hers. The anticipation of a higher salary had enticed her to sign a lease on a new Lexus just last week—the culmination of her efforts was everything she'd dreamed of for years. For one glorious week, she was indispensable and invincible. Her professionalism and discipline had paid big dividends. Now, she was canned.

Why had she drunk so much at the party last night? Why had she laughed at her boss's wife and described her to an executive partner as "a crashing jumbo jet"? Yes, Judith was obese and staggering drunk, and the remarks had seemed funny—even clever—at the time, but Mrs. Jumbo Jet had overheard. Just one look at Olivia and then at her husband had sealed the demise of Olivia's career.

She began clearing out her office. There weren't many personal items. No family pictures or graduation diplomas hung prominently on the wall. Olivia grabbed a small box and dumped her things into it. She deliberately left the lights on. Then, her fury turned to the wastebasket. She backed up, took aim, and violently kicked it. Crushing the metal can gave her a little thrill.

She strode over to the corner office that would have been hers as vice president. She looked at it and thought about the future she'd envisioned. Then she spotted another wastebasket. It received the same punishment as the first. *Bam*—another perfect kick.

Rory Shannon's office was next. The door was unlocked. Excellent. She was going for the hat trick. Olivia sized up the brass wastebasket beside his desk and moved in for the kill. A running leap at the can, perfect placement, and a monster dent. The contents spewed all over the office. Retaliation felt good, even if she'd rather be smashing Rory Shannon's face than his wastebasket. It was small payback for last year's Christmas party when he'd gotten drunk and crawled all over her. She'd spurned his crude advances but hadn't told anyone about his behavior. Where was the company policy on drunken indiscretions then? Conveniently overlooked. He was the owner and got a pass. End of story.

Olivia exited the parking lot in her Ford Escape. *Crud. Tomorrow I would have been driving a Lexus.* Another reality hit her—the lease on that new apartment at Bonham Point. Well, that wouldn't be happening. She had to be out of her current apartment by the end of next week. They had already notified her that it had been leased, and the new occupants wanted in by next weekend. Now she was obligated to vacate. Olivia was jobless, and now she would be crowding the homeless for space on the street. *One moment I'm on top, the next I'm in the gutter. It's not supposed to happen like this.*

Her phone rang. Four Seasons was calling, the place her father lived. It was an apartment complex that offered month-to-month living. Their standards could be higher, her father would complain no matter where he lived. Even when her mother had slaved away keeping a nice house for him, he'd taken it for granted. Now that her mother was dead, Olivia wasn't about to step into her shoes. Doing anything for her father was a thankless waste. Her career had always been far more rewarding—up until this week.

The call from Four Seasons concerned, as always, her father's irascible behavior. Olivia agreed to come over and confront him. She pulled up to the main office and noticed that all the convenient spaces had been taken by the complex's employees. Typical. She parked in a remote area of the lot and began walking to the office, wondering how long this inconvenience would take.

In the corner of her eye, she saw what appeared what be a hapless vagrant. As she picked up her pace and passed him, the man spoke.

"Good morning. What a nice day God has given us." She ignored him. He spoke again, louder this time. "Good morning! What a great day the Lord has provided."

Olivia spun around and faced him. "Excuse me, are you talking to me?" Her tone was deliberately irritating. Olivia looked closer and realized that the man was wasn't very old, even close to her age. Probably one of the thugs who lived under the nearby bridge. "Does security know you're loitering out here? They lock up reprobates like you."

"Maybe I'm untidy right now, but I assure you that I'm not a reprobate. Look at both of us. Which one is smiling?"

Olivia wanted to flip him off and get away from the creep, but he raced ahead and opened the door for her.

"Beat it, jerk" was her parting remark. Olivia walked inside, never looking back. She thought perhaps she should alert someone about the man lurking outside. Continuing down the corridor to the office of Zelda Gambier, the general manager, she knocked briefly and walked in. "I got here as quickly as possible."

Zelda looked up from her desk, apparently surprised. "Good morning. Thanks for coming so promptly. I hope this doesn't affect your work day?" Olivia ignored the remark.

"What has he done now?" She coolly asked.

"Just the same as usual."

Olivia's instinct was to reply that they were not discussing a second-grade student's bad conduct, but she dismissed those thoughts.

"I dislike speaking of your father unfavorably, but he can be difficult—even belligerent—and his neighbors have been complaining. Frankly, Miss Hood, if he doesn't cooperate, we may have to ask him to leave. We have a substantial waitlist. Our staff would welcome some new residents with a little more tact."

Olivia could win this confrontation handily with a few choice words, but she resisted the urge. "Let me talk to my father. I ask your patience with him. At the moment, moving him is not convenient for me as I'm in that process myself."

"Yes, please talk to him. Forgive me, but I often wonder if he's troublesome because he's lonely."

She thought about setting this woman straight on her father's true character; she needed to back off.

"Olivia—may I call you Olivia?"

"Go ahead."

"Again, please forgive me, but you appear to be burdened." This lady has no borders on intrusion.

Normally, Olivia would say something along the lines of "keep it all to yourself, lady." But this time she didn't. "I don't mind you asking. There is a lot of friction at work right now, but I'm in control. I'm putting feelers out with some other companies. You never know when any of us might get a sudden dismissal and be on the street." She sat up a little straighter. "Of course, I'm still doing very well. I'll be moving to Bonham Point."

"That's a very nice area."

"I work hard and put in the hours. It has its rewards."

Then Ms. Gambier asked another question, her eyes making direct contact with Olivia's. "How can I pray for you?" More crossover intrusion, will it ever end, she thought.

Olivia had never been asked that before. Wasn't prayer something personal that you kept to yourself? She fumbled for a reply. "I suppose you can pray for my job to go well . . . and even my relationship with my father." She regretted the last request. Her relationships were no business of Zelda Gambier's, and her father was beyond the impact of any prayer that she was familiar with. She decided to leave and made a departing remark.

"I was bothered by a young man on the way to your office. Scruffy looking, probably homeless. Has anyone else complained?"

"Was he friendly, possibly overly friendly?"

"I wouldn't refer to it being friendly, but that's him. Do you know him?"

Zelda smiled. "I do know him. That's Billy Ashby. He is a decent young man, old-fashioned and outgoing. Billy works part-time for our maintenance contractor and does mowing and trimming. Today, they were spreading tons of mulch around our courtyards, pool area, and outlying buildings. He's always hands-on. Probably covered with that nasty black stuff."

Olivia's stomach sank. What had she called him? She couldn't remember the last time she'd felt some shame; not even her scorching comments about Rory Shannon's wife had the same sting. This was all so strange.

"He's new with maintenance. He formerly worked for one of the auto supply chains over in Indianapolis. I don't know many of the details, but his employer was involved in a merger. Evidently, he got cut to trim expenses."

No way, Olivia thought. Could it be the same merger she had facilitated? She knew how the merger process worked. Job cuts would temporarily enhance the bottom line and add to a deal's attractiveness. Some positions would strategically be eliminated to achieve that goal. But for the sake of the deal, it had to be done. *I guess this guy could have been part of the fallout.*

She had never met one of her victims before. Maybe she'd misjudged the mulch guy. *Am I suddenly mellowing at age twenty-six? I will be eaten alive in the predatory domain of mergers and acquisitions.*

"Are you OK?"

Olivia started. "I'm fine. Thank you for the chat. I will try to reason with my father. Thank you for your thoughtfulness to pray for me." She excused herself and headed for the encounter with her father. *There are two ways to approach it. I can be confrontational or show a little kindness. If the latter doesn't work, I can always blast him.*

She walked to unit 405 and tapped on the door.

CHAPTER TWO

Oliver Hood was in his early sixties, retired, and at war with everyone. He was like a cactus—prickly in all aspects of life. He had no desire to be sociable with anyone, including his family. He was convinced that everyone was attempting to conspire against him. He met them all head on and basked in it.

He was prejudiced against anyone who didn't look, speak, or dress like him, but he'd flatten anyone who dared call him a bigot. After all, he had married a Puerto Rican woman. That proved he was no racist. However, the fiery temper that had begun to rage shortly after their brief honeymoon had lasted all through the marriage and beyond his wife's death two years previous.

That same rancor had throttled his career as an assembly line worker at a tractor and implement company. He was ostracized by his coworkers and spent most of the workday alone. That was fine with him. It gave him the freedom to bitch to himself and not listen to any of their complaints. Management slotted him for the quickest possible retirement.

Olivia had found a needed respite in going to college and seldom visiting her parents. She always felt a pang of guilt at leaving her mother alone with her father, but academics took over as Olivia's priority. When her mother died, she immersed herself in her career, and her resentment toward her father compounded.

She knocked on her father's door and ignored his surly response to go away. "Dad, it's me. Unlock the door."

"What do you want?"

"Open the door. I want to talk to you." She heard the TV go off and the old recliner creak, and then the door opened.

"Well, come on in." He turned around and shuffled back into the stuffy apartment. Picking up some clutter from the sofa, he pointed to a bare spot. "Sit down. What's wrong now?"

"I just came from Ms. Gambier's office."

"I knew it. What are they complaining about now? My TV is too loud, or my truck is parked in the wrong spot, or it's straddling the yellow line? Maybe they don't like me shouting at those maintenance people who start mowing at seven in the morning and stomping around outside my windows throwing mulch everywhere. Wait, I know—I'm not recycling my trash. That's it, isn't it?"

"None of those were brought up, but I am sure you're guilty of all of them."

"If you have nothing more than that to say, get on out of here and leave me alone."

Olivia was tempted to satisfy him by storming out, but she didn't. She offered a suggestion. "I thought we could get lunch and spend some time together."

"Then pick me up tomorrow for breakfast."

Olivia was taken aback. "OK, I'll be here at eight o'clock."

"Won't that make you late for work?"

"I have it covered. Nothing to worry about." On an unfamiliar impulse, she went over to give him a slight hug and then waved goodbye and left.

Olivia got in her car and slowly drove through the parking lot, hoping to spot Billy Ashby. She saw him in a green space next to the pool area, arranging black mulch with his rake. She stopped, lightly tapped her horn, and waved. Billy looked her way, hesitated, then dropped his tool and walked toward her car. Olivia got out and went to meet him.

"Billy, this doesn't come easy for me, but I owe you an apology. And, in case you haven't noticed, I am smiling this time."

"How did you find out my name?"

"Ms. Gambier gave it to me."

Billy seemed to relax. "No need to apologize. I guess this black mulch does give me a freaky appearance. We're almost done with the mulching, and then maybe I can look normal." Olivia thought she'd like to see that. Those blue eyes peering through mulch smudges on his face were promising. *He may be even cuter when he's finally cleaned up. And I haven't seen a man this laidback since I started working for Shannon and his cronies.*

"I get off work around five thirty today. Would you like to meet later and get a bite to eat?"

Billy's request surprised her. Olivia stood there, knowing there was a time when she would have spurned an offer like this immediately. She was an executive—or at least she had been. *What the heck? I'm unemployed and about to be removed from my apartment. I can't sink any lower.* "I guess I could fit you in." Her smile softened the sarcasm, but it didn't come naturally.

"Ever been to Frankie's Place?"

It didn't sound like a place she would take a client for a business lunch. "I've never been there, but it sounds fine to me. Aren't they over on South Fourth Street, close to that military surplus store?" She detested that filthy place, but this guy probably had a wardrobe full of camo from there.

"That's them. How about we meet at seven thirty, or I can come by and pick you up."

"No, I can meet you there." No way would she divulge her location.

"I like to know the names of ladies I dine with."

At that moment, Olivia realized she'd never introduced herself. "That's a fair request. I'm Olivia Hood."

"Olivia . . . that's a pretty name. It was used by Shakespeare in one of his plays, possibly *Twelfth Night*. The male counterpart is Oliver."

She was impressed by his knowledge of Shakespeare but knew her name had nothing to do with theater and everything to do with her self-obsessed father.

"I need to get back to work. Please excuse me," Billy told her.

"You are excused, and I will see you this evening at seven thirty."

*   *   *

As his new acquaintance got back in her car and pulled away, it occurred to Billy that he didn't even have her phone number. Hopefully, she wouldn't be a no-show. He went back to the bags of mulch, but he was thinking about the girl he'd just met.

At 5:45, he dropped by Zelda Gambier's office. "The mulching is done. Please tell Mr. Landis that I will finish the mowing and trimming first thing tomorrow."

"I'll tell him. Billy, you're a mess. You certainly got the attention of a visitor earlier today."

"You must be talking about Olivia."

"Oh, you know her name?"

"Naturally. We're having dinner this evening over at Frankie's."

"She's going out with you? You resemble something that just emerged from a toxic landfill. Get out of here and clean yourself up! You're going to need some extra time." Billy moved toward the door. "Hey, Billy. Have fun tonight."

"It is going to be interesting," he told her.

Billy got to the parking lot and tried in vain to knock the mulch from his clothing and shoes, then gave up and climbed into his car. He was positive that the air conditioner would work this time, but it sputtered as usual. He powered down the windows and headed home, wind in his hair, sun in his eyes, and pieces of mulch swirling around the car. He was looking forward to dinner and the chance to get to know Olivia better.

*   *   *

They arrived at the restaurant simultaneously, and Billy was the first to speak.

"You look pretty good for Frankie's Place." He seemed to be referring to her dress, but Olivia wondered if he was admiring more than that.

"You clean up well too." He had his cleanest jeans on, along with a golf shirt. At least it wasn't camo.

Olivia followed Billy into the eatery, and they settled into a red vinyl booth. She decided to plunge right in. "So, how did you get into the mulching business? Zelda Gambier told me you used to work for an auto parts supplier in Indianapolis. Any chance it was John Murphy Auto Supply?"

Billy looked taken aback. "Yeah, it was. I worked summers there during my college years at Butler. After graduation, they offered me a position at their main distribution center."

She had assumed that he'd been a blue-collar hourly worker. She regretted that now. "What is your degree in?"

"I studied business with an emphasis on finance. I kicked around the idea of maybe going on to law school. I still think about it at times, especially during mulch season." Olivia smiled.

The waitress came alongside their table to take their orders. Both chose the double cheeseburger platters with iced tea. Olivia was pleased to see there was no alcohol was on the menu. Her "jumbo jet" remarks were still fresh in her mind. Let it all lie still.

"So, what pathways are you contemplating?" As someone whose own career had just boomeranged, she had a sincere interest.

"Ideally, like a lot of people, I would like to have my own business, but it's all just lying on the table for the time being. I have no sense of direction, but my mulching days will rapidly be coming to a close and won't be renewed.

Olivia smiled and was silent for a few moments, swirling the straw in her tea, trying to think of a clever way to phrase her question and failing. Finally, she asked, "Why were you dismissed at Murphy? If you prefer not to discuss it, I understand."

Billy didn't hold back. "I was too close to the inventory control programs." Olivia looked confused, and Billy opened up a little more. "I don't know your background, but inventory management is huge in a business operation. Miscalculations will have a big impact on profitability. Spreadsheets are critical and give a lot of information, but they can be easily altered or disappear for . . . convenience." Billy paused. "In my particular incident, I got too close to some questionable issues. My boss said they were 'gray areas.' I didn't agree."

"I'm with you now. Go ahead."

Billy abruptly changed the subject. "You have a lot of interest in my career with Murphy. What's up?"

She decided to be transparent. "Like you, I have a business degree and an MBA in finance. I've been working in mergers and acquisitions for the past few years. In fact, I was deeply involved in the Murphy and Blanton merger. I was the lead person and reported directly to Rory Shannon."

Billy tensed up for a moment, but just then their drinks arrived. When the waitress had gone, he looked calm again. "You just spoke in the past tense about your job."

"You caught that, hmm? As of yesterday, I am gone from Shannon Corp."

"Did you get too close to a situation, like me?" His eyes and smile touched her.

Olivia returned his smile. "Way too close. I'm not much of drinker, and I went overboard at a work function. I made an ass out of myself in front of all the right people and was summarily fired."

Billy began chuckling. "I saw that side of you this afternoon. I prefer your current demeanor. It's more tolerable."

She didn't know if it was the casual diner atmosphere, or this man's engaging smile, or the fact that she had little to lose, but she felt at ease with Billy. "Prior to the celebration carnage, I signed a lease on a new Lexus and an apartment in Bonham Point. I gave notice on my current place, and now I have to vacate. They have no other units available. Booked solid."

Billy jumped in with advice. "The dealership will rescind the Lexus lease once you explain your job status. The apartment is another challenge. Most places do a credit and background search. Since you are unemployed, it may be difficult to find a new apartment at short notice. I do know of one opportunity. Are you familiar with the near north end of town, a place called Glacier Village? It's a transitioning area. Some streets are going through urban growing pains, but the majority of it is still popular and a decent place to live.

Olivia sensed his direction. "I am in no position to purchase a house or even lease one."

"Please hear me out, OK?"

Billy seemed eager to help her, something Olivia hadn't experienced in a long time. "Very well, I'll hear you out."

"I have a friend who owns four homes in the Glacier locale. Two are currently rented, and a third is close to being occupied, but the house adjacent to that one is available. Personally, I think it's the nicest of the bunch—a classic two-story, four bedrooms upstairs, three and a half baths, family room, dining room, living room, two-car garage, and a screened-in porch."

"You sound like a real estate agent. Is there a big close coming?"

Billy laughed. "I can put you in that gem for around $1,200 per month, and month-to-month, too."

"Why so reasonable?" Before he could respond, the waitress popped up at their table with a basket of rolls and their cheeseburger platters. Billy asked Olivia to join him in giving thanks, and he prayed a short blessing over the meal. She had mixed emotions but bowed her head, peeking over at him.

Olivia hadn't eaten all day, and she welcomed the monster cheeseburger. Between bites, she continued the house talk. "Why is the rent so attractive?"

"Tyler buys on speculation. He's looking for market appreciation as well as rental income. It's in his favor to keep the houses occupied. Insurance companies prefer them that way, and it reduces the chance of vandalism." Billy took a bite of his huge cheeseburger, chewing as politely as possible.

"How's your food?"

"My food is excellent. My time with you is just as good." Olivia liked his response. For the first time in the last few years, she was enjoying the company of another person. Her collegiate life and business career had always been about fast-tracking. The next rung on the ladder forever dangled in front of her, clamoring for her grasp.

"Olivia, I have only known you for a couple of hours, but I feel at ease with you."

She recognized a come-on move but played along. "I'm at ease with you as well, Mr. Ashby. Anything else you want to sell me?"

"In a way, maybe. This might come across as bold, but here it goes. I have a burden for your father."

Olivia stopped him. Her flirt-mode was off. "How do you know my father, and why should you have a so-called 'burden' for him?"

"I saw you go into his unit, and I put two and two together. Maybe a *concern* for him would have been a more appropriate term than *burden*. He's pegged around the complex as being totally abrasive. I don't see him that way at all. I admit that I'm a finance dude and know nothing about psychology, but I sense he's lonely and just frustrated with life."

"Sounds like you've been talking to Ms. Gambier."

"Not really. I just hate to see him alienated from the other residents. I've reached out to him at times, but I got nowhere. What's sad is I've seen him peeking out his blinds as the other folks load into the minibuses for group excursions."

"So, you're spying on him?"

Billy laughed awkwardly. "I know it sounds like spying, but I just happen to catch glimpses while I'm doing my outdoor maintenance. They keep me busy all over the complex."

"Apparently not busy enough if you have time to keep up surveillance on my father's activities."

"Come on now. I have a little compassion for your dad. Nothing more and nothing less. It's disheartening to see him so down all the time." He seemed sincere in his consideration for a man he hardly knew. Olivia wasn't sure what to make of Billy Ashby. She gave him some more rope.

"I guess you're harmless enough. You just have no idea what my dad is like."

Billy changed the flow of their talk. "Do you know what he's paying for rent?"

"I have no idea."

"Well, I happen to know those one-bedroom apartments rent for $1,000 per month."

"You're kidding. That's exorbitant for that place!"

"Now, I won't ask what you are shelling out monthly, but I can think of a pretty good way for you and your father to save some money, if you get my drift."

Olivia sat back and crossed her arms. "You are implying that my dad and I could share that house. Billy, you have no clue about the relationship between us. It's been a problem for years. There have been times when we couldn't even share the same state, let alone the same house. You might think my dad is lonely and needs some TLC, but that doesn't justify me living with him." She wanted to say more. *You are way of bounds here. Back off!* But she bit it back. The despair from years of family trauma and mental pain was suddenly weighing down her heart and choking up her throat. Billy looked as if he were on the verge of making an apology, but she cut him off. "Let's drive by this house. I want to check it out."

"I can drive, but my air isn't working."

"We can take my car. It's no Lexus, but the air does work." A couple of hours ago, she had total disdain for the unkempt man in front of her. Now she was getting into a car with him and checking out a vacant house in an unfamiliar part of town. It felt natural.

CHAPTER THREE

Olivia pulled off North Cooper Road into a short driveway. Her first impression was positive. The two-story house was typical of homes built all over the metro area in the seventies and eighties. The other houses on the street were tasteful, and she agreed with Billy that the neighborhood still retained a lot of charm and didn't appear threatening.

She knew there were a lot of factors to consider. Moving from an apartment to a house, this particular location, possibly sharing a home with her father. . . . Billy interrupted her thoughts by punching in the code on the security keypad. "I can't believe Tyler didn't change the code! I thought it was a joke." That smile never seemed to leave his face. Olivia shook her head and entered the house.

They headed through the foyer into the kitchen. Olivia noticed a slight musty smell, but that could be alleviated with a good airing. As they toured the home, it was obvious that the paint scheme and wallpaper were dated. They viewed the downstairs and upstairs rooms. Olivia kept her distance. They came back down and went into the family room. Billy unlocked a sliding door, and they went out to an enclosed porch.

He cranked out two of the windows for ventilation. "This would be a really cool place to read and meditate." Olivia knew that wouldn't apply to her or her father. Oliver would be out there cursing the nearest neighbor—or anyone else within range. She seldom read, and she certainly didn't have time for meditation. Her career had never provided any time for hobbies. Olivia felt a pang as she thought of that career, the one that was now buried in Rory Shannon's personal dumpster with the lid shut and a jumbo jet resting on it.

They closed up the house and headed back to the diner. Billy didn't press her to make a quick decision. As they pulled up next to his car, he said, "I enjoyed our time together. I hardly know you, but I know you're feeling overwhelmed by all that's happened. I want to see you bounce back to a higher level."

"Thank you, that's sweet. I think."

"Can I share something with you?"

"Certainly."

"I have had some impediments in my life, but I know the barriers and problems don't matter, only how I face them. Simply put, it's through the power of Jesus Christ."

Olivia was caught off guard but let him continue.

"The book of Mark, chapter 8, says what good is gaining the whole world and yet forfeiting our souls? All our successes mean nothing in terms of our eternity."

Olivia graciously smiled. "I will fact-check that passage. Thank you for sharing it." It meant nothing to her. "Well, I'll think about that house, but it's getting late, and I need to be heading home."

"Sure." As Billy got out of her car, he asked to see her again.

"That would be nice."

This time, he got her phone number. Pleasantries were exchanged, and they departed their own ways.

*   *   *

Olivia returned to her apartment. As she was climbing out of the car, she noticed a little paper tract next to her. Billy must have planted it there. It was an illustration of "The Way of Salvation: The Romans Road." She smiled and put it in her purse.

She walked up the steps to her second-floor unit and the reality of moving ambushed her. But things were different than they had been just that morning. This problem would be faced with a new ally. She wasn't alone. Maybe that house could be feasible. She entered her apartment, and the first thing she saw was the wastepaper basket by the door. She smiled; it wasn't going down with one of her specialty kicks.

Surveying her apartment, she began making mental notes on what she could purge before her move. She started in her bedroom closet. On a shelf were two boxes of her mother's things. They'd been in her possession since her mother died, but she had never opened them. It would be a small start, but maybe the contents could be pitched.

She pulled one box down and placed it on her bed, removing the tape and pulling the flaps open. On top of the contents was a Bible. *Odd*, she thought. *I've never seen this.* Olivia opened it to the first page. "Presented to Angelina Maria Hernandez, August 16, 1960, by Pastor Stanley Belvedere, First Fellowship Church. 'May you always walk in His path, and may His word be a light unto that path.'" There was a note of the date she'd accepted Christ and a baptism date.

Olivia recalled her mother's dedication to spiritual matters. Her attempts to take her daughter to church had always been spurned by Oliver. Over the years, both father and daughter had mocked Angelina's faith, never giving her any support. Olivia traced the handwritten dedication with her finger and felt a wave of sadness. Billy might have called it a "burden" for her late mother. This Bible had meant so much to her, and she'd kept believing no matter how much her family had discouraged her. She had her own form of dedication similar to her daughter's allegiance to her career.

Olivia was hurt as she thought back on all the grief and pain she had caused her mother. She thought of her own folly in seeking a better position, a newer car, a bigger apartment, all the while neglecting her family. Neglecting her soul.

She felt compelled to read the tract that Billy had given her. She picked up her mother's Bible and fumbled through it, finally finding the book of Romans and reading through the key verses one by one. In her own way, Olivia began praying as a new disciple of Christ.

The past was the past, but she knew changes could be made that would affect the future. She and her father could improve their relationship by following her mother's example. She put the Bible on the nightstand beside her and returned the box to its shelf. It would be moving with her wherever she ended up—rental house, apartment, or street corner.

Her phone rang, and the caller ID showed Billy Ashby. She answered.

"Are you still up?" Billy asked her.

"I am."

"I wanted to invite you to church this Sunday. I attend Highland Park Assembly, over on Carson Avenue."

"This seems a little sudden. Let me get back to you."

"Oh, come on, you will enjoy it. I would like to see you again."

Olivia liked that thought. "OK, I can join you. What time?"

"First service starts at nine o'clock. I can pick you up."

Remembering his car, she declined. "Why don't I meet you? That would be easier, and maybe safer." Billy caught the weak attempt at humor.

There was a pause. "Olivia, I have a better idea. It's only Wednesday evening. I would actually like to see you before Sunday." Initially, she wanted to decline, but gave in.

She liked that arrangement. "Let's meet tomorrow evening after your work. Now, it's getting late, and I have to get up early and meet my father for breakfast." Her halfhearted attempt to truncate the call failed, and they talked past two in the morning.

CHAPTER FOUR

Earlier that same evening, Oliver had sat in his apartment and stared at the wall with brooding eyes. He was miserable, and for the first time in his life, he knew it was his fault and no one else's. He could cast the blame over a wide area and target a lot of people, but it would be in vain. He had to take ownership of his life and his actions.

His daughter—his little girl who he'd always been proud of against his will—wanted to spend time with him. She'd even given him a hug. No one had hugged him since Angelina passed away. He and his daughter had been pushing each other away for years, and now she wanted to get breakfast with him.

Oliver's eyes wandered to a photo of his wife, and he thought of the qualities in her that he'd always despised as weaknesses. Angelina was gone, but maybe he could mend the shattered bond with his daughter. However, there was something inside holding him back. Something had always held him back.

Shrill, blaring music from next door jolted him. Oliver jumped out of his chair and went over to the wall, about to pound it with his fist and exercise his unique vocabulary of profanity. He hesitated halfway across the room and came to a standstill. *OK now. If you want to make a change, start right here.*

Oliver went outside instead. The fresh air was invigorating, and he decided to take a walk, something he hadn't done for months. He had just beaten his inconsiderate neighbors at their own game. They weren't going to jam his airwaves with their aggravating music. He continued into the adjacent neighborhood and noticed people sitting on their front porches. He envied those folks. That would be a nice experience—if he had a porch. He waved at one couple, and they returned the gesture. The same arm that had been raised countless times in anger proved it could be used in a friendly manner.

His thoughts then turned to that pesky young maintenance man who always had cheerful remarks about a beautiful day and other trivial stuff. Maybe he could exchange some pleasantries with that kid. He wouldn't be hard to find; he was always popping up with words of good cheer, and lately seemed to be near all of the mulching activities.

*   *   *

Olivia hadn't expected to see her father waiting out front. Usually, she had to knock on his door, identify herself, and wait to be let in.

Oliver waved and got into the waiting car. "I'm hungry. Where are we going?"

"A friend of mine and I ate at Frankie's Place last night, and he mentioned they have a good breakfast."

"Oh? Who's the fellow you went out with?"

Her father had never asked about her social life. No way was she going to disclose that it was the maintenance guy who had tried to befriend him. It was too early for an angry rant.

"Just an acquaintance, nobody special."

The diner was busy, but they found a table near one of the front windows. As soon as they sat down, Olivia had a sinking feeling. The waitress coming to their table had creamy brown skin, and her name badge read "Valentina." Olivia silently prayed the best way she knew how, dreading the spectacle her father was sure to make.

"Good morning, folks. My name is Valentina. Would you like to start with some coffee?" Olivia was frozen to her chair. She closed her eyes and dug her hands into the upholstery.

"Yes please, Valentina. That is a lovely name. Are you from Puerto Rico?"

"Yes, sir. All of my family is from there."

Olivia was already cringing, anticipating a crude comment. Puerto Rico was about to experience a hurricane named Oliver.

"My late wife was from Arecibo. I lost her two years ago. This is our daughter, Olivia." Olivia opened one eye and reached out to take a menu from Valentina.

"I am sorry to hear of your loss. Your daughter is very pretty. I bet she takes after your wife."

Oliver sat up a little straighter in his chair. "Fortunately, she didn't get my looks. My wife was an attractive lady, and they do favor each other." He gave Olivia a wink, and her thoughts spiraled into confusion. Valentina poured the coffee, took their omelet orders, and then left for the kitchen.

"Dad, you really surprised me. You were polite to Valentina. I'm impressed."

Oliver grinned at her. "I'm trying. I don't want to be a pain in the butt *all* the time. I admit, I'm usually no joy to be around." He looked down at his hands and mumbled something, bending and re-bending the menu.

"What was that?"

"Olivia, I know you are twenty-five, but you're still my little girl."

"Dad, I'm twenty-six."

"Really? Anyway, I want to be a father to you." He finally looked up, and they sat studying each other in silence for several minutes. Olivia couldn't say anything, but she felt a piece of her heart melting. Their eyes said that they would be there for each other. Oliver reached over and took his daughter's hand.

"Everything OK, folks?" Valentina had brought their coffee.

"Perfect," Oliver said. The hurricane had burned out.

They both enjoyed the meal. Usually, at this hour, Olivia would be well into her day, and her father would be wolfing down a bowl of cereal in his apartment and watching a local news program (all the while loathing his neighbors and defying them to make any noise distraction).

After breakfast was finished, Olivia shared two items with her father. She spoke briefly about her job loss, and then she told him about her housing situation and the place for rent in Glacier Village. Oliver reassured her that, with her qualifications, she would bounce back in the job market, but he surprised her by putting more emphasis on the house than her job loss. Oliver asked questions about the house and sounded very interested in the porch. It was clear that he wanted to see it firsthand.

Olivia texted Billy for permission and the code for the door. He promptly got back to her. He agreed to give the code if she would meet him that evening to join in a special ministry he was involved in. She agreed, and he sent the code. 1234. *Brilliant*. Olivia laughed and shook her head. Their meeting was on for 5:30 p.m.

"That was a lot of communication just to get a passcode," Oliver told her. She smiled but didn't reply. Her father left a generous tip for Valentina, and they drove toward the house on North Cooper Road.

During the short drive, Oliver talked about his neighbors' terrible taste in music and how he'd been thinking a lot about porches lately. "You know, somewhere I could relax. A place to have some peace and start to enjoy life."

Olivia glanced over at him and said, "Are you hinting at something, Dad?"

"Hinting? Me? What would I be hinting at?"

"I have to move out in a matter of days, and you'd like nothing better than to leave Four Seasons."

"I would welcome another place to live." Oliver turned to face her as if just struck with an idea. "Hey, maybe this house would be good for both of us."

"It would be nice if we could make it work, even for the short-term," Olivia said.

They reached the house, entered the diabolical code, and toured the house. Both liked the layout and the price couldn't be beat. They decided to go for it.

Olivia texted Billy to say that they wanted the first option on the house and asked about the next steps. He replied that the next step was to meet him at Highland Fellowship Church at five thirty. He would bring a couple of sandwiches for their supper. The paperwork would come in due time.

Oliver bugged her about the mysterious texter all the way back to his apartment.

CHAPTER FIVE

The Wednesday church service schedule began at seven o'clock, but Billy's ministry started at half past five in the church parking lot. He and Olivia walked over to an old converted school bus. It was painted in soft pastel colors with the church name and address highlighted in blue and pink letters. Olivia noticed that the name "Joshua" was painted at the top of the cab, between the roof and the windshield. She assumed that Joshua was the driver, but she quickly learned that Billy was the man at the wheel.

He plopped down behind the wheel and pointed to a seat behind him for her to occupy. Olivia made herself comfortable and looked around the interior of the bus. The outside was pleasantly colorful, but the interior still bore the look of a school bus. However, Bible verses were written on the ceiling and some of the wall space. The calligraphy was excellent. Someone had taken extra care to do a good job with the inscriptions. Billy reached under the driver's seat and pulled out a card that he inserted in a plastic pocket above the windshield: "Tonight's driver is Mr. Billy."

"Are we taking a bus tour, Mr. Billy?"

"Yes, ma'am, we are."

"Do tell, Mr. Billy—will Mr. Joshua be joining us?

"He won't be tagging along this evening. This bus is named after a spy named Joshua who with Caleb and some other spies, was sent ahead of the Israelites to scout out the Promised Land and report back to Moses. Joshua and Caleb returned with positive input and praised God for the land he had promised. There were some obstacles, but they knew God would get them through all of them."

Billy slapped Joshua's dashboard. "This old gem is a 2001 seventy-one passenger International. In its previous life, it was used hard, but we have rebuilt all the mechanicals. It's running smoothly and is powered by God's grace. Now that we have our Joshua, we are praying for a Caleb." Olivia decided to make no further comment. She would let the evening unravel itself. Buses, biblical names, and spies were of no consequence to her.

"Our journey this evening begins here, and we cover about a ten-square-mile radius of the church. We pick up kids, usually junior-high age and younger. Our mission is to bring them back to the church, give them a meal, have devotions, let them play some sports, and get all of them back home by a quarter to ten. A lot of these kids are in need of someone to love on them. I give you fair warning—they can melt your heart. Of course, that's on the condition you want to make the journey with us this evening."

She gave him a pretty smile. "It appears to be a nice evening for a bus trip."

"Good, because I wasn't going to let you get off. We'll have some others joining us. Here they come now." Two more couples climbed onto the bus, and Billy made the introductions. He fired the old International up, let it idle briefly, then he looked in the rearview mirror and winked at Olivia. Billy prayed, and they were off.

In the first thirty minutes of the route, Olivia counted thirty-two kids. Billy gave each one a high five as they entered the bus and found seats. It was a diverse group of children, and they were noisy but respectful. They knew there were fun times ahead that evening.

As the bus navigated its route, Olivia noticed that it was skirting the Glacier Village area. They were close to the house she had just agreed to rent.

Billy made another stop, and a little preschool girl climbed on the bus. She appeared to be unattended. She climbed the steps, looked around at the faces staring at her, and quickly sat down on Olivia's seat, snuggling close to her.

Billy was watching in the mirror. "Esi, if you are going to stay in that seat, please hold on to Miss Olivia so you don't fall off it." The girl grabbed Olivia's arm and snuggled closer.

"Hi there. I am Miss Olivia. What's your name again?"

"I'm Esi, and I am from Ghana. That's in West Africa. Have you ever been there?"

"No, I have never been there. Maybe someday I can visit."

"If you go there, can I come with you?" The little girl's face was serious. "My mommy and daddy are there. I miss them." Olivia caught Billy's reflection in the mirror. He was trying to give her a silent lip message and shaking his head. She didn't know what he meant, but it seemed to be important and definitely involved her seat companion.

Joshua made a few more stops, and a couple of kids got on board each time. Billy continued his high fives, and all of the newcomers patted Esi on the head as they moved back to their seats. Esi liked the attention and showed it with a precious smile.

When the route was complete, Billy maneuvered the big International bus into the church's side parking lot next to a playground and basketball court. Two of the crew had a roster and checked off names as they departed the bus. There were eight new kids on this trip, and the info was transferred to the master list. Attendance for the evening was fifty-one, a new record for the Wednesday night activity.

The kids were given ten minutes of game time before their meal. Billy and Olivia joined the food worker's line, serving the kids. Once they were stationed side by side, Olivia was finally able to ask about Esi.

"Why is she here if her parents are still in Ghana?"

"Esi's parents are buried in Ghana. They were martyred by a renegade sect about six months ago. She has never been told about any of it. Personally, I disagree with not disclosing the details to her, but it's not my call. Her guardians have the control, not me."

"How did she make it to America?"

"The American Consulate got involved and facilitated her immigration through our State Department. She was accompanied by her aunt and the aunt's family. It's amazing what can happen when people have real concern for others. I know God was overseeing all of it."

"Why was she alone when we picked her up this evening? She's too young to be left by herself."

Billy laughed. "Believe me, she was not alone. They tend to remain in the background, but her family was keeping watch. Those folks are definitely family-oriented and protective of each other, especially their children, although they let the kids have some freedom. Esi is loved by them, and her care is top notch. Maybe you'll meet her family sometime."

"That would be interesting." Olivia was already fond of the little girl. Now that she knew she was an orphan, her heart began to ache for Esi. She looked around at all the other kids they had brought in on the bus. *What is going on in their lives? Neglect? Abuse? Hunger?* Her personal problems now seemed minuscule. Billy nudged her and said to pick up the pace—there were more mouths to feed.

She nudged him back. "Watch it, buddy." She brandished the serving spoon at him, and Billy got the point. He gave her a little bow and kept scooping out the macaroni.

The evening passed quickly, and then they all got back on the bus. The kids were obviously tired. Some had been up early that morning, and it had been a long day for them. Olivia returned to her seat behind Mr. Billy, and Esi curled up next to her and fell asleep.

Olivia wrapped her arm around the resting child. The flicker of passing streetlights glistened on Esi's face, showcasing her contented smile. The same flicker highlighted Olivia's face, and she caught Billy sneaking looks back at her. She gave him a teasing wink. After so many years without feeling a shred of affection for anyone, now she felt attached to this bus driver, the little girl snuggled next to her, and—strangely enough—her own parents.

The bus eventually stopped at Esi's home. When the door was opened, there were two men and a lady waiting to retrieve the little passenger. Olivia assisted the groggy Esi down the steps. A large man in colorful Ghanaian garb reached out and took Esi's hand while the other two, also dressed in traditional attire, thanked Billy. The lady spoke "blessings" to Olivia, and they all retreated into the house. Olivia stood staring at the house.

"Come on, lady, back onto the bus. We have to complete the course." She climbed back into her seat and Billy said, "How's your sense of geography right now?"

"Blurred. Why do you ask?"

"Esi's family lives on North Williams Street, which runs parallel with North Cooper. Your new house is close by. Tyler owns their place too. He took some flak from the other residents when he leased to the Ghana folks, even though there are laws against discrimination in renting. They underestimated Tyler and his wife. They are businesspeople, but they're also very considerate."

Olivia was trying to process all Billy was conveying, but it would require some more explaining at another time. Which was good, since it would provide another occasion for them to hang out.

By half past nine, the bus was sitting in the church parking lot, empty. Billy and Olivia were now alone, standing by her car. There was an awkward silence, and then Olivia invited him over to her place for a late-night snack. Neither was hungry, but the invitation spoke for itself.

As soon as they arrived at her apartment, Olivia began having second thoughts. This wasn't going to be a casual get-together—they were both too tense for that. She got out some cheese and crackers, but they were more of a distraction than anything else. Too bad Billy wasn't covered in black mulch, then she could easily have easily sent him home. His steady gaze was making all of it more difficult.

Finally, Billy spoke in a slightly choked voice. "Olivia, I'm going to be honest. I find you very attractive, and I need to get going before I attempt something stupid."

She understood completely. Her emotions were high as well, and she had uncomfortable thoughts. "I agree, it's getting late." Billy leaned over and gave her a soft kiss. She responded by embracing him.

Billy said, "Thanks for helping out tonight. Call me tomorrow with the moving timeline."

"I will. Good night." Billy walked out the door, and Olivia watched through the window as he drove away with the windows down—a dead giveaway that the AC wasn't working.

She was weary, but a good weary. This day had been amazing—a pleasant breakfast with her father, spending time with Billy, meeting Esi. Although she was tired, she followed some advice she had heard at the devotion that evening and picked up her mother's Bible. She again found the book of Romans.

The bitter edges of her life were rubbing away. She reflected on Billy's request to call her with the moving details. She was allowing him to close the deal.

CHAPTER SIX

Earlier that same day, Oliver returned to his apartment. He was satisfied from the big breakfast with his daughter and plopped down in his slouching recliner. It tilted sideways and then fell backward. As he sat in stunned silence, slumped at an angle, he looked around at some of the other furnishings in his apartment. He decided to dump the old stuff. Why even move it? Better to sack it and be done. He and Olivia were going to a new place; why not get some new furniture?

He walked over to Zelda Gambier's office and gave notice that he would be vacating in the next forty-eight hours. Zelda looked more startled by his pleasant smile than by his short notice of leaving. Oliver explained that he would be moving in with his daughter and then wished the manager a good day, leaving her staring blankly as he left her office.

Oliver had never shopped for furniture, but a brief drive around the downtown brought him to a store on South Front Street: Benny's Furniture Depot. "Everything in stock and guaranteed next-day delivery." Maybe he was getting ahead of the game, but the move appeared to be a go. If there were any snags, he was sure Olivia's anonymous texting friend would sort things out.

Typical of most furniture stores, there was a sale in progress and discounts on top of discounts. The owner, Benny Hatfield, met Oliver at the front door and gave him a big welcome. Benny informed him that somewhere between the main floor and the clearance room there was a deal to be made. Oliver wandered the store with Benny right behind him. He expected the usual salesy chatter but was surprised when Benny steered him away from certain pieces that were higher priced but didn't afford the best quality. Oliver liked Benny's style. He selected his new furnishings without any pressure from the owner.

After Oliver signed the paperwork, Benny asked for the delivery address. Only then did it occur to Oliver that he didn't have it. He apologized, saying that the house was in Glacier Village, on North Cooper, but he would have to call for the exact number.

"Is it one of Tyler Vance's houses?"

"I believe so. Do you know him?"

"I do know him and his wife, Nancy. They're part of our fellowship at Highland Church. No need to call me back; I can get the address from Tyler. We can be there between one and four tomorrow afternoon. Will you or someone be around to receive the delivery?"

"I will be there."

"Do you have plans for your old furniture? We've got a connection with the local furniture bank, and they'd be grateful for anything you'd care to donate."

In the past, Oliver would have trashed his old stuff, regardless of its condition. Now he thought about the young couple who had recently moved into the apartment above him; they had mentioned something about losing their jobs and getting their furnishings from a local furniture bank. He'd called them worthless freeloaders at the time, but his thinking had begun to shift. His daughter had lost her job. It could happen to anyone.

"Yeah, that sounds all right. It's not much, but I'll donate everything if they come and pick it up."

Oliver returned to his apartment, moved aside the broken recliner, and set up a lawn chair in its place. Before turning on the TV, he reviewed his receipts for the furniture. Inside the packet, Benny had inserted a tract titled "Where Will You Spend Eternity?" Leaning back in the old lawn chair, Oliver read the little booklet. It was a long time before he turned on the TV. He was analyzing himself and meditating on the turns his life was taking. Hopefully, any speed bumps would be minimal.

*   *   *

Olivia began her morning with the task of canceling the two leases. She contacted the car dealer first. The leasing manager understood her job predicament and worked with her. He, too, had been out of work at one point, and he offered some consolation. Then he continued the sympathetic approach and offered to meet with her after his business day. An evening out together, a nice restaurant, and some wine would provide them an opportunity to get to know each other and pursue some options. Olivia thanked him but declined, informing him that she had someone in her life.

Bonham Point was a different story. The leasing agent insisted the lease was binding and Olivia had to fulfill her end of the contract. Her hardball approach continued until Olivia bluntly reminded her that she had lost her job and was in no position to get involved with a lease. The representative continued to press her, advising her to go ahead and move in; she would ultimately find employment and manage the lease. Olivia heard her out before advising her of the folly of such a plan.

Finally, the agent backed off and agreed to cancel the lease, only after calling Olivia a pathetic loser who was in way over her head. The victim of that crude remark let it slide. The former Olivia would have trashed the woman, quick and lethal, but she held back. Before she ended the call, Olivia asked her antagonist how she could pray for her. The response was a swift hang-up. Olivia thought, *Who is the actual loser here?*

Next, Olivia faced the ordeal of packing. She had some decent pieces of furniture, and all of it would fit into the house. She knew her father's furniture was of no great value, but they would blend them together. Her wardrobe would be the biggest challenge. She was sorting garments when Billy called. He and friends with a van from the church would be over in the morning, and the plan was to move her and then her father in the afternoon. Olivia picked up the pace.

* * *

Oliver arrived at their new location around noon, ahead of the scheduled furniture delivery. He made a note of the house number and then entered the code on the lockbox and went on in. It all felt so real. He had a sense of inner peace—that made for a good change.

His first step was to go to the garage and raise the double-car door. As the door opened, he visualized tinkering on his truck and puttering around the work bench the way he had years ago. Then he heard a muffled noise. As he turned around, he saw a small child standing about five feet away. She had walked into the garage. They looked at each other without speaking.

Finally, the girl said, "My name is Esi. Are you going to be our new neighbor?"

"I'm not sure. If you live nearby, I might be your neighbor. Do your parents know where you are?"

"My daddy and mommy are in Ghana. I live with Aunt Akua and Uncle Kojo, back over there." She pointed in a general direction behind them.

"Do they know where you are? Maybe they're looking for you."

In typical childlike fashion, she said she was afraid to walk back home, and could he walk with her? Oliver stood there for a moment, knowing there was no use in discussing the fact that she had gotten there OK and could certainly find her way home without incident. He agreed to escort her back to her home.

Esi wanted to take a shortcut through the backyards. Oliver hedged at that notion and decided to take her down the street in full public view. After a few steps, she reached up and grabbed his hand. He felt uneasy. He didn't know the child, and the situation could be misinterpreted by anyone who knew the little girl. He picked up the pace, wanting to get this over with. He had to meet the furniture delivery.

The little girl took him right up to her front door and banged on it. Seconds later, it opened, and Oliver was staggered by the size of the man who greeted them. He was at least six and a half feet tall, of immense build, and dressed in a bright orange tunic topped off with a vibrant hat. Right behind him were six other figures, all wearing similar colorful clothing.

Oliver stammered, "Excuse me, folks, but this little girl was at my house, apparently lost, so I escorted her home." No one spoke. The silence made him jittery.

Finally, a woman dressed in luminous green came forward. "Esi, come in here." She reached out and took the girl by the hand. As soon as they walked through the door opening, the woman turned and spoke to Oliver. "I am Akua, Esi's aunt. Thank you, sir, for bringing her back." The big man who had greeted Oliver stepped forward and closed the door. Oliver stood there, dazed, for a moment. Then he turned and hurried down the walkway. The sooner he got out of there, the better he would feel.

When he reached the sidewalk, he felt a heavy tap on his shoulder. He turned, and behind him was the door greeter, looking more ominous than before. Oliver took a few steps backward, unsure of what to expect.

The man spoke in a deep voice. "Come. You eat."

"Excuse me?"

"Come, you eat," he repeated. Oliver guessed it was an invitation to lunch. He had no desire to have lunch and needed to get back for the delivery.

"No, thank you. I have to get back to my house." There was no reply. Each of them looked the other over. Then Oliver met the man's eyes and was moved by the hurt he saw. This stranger was offering him a gift, and Oliver was rudely declining.

"Oh, sure. Why not?"

This produced a beaming smile from his new acquaintance. "OK, come. You eat." They both headed back to the front door.

Oliver was anticipating some cold cuts and chips. A quick snack and he would be on his way. They entered the house and walked down a hallway, through a kitchen devoid of any food, and out onto a wooden deck. Oliver saw a large, deep black pot simmering over a wood fire in the middle of the yard. There was a group of people sitting behind the kettle. All were attired in colorful clothing, and they were looking at Oliver. They were ready to eat but were waiting for their guest to be seated, a friendly sign of hospitality and respect.

Oliver caught the sound of the kettle's contents bubbling. The air around them had a sharp aroma. He guessed the kettle held a blend of vegetables and some type of meat, but that was only speculation. Oliver was so fixed on the bubbling kettle that he didn't notice a man stand up and approach him. He stood in front of Oliver and introduced himself.

"Welcome. My name is Kojo. You met my wife, Akua, at the front door. Thank you for bringing our Esi home. Please have a seat next to me, and we will have our meal." Kojo motioned for Oliver to sit next to him, on his right, between him and Akua. He sat down and then looked around at all the eyes focused at him. Kojo reached over and took Oliver's hand; Akua grabbed his other hand. The others situated around the kettle followed their example. Kojo then said what sounded like a prayer in his native dialect. He closed in English, "In Jesus's name, thank you."

The group then clapped and urged Oliver to go first. He had no clue about the protocol. Akua realized his hesitancy and pulled him to his feet. She led him over to several bowls of bread chunks, reached down, and grabbed two large pieces. She took one and gave Oliver the other, then pulled him to the front of the kettle and submerged her bread into the soup. She let it soak for just a few seconds, pulled out the saturated bread, and took a large bite.

Oliver grasped the drill. Dip the bread, keep it under briefly, pull it out, and enjoy. He knew they were all hungry and didn't want to delay their meal. Without any further hesitation, he rolled up his shirt sleeve, dipped, retrieved, and put the soppy bread up to his mouth. The temperature was perfect. He took a bite and was encouraged by the group to dip again. Evidently, there was no policy against double-dipping. His shirt sleeve fell into the broth, eliciting some laughter from the others. He smiled at the group and then finished off the dipped bread chunk. They laughed and then formed a line to begin their own bread dunking.

Everyone ate their fill and settled back down on the ground. He didn't dwell on what the kettle's contents might be or possible sanitation issues; he just enjoyed the moment of camaraderie with his new neighbors. Oliver learned that his dining companions were part of a Ghanaian Christian fellowship in the city. They were able to keep up a broken kind of conversation, discussing the house where Oliver would be living and the neighborhoods of the Glacier Village area.

Oliver's cell phone rang, and he reached for it with his dry hand. It was Benny telling him the truck would be there in twenty minutes. He stood up and explained that he had to leave and meet a delivery at his house. He had been so caught up in the outdoor dining experience that he'd lost track of time. He watched as a line formed, and each person came forward to give him a big embrace. Esi was last in line, and she wrapped her arms around his waist. Oliver reached down and put his arm around her. This was all new to him, and an experience he would never forget. He expressed his goodbyes as best he could and began walking to the front yard. Kojo accompanied him.

When they reached the front walk, Akua appeared at the front door and called out to him. "Please, Mr. Oliver, take this with you." She was holding a large bowl of fruit. Oliver recalled the first experience of refusing hospitality and didn't want to offend her. He accepted the fruit and immediately noticed the ornate bowl that contained it. It was a striking hand-carved work of art. "Please keep bowl too. Our gift to you." He was speechless for a moment, then he thanked Akua, and she hugged him. Kojo shook his hand.

"Thank you for the meal and this lovely gift." The thanks came unexpectedly from him.

"Please come back and see us, and we eat again."

"I really would like that." He started back to his new home. His thoughts were racing. He chuckled at the possibility of anyone from his past seeing him with Kojo and the others. "What is that racist bigot doing with those people?" That's what they'd say.

He walked a little faster. The delivery was coming.

CHAPTER SEVEN

While Oliver was having his guest luncheon with Esi's friends and family, Billy and his moving crew arrived at Olivia's apartment. She informed them that they would make a charity run first and return for the rest, then it was on to the house. Olivia looked at their van and gauged three trips, including the donation drop-off. She was ready to get it all done.

The charitable trip was made, and they went back to the apartment for another load, then on to North Cooper. Billy pulled up in front of the house and remarked on the truck from Benny's Furniture Depot blocking the driveway. Oliver was directing the unloading and placement of the new goods in the house. Olivia got out of the van and walked over to her father.

"What's all this?" She watched a leather sofa come down the ramp. Olivia moved behind the truck and saw the other furniture.

"I decided to dump all my old junk."

Olivia watched another piece go down the ramp and disappear inside the house. At least it was decent-looking stuff.

Then Billy made his presence known. "Mr. Hood, I am Billy Ashby, a friend of Olivia's."

They shook hands, and Oliver looked him over. "You look familiar. Have we met before?"

"You may know me from Four Seasons. I help with the outside maintenance there."

"Yeah, that's where I've seen you. How do you know my daughter?" Olivia kept mum. She was curious to see how Billy would respond.

"I met her at Four Seasons the other day. It's interesting, we both have a common background."

"Excuse me, my daughter has never done lawn maintenance. How can you have a common background?"

"Dad, Billy has the same educational background that I do. He's rerouting his career and working at Four Seasons temporarily."

"Sounds like you lost your previous job, but nice to meet you." Oliver walked into the house and continued his supervisory role.

* * *

Benny's crew was soon finished, and Oliver signed the delivery receipt. Billy got into the church van and backed into the drive, parallel to Benny's truck. They began unloading. Olivia now supervised her portion of the move. One more trip and the moving was done. The next leg was back to Four Seasons for Oliver's leftover essentials. At the last minute, Oliver asked Olivia to stay behind and jumped into the passenger seat of the van. Billy seemed surprised, but he kept driving without comment.

They made the trip to Oliver's place. Since the bulk of the furniture had been donated, the remaining things were easily loaded up. The task was minimal and gave Oliver time to interrogate his daughter's new friend. It was the first time he had ever had concerns regarding his daughter's social life. Oliver was temporarily appeased by Billy's responses.

Both apartments were emptied and left in return-deposit conditions. The movers then rendezvoused back at the house. Food was ordered, but Oliver abstained. He mentioned that he had eaten out for lunch. Olivia asked if he could recommend the place, but all he would say was that it had outdoor dining, a good atmosphere, and not far away. She looked at him but didn't pursue any of it.

Once the food delivery was gone, Billy's crew began to leave. Oliver offered to pay them, but it was declined. Billy and Olivia lingered outside briefly, and Oliver tried not to be conspicuous as he peered at them through the window. Billy left, and Olivia came into the house.

She commented on the new furnishings and seemed impressed with his taste. She was enamored of the sixty-five-inch flat-screen TV. She had neglected TV in the past as she focused on her career. She and Oliver sat down and discussed the placement of the furniture, and soon, Oliver was opening up to his daughter.

"I am thrilled to be away from Four Seasons. I regret being so cantankerous with everyone there. I was really a pain to the management people. That Gambier lady was always pleasant, but I gave her a lot of heartburn. I have to change my disposition." Olivia listened but changed the subject.

"What do you think of Billy?"

"I don't know him that well, but he seems to have some good qualities. He needs to focus on his career path." Oliver paused, mulling over his thoughts. "I have a strange feeling that your mother would have approved of him. I know you kept your mother's Bible. Any idea where it might be?"

"I will be right back." Olivia went upstairs and came back with a familiar old box. She sat next to her father on the new leather sofa and handed him the Bible.

"I wonder where I would begin on the subject of eternal security." Benny's tract was still in his thoughts. Olivia leaned over and pulled out the Romans Road pamphlet from between the onionskin pages.

"Let's begin here." After half an hour of talk, they agreed to call it a day and headed upstairs to their rooms. Oliver continued reading the Bible late into the night. It was a new venture for him, but he persisted. He was fascinated by his wife's personal notes.

* * *

Over at the offices of Shannon Mergers and Acquisitions Corporation, Rory Shannon and John Murphy were in the CEO's suite and well on their way to getting tanked. John Murphy asked about the hot chick who had worked on the Blanton merger.

"You mean Olivia Hood? I had to let her go. She had a drinking problem."

Murphy laughed. "You had to dismiss an employee for drinking? That's hilarious. Where can I find her? I would give her a job on the spot. Know what I mean?" They both smirked.

"I heard that she's moving to Glacier Village."

Murphy made no comment; the locale meant nothing to an out-of-towner. "How did you know she was moving?"

"I have my contacts." He didn't reveal his association with a certain lady staff member at Bonham Point.

Murphy said, "How about we go find her? It's late, but if she's a party animal, she'll enjoy our company."

After more drinks, the two men found themselves in Shannon's car weaving toward the north end of town. They were seeking Olivia.

* * *

At 3:30 a.m., Olivia was startled out of bed by the combination of a doorbell and heavy thuds on the front door. She heard cries of, "Mr. Oliver, Mr. Oliver, please open the door." A moment later, her door opened, and her father came in, warning her to stay there and be ready to summon the police if necessary. He fumbled for the stairway light and was halfway down the steps when Olivia shouted to him.

"Dad, whoever it is, they know your name." Her father didn't reply.

"Mr. Oliver, please open the door. It's Kojo. Please hurry."

"Dad, don't open the door. Let me call the police."

"No, don't call them, it's OK. They're a family from Ghana and live just behind us. I know them." Olivia then began to make the connection. *Was this Esi's family?* She heard her father open the door and someone come inside.

"Mr. Oliver, come to our house. We need help."

"Kojo, slow down. What's the problem?"

"Two men crash a car at our house." Oliver agreed to go with them to see the scene.

Olivia called down the stairs, "Dad, I'm going with you." She quickly got dressed. Oliver grabbed a shirt, and they went with Kojo through the shortcut to his house.

When they got there, a group of people was standing in the yard in front of a dark-colored sedan. Esi stood on the porch steps looking out at the commotion, and she waved as Olivia and Oliver walked up.

Olivia saw the car's vanity plate: SHANNON. She felt numb. It was the Lexus she had always idolized. Now, it didn't appear to be so lavish—the hood was bashed in, and something had cracked the windshield. Even the darkness couldn't hide the deep tire ruts in the yard and the utter destruction of a beautiful flowerbed. The Lexus had taken out the mailbox and was close to hitting the front porch. What a disaster.

She recognized the men inside the car—Rory Shannon and John Murphy *What on earth are they doing here?* They looked half-asleep and kept making exaggerated hand gestures. They might have been a little scraped up, but Olivia had no sympathy for either of them. The "victims" of the accident seemed less in need of an ambulance and more in need of a police officer.

Her former boss saw Olivia and leaned out the driver's window. "Olivia! We found you. Good to see you." Oliver looked like he could possibly do some damage to this stranger who seemed to know his daughter.

Olivia decided to call Billy. He answered on the second ring.

"Sorry to call you so late, but there is a mess over at Esi's house. I can't explain it all over the phone, but I would appreciate it if you could come right over."

"Is it an emergency?"

"No, but it could escalate."

Billy would be over in a few minutes.

"Should we call the police?" Kojo asked Oliver. He agreed, but Olivia intervened.

"Dad, let's hold off for a moment. The driver is a man I used to work for, and unfortunately, I know the other guy too. They'll face some serious charges for this, but I want to talk to them first."

"I can't speak for Kojo. He's the one affected by all this."

"Mr. Oliver, I will make them strong coffee and get them right." He went inside his house.

Billy arrived, and Olivia brought him up to date on the incident. They stood and looked at their respective former bosses in their pathetic situation. She whispered to Billy that the two sots seemed to have been in the area to find her, but she had no idea how they knew where she lived.

Kojo and Acuna came out from the house, one carrying a large carafe of a potent West African coffee and the other a tray with china cups, saucers, cream, and sugar. Olivia filled one of the cups with the rich black coffee and thrust it into Rory's face.

Rory sniffed the fumes, and the hearty brew did its job. His eyes focused on Olivia, and he repeated, "Hi there. We were looking for you." Rory then looked around at all the people standing there in colorful clothing.

Olivia spoke to him. "Rory, chug this coffee. The quicker, the better. You are involved in a major mess." He was oblivious to her remark.

"You brought me coffee! Thank you, darling." Olivia heard her father make a growling noise and saw his fists clench. Kojo opened the passenger's-side door and handed a cup to Murphy. The big man's intimidating presence got the point across to Murphy. He took a gulp. He glanced over at Billy and looked as though he was trying to remember his face.

Meanwhile, Rory was slowly coming back to reality. "Where are we? What happened? Should I get ahold of Whetstone?"

Olivia knew that Randall Whetstone was Rory's attorney. "It may come down to that. You are looking at a possible DUI and property damage. But it's not my call." She pointed at Kojo and Acuna. "It's their call."

Murphy leaned as far away from Kojo as possible, nearly falling into Rory's seat.

Rory was quick on the uptake. "I suggest we agree to correct all this and make these folks happy. We can take care of everything—no need to get the attorneys involved." In a quieter tone, he whispered, "Or the police." He leaned closer to Olivia and said, "If we can avoid the police, that would be my preference."

Olivia said, "Don't talk to me. It's Kojo's property."

Rory glanced over at large man standing a few feet away. "I will take care of all damages," he told him. He then humbly asked to use the bathroom.

"Follow me." As both of the revelers followed Kojo into the house, Olivia saw Billy put away his phone.

"Got it all on video. They won't be able to go home and pretend this never happened."

After the men came back out, Acuna made more coffee and offered to feed them, but neither had any appetite. Rory and Murphy returned to the Lexus.

Rory stood in front of the car and surveyed the ruts and the destruction of the mailbox. He asked for help with getting his vehicle out the ruts. He started the car, and two men eased it out of the grooves. Rory carefully backed out to the curb and then into the driveway, then he got out to stand beside Murphy. More phones were recording their every move. Some men gathered around the sedan as if admiring it, deftly blocking Shannon and Murphy from getting back into the car.

Olivia then took control. She sternly looked at both of the men and reiterated the business at hand, especially their obligation to resolve it all to Kojo's satisfaction. The agreement was that they would be back by noon to make all the repairs. They could do it themselves or send a crew. It didn't matter. She wrote out the address for Rory Shannon and gave it to him.

"Don't welch on this, or there will be a search for the guilty. This is bigger than a jumbo jet going down." Olivia looked capable of lynching both men right then and there. She enjoyed the power she was grasping, and the dejected look the two had on their faces. She wanted to make them squirm a little more.

Rory surveyed the damage one more time and then handed his coffee cup back to Acuna with a sheepish expression. "It'll be taken care of by this afternoon, if not sooner." The men gathered around the car moved aside, and Rory and Murphy climbed in. Olivia heard Rory murmuring about what his wife would say when he got home. The Lexus slowly backed out of the driveway, and the little group that had formed then dispersed. Billy had to go to work, and Oliver and Olivia agreed to come back at noon to monitor the repairs.

CHAPTER EIGHT

Rory and Murphy didn't renege on their promise and arrived as agreed. They were bound by their word, and the phone recordings sealed it. They were wearing jeans and t-shirts, and the Lexus had a new mission—it was loaded with a wheelbarrow, post-hole diggers, shovels, mortar mix, and an upscale mailbox kit. The premium vehicle had become a work truck.

A while later, a local landscape company brought over a load of topsoil and fifty bags of black mulch. Olivia was disappointed that Billy missed the sight of the two tycoons spreading mulch. Surprisingly, Shannon and Murphy jumped into the project with both hands. Perhaps it was a show of honest contrition, or they were hoping that their penance would make things turn out better in a courtroom, should it come down to that. Either way, the two of them got the project done. The topsoil and mulch were spread by the mailbox, the flowerbed in front of the porch, and around the perimeter of the house.

After the men were finished, Olivia surveyed their work. She had to hand it to them—they were close to making up for the destruction of last night.

"I'll be honest, Rory. You surprised me with your talents." Olivia taunted him.

Rory looked a bit proud of himself. "My father owned a hardware store, and I grew up around all the tools and materials we used today. Brings back many memories." He started loading the nostalgic tools back into the Lexus.

It was then that Olivia saw Esi run out of the house. "Come! Come to the backyard!" She grabbed Olivia's hand and dragged her toward the back of the house.

Olivia, Oliver, Rory, and Murphy followed her to the backyard and saw the strangest sight. Even on this warm day, a fire was burning in the middle of the yard, and a huge black kettle was set over it. Acuna was coming out of the back door carrying a large basket of bread, followed by three ladies with trays of food.

Kojo called out with his booming voice, "Come, you eat!" A line formed at the kettle. Kojo asked for silence, gave thanks, and then the feast began. A confused Rory and Murphy were herded to the head of the line. They were now guests. They looked uncomfortable but weren't about to second-guess their hosts. Soon, they were all partaking in in the dunking and eating. Olivia watched her father during the dipping process. He acted as if he had done it before. She stayed in the background and didn't eat.

The upscale bigshots sat on the ground and ate. Before they left, they were on the receiving end of embraces from Kojo and the others. Kojo invited them to come back again, just not in the early-morning hours.

Before Rory Shannon left, he took Olivia aside. "Would you be able to stop by my office tomorrow? Maybe we can sort things out and get you back on the team. Don't worry about my wife. She's more worried about my antics than yours at this point."

Olivia hesitated. "Rory, I really need to think it over." She was deliberately hedging. She felt unprepared for more corporate entanglements. She and Billy would discuss it. Rory Shannon left without any commitment from her. The Lexus pulled away with the trunk lid banging up and down on the wheelbarrow. Rory steered the former luxury sedan while gazing through the cracked windshield.

Olivia and Oliver went back to their house. As they approached the driveway, both noticed a car parked in it. Another Lexus. Olivia recognized it immediately. The car belonged to Judith Shannon, and her head leaned out the driver's-side window as they approached. How had she found their new place?

Olivia whispered to Oliver as they got closer. "Dad, this is Rory Shannon's wife sitting in the driveway. I have no clue what she wants, but she is totally uninvited."

"I'll run her off. I have had enough of these jerks in their empty suits and fancy cars," Oliver blurted out.

"Let me handle this. Just ignore her and go on up to the house." Oliver went to the porch, grabbed his aluminum lawn chair, and plopped down well within hearing distance.

Olivia walked up to the car. "Judith! I am surprised to see you here. What can I do for you?"

"Please spare me the pleasantries. Were you with my husband last night?" The callous question was a blow to Olivia, but not a knockout punch. Anger swelled inside her, and an offensive comeback was brewing. *Get this, Judy. I have never been with your husband. I find him despicable and crude. If you can't control him, make some changes in both of your lives. Now get out of our driveway. Beat it, lady.*

She leaned in closer to Judith's face, but she couldn't bring herself to say the nasty words. Instead, she felt almost sorry for this woman. Being married to Rory was enough to win any woman's sympathy. "I am sorry that you believe I have something going with Rory, but it's not true. I suggest you both get some counseling and work things out."

Before Olivia could continue, Judith Shannon powered her window up, backed out of the driveway, and squealed her tires down the street. Any possibility of Olivia meeting with Rory Shannon and coming back into the business went down the street with Judith's frustrated departure.

She sighed and walked up onto the porch to join her father.

"You were really gentle with her. If only I could have heard similar advice about my relationship with your mom, or even you, and many others."

Olivia smiled. "It's OK, Dad. It's all in the past. You know, I really wanted to nail Judy, but something held me back." Olivia then spotted Esi coming down the street on her bike. *A breath of fresh air*, she thought.

* * *

One year later, on their wedding day, Billy and Olivia greeted the eclectic group of guests at their reception. One of the more notable couples invited was Rory and Judith Shannon. A month after the incident at Kojo's house and Judith's encounter with Olivia, they had reached out and apologized to Olivia. All had been forgiven on both sides of the fence. The Shannons were in a recovery process and both had been dry for twelve months.

Olivia had formed her own consulting agency, specializing in mergers and acquisitions. Her integrity went before her, and her skills were in demand. Rory was her first client.

Billy's career took an unexpected twist. He was contacted by the furniture dealer, Benny Hatfield, regarding his inventory control problems. They worked jointly for a period, and then Benny confided in him that he was looking at retirement. Billy had learned about the business and was aware of its profitability and sound management. He agreed to assist Benny's transition out of the business, but Benny had an alternative solution. He gave Billy a generous buyout proposition and agreed to fund it. Billy and Olivia realized the benefits of the offer, and Billy's desire for self-employment was fulfilled. He was immersed in the world of retail home furnishings, and Benny was a happy retiree—everyone got a deal.

Esi, the flower girl at the wedding, had been formally adopted by Kojo and Acuna. She was also a frequent guest at Olivia's house.

Olivia and Billy had purchased a place of their own before the wedding, and Oliver Hood would continue living in the house in Glacier Village. He'd developed a strong friendship with Kojo and Acuna, and he had another friend—Zelda Gambier. They'd been spending more and more time together, and she was his date for Olivia's wedding.

Back at Benny's Furniture Depot, Olivia maintained an office where she ran her consulting firm. Displayed on the far wall were three dented metal wastebaskets, given to her by Rory Shannon. Each time she looked at them, she remembered the fateful time she'd been fired. Now it symbolized the hat trick she'd found since that day: her marriage, her business, and her relationship with God.

PAPER FILES—REAL PEOPLE
INTRODUCTION

Pat Crocker opened the top drawer of the large four-drawer file cabinet behind his desk. The top two drawers contained twenty years' worth of carefully typed documents, each recounting the details of the pastor's interactions with the people who came to him for help and spiritual insight. He was an old-fashioned man, so the files were on paper rather than typed up in a computer database. The files were painstakingly labeled and sorted. They were a dossier on the lives of people who were repentant and committed to restoration and clean, sober lives. Unfortunately, there were also some files for those who continued living under the load of hardened hearts. Pat was protective of the information and kept only the hard copies; none of it was on a computer.

Each file bore a name, and even after a couple of decades, each one still resonated with him. Pastor Crocker's plan for the sleepy Thursday afternoon was to peruse the files and read the collected notes. Casually thumbing through the records, he stopped at the name of Portia Flickinger. He pulled the folder up from the drawer and slowly opened it to look at his notes from fifteen years ago. The details were still fresh in his mind as he reviewed the events in Portia's life. He returned to the desk, kicked back in his chair, and immersed himself in memories.

PAPER FILES—
REAL PEOPLE

CHAPTER ONE

Pat Crocker and one of the associate pastors, his close friend Bruce Summit, were coaching youth baseball for first and second graders. Their team, the Simmons Point Rangers, was one of a dozen teams in the same bracket. Pat and Bruce's coaching techniques were developed to instill confidence in their players, and their approach with the kids won the approval of most parents, although there were exceptions. There were always the excessively eager parents who were convinced their prodigy children were the most gifted players on the team, or perhaps even in the league. Fortunately for Coach Crocker, he had years of pastoral experience that enabled him to deal with the parents at all levels. Coach Summit followed his lead. Their wisdom defused most of the incidents with the few over-involved parents, but the harder issue was the case of one under-involved parent.

Portia Flickinger was the mother of Timmy Patterson and Tammy Bryant. Pat Crocker knew little about her other than her name, since the mother not only avoided practices but also steered clear of every game. She never picked up her children like other parents; instead, both had permission slips to leave the park and meet her on the extreme southwest edge of the vast park complex. Their trip to her waiting car was a long walk, and it created some anxiety for the observing coaches. They tried to keep the kids in their sight as they went across the park.

The next game for the Rangers was a thriller. The players, parents, and coaches of both teams were shouting encouragements to the kids. In the last inning, Tammy doubled and drove her brother in from second base for the winning run. After the victory celebration, both of them looked hopefully into the stands, hoping their mom was there, and then out across the park where their mother normally parked, but there was no car in sight. Pat and Bruce both knew the kids were looking for Portia. Pat assessed the situation and made a decision he had pondered for weeks.

"Kids, don't leave just yet. I want to walk you over to your mother's car." Both of them looked at the ground, and then Tammy spoke up.

"Coach Pat, Mom…she don't like preachers." Pat was surprised by the girl's candor, but he had heard much worse during his years in ministry. He wasn't deterred.

"How does your mom feel about youth league baseball coaches? I want to tell her about the good game you played today and let her know that I enjoy having you two on the team." There was no comment; both kids attempted a smile, but they had doubt on their faces.

Pat walked over to Bruce and informed him of his plan to walk the children over to Portia's car. "I think it's time we met each other."

Bruce gave him a wry smile. "How can I pray for you?"

"I'm not sure."

CHAPTER TWO

The pastor in coach's clothing chatted with the brother and sister as they approached the waiting car. Pat saw that it was an old Buick wagon from the Seventies parked across the street and facing away from them. Portia was looking at them in the rearview and side mirrors.

Pat felt apprehensive. He walked up to the car, but before he could even say anything, Portia Flickinger got out and stood in front of him. He had never met her, but in his imagination, he'd pictured an overweight, sluggish woman. That assumption was quickly dispelled. Portia was tastefully dressed, younger than he'd anticipated, and reasonably attractive.

"Mrs. Flickinger, I'm Pat Crocker, one of your children's coaches. They both played well today." She didn't return his smile.

"It's *Miss* Flickinger. I've never been married." Her stare was intense. "So, you are their coach. Aren't you leaving something else out of your background?"

"Excuse me? I don't follow you."

"Well, coach Crocker, what's your livelihood?"

Pat recalled Tammy's comment. "I'm a pastor at Ridge Hill Bible Church here in Simmons Point. I've been there for ten years in the lead pastor role."

"That's nice, but I don't much care for preachers."

"That's painting things with a broad brush. Why do you feel that way?"

"I have my reasons, and they are valid." Her voice was sharp and reeked of bitterness.

Pat took a step closer to the Buick. "May I call you Portia?"

"I can't stop you."

Man, she is a case, he told himself, but he remained cordial. "Thanks, Portia. I came over here for two reasons. First, I wanted to let you know your kids played a great game this morning, and second, I wanted to meet you. If this is an intrusion, I apologize."

"No apology needed. You've met me now. Anything else, Preacher? Maybe you want to use my kids as bait to get to know me better, then hit on me and follow me home. Is that it?"

Pat was stunned and embarrassed that her kids could hear all the dialogue. "Miss Flickinger, I am a happily married man, and I take my calling as a pastor seriously. All I wanted to do was meet you and congratulate you on your kids. Have a nice day. Goodbye, kids." Pat turned to leave and was saddened by the look on Tammy and Timmy's faces. He knew they were humiliated. Their joy of winning the game was lost. He looked at Portia, expecting her to grab the kids and speed off, but it seemed her fierce countenance was starting to wane.

"Kids, wait for me in the car." Portia motioned for Pat to step away from earshot of the car. He was expecting another bitter salvo, and she didn't disappoint him.

"My old man was a pastor back in Kentucky. He preached what he called 'the Word' and was prepared to help people out. Even to a fault."

"To a fault?"

"He fell over himself to help a pretty young divorcée in his congregation. Call it a trap on her part, or enticement, or his stupidity for being sucked in. Take your pick. Everyone knew about his affair except my mother. Soon it all came out in the open. It devastated her, and then my preacher father deserted us for that bitch. Pastor Blake Flickinger took off with his new toy, and we never saw him again. The church never recovered. My mother was flattened."

Pat felt a burning in his stomach. He had heard of many travesties similar to Portia's. It was ugly to see the ministry of Jesus Christ stained that way.

Portia wasn't finished. "My mother died when I was eighteen. I had no other family and was on my own. There was a big void in my life, and men helped me fill it with drugs, alcohol, and false love. By twenty-one, I had gone through an abortion, a miscarriage, and birthed those two sitting in the car. So don't give me your piety about your marriage faithfulness and your devotion to God. And please, don't stand there in contempt of me. I ain't buying any of it." She walked away, got in the old vehicle, and drove off, producing a bluish-black smoke cloud from the car's exhaust.

Pat stood in the middle of the sidewalk for several long minutes. He had taken a lot from Portia but sloughed it all off. He knew a pastor had to be thick-skinned, but he had concern for her and her kids. He walked back across the park toward the empty ballfields and sat down in one of the dugouts. The crowds were gone, and Pat welcomed the serenity. It didn't remain.

He heard a noisy car pull up behind the bleachers. The doors slammed, and then he saw a shadow fall across the front of the dugout. Portia was back. She told her kids to go over to the playground.

"I need someone to talk to. Looks like you are available."

Pat gazed up at her from the darkened dugout. "I have some time. What's on your mind?" He was tired and hoped he could hold up through another barrage. He motioned for her to join him on the bleachers. They sat down where they could watch the kids, and Pat kept a wide space between them.

Portia began. "This is nuts. Maybe you preachers call it conviction, but I have felt some pressure inside me ever since I unloaded on you. It's gnawing at me, and it's not a good feeling."

Pat knew her analysis was spot on, it was conviction, but he only said, "Portia, when was the last time you communicated with your father?"

"It's been years. Don't start that love-your-father routine, because it's not in me."

Pat then took the lead in their dialogue. "Please allow me to share something. I will get to the point. I had an abusive father and suffered many times from his drunken rage. I saw him turn on my sister and mother as well. I scoffed at my mother for taking his abuse. She kept telling me to pray for him. I did pray—that he would choke on his whiskey or fall down the steps and crack his skull. Mom was encouraged by others to leave him. She admitted more than once that she considered fleeing, but she remained in the house with him and kept on praying. She was strong, but she struggled beyond belief. I was jaded by it all.

"One night, I overheard her praying. She was on her knees by her bedside. She was crying and telling God that she couldn't take much more of the mistreatment from her husband. I was only nine years old, but at that moment, I knew my mother was hanging onto the hope that God would change my father. I quietly joined her and put my arm around her shoulders. My heart talked to Christ, and for the first time, I realized that prayer could change things. I no longer sought vengeance against my father. I also asked God to change him."

"This is all very touching, but I don't see how it involves me."

"Hear me out, OK? Two days after my mom and I prayed together, my dad was picked up on a drunk driving charge and locked up. The next morning, a Sunday, the sheriff's chaplain came in to see the prisoners. My father was one of the few listening to the chaplain that morning. He was straightforward and laid it all out for my dad and the other prisoners. You mentioned conviction earlier— that was exactly what Dad experienced. He began a journey with Christ that day.

"It took time, but through discipling and study of the Bible, he became the husband and father that God had intended him to be. He even became a pastor, and he never deviated from his ministry. He talked up the need for repentance, the wrath of God, and the day of judgment. Yep, he was a preacher." He smiled at Portia, but she gave him a stern look.

"Where's your father now?" she asked him.

"He passed away two years ago. My mother lives in Florida but spends summers up here with us. Incidentally, she's visiting us now. Would you like to meet her?" Pat didn't wait for a reply. "Why don't you and the kids come to our home for supper this evening? Tabby and I are empty nesters and would enjoy having all of you over."

Portia's first inclination was an emphatic no. There was no way she was going to associate with a preacher and his family. No good could come from it. "Maybe some other time. Tammy, Timmy—get in the car."

Pat watched as the kids climbed into the back seat of the old station wagon. Portia started the car and another puff of colored smoke spewed forth. The car idled for a few moments, then Portia opened her car door and got out to speak to Pat.

"What's your address?"

He gave her the address.

"Let's make it five o'clock."

CHAPTER THREE

Pat's wife, Tabitha, was an excellent cook, and she had her mother-in-law's help. But the quality of the meal was surpassed by the caliber of the conversation. Portia impressed them all with her intellect. She didn't have college training, but she could clearly express herself. Her typical rancor was absent, but she asserted confidence.

Her admission that she was estranged from her father got the attention of Pat's mother, Darla. Portia decided to indulge the elderly woman and engaged her in conversation.

"Did you ever just want to give up and leave your husband or boot him from the house?"

Darla laughed. "Many times. I also thought about strangling him in his sleep, but I didn't want to clean up the mess." Portia appreciated her humor. "Admittedly, as a follower of Christ, I never should have married a non-believer. I was young and naïve, and I was determined that I could get him converted, but my beliefs only became a wedge between us. I couldn't undo the marriage, and we soon had two kids. Prayer was my resource. It helped erase the bitterness and gave me continual hope. Anyway, enough of that. He found Christ, preached the Bible, and he's in heaven. I have nothing but good memories of our marriage."

"I am gathering from all this that I should reach out to my father and make peace. Doesn't the same principle apply to him? Let him contact me. Maybe he could get to know the two grandkids he's never met," Portia told them. She was getting heated up. Pat got up and quietly took her kids out into the front yard. Fortunately, some of the neighbor kids were out there, and Pat introduced the two to the group. He then went back up on the porch and sat down. His presence at the table was no longer necessary. Experience had taught him that his wife and mother would know just what to say to Portia.

Both women were convinced that the resentment and bitterness afflicting Portia was the result of her empty quest to find a father figure. Tabitha attempted to fill part of the void. She wanted Portia to view her as someone who could provide nurturing and support. Darla desired the same role, only more as a grandmother than a friend. Portia was moved by their grace. It was a refreshing experience for her.

After that first encounter, the three women met at least once a week. In a short time, they went from strangers to solid friends. Portia's attempts to find an authoritative figure in her life ended. Also, her untapped potential as a person was bolstered by the fellowship. Portia enjoyed having someone to guide her and provide answers to her frequent questions.

* * *

Pat Crocker finished perusing the notes in Portia's file. It had been fifteen years since his introduction to Portia Flickinger, yet their fellowshipping that evening at his home seemed only days ago. Finally, he looked at a notation at the bottom of the last page of her file. Portia had contacted her father and restored their damaged relationship. He also smiled when he read the familiar note that her son, Timothy, had completed college and seminary and was pastoring in Kentucky. Portia, the onetime dissident, now had a pastor for a son. Tammy was married to a state patrolman, had two children, and was teaching middle school and coaching softball.

Pat thanked God for calling him into the ministry. Sure, there were challenges and disappointments, but all of it was offset by the opportunity to make a difference in people's lives.

He looked into the cabinet again. Tony Wyndham got his attention. He opened the file and was amazed at the date. Twelve years ago. Tony had come to the church with a strange request and had gotten much more than he'd asked for.

CHAPTER FOUR

Twenty-four-year-old Tony Wyndham casually walked into the reception area of Ridge Hill Bible church. He had a simple purpose in mind—a request for money. He was almost sure that the appeal would be rejected with the usual reply that they did not give out cash, only vouchers for food or gas purchases, but he made the effort.

Tony appeared to fit the stereotype of those seeking a monetary handout, but his solicitation was unique and unlike any other previous plea for money. It was a slow day at the church office, and his request was so original that the receptionist referred him to Bruce Summit, the associate pastor for the church. Bruce, in turn, bumped the matter up the ladder to Pat Crocker.

Pat Crocker wasn't having a slow day. He was absorbed in preparing for the quarterly elder meeting. His agenda was to work for several more hours behind a closed office door. Bruce respected his need for seclusion but insisted that Pat meet a certain young man. Pat paused his work and walked with Bruce down the corridor. In the reception area, he saw a tall, disheveled man. Beside him was a young lady, probably his girlfriend. They looked like flower children—fresh from the 60s and the Haight-Ashbury San Francisco hippie movement. If they weren't hippies, they definitely led a bohemian lifestyle.

Although the church's no-handouts policy was strictly enforced, another policy was more important—if a stranger entered the church, they would be treated as friends. No exceptions.

"Good morning. I am Pat Crocker, the lead pastor here at Ridge Hill." He extended a hand of welcome to the visitors.

"Hi, I'm Tony Wyndham, and this is my friend, Mira." He stepped aside to make her more visible.

"Nice to meet you. Pastor Bruce has indicated that you two are in need of some funds. Unfortunately, we have a firm policy of not disbursing any money, but we can arrange for a gas purchase or a food voucher." Mira began pulling on Tony's arm, indicating it was time to leave.

Pat had a feeling these two were not substance addicts but simply free spirits, perhaps a bit irresponsible. He decided to probe a little deeper and be blunt with them. "What do you need the money for?"

Tony Wyndham never broke eye contact. "I need to get my sax out of hock." Pat was taken aback, but Tony kept talking before he could ask for details. "I will treat the money as a loan and pay it back in full, within two weeks or less."

"Don't you have family in the area that could help you out?"

"No, no one at all." Mira tugged harder on his arm, but he wasn't paying attention. Finally, she spoke.

"Tony, let's go. We don't need to waste any more of their time. These folks must have to get back to work."

"Sure, babe. Let's go."

They both turned and headed for the door. Pat quickly assessed the money demand.

"Tony, how much do you need?" His offer was based on his character assessment of the couple. Tony turned and met him with the same steady gaze. Pat silently prayed that his gut instinct was in sync with what God would have him do in this unusual situation.

"Forty-seven dollars and sixty-five cents," Tony told him. Pat had been anticipating a demand for a couple of hundred dollars. He didn't want to use church funds in case his judgment was wrong, but he happened to have cash on him. He reached into his wallet and produced forty-seven dollars. He asked Bruce for the sixty-five cents. Bruce complied, and Pat extended the money to Tony.

"Pay me back when you can." Tony glanced over at Mira, who looked surprised and grateful.

"Pastor, do you want me to sign an agreement?"

"No, but I'd like to shake on it."

Tony reached out to him. "I won't let you down, and I won't stiff you."

Mira spoke again. "No, sir, we won't burn you." They headed for the door.

After they left, Pat turned to Bruce and shrugged his shoulders. "Well, there you have it." Bruce didn't comment but was interested in the continued development of this unique situation.

* * *

Pat returned to his office, aware that he was behind in his meeting prep. He passed through the outer office and nodded to his assistant, Tess O'Bannon. She knew that look. He was now in do-not-disturb mode. That lasted all of forty-five minutes.

Tess pecked gently on his closed office door. "Pastor Pat, can you come out here?"

Pat stretched his arms over his head and got up from his chair, walking into the outer office. "Sure, what's up?"

"Listen, can you hear that music coming from the main entrance.?" He heard nothing, but he went out into the hallway. Bruce passed him, headed in the same direction. Pat then heard a saxophone playing "Amazing Grace." Accompanying the music was a female voice humming the tune. Other staff had heard the music and were gathering in the main lobby to listen. It was a welcome break in the slow day, and unique on any given day.

Pat was not a music critic, but he knew some of the notes were a little out of tune. However, the melody blended well with Mira's voice. Tony stopped playing and was greeted with a soft round of applause. He and Mira slightly bowed to the small audience, and then both looked over at Pat.

"That was for you, Pastor."

Pat was flattered. "Thank you, Tony and Mira." He went ahead and introduced the duo to the church staff, who repeated their soft applause. Pat then walked over to Tony.

"That was beautiful, but why didn't Mira sing the lyrics? She has a pretty voice."

"Neither of us knows the words, and I struggle with the tune."

"Really?" Pat asked him. "How did 'Amazing Grace' find its way into your repertoire?"

Tony hesitated, but Mira said, "Go ahead and tell him."

"I heard the tune up in New York City, around 42nd Street and Broadway. It was being played on a sax by a street pimp. He had a bucket in front of him for cash donations."

"How do you know he was a street pimp?"

Tony gave him a pitying look. "Trust me, Pastor, he was a pimp. I know the dude. Anyway, I heard him playing the tune, and I liked it. I have no idea what the song's about, I just like what I heard. I can't read music, but I play by ear."

Standing behind him was Jason Albright, the church's worship leader. "That is some talent you have. Quite a gift. Do you play any other instruments?"

"I can play the piano and a little guitar, but Mira is the real guitar player. She even reads music." His smile was noticed by everyone.

Pat lost sight of his upcoming quarterly meeting. This was more interesting. "Tony, Mira, do you have time to come back to my office for a quick chat? I want to discuss the song you've been playing." Before they could answer, he invited Bruce and Jason to join them. Tony shrugged his shoulders and looked at Mira, who was nodding her approval. Neither had an agenda.

The five of them walked down the hallway. Tony had the saxophone slung over his shoulder and was talking music with Jason. When they reached Pat's office, they sat around a small conference table. Mira snuggled close to Tony.

Pat began. "The song you were playing, 'Amazing Grace,' is a cornerstone hymn in Christianity. The author was a slave trader, but he came under conviction of his sins and made a 180-degree turn in his life, becoming a follower of Christ. He knew he didn't deserve it, but he found God's grace." Pat concluded his story with an invitation to Tony and Mira to share in God's grace. They shifted in their seats and looked uncomfortable.

Tony said, "Pastor, there is a lot for us to consider here. You probably guessed we aren't married, but we do live together. I know you likely disapprove of that kind of arrangement. We really need to think this through."

"I certainly can't condone your relationship, but I won't be judgmental regarding it. All I can say is it's not honoring to God."

"Fair enough." Tony stood up. "We have to get moving."

Before they left, Pat gave them literature supporting his conversation on grace and forgiveness. "Take these two pamphlets with you." Tony tucked them in his back pocket, and he and Mira excused themselves and went out to their car.

Mira was concerned and started talking as soon as they got into the car. "Tony, I'm not happy."

"What's bothering you, babe?" Her look of unbelief got Tony's attention.

"We're going nowhere. Absolutely nowhere."

"It'll get better, I promise." He tried to start the car, but Mira stopped him. "What are you doing?"

"We need to just sit right here and talk."

"OK, talk about what?" Tony was getting agitated.

"Look at us. We are about to go to that pit of a rental house, plop down, and look at the walls. I'm tired of it. I need a change, and just maybe I want out."

"Hey, give me some time, and we'll be OK."

"Really? I don't think so. What is all this about? We hang out on street corners and panhandle for money while we play songs we don't even understand. If that comes up empty, we move to a freeway intersection and beg for money. Tony, I'm sick of it. What happened to your vision of getting into the music business? You're talented, but you're literally flushing it all down a toilet. I feel like we're living in a dumpster, and it's about to be picked up—with us in it."

"That pastor was very kind to us, and he talked about grace. He gave you money to get the sax out of hock, no strings attached. Maybe that's some of the grace he's referring to. Also, I'm feeling ashamed that we've lived together without any intentions of getting married. My back is bent over as far as I want to go. I need to be able to stand upright and face this crap trap that keeps on kicking us around. I want some structure and stability in our lives. That pastor convinced me that God can and will fill the void that is plaguing us. I'm going back to his office, and hopefully, he will see me. I have a lot of questions. Are you coming with me?"

Tony was staggered by her words, but he knew them to be true. He looked around at their surroundings. "It is like living in a dumpster. And it's time to climb out. Yeah, babe, I'm going with you." He put his arm around Mira and pulled her close. "You are amazing." He smiled at his awkward pun.

"I hate that name, "babe." Don't use it anymore, OK?"

* * *

"Pastor Pat, you have two visitors who would like to speak to you." Pat dropped his pencil and shoved the legal pad away from him.

"Who is it, Tess?"

"It's the couple with the saxophone."

Pat perked up. What were they doing back so soon? The final touches to the elder board meeting would have to be put on hold. "Send them back." Ministry always took precedent over agendas.

Their meeting was fruitful, and spiritual decisions were made. Pat prayed with Tony and Mira. When they were ready to leave, Tony stood up and made a request.

"I have to go to New York City, but I feel uncomfortable leaving Mira alone in our rental place. We aren't in the best part of town. Is there any way someone could give her a place to hang out while I'm gone?" Pat was naturally intrigued by Tony's plans. Why would he suddenly make a trip five hundred miles away? Then he redirected his thoughts to the need for hospitality. Mira was smiling at her partner.

"Mira is welcome to stay with my wife and me while you are gone."

"Thank you, Pastor." Tony went to Mira, leaned over, and whispered in her ear. She looked surprised but smiled as she watched him walk out the door. Pat realized that Mira was now stranded in his office alone with him. He reacted quickly.

"I'll ask Tess if she can take you back to your place. Go ahead and get your things together, and my wife and I will pick you up later this evening. I need your phone number, and we will call you. Maybe plan on around six o'clock."

"Thanks." Mira and Tess soon left, and Pat called Tabitha to inform her of their upcoming houseguest. After he completed the call, he again began questioning Tony's trip to New York. What was the urgency?

* * *

At 5:55, Pat and Tabitha arrived at 323 Winter Street, a ramshackle rental in a questionable neighborhood. As they went to the front door, Pat could see some of the neighbors peeking out behind their shades at him and his wife. Once inside, he felt a temporary feeling of relief. He didn't want to linger and was direct with Mira. He suggested that she leave nothing of value behind.

"We have nothing valuable. Only our two musical instruments." Pat saw that her guitar was in a case next to her along with one large suitcase, an overnight bag, and a paper bag that smelled of fresh baked goods. She extended the bag toward him.

"I made these after I got home. They are for you and your wife." Pat looked in the bag and saw huge oatmeal raisin cookies. His favorite. Then Tabitha introduced herself to Mira. The two ladies shook hands as Pat clinched the cookie bag in his teeth and grabbed the suitcase and overnight bag. Tabitha reached over and relieved him of the bag of cookies, and Mira carried her guitar. The scrutiny of the neighbors followed their steps to Pat's car. Once inside, Mira finally shared about on Tony's trip.

"Pastor Pat, I'm sure you are questioning Tony's trip to New York. I know it seems weird."

Pat shrugged his shoulders and glanced into the rearview mirror. "It crossed my mind, but I didn't want to pry into his personal business." He was awaiting her tale.

"Tony is going into the heart of Manhattan to find Apollo White. He's the pimp he mentioned this afternoon. You do remember Tony mentioning him, right?"

How could he forget? "I do recall that. What's so urgent about contacting him?"

"Tony wants to share the meaning of 'Amazing Grace' and share Jesus with Apollo."

Pat's knee-jerk reaction was to slam on the car's brakes.

"Mira, excuse me for prying, but where did he get funds for his impromptu trip?"

"My parents sent me a $200 gift card for my birthday."

"When was your birthday?" Tabitha asked her.

Mira hesitated. "Tomorrow."

Pat then realized that Tony had hocked the saxophone to get Mira a gift. A quick glance from his wife told him that a little celebration would be appropriate for their guest.

CHAPTER FIVE

Mira was humbled by the glowing warmness toward her. Their home was a stark contrast to the rental house.

Pat eventually excused himself to give the ladies a chance to talk. He took an extended stroll through the neighborhood, praying hard. He thought of his wife and Mira, Tony's trip, and Tony's pending encounter with Apollo. He wondered if Apollo was his actual name or a street moniker.

He returned to the house and was pleased to see his wife and Mira still chatting. Tabitha had her Bible open, and there was another Bible beside it. He knew that one would be a gift to Mira. He went upstairs and briefly watched a baseball game on the TV. Tabitha and Mira continued to talk until midnight.

Tabitha did give Mira the Bible along with notes on suggested Scripture readings. Later, in the solitude of the guest room, Mira plunged into reading. She turned off her bedside lamp at three in the morning.

Before breakfast, Mira talked to Tony on the phone and shared the news with her hosts. "He made it to New York in eight hours and even found a parking space in Manhattan, a couple of blocks off Broadway. Tony is a quick learner, and he reviewed those pamphlets you gave him as he walked to Apollos's turf."

"Did he find Apollo?" Pat asked her.

"Yes, he found him in his usual haunt along with his collection of procurer friends. One thing you have to know about Tony—he's a Type A personality, and he's not intimidated. He shared what you told us in your office and gave them the Bible handouts. He told me that he was planting seeds."

"He went all the way to New York just to plant some seeds?" Tabitha asked her.

"Yep, that's Tony."

"When is he returning?" Pat asked.

"He should be back early this evening. I know he wanted to get out of there before daybreak."

"I hope he will arrive in time to join us for a little birthday bash for you."

"Really? That is so thoughtful of you two." Her tears went unnoticed by her hosts.

"Tony will be racking up a lot of miles. Hopefully, he will find the pullout sofa bed comfortable," Pat told her. Mira got the hint. There would be no sharing a bed in the pastor's house. She was comfortable with the arrangement.

* * *

Pat Crocker closed the file and thought back on the evening of Tony's return from New York. Tony was tired, but he'd talked with Pat for hours that night. Pat admired Tony's gutsy venture. The escapade was one to never forget. He also remembered Tony sharing his aspirations of getting into the concert venue business. He wanted to get acquainted with a concert producer start working on a career. Pat asked what was standing in his way, and Tony acknowledged that he himself was the only obstacle. Nothing else.

Pat had him contact a friend that networked with a variety of concert producers. Tony landed a job within a week with a Christian concert promotion group. After two years of learning the nuances of the business, Tony the quick learner developed his own company.

He and Mira had gotten married, and they became productive members of Ridge Hill Bible Church. On occasions, Tony played the saxophone accompanied by Mira on her guitar.

Tony's production business grew exponentially each year. He made significant donations to build a new musical center for the church. The new gathering place was dominated by the Apollo Coffee Shop in the rear of the large room. Only a few people knew the backstory of the neon "Apollo" sign that shone from the back wall. In front of it was a platform that could accommodate a few musicians, and performances were frequent.

Each time he saw the light turned on, Pat recalled his own face-to-face meeting with Apollo.

Apollo had found his way to Ridge Hill and sought out Pastor Crocker. The big man had smiled as he told Pat that the word was out that he was an easy touch for money. He needed funds to get his sax out of hock. He also said he'd been informed that Pat was an easy touch for teaching about grace. Apollo didn't get the money, but he did hear the message of grace.

That encounter was documented in another file in Pat's file cabinet. It was one of many that Pat often thumbed through.

CLOTHES CLOSET
GAMES

CHAPTER ONE

The clothes closet of Victory Hill Fellowship was jammed with shirts, dresses, blouses, suits, and kid's clothes awaiting their new owners. To the right of the room was sports attire for all ages, from youth to the wannabe senior athletes. Every inch of the six hundred square feet assigned to the clothes ministry was smothered in donations.

The clothes closet's mission was simple—donated clothes were given out to those in need free of charge. However, in practice, things were more complicated. Donations were generous, but an overzealous generosity occasionally proved to be a fault. There was no filtering of the dropped-off items, and realistically, some of the donations should have been consigned to a recycle center or given a new function as cleaning rags.

Janet Ziegler, the pastor's wife, was aware of the disorder in the clothes closet, but she had priorities, and the closet was at the bottom of her list, way behind filling the children's ministry positions for the upcoming fall. That seemed far more important, but there were some in the congregation who didn't share that viewpoint. Two micromanaging elder's wives changed the game plan, using their influence with their husbands to pressure the elder board into passing a motion to remedy the clothes closet situation as soon as possible. However, no one had any suggestions as to how to correct the problems of disorganization and unacceptable donations, so the matter was delegated to the lead pastor, Carl Ziegler, who graciously deferred to his wife, Janet. She agreed to help. The need for volunteers was posted on the church website. The elder's wives who had instigated the whole business neglected to offer their assistance. Only two persons responded to the call for help: Lucy Davis and Bonnie Wheeler. Janet was thankful for the two candidates and looked forward to fast-tracking them through the process.

Lucy Davis was in her late fifties, retired, and distanced from her habitually golfing husband. Their alienation from each other was bolstered by Lucy's habit of beginning each day with the goal of hacking people off. Lucy was miserable and frustrated with her life in general. Her husband found his sanctuary on the golf course. Many times, she ignored the practical solutions to her acrimony and chose to wallow in the mire of it all. She was now hoping that volunteering would help her become less edgy, but she was mired in her current disposition.

Bonnie Wheeler, same age, an ordinary woman who was middle-of-the-road in her thinking, but she followed Lucy devoutly. Lucy knew Bonnie's weak personality and capitalized on it by influencing her every time they were together. Bonnie was always a willing accomplice for Lucy.

A face-to-face meeting was arranged between Janet and the two applicants. Janet reviewed the functions of the clothes closet, emphasizing the need to check the quality of the donated items. Anything donated that the two volunteers would choose as unacceptable would be routed to the recycle center. Approved garments would be placed according to general sizes and application. Their job would also require policing the visitors to the closet. "Sometimes it's necessary to limit the number of items a customer takes home," Janet said, "but please be as tactful and diplomatic as possible if you do need to take that approach."

Finally, Janet mentioned the "unlocked door syndrome" that plagued the clothes closet. Generally, the doors were secured during non-operational hours, however, at times the door locking was carelessly overlooked. Invariably, the unlocked doors served as an invitation for anyone to come in, and huge quantities of clothing disappeared. Unfortunately, some people were taking the clothing to sell online or to resale shops.

Lucy and Bonnie grasped the basics of the operation and were anxious to get started. Janet said they could have flexible hours during the week but urged them to be present at specified times during church services. "Ladies, here are the keys. Thank you both so much for stepping up. Let me know if you have any questions."

The new volunteers unlocked the door and stared at the piles of clothes heaped around the room. They shrugged their shoulders and started rummaging, sorting the donations into piles. After an hour, they stepped back and looked at their accomplishments.

"Bonnie, all we need is a couple of more uninterrupted hours, and we will change the whole complexion of this place."

Just then, Miriam Rucker and her toddler daughter made an appearance. As long as the clothes closet door was unlocked, the "closed" sign on the door never deterred her. The new guardians of the clothes closet watched as Miriam ransacked the piles of toddler clothing that they had just arranged. She began piling up both girl's and boy's outfits.

Lucy couldn't hold back. "Excuse me, Miriam, but you only have one daughter. You've stacked up enough stuff for a dozen kids."

Miriam barely gave her a glance. "Who put you in charge?"

Bonnie intervened. "Lucy and I were selected by Janet Ziegler to clean this mess up, and you aren't helping by busting in here. *Hello*, the sign says 'closed.'"

Miriam glared at her. "Back off, Bonnie. I have good reason to take this stuff. My Amy will grow through these things, and I will need replacements. I'm taking them now because they may be gone in a couple of days."

"Yeah, someone your type might come in here and grab it all up," Lucy said. "I am in charge here. Put most of those clothes back and come see us when Amy's grown out of them. Maybe, in the meantime, you can have some sons for those boy's items you selected." Lucy started grabbing clothes out of Miriam's arms and tossing them back onto the jumbled piles.

Miriam's voice rose to a high-pitched scream. "Listen to you two! I can't recall either of you doing anything around this church, and now you are acting like the big hogs at the trough." She pulled her little daughter through the stacks of clothes and went out the closet entrance with a parting salvo: "This isn't over."

"Come back anytime," Lucy told her. She then craned her neck from the clothes closet door to see which way Miriam was headed. Lucy was relieved that she exited toward the main parking lot rather than the pastoral offices. Lucy whispered to Bonnie, "Can you believe her attitude? She has a lot of growing to do."

"Absolutely," Bonnie commented in her usual manner. They looked around at the disarray and decided to leave. The stacks of clothes would be there tomorrow.

CHAPTER TWO

Lucy and Bonnie met at the closet the next morning at ten o'clock. As usual, Lucy was in attack mode and Bonnie was in following mode. Lucy had seen Polly Combs earlier that morning in Polly's front yard caring for her flower beds. Polly's apparent carefree downtime resurrected Lucy's longstanding angst toward this lady she barely knew and contributed to the mountain of contempt Lucy harbored against her. She devised a plan of attack. Standing ankle-deep in some recent donations, Lucy began to share her disdain for Polly with Bonnie.

"You know how I dislike Polly Combs, right?"

"I never knew you didn't like Polly."

"Well, who doesn't dislike her? She struts around this church like it revolves around her. It's like she's saying, 'Look at me, look at me!' Then she's always cooing about how great her kids are and flaunting her flower gardens."

"I've never noticed it."

"Come on, Bonnie. You miss a lot of things around here. More than likely, you miss the points of Pastor Carl's sermons."

"I get quite a bit from his teaching."

"Whatever. You don't show it." Bonnie refrained from making any further comment.

"Anyway, I found some almost new, really cool designer stuff in one of the bags. It won't fit us, but I want to bait Polly with it."

"I don't follow you at all."

"I want to bring her down to earth, remind everybody that she's no better than the rest of us."

"Lucy, is that really necessary? Come on, it's not worth it."

"Oh, knock it off. I just want to have a little fun. It's all innocent. All I want to do is get her to take some of these clothes. Then, at the right moment, I'll confront her and compliment her on how nice the clothes closet garments look on her. It would be nice to have a crowd around. Just a little joke. She needs to be knocked down a couple of pegs. Vicky Tanner is also on my hit list."

"What has Vicky Tanner done to you?"

"Nothing, but it's obvious she's another one of those gold-dollar swagger queens. Maybe worse than Polly. Promenading around here big time." Lucy was in high gear, her mind swirling with ideas. She had a plan and was patient. Bonnie was questioning all of it but didn't pose any more objections.

Later that morning, fate intervened and Lucy was ecstatic. Polly Combs stopped by the clothes closet. Lucy hastily pointed out some garments to Polly that she'd purposely put aside for that perfect moment. The first trap had been set and sprung. Polly accepted the clothes and took them out to her car. She then returned with two bags of donations from her mother-in-law. Lucy and Bonnie had stepped out a few minutes. The door was unlocked, as usual. Polly dropped the bags in the room and left. When Lucy and Bonnie returned, they found the anonymous donations, and went through the bags. They liked what they saw.

Later that week, Lucy and Bonnie succeeded in demeaning Polly Combs at a church gathering. The entrapment went way beyond their expectations. Lucy then brought up Vicky Tanner's name again. She was next on the hit list.

Lucy knew very little about Vicky but was convinced that she couldn't afford the glitzy attire she wore. Her personal observations were not to be tangled up by bothersome facts or clouded by conviction. The clothes closet continued to slip further away from being a ministry and moved closer to becoming to a grudge-machine operation.

The first step of the nefarious scheme was to bring handpicked garments to Vicky's attention. The next Sunday morning, before the first service, Lucy told Bonnie to arrive early and join her for duty in the clothes closet. Lucy's wide-eyed plan began with a search for name-brand pieces. Next, they carried piles of that selected clothing down the annex hall, past the visitor's center, and on to the main entrance of the building. During their treks through the hallways, the designer labels were to be prominently displayed. Each would make the trip and then turn around and head back to the clothes closet, all the while keeping an eye out for Vicky Tanner. Ideally, she would arrive early and take the bait and not disappoint them. They knew the constant parade would be an endurance test for them; both were calorie challenged. After the third trip of transporting the designer apparel up and down the hallways, with no sign of Vicky, Bonnie called a halt and plopped down in a pile of clothes just inside the clothes closet.

"I can't take any more of this, Lucy. I'm exhausted. After I catch my breath, I am going for coffee and a pastry. People are giving us strange looks."

Lucy, however, was more determined than ever. Victory was still in sight.

She watched her friend slowly sink into the stack of garments. "You do whatever you want, but I'm pressing on. Grab me a couple of pastries on your way back here." Lucy then picked up some of the clothing that Bonnie had been toting, put them on her load, and stoically began another lap through the hallways. She hoped she would find Vicky on this trip, as the clothes were beginning to weigh on her. As she struggled down the hall, she didn't notice that she was dropping a few pieces behind her. She continued to attract bewildered looks.

A voice caught her attention. "Excuse me, but you are dropping clothes all down the hall."

Lucy spun around and dropped even more articles. "What did you say?" She came face-to-face with her targeted victim. It was the first time either had personally addressed the other.

"Here, let me help you," Vicky offered.

Lucy was surprised, but she stuck to her game plan. She blurted out, "Hey, do any of these things catch your eye, do you want any of them?"

"No, thank you."

"Take a closer look. Aren't these big name brands your thing?"

"I really don't have any interest in them. I'm guessing these are from the donations made to the clothes closet. They would be of more use to someone in need."

Lucy kept it up. "But these are your brands! You wear them all the time."

Vicky stepped back and gave her a peculiar look. She didn't know this lady carrying the clothes, and she didn't like her persistence, but she remained congenial. She decided to introduce herself. "I'm Vicky Tanner. Can I ask your name?"

"I'm Lucy."

Vicky extended her hand, but Lucy was busy shifting her load. "Lucy, I'm flattered you think I'm such a fashion icon, but actually, I'm just a dedicated bargain hunter. There's a thrift store located on south Barger Pike. It's owned and operated by Belmont Church. Evidently, someone in that church has a good connection with a clothing chain. The chain receives a lot of customer returns. Instead of sending most of them back to suppliers, they go to the Belmont thrift shop. They stock beautiful clothing at deep discounts. The Belmont store could definitely get higher prices for all their stock, but they have chosen to make it a ministry, not a profit center. It's like the ministry model Pastor Carl and Janet have chosen for our little clothes closet operation, except we do not charge for the goods." She gave Lucy a concerned look. "Please let me help you get this clothing back to where you were headed." They both scooped up the clothing that Lucy had been flaunting up and down the hall. "Are you staffing the clothes closet today?"

"Yep, it's my turn in there. My friend Bonnie is helping me."

"Bonnie Wright?" Vicky asked.

"That's her. Do you know her?"

"I do know her. I see her at the Belmont store frequently. She always has a full cart. She can really spot a bargain."

"Oh?" Lucy felt slighted by her cohort. Bonnie had never mentioned the Belmont store.

When they got to the clothes closet, they saw Bonnie jump out of her seat and blush bright red. She had given up on the scheme and wasn't expecting to see Vicky.

Vicky looked around the interior of the room. "You two have done a great job setting all this up. I've never been in here, but I've passed by many times and seen the clutter from the hallway. It really looks nice. You two are to be complimented on your ministry. Such dedication."

Lucy looked at her blankly. "It's a gift we both have."

"Unfortunately, not everyone at the church seems to appreciate this clothes closet. I heard about the incident involving Polly Combs," Vicky told them.

Lucy started beaming inside. Her big scheme had been successful—the details of Polly's sting seemed to have spread.

"Really? What happened?" she quietly asked.

"I need to choose my words carefully. I don't want to gossip."

Lucy covertly winked at Bonnie, indicating that this was the big bullseye.

"You see, the Combs family is on a tight budget—Polly would tell you that herself. They homeschool three kids and have two more in college, so obviously, they watch their expenses. It seems Polly came into the clothes closet one morning and found some very nice clothing. She chose a couple of items, one of which was a blue paisley dress. She wore it to the reception for those missionaries from Nicaragua. The whole episode ended with the possibility that Polly had been set up."

"What do you mean?" Lucy asked. Inside, she was thinking, *This is awesome.*

"When Polly arrived at the reception, she joined a group of ladies. I'm not exactly sure who they were, but when they noticed her dress, the comments got snarky. One zinger hit Polly pretty hard. 'Nice dress. Looks like the church clothes closet was open this morning.' Other cheap comments followed, purposely targeting Polly. She was hurt, but she showed some class and simply excused herself and went home early."

"She must have been devastated," Lucy said, smirking.

"She was feeling down, for sure. Polly called me that afternoon, and we talked through the whole senseless matter. It's hard to believe, but she had no malice toward any of those narrow-minded witches who made the comments. She is a mature Christian lady."

Vicky noticed neither of the volunteers was making eye contact with her. "You two OK?"

"We're fine," Lucy said. Bonnie was silent.

"Here's the backstory—I think it's so cool. The day before the reception, Polly had dropped off some donated items from her mother-in-law. That lady is very chic and only purchases the best—no thrift store shopping for her! Her stuff was all plus sizes, nothing to fit petite Polly. Well, it turns out that two of ladies who ridiculed poor Polly were unknowingly wearing sweaters that Polly had taken to the clothes closet! The best part is that Polly never said a word about them. I am sure she was tempted, but she kept quiet."

Lucy and Bonnie both recalled the donated sweaters. They'd had no idea that Polly Combs had dropped them off. Both of them had taken a few pieces from that bag. Polly had seen them wearing her mother-in-law's clothing. She could have shamed them in front of everybody, but she'd chosen not to.

The music of the opening worship song came over the speakers and Vicky jumped. "Oh! The service is starting. Sorry, ladies, got to run. Thanks again for all you're doing. Keep it up."

Lucy and Bonnie were left speechless and simply looked at each other.

HEIRLOOM: GOING ONCE, GOING TWICE

CHAPTER ONE

Chip Hollister, a man in his 60s, stood at the top of the stairway and looked at the broken table at the foot of the stairs. How could he have been stupid enough to try getting the table down the steps without help? He knew the old table was heavy and awkward, but in his haste and male pride, he'd attempted to maneuver it downstairs on his own.

He had felt a spasm of pain each time the table hit a step on its descent to the stair landing. Each thump represented ten years of history of the old table being in the Hollister family. Now the heirloom was in pieces.

Chip's wife, Haylie, had wanted the table moved downstairs, and Chip had wanted to surprise her by moving it before she returned from her morning errands. Well, she'd have a surprise all right. Chip kept staring at it without moving. He tried to remember how many times he had offered the table to one of his children. That piece and other vintage items were always rejected. They were labeled as "old-fashioned" and had no place in modern homes. His trance was interrupted by Haylie coming into the house from the garage.

"Chip, I'm home. How was your morning?"

CHAPTER TWO

In the fall of 1879, Ezekiel Hollister took a break from the labor that often confined him to his farm. Now it was Saturday night, and he was going to break free. Zeke's first stop would the infamous corner saloon, Mable's. Relax, play stud poker, have a few beers—or more. It was Saturday night, and there would be a crowd.

Zeke dismounted his horse, tied it to the rail, and brushed the dust off his shirt. He walked to the front door of Mable's, stopped, and looked in. Zeke was not a talented gambler, and his lack of card skills preceded him. An easy mark was always welcomed at the poker table. He spotted his main running buddy, Willy Horton, seated at one of the stud tables in the back. He was about to holler a greeting and go join Willy when a voice spoke behind him. It was a soft, musical voice, and it was speaking to him.

"Shame on you, sir, for even thinking about going in there and tightening the devil's grip on those unfortunate people." Zeke spun around. No matter how pleasant that honey-coated voice was, nobody was going to question his right to a few beers and a round of poker.

Then he saw the angelic creature who had spoken the words standing only ten feet behind him. The early evening glow was shining on her. She was the most enchanting girl he had ever seen, and she was smiling at him. Her softly curling hair was the same color as her pale-yellow dress, and her blue eyes were intensified by the color of her bonnet.

"I am sure you labor hard for your money, and it would be pure folly to dump it in there. No good will come from any involvement in that pit." Zeke was amazed at the brashness of this girl who barely reached his shoulders. He backpedaled on his evening's intentions.

"I was going to just meet a friend, chat for a while, and get on back home. I still have chores waiting."

The girl didn't look as though she believed him. Then she said, "After you meet your friend, I suggest you stop by Shiloh Missionary Church just around the corner. We're having a revival meeting at seven o'clock, and the meetings will be held every evening next week. I'm Lydia Sharp, daughter of Reverend John Sharp. He's working with a traveling evangelist from Center City." She paused, directing her sparkling blue gaze straight at him. "Keep your money in your pocket while you're in there, sir, provided you stay."

He removed his hat and bowed low toward her. "Miss, I do plan to hold onto my money. And what Zeke Hollister says, he does."

"Well said, Mr. Hollister." She smiled and turned away in the direction of Shiloh Missionary Church. Lydia looked over her shoulder. "Good evening, sir."

Zeke had heard there was a new preacher in town, but he hadn't given it any thought—until now. Lydia was outspoken but attractive. He knew he wanted to see her again, and he knew where to find her.

He walked into Mable's and moved toward the open seat next to Willy Horton. Everyone at the table greeted him and encouraged him to get his money out. They needed a chump. Zeke sat down, reached into his jacket to pull out his wallet, and then visibly hesitated. Willy and the others detected his reluctance, and his smile confused them.

Willy tried to antagonize him. "You OK, buddy? You sure got a funny look. You ain't thinking about keeping your money, are you?" That remark drew laughter from the others.

One of them said, "Why don't you just drop all your cash now and spare yourself the sorrow of parting with it?" More ribald laughter came from the group.

Zeke looked around the table and began to realize that he didn't belong there. Were these gents friends or vultures ready to tear into his money? Even if he won some dough tonight, it would all be sucked up by drinks around the table and other jackals lingering in the background. All of a sudden, he didn't want any part of this camaraderie.

"You OK?" Willy asked again. Zeke simply stood up, bid them all goodnight, and walked out the door.

"I hope that boy hasn't fallen for any of that religion stuff that's floating all over town," Willy told the group.

Zeke didn't hear the comment. The creaking of the saloon doors as he exited drowned the remarks and laughter out. He now realized that Willy had just been elevated to the role of chump at the poker table.

* * *

Once outside, Zeke untethered his horse but didn't mount up. He just walked his gelded palomino in the direction of the church. When he reached it, he was amazed at the number of buggies and horses gathered in front. As he tied his horse to the rail, he heard a soft singing voice and a gentle tune on the church piano. Zeke walked up to the front door, removed his hat, and walked in.

Lydia Sharp was singing and accompanying herself on the old church piano. She saw Zeke taking a seat in the last pew in the back and cast a smile meant for him only as she continued her hymn. Zeke nodded sheepishly in her direction and then acknowledged the couple next to him. Zeke was relieved that his attire—intended for the saloon and poker table—was appropriate for the church meeting.

Reverend Sharp got up from one of the two hand-carved chairs that had been placed behind the pulpit. The other chair was occupied by the visiting evangelist, who Sharp introduced as Desmond McPierson. Zeke saw that John Sharp was a big man, and he wondered how this man could have such a petite daughter. McPierson was much smaller, yet he had the look of someone who belonged behind a pulpit. His gaze at the audience sent the message to stay alert and heed his Biblical message. Zeke Hollister didn't escape McPierson's look. John Sharp prayed, thanked the gathering for coming, and then stepped aside for the itinerant evangelist.

Zeke Hollister had heard the proverbial fire and brimstone message from a pulpit before and was prepared to tune the little man out. Now that the singing was over, he'd gotten uncomfortable started looking for a discreet way to exit the church. His restlessness caught Lydia's attention, and again, she smiled at him as she left the piano stool and sat down next to a lady who Zeke guessed was her mother. Her identity was confirmed when Lydia pointed Zeke out to her. The lady looked back at him, and she wasn't smiling. Zeke squirmed in his pew as Desmond McPierson began preaching the gospel.

The visiting evangelist was short in physical stature, but his oratorical gifts compensated for his size. He began with some humor, anecdotes, and illustrations, and then ended his Biblical treatise with salvation through the atoning work of Christ on the cross. Zeke kept fidgeting in his seat as he listened. The message ended with an altar call urging those seeking forgiveness to come forward.

Zeke hesitated, but his heavy heart lifted him out of the last pew and took him down the aisle to a kneeling rail in front of the pulpit. John Sharp got up and went over to kneel beside him.

"How can I pray for you, son?"

"I want the forgiveness of my sins that only Jesus can provide." John Sharp asked him a few questions and then prayed with him. They stood up, shook hands, and the two strangers embraced.

"What's your name, young man?" Before Zeke could reply, a voice interrupted him.

"Dad, this is Mr. Zeke Hollister." Zeke turned and saw Lydia standing behind him. Beside her was her mother. She was scrutinizing the young man next to her husband, still with no smile.

McPierson came up to Zeke at that moment and introduced himself. He and Reverend Sharp explained the need for Zeke to be baptized. It would show others his commitment to be a disciple of Christ. Tomorrow was Sunday, and the baptismal service was planned at Honey Creek directly after the morning service.

As the crowd dispersed, Zeke asked permission to walk Miss Lydia home. She consented, and they stepped outside. Lydia grabbed his arm, and they began to stroll down the path away from the church. After just a few steps, she stopped and thanked him. He was confused, then he realized that Lydia lived with her family in the parsonage adjacent to the church. She held out her hand and gave him a gentle handshake.

"Goodnight, Mr. Hollister. See you at the ten o'clock service tomorrow morning." Lydia then pulled away from him and walked up to the front porch and into her house. Neither knew that her mother was standing in the shadows of the darkened front porch. The protective woman's slight smile was concealed by the darkness.

*   *   *

Zeke didn't even recall walking back to his horse. He was replaying the whole evening again in his mind. He'd made a decision for eternal life, and Lydia Sharp had entered his earthly life. He reached for the reins of his horse, and a voice startled him. It was Willy Horton.

"You did get religion, didn't you?" Zeke knew right away he was drunk. He'd sprawled out on the side of the road and was holding an empty bottle.

"Willy, look at me." Willy raised his head slightly.

"OK, I'm looking at you. What do you want? Make it quick."

"Willy, something happened to me tonight. My very soul was moved by God's Word. I got more than religion—I have a new life in Jesus Christ." He looked down on his friend. "And I still have all of my money, except for the little I put in the offering." His feeble attempt at humor only hammered Willy a little lower to the ground.

"Lucky you. They cleaned me out tonight."

Zeke was aghast. "What? How much did you lose?"

"A lot."

"How much did you lose?" Willy dropped his head even lower and mumbled. Zeke couldn't understand anything he said. He reached down and grabbed his friend by his coat collar, pulling him up onto his feet. Looking directly in his face, Zeke asked again, much louder.

"How much did you lose?"

"I lost $250. They cleaned me out. "

"Willy, how could you be so stupid? Didn't you see it coming? You were the sucker tonight."

"Sure, I was, because you walked out." Zeke ignored the remark. He wanted retribution for his friend. Willy had been fleeced, and in a rush of rage, Zeke reached for the rifle he kept tucked behind the saddle. He was going back to

Mable's to get Willy's money back. Before he could draw the rifle out, a big hand clamped onto his and held it on the butt of the rifle.

"Zeke, don't be too hasty and regret a foolish move." He spun around and came face-to-face with Reverend Sharp. Sharp let go of Zeke's hand and gripped Zeke's shoulder. "I heard you two talking. You got a little loud." Zeke simply pointed over to Willy, who had fallen back onto the ground.

"That is my friend Willy Horton on the ground over there. He recklessly lost a lot of money tonight. All his money."

The preacher extended his hand to Willy and pulled him up on his feet. The stench of alcohol was powerful, but Sharp ignored it. "Mr. Horton, I am Reverend Sharp. I'd say you have had a rough evening. I want you and Zeke to come to my house, and we'll have some coffee and get to know each other." He and Zeke propped Willy up and got him onto the porch and into the house. As they passed through to the kitchen, Zeke looked around, hoping to catch a glimpse of Lydia.

The coffee was soon brewed and served. The kindness of the preacher calmed Willy, but the reality of losing his money ate at him.

"Willy," said Sharp, "I was once a heavy drinker, brawler, and gambler. Nothing bothered me. I always looked forward to the next drink, another card game, and any opportunity to clobber someone who stood in my way. Then I met the man who spoke at our service tonight, Desmond McPierson. Out of love, he boldly challenged my life choices and explained that someday, I would be held accountable and required to explain my life to God. I was drunk at the time, but his words battered my rebellious soul and reached into my heart."

Willy hung on to every word the preacher spoke, then said slowly, "I have a rebel soul, and I need help." They prayed, and one more name was added to the baptism list for Sunday.

Later, as the two friends left the parsonage, a voice whispered from an upstairs window.

"Goodnight, Mr. Hollister." Zeke turned around, removed his hat, and bowed toward the open window.

Willy saw it all. "Who was that?"

"You will meet her tomorrow morning."

CHAPTER THREE

Willy Horton was a skilled furniture craftsman, and naturally, he did his best work when sober. His encounter with John Sharp changed his life, and sobriety became his standard. Mable's became only a memory of the past, and he created a new bond with Shiloh Missionary Church. One of his first contributions to the church was a handmade altar table personalized with the church's name. It was placed on the platform behind the altar rail and served as a silent testimony to God's grace in Willy Horton's life.

Willy's furniture business flourished. The demands on his time were great, but he took the time to create another personal piece: a striking cherry drop-leaf table with a decorative inlay. The table had a very special purpose, but it was kept under wraps. No one but Willy knew of its existence.

Zeke Hollister also developed a new lifestyle. He gave up his vices and fostered a growing relationship with Lydia Sharp. Six months later, he gave her an engagement ring. That event was celebrated by her family and produced a lasting smile from the protective mother. Zeke had been accepted.

Zeke began updating and expanding his farmhouse for his future bride. He was also concerned that he needed more suitable transportation for her. The farm wagon was not appropriate for carrying his lady.

He wrangled a deal with a slick trader named Hiram Bessemer for a two-person carriage. The haggling between them was fierce, and the final price called for Zeke to throw in four pork slabs in addition to a cash payment. The deal was struck, and Zeke returned to his farm to get the pork while the smiling Hiram prepared the carriage for delivery.

Zeke picked out four good slabs of the smoked pork and set out for Bessemer's place. He was in a hurry, looking forward to getting the carriage. As he rode past Abraham Jones's shack, he noticed the family out front in their garden. He knew they were sharecroppers, and no matter how hard they worked, life would always be a struggle for them. Zeke slowed down his horse when he saw all the kids waving at him. Many times he would ride on by and ignore them, but today he felt compelled to stop. As he dismounted, Abraham and his wife, followed by their seven kids, all walked out to greet him. Zeke removed his hat and spoke. "How's the Jones family these days?"

"We are all fine, Mr. Zeke."

"Please, just call me Zeke."

"Yes, sir." The kids were huddled behind their parents and peeking out at him. Zeke smiled at them.

"Mr. Zeke—I mean Zeke—we hear you got baptized some time ago, and Mr. Willy too."

"You are right, Mr. Abraham."

They laughed at his formality. "Praise the Lord," said Mrs. Jones.

Zeke began to feel an urge to give them the pork slabs he was transporting to Hiram Bessemer. It was a strange feeling, but he didn't question it.

"Abraham, I have some hog slabs with me. I would like you folks to have them."

"I'm sorry, sir, but we are still waiting for the harvest, and we don't have any extra money right now."

Zeke smiled. "Abraham, it's a gift to you."

The man hesitated. "You are a kind man. I not only see the Lord in you, I can feel Him." Zeke stepped over to the horse and united the pork slabs. He called the kids over and handed the meat to them. He worked quickly, knowing he had to return home and get more slabs for Bessemer.

"I have an important meeting and need to get on my way." He waved good-bye as he rode off.

Returning home, he grabbed some more slabs and then set out again for Hiram Bessemer's buggy shop. He and Hiram sealed the agreement. The carriage was his. The money and pork went to Bessemer. He hitched his big gelding into the harness and gently urged the horse to begin pulling the carriage. It was a sharp contrast to the wagon. The big palomino reared his head back and began a prancing trot unique to him, transporting Zeke to the Sharp home. Lydia was waiting on the front porch as Zeke pulled up in the carriage.

"Zeke Hollister, where did you get that carriage?" She didn't let on that she was impressed, but Zeke sensed it.

"Hope you like it because it belongs to us." Lydia politely chastised him for his venture but accepted his reasoning that he had gotten a good deal. They chatted for a while up on the front porch, and then she accepted his invitation to try the buggy out. She retrieved her bonnet (Zeke's favorite), and he helped her into the rig. The horse was still contesting the harness and the buggy but dutifully stretched against the confines of the harness and got the carriage moving. They passed by Abraham Jones's place, and Lydia commented on the delicious smell of roasting pork in the evening air.

* * *

Three months later, John Sharp performed the wedding ceremony for Zeke and Lydia. Desmond McPierson also there with his wife and three daughters. The oldest daughter, an uninhibited and outgoing girl named Willa, was attracted to Zeke's best man, Willy Horton. He was drawn to her as well.

After the ceremony, gifts were presented, and the wedding cake was served. Willy excused himself and, with the help of Abraham Jones, carried in a very impressive handmade cherry drop-leaf table and presented it to the married couple. Lydia slowly stroked her fingers over the grain of the wood, and Willy smiled at the look of pleasure on her face.

Others gathered around the table, and Willy took a couple of steps backward. He practically fell over Willa McPierson, who was standing right behind him. Perhaps it was no coincidence, but Willy grabbed her hand to keep her from falling, and she clutched his, and then she led him away from the others while complimenting him on the beautiful table he had created. Later, they sat talking on one of the church benches outside in the late afternoon air, Willy listened as Willa chatted away.

CHAPTER FOUR

The cherry table entered the Hollister family in the spring of 1880, and the wedding gift from one friend to another became a family heirloom. The family custodians provided loving care for the table, with the exception of a few scratches and two infamous cigarette burns.

The smoking culprit was never identified, but the burns were attributed to chain-smoking Chalmers Hollister. Chalmers was innocent but took the blame in a good spirit. He knew the guilty persons. They were his daughter Elizabeth and her cousin Ethel. The two had partaken in the taboo of cigarette smoking and then gotten distracted and accidentally left the smoldering cigarettes laying on the edge of the table.

The damage was done, the girls were reprimanded by Chalmers, and the incident was never discussed again. He playfully lived with the blame. Ironically, the table was handed down to Elizabeth, and the burnt marks at the edge of the table always reminded her of her father's admonition. After her passing, none of her family had any interest in the table, so it was claimed by her brother Clyde Hollister, remaining in the family.

Over the years, Willy's wedding gift to Zeke and Lydia served as a breakfast table, a tabletop to roll out bread dough, and a cutting board for vegetables and other ingredients. The care and concern for the table decreased with each generation.

In the 1940s, it held a tabletop radio flanked by pictures of Nellie Hollister and her brother Cameron. Later, it became a TV stand for the state-of-the-art Sylvania Halo Light black-and-white television. Then console TV sets took over, and the table was demoted to the basement of Norman Hollister, Chip's father. Another set of newlyweds was next in line as keepers of the table.

* * *

A year after they were married, Chip and Haylie were rummaging through his parent's basement and found the table tucked away in a corner.

"Chip, I love this table. Will your parents be willing to part with it?" Chip recognized the table, but he knew little about its history with the Hollister family.

"Since it's tucked away down here, I'm sure they have no use for it."

"I love the workmanship. It's definitely handmade." She ran her hand over the texture of the grain and the inlaid panels. Chip's father, Norman, overheard them.

"Anything you find down here, please take it." Haylie claimed the table. Chip and his father carried it upstairs and out to the backyard. There was some mold in the crevices and rust on the hinges, but the cherry wood glowed in the sunlight that the old table hadn't seen in years. Haylie was thrilled and began wiping the table down. Then it was loaded into their Oldsmobile station wagon.

Chip's father commented, "I have something that would be of interest to you, Haylie." They all returned inside. Norman went to his desk and retrieved what appeared to be a very old letter. Haylie opened it and began reading the contents aloud. She was surprised that the faded ink was still legible.

This cherry drop-leaf inlaid table was made by Mr. Willy Horton during the winter of 1880. It was finished in April 1880 and presented to Ezekiel and Lydia Hollister as a wedding gift. Willy Horton was my husband's best man at our ceremony.

Zeke and I have cherished this table. We spent countless hours reading the Bible under the kerosene lamp perched on top of it. This table has also served as a desk for our six children to use as they read, study, and tutor each other. Perhaps this is selfish, but our wish is that this table would remain in the family for generations after us.

Lydia Sharp Hollister—April 20, 1910

"Dad, I had forgotten about that old letter. Lydia definitely had a purpose in mind for that table. Haylie and I will be the caretakers from now on. No offense, but it's too bad the family's interest headed south over the years."

"Son, ancestors and their things simply become items of the past." Norman paused. "We do have the lamp Lydia mentioned in the basement." Haylie jumped up and headed back to the basement.

"Let's go find it. I would love to have that too." They all followed her back down into the basement.

Norman pulled a stepstool from behind the furnace and walked over to a suspended shelf hanging from the ceiling. He stepped up and pulled a box down. Chip took it from him and placed it on the workbench, and Haylie had the exuberance of a kid unwrapping Christmas presents. She unboxed the lamp and other assorted glassware. She found a pair of gold-rimmed glasses, old church bulletins, and at the very bottom, Zeke and Lydia's family Bible.

Haylie tenderly picked it up and began turning the pages. Like most Bibles of the period, there were pages of records of marriages, births, and deaths. Lydia had done an excellent job of recording the family details. The practice was carried on by Zeke and Lydia's oldest son's wife, Lois Anna (Horton) Hollister. Lois was the oldest child of William and Willamena Horton. Haylie couldn't ignore the name combination.

"Can you imagine a married couple with the names William and Willamena? Willy and Willa must have created a lot of confusion. Hopefully, they had pet names for each other." The reading glasses, lamp, and Bible were reunited with the table. Chip and Haylie took all of it home. Now it was all was in the hands of the next generation.

CHAPTER FIVE

The table, lamp, Bible, and the gold-rimmed reading glasses became a fixture in Chip and Haylie's living room. The vintage package provided a lot of information about the Hollister lineage, but none of it impressed their three children. They respected the family history, but none of them were drawn to the old stuff. None wanted to live in the past.

Their youngest, Isabella, was a schoolteacher and married to a pharmacist. Neither had a passion for antiques. The middle child, Deborah, was an attorney with no time for home decorating or a social life. The oldest was Liam. He and a fellow college classmate had partnered in a robotic prototype that revolutionized assembly-line production and become a profitable business for them. All three siblings were successful and adored by their parents, but no one had any interest in family heirlooms.

They all knew that each trip to their parents' house would include an attempt by their dad to foist the old stuff on them, particularly the cherry drop-leaf table. Dad had resolved that the table would go to one of them, and the tradition would endure. Just as resolutely, they all declined, urging their parents to just donate all of it or send it to auction.

* * *

Chip stood at the bottom of the stairs. Haylie was trying to look over his shoulder at the table that had just made a free fall down the steps.

"Chip, step aside." She scrutinized the table. "You might be in luck. The carnage may not be all that bad." Chip liked her positive thinking but remained silent. "I know someone who might be able to help us. Now, how many times have we moved that table, and it always took two people?" Chip was mute.

They picked the table up and placed it in the front room. Chip looked at it and felt a knot in his stomach. Haylie didn't dally. She searched for Jerome White, a.k.a. "The Furniture Doctor." Dr. White arrived that afternoon. His promptness gave them the impression that either he was not busy or his services were overpriced and rejected by most people.

CHAPTER SIX

Jerome White studied the damaged table.

Chip couldn't help asking, "How bad is it, Doc?"

Haylie elbowed her husband. "It's a piece of furniture, not a dying relative!"

The furniture doctor laughed and then bent down to the table, placing his ear on the surface. "Shh, can you hear that?" Chip and Haylie gave him a funny look and then wondered if the table could be infested with termites, or something worse. Jerome grinned at them. "Just kidding. Works every time."

The Hollisters were not amused, and they encouraged Jerome to get to the business at hand. "It's not as bad as it looks. The legs that are almost disconnected came apart at the joints and can be easily reattached. The newer scuff marks can be rubbed out, and I can straighten the drop-leaf hinge." Chip was elated. The table would make it after all. "Whoever made this piece was an excellent craftsman and put long hours into creating it. It could have been a gift, judging by the quality." Chip was impressed with his assessment.

"What would you say the value is?" Chip asked.

Jerome didn't hesitate. "At auction, with a perfect storm, maybe $300. Retail, possibly $400. These units are nicely made but not popular in today's market. Today's buyers want glitz, colorful stuff. Antiques are ignored. Young buyers forget them." Chip and Hayley knew this from experience.

Jerome took the table with him. The repairs were routine for him, and he sent it back to Chip the next day, along with the bill.

Later that day, Chip and Haylie began to talk about downsizing again. It had been discussed many times before, but this time, it got more priority. They understood that some of their possessions had to go, including furniture. Chip decided to put the table in that category.

"I am going to call all three of the kids one final time and try to reason with them on taking some of the family items. Hopefully, one will step up and claim the table." Haylie didn't comment, since she knew what the outcome would be. "No thanks, Dad."

Chip ignored all his children's previous pleas to text or email them and picked up the phone. He was lucky enough to get in contact with them. All three admonished him in a fun way and told him to find another outlet for the stuff. Chip was disappointed. He wanted the table to remain in the family, but he was now convinced it wasn't going to happen.

After much thought, they donated the table to the church charity fundraising project. Chip hoped it would bring the estimated $300 at auction. The funds would benefit the church. Chip had previous experience with auctions. He knew the old adage, that "corn is up, and wheat is down." That principle was explained to him by his auctioneer friend, Roger "Red" Monaco. Red was the auctioneer assigned to the church fundraiser. He echoed Chip's children, reminding him that some of this stuff just wasn't "cool" in today's environment. Chip knew that and only shook his head at the reminder.

Liam, the robotics magnate, and his family were visiting his parents on the day they were to transport auction items to the church. The auction was slated for the upcoming Saturday. After the table was loaded up, Liam asked a question.

"Dad, why are you so attached to this old table?"

Chip paused before carefully replying. "I confess, I am overly sentimental. I think back to all the labor that went into producing the table for my great-grandfather and the joy it must have brought as a wedding gift to him and his bride. I try to imagine all the hours of conversations spoken by my ancestors as they were seated around it. I know there were many moments of meditation spent there and maybe some confrontational episodes. Too bad you couldn't see your mother's face when she first saw it in your grandpa's basement. She spiffed up that old table, and it was the centerpiece of our home. But I understand that things change, and I'm now beginning to accept it. We need to downsize anyway. It's time to move on."

Liam admitted to himself that he and his siblings had never fully appreciated their father's sentiment for the old table. "I hope it fetches a good price. If you don't mind, Kim would like to have the lamp and the old reading glasses that always were laying on the table next to that old Bible." Chip was pleased by his daughter-in-law's interest in the pieces and gladly offered them to her.

They got into the pickup and made the fifteen-minute trip to the church. Once there, the table was unloaded and immersed in a vast array of donations. Nestled around it were other pieces of furniture, fishing gear, golf clubs, some vintage toys, antique firearms, a huge assortment of glassware, and a lot of junk.

*   *   *

The Saturday auction started on time, and as might have been expected, the first few items struggled to bring fair prices. But the momentum grew. The bidders got caught up in bidding frenzy—and it was all for a good cause. The prices were going up. After about forty-five minutes, the Hollister table was on the block. There was some interest, and the bid reached $200. Chip and Haylie were pleased, but Chip was silently praying it would bring $300. *Come on—let's have a perfect storm.* The demand for table stalled at $225 and only got a $5 bump.

Few noticed a nervous Pastor Woody Bennet standing beside the platform. He was tracking the bidding, and then as if on cue, he moved up to the podium. He asked for the microphone from Red Monaco. This was not auction protocol, and Red was none too happy about the interruption. It could hamper the auction's momentum. Chip and the rest of the crowd watched as Woody took the microphone from Red. The preacher was noticeably jittery. He took a deep breath before speaking to the crowd—surprising for a man accustomed to addressing hundreds of people every Sunday. Some thought this might be an emergency announcement.

"Ladies and gentlemen, please let me have your attention." He waited for the murmuring to subside. "I have received by phone a guaranteed bid"—he paused and took a deep breath—"of $100,000 for this cherry table."

There were gasps from the crowd, combined with some laughter. Someone said it must be a practical joke. Woody reiterated the validity of the bid. It was no joke.

Maddie Joseph, sitting in the front row, cried out, "Who is the bidder?" Others asked the same question.

Woody kept his composure. "Please, everyone, listen to me. The bidder has asked for total anonymity, or the bid will be rescinded. They have agreed to wire the money at the beginning of business on Monday morning." Then Woody stepped back with a smile on his face. "He's agreed to wire the money only if he's the winning bid."

Red Monaco jumped in. "Do I hear $100,005?" There was no response, not even a chuckle, from the numbed crowd. "Going once, going twice…fair warning, folks…sold, sold, sold!" The bidding was closed.

Chip cautiously approached Woody Bennett and asked him about the anonymous bidder.

"Sorry, Chip, confidential. I can't share any details. If I did, it would nullify the offer. You don't want that to happen, do you?" Chip had no reply. He went back to his seat next to his wife.

"Who's the big-time bidder" She whispered to her husband.

"Don't know. Woody has clammed up. Unusual for a preacher to be lost for words."

"Woody isn't budging?" She asked him.

"Nope, complete confidentiality. He wouldn't disclose anything. It was part of the agreement, and I am OK with it."

"You better be, Mr. High Seller of the day." Chip squeezed her shoulder and gave her the same affectionate look that had been present for all of their years together.

"Yeah, how about that. I was praying for $300 for the table and was unsure that it would even bring that. It's a good moment, but very humbling and strange."

The remainder of the auction was closed out. Pastor Woody and his fund-raising group were blown away with the proceeds.

* * *

On Monday morning, Chip was apprehensive about the money transfer and called Woody Bennett at ten o'clock. Woody confirmed that the money had been wired and a transport company would be there before noon to pick the table up. Chip again asked for the identity of the buyer, but Woody stood his ground and remained silent. There was no way he would jeopardize the deal, and he again reminded Chip to just be content with the sale. It was gnawing at him, but Chip Hollister backed off. He contacted their kids, and they all laughed at his mention of the outrageous bid price for the table. One teased him that he should have kept it, if it was that valuable. He took it in good spirits. His thoughts moved on to an upcoming trip with Haylie to Liam's new home. They were anxious to see the new build up in Michigan.

Liam and his wife, a tax attorney, had chosen to build a new home away from the typical suburban environment. Both needed a getaway from the corporate pressure. Their new home was designed to be a sanctuary where their careers could be put on hold. Spacious guest quarters were included in the floorplans, and Liam had assured his parents that it would be a fun place for the whole family to hang out.

Chip and Haylie drove up the long, curving driveway of stone and paver bricks. They already knew that Liam had downplayed the opulence of his new home. They parked in the spacious circular driveway and sat staring for several minutes.

"I can't believe those massive front doors. They certainly didn't include all this when they sent us pictures," Chip said. They got out of their car, and the two big doors opened. Their two grandkids ran to greet them, Liam and Kim were right behind. Chip then went to the rear of their vehicle and popped the trunk latch.

"Have you got someone to fetch the bags, possibly a butler?"

Liam grinned. "Just me, Pop. Give me the bags."

Kim reached in and grabbed some of the loose things laying on the back seat, including Lydia Hollister's Bible. Haylie explained the significance of the family heirloom and said that it was a gift; she wanted the Bible to be reunited with the lamp and the old glasses that Kim had gotten from them. Kim acknowledged the gift with a coy smile.

They all proceeded to the large sunlit foyer. Haylie was attempting to be discreet as she took it all in, but the interior of the home was breathtaking. Contemporary art adorned the walls, and soft, mellow-toned leather furniture was in all the rooms. The open concept prevailed throughout the main floor, with one glass wall separating the family area from a multi-seasonal windowed room that stretched out into the large backyard. It was challenging to absorb it all.

Eventually, the home tour was over, and the bags taken to the guest quarters. After freshening up, Chip and Hailey went to the kitchen area for some snacks, nearly getting lost on the way. Chip whispered to his wife that a St. Bernard would be useful to help them navigate the huge home.

He greeted his son and daughter-in-law. "Where are you going to find room in this place for the Bible we just brought you?"

Kim laughed and said, "I just placed it on a table in the family room.'"

"There is an old letter inside the Bible, and I want to show you. "Steer me in the right direction?" Haylie asked her.

"That way," Liam said, pointing his finger.

Haylie got up and went into the room. A moment later, she called back, "Chip, could you please come here?" Chip got up, anticipating another spectacular room or a million-dollar view. He walked in and stopped next to his wife.

Liam asked, "Hey, did you two find the Bible?" He glanced at his wife.

Chip didn't answer. He and Haylie had found the Bible. It was lying next to a familiar oil lamp and gold-rimmed reading glasses, all resting on Zeke and Lydia Hollister's wedding gift—the cherry drop-leaf table.

Liam asked again if they'd found the Bible. Chip drew Haylie to his side and squeezed her gently. His voice cracked as he said, "Yes, son, I see it. I see it very clearly. I see everything very clearly."

Andrew, their four-year-old grandson, came up to them.

"Grandpa, what do you think of our new table?" Chip reached down and picked him up. He noticed a ray of sunlight shining on the table. Momentarily, he thought of the table's origin, its survival, and its new home.

"I like it, Andy."

HOMECOMING VIA MERIDIAN

CHAPTER ONE

Bradley Kincaid pulled his car into a handicapped spot at the Blendon Skilled Nursing Facility for seniors. His arrival was observed by a few of the residents seated under the porch canopy. They watched as the eighteen-year-old visitor emerged from his vehicle, then got into his wheelchair, and approached the porch.

Bradley was no stranger to the facility, and his visits were welcomed by the residents and staff. The sticker on the back of his wheelchair, "I Would Rather Be Running," always elicited a smile from observers. The friendly young man had a positive effect on everyone, and that made him popular at the facility.

Most knew that Bradley was the victim of a speeding car that had veered into his bicycle's path. The force of the impact had caused traumatic paraplegia. At age fourteen, he was thrust into the stark reality of continuing his life in a wheelchair. He had a supportive family, but Bradley remained an independent soul and made himself available to serve others who needed support. He was particularly interested in helping those who had been ignored by their families.

One of the porch residents called out to him. "Good morning, Bradley. Is it hot enough for you?"

"I'm OK. How are you holding up?"

The resident simply waved and smiled. Another asked, "After you see Micah, how about a game of checkers?"

"Only if you take it easy on me."

Bradley and Micah had met a couple of years before, and their many conversations had given the young man insight into a time long gone. He knew all about Micah's service in WWII and how he and other black soldiers had volunteered as replacement troops for the previously all-white units. They had performed admirably during the Battle of the Bulge and were personally decorated by General Eisenhower. His stories were fascinating, and Bradley never tired of hearing them. He knew there was no revisionist history coming from Micah.

He tapped on Micah's slightly ajar door and heard an immediate answer. "Good morning, Bradley." He wheeled himself inside.

As the old man turned to face Bradley, he replaced a framed photo on his table.

"Good morning. Did I interrupt something?"

"Oh, no, I've just been sitting here thinking about my old hometown. Meridian, Mississippi—Queen City." Bradley had heard about this before but politely indulged his friend.

"Yeah? Tell me about it."

"I can't believe it's been over seventy years since Dottie and I left there and went up to Detroit." Micah turned to look at a black-and-white picture of a lovely woman dressed in a flower-print dress and pillbox hat. "The railroad jobs were going away in the Meridian area, so we decided to come up North for the auto jobs. Thank goodness I didn't keep doing that forever."

Bradley knew enough to fill in the blanks. Micah had attended night school, and in spite of the grueling assembly line hours, he managed to complete undergraduate work and postgraduate work in behavioral science. He began a new career with Wayne County teaching and counseling underprivileged youth throughout the Detroit area.

"I helped a lot of teens and young adults over the years, but It's still a mystery how our son got away from us." Micah picked up a picture of four faces—a mother, father, and two grinning little girls. "Rondo undervalued his marriage and his children…don't know where he learned to live that way." After retiring, Micah and Dottie had moved a little south to Toledo, Ohio, to be nearer their son and his family. They'd idolized their two grandchildren.

Micah seemed to forget that Bradley was there, staring at the faded photo, but he continued thinking out loud. "He had this urge to go to California. Why California? Beats me. He and Sabrina made that trip, but they left their girls with us. They would send for the girls once they got settled out there. Once they found their dreams. We never heard from either of them again." He shook his head and replaced the photo on his table. "We raised the two girls, they left us after college, and then, well.…"

Whenever Micah started talking about his family, Bradley thought of finding them via the internet and social media, but every time he brought it up, he was rebuffed with the same reply. After all these years, Micah didn't want to know. He'd gone through the pain of losing touch with his son and daughter-in-law, and then his granddaughters had taken a similar path, vanishing away up the West Coast. And yet Micah only ever expressed sadness, never bitterness.

Bradley knew it was time to steer clear of the past and change the flow of the conversation. "Micah, I brought you something." He handed him a foil package of premium ground coffee. Micah was a coffee purist and relished quality beans. The ho-hum variety served at the facility was several levels below his taste. Micah was pleased and handled the package lovingly, opening the top just a little to inhale the rich scent. He thanked Bradley for the gift and went over to his coffee pot to make what he considered to be *real* coffee. As it brewed, Micah turned around to look square at Bradley.

"Do you believe in bucket lists?"

"Somewhat. Why do you ask?"

"Well, I have one. Not much on it. In fact, just one item."

"Oh, really?" What could someone like Micah want to do? From his stories, he'd done just about everything he'd ever set his mind to. Bradley thought perhaps he wanted to spend a weekend in Vegas or possibly take a trip back to whatever European country was the site of the Battle of the Bulge. It turned out to be neither.

"I would like to go back to Meridian and chase down some good ol' memories. But it's just a thought." He got up and poured his coffee and sat back down. He was in a reminiscing mood and didn't seem to notice that his conversation skipped around a bit. He started talking about the Negro baseball leagues and the civil rights movement. For two people with such dissimilar backgrounds and cultures, Micah and Bradley communicated well. Bradley was fascinated by these subjects—talented players with major-league skills who were denied opportunities to play because of color barriers, social injustices in the times of Martin Luther King Jr. and Rosa Parks. Bradley's thoughts were soured by the accounts of white Christ-professing Christians who'd practiced crude racial bigotry. Micah called them out as wolves in sheep's clothing circulating among the flock.

As Micah moved from story to story, Bradley's mind wandered to Meridian, Mississippi. How far was it from Toledo? He wasn't so quick to shelve the idea of an old man's fantasy. Of course, there were obstacles that could possibly kill the idea, but they were not his focus. He was pondering the possibilities.

CHAPTER TWO

Bradley, his family, and Micah Johnson were all part of the fellowship of Northside Bible Church. The church had been planted forty-five years ago by Jake Standler, a visionary man with unstoppable energy. Jake had worked full-time as the church's lead pastor until the age of seventy-five when he'd realized it was about time to start slowing down.

Jake had intended to remain on staff as a teaching pastor and assist with the transition, but the majority of the prospective replacement candidates viewed this as a big negative. Only one applicant understood the value of having Jake Standler one office away and welcomed his accumulated years of wisdom. Harper Wolfe was contacted by the search committee, passed all scrutiny, and preached both services for two consecutive Sundays. Jake and the committee endorsed him, and he was approved by the congregation.

Harper was two years out of Dallas Seminary and had been mentored by Lucius Stone, a seminary classmate and friend of Jake's, but he was better known to his new congregation for being a second-team all-American basketball point guard for the Tuskegee Golden Tigers. That was enough to stir up plenty of curiosity and excitement among the people of Northside, and they looked forward to knowing him better. Harper always played down the basketball achievements.

* * *

Harper arrived at Northside and quickly embraced the tutelage of Jake Standler. He made it a top priority to get assimilated with his congregation and developed solid relationships in a short time. One of the people he met in his first week was a young man in a wheelchair, Bradley Kincaid.

On Sunday afternoon, they met at a coffee shop to get to know one another better. After a few minutes of casual chitchat, Bradley leaned in and said, "Are you planning on returning to Alabama in the next couple of weeks?"

Harper sipped his cappuccino while deliberating the unexpected question. "I do need to return and clean up some personal matters and finish the moving process. Why do you ask?"

"I have this friend who is from Meridian, Mississippi. He needs to make a trip down there. It's sort of a nostalgia thing with him. Since Alabama is close to Mississippi, maybe we could arrange a trip for him?"

Harper was puzzled by the strange request but intrigued enough to learn more. "I know the area. I grew up in Western Alabama, about twenty miles east of Meridian. Who is this friend of yours?"

"He's old—ninety-three. The medical people are telling him it's only a matter of time before he's placed on oxygen, which could hamper his ability to travel. Personally, I would love to drive him down there, but my parents would nix that plan." Harper didn't comment on the obvious challenges.

"Bradley, let me ask you something. First of all, what is your friend's name?"

"Micah Johnson."

"You want me to drive Mr. Johnson all the way down to Mississippi?"

The young man grinned. "That's exactly what I had in mind, with one exception."

"And what would that be?" It was a rhetorical question, as Harper thought he already knew the answer.

"I would like to come along."

Harper thought Bradley was a gutsy young man, asking such a favor of someone who was practically a stranger, but he admired his moxie, and it seemed to be for a good cause. "What is Mr. Johnson's timeline, and how much notice will he require?"

"He's prepared to leave at any time." Bradley began to give Harper some details about Micah. Harper was moved by his lonely situation. He had seen that kind of scenario played out before and sensed the heartache that Micah had experienced.

Bradley's phone vibrated and he glanced at the screen. "My mom is reminding me to ask you to supper. That will give us a chance to discuss the details of the trip. Pastor Jake and his wife will be there also."

Harper accepted the invitation, and Bradley gave him the Kincaid's address. Then he wheeled himself out of the coffee shop and to his car, carrying a gift bag of coffee for Micah. Harper followed and watched as Bradley deftly maneuvered himself behind the steering wheel. As he watched, he imagined himself, a disabled teen, and a ninety-three-year-old man all bound for Mississippi via Alabama.

He got into his own car and leaned the seat back, staring out the window and asking for God's input. It would be convenient to have all his stuff up here in Ohio. And he also had a desire to know Bradley and Mr. Johnson better.

*   *   *

Harper arrived at the Kincaid home and was welcomed by Bradley's parents, Roger and Meg Kincaid. He had casually met them previously and welcomed the opportunity to get to know them better. He shared his admiration and respect for their son. Jake Standler and his wife, Carmen, were dinner guests also, along with Micah Johnson himself. Harper suspected that the road trip had been previously discussed, but Micah made no reference to it as they sat down to dinner.

Meg Kincaid deserved her crown as the culinary queen of Northside Bible Church. The meal was a success and was topped off with a blackberry pie from Carmen Standler. The table talk ran the gamut from Jake's colorful ministry moments to Micah's historical anecdotes, and a reluctant Harper Wolfe was encouraged to share some basketball tales. Roger Kincaid attempted to tell some stories of his exploits as a quality control engineer, which sounded rather mundane in contrast, but everyone graciously listened.

There was a lull in the conversation, and then Jake began to speak.

"Mr. Johnson, it seems that just about everything swirling around a church soon reaches the pastor. Some good and some bad." He smiled gently. "But this is good. I am aware that you have a desire to make a trip to Meridian, Mississippi. The church staff, with your permission, would like to accommodate you in that venture."

Micah had just finished his blackberry pie and was wiping his mouth. The napkin fell into his lap, and he stared at Jake for few moments before saying, "You heard about that." He looked at Bradley. "I have thought about returning to Meridian many times, but reality seems always to be in the way. It's just an old man's dream, and I certainly don't want to burden anyone with it."

Jake said, "Micah, we have discussed the details, and it's our desire to make it happen."

Micah just shook his head and smiled. "I don't know what to say, other than I feel like the winner of a game show." His comment sealed the deal. Jake looked over at Harper.

"Then it's settled. Harper?"

"Yes, sir?"

"It would be nice if you could be the driver for Micah, but I am asking and not directing you. It's your call."

A brief silence prevailed while Harper thought the matter over. "I would be honored to help out in any way I can. I do have a request—may Bradley join us?" Bradley's parents looked at each other. Meg nodded her approval to her husband, who nodded back, and it was confirmed.

"Perfect," Bradley said. Jake then took the lead.

"Harper, your schedule has not jelled yet, but it's coming. You will be busy. I suggest that you leave in the next couple of days; give Mr. Johnson the necessary time and collect your gear, but limit the trip to no more than a week." Harper glanced over at Micah.

"Sir, are you OK leaving in the next few days and returning within the week?"

"The plan seems good to me! I can leave tonight, but don't want to rush you young folks." Micah's remark brought smiles.

It was decided they would leave that Tuesday and arrive in Meridian late Wednesday afternoon. Roger Kincaid agreed to fund the trip. Jake offered one of the church's fifteen-passenger vans—large enough for the three travelers and with plenty of room to bring Harper's things back with them. Micah was next, and he insisted on paying for everything. Roger closed the conversation.

"Here's the bottom line—I pay all expenses, Northside furnishes the van, and you two"—looking at his son and Harper—"will take care of Micah. And for sanity's sake, everyone get your own hotel room. You will spend enough time with each other on the road, and you will need your space."

Jake said, "Amen!"

As they departed the Kincaid home, Jake called Harper aside.

"Thanks for stepping up."

"My pleasure. Micah Johnson is a man with a lot of experience. I can learn from someone who faced racial bitterness in the segregated South, served his country in combat, and taught in the inner-city schools of Detroit. I understand he's gone through some serious family issues as well. He's been challenged many times but seems to have got through it all in a mature, Christ-honoring way. That's the kind of saint I want to teach me."

Jake gripped his shoulder. "I'm glad you're joining us at Northside, Harper."

* * *

On Tuesday morning, the blue Northside Bible van was packed, and prayers and goodbyes were said. The three passengers boarded, and Harper turned south on Blazer Road, heading for I-75 South. The goal was to reach the north end of Atlanta that evening. Micah was awake the entire trip telling stories about his travels before the interstate system. He mixed in personal tidbits about his family. Harper asked him the names of his granddaughters, hoping he wasn't stirring up any bad memories.

Micah obliged him. "The oldest is Cecilia, and her younger sister by one year is Samantha. We called them Sissy and Sammy. I haven't heard from them for years, but I keep praying for them."

"Mr. Johnson, you know it would be easy to search for them on social media. You might be able to contact them that way. I can assist you."

"Thank you, Harper. Bradley has offered the same advice, but I just want to keep it all unknown. I don't think I could handle the truth. At least not at this time. And please—call me Micah."

The van got silent. Harper could see a soft gleam growing in Micah's eyes as they headed south, drawing closer to Meridian. They had a late lunch; Micah seemed distracted and only picked at his salad.

* * *

They stopped in the early evening and found a hotel. Micah appreciated having his own room; the other two men were excellent company, but he was used to being alone, and it was good to have some time to himself. Micah had no one to call and give updates to, so he busied himself with the nuances of his room's cable TV system. He was soon frowning at the raunchy pay-per-view choices that kept popping up on the screen. *Evil is all around,* he told himself.

A tap on the door told him it was time to meet the others for supper. Micah followed Harper down the hall, and they met Bradley in the lobby. The choice for supper was Mexican. Micah settled for another salad, which he could hardly touch. He'd felt ill all day but hadn't said anything. He didn't want the others to worry or take trouble about him. When Bradley asked how he was feeling, Micah deflected and brought up the pay-per-view trash he'd discovered on the TV. Harper said he knew it was profitable for the hotels and the cable providers, and the love of money often squeezed out any thoughts of accountability. Profits above morality.

Early the next morning, the Northside Bible Church van headed south again. Around mid-morning, Harper spotted a sign for a small restaurant chain that featured chicken biscuits and steak biscuits with gravy and suggested a stop. Micah agreed, but Bradley was uncertain. This cuisine was new to him. Micah assured him that he would love the combination and quipped that gravy had been his favorite beverage up to the time he left for the army, and then he preferred cold coffee. Bradley was so impressed by the meal that his breakfast habits were instantly changed. He texted his mother of his newfound love for Southern breakfast fare, and she agreed to research the recipe and make it all from scratch.

The trio continued to Birmingham. Once there, they drove by Harper's former pastorate, Evangelical Fellowship. He considered stopping but headed west toward Meridian. Micah felt his heart racing.

They arrived around a quarter past three, and Harper and Bradley told Micah he had free reign to direct the van anywhere he wanted. He remained silent as they drove into his old hometown. There had been many changes—which he'd expected—some good and some bad. He sat back and took it all in.

They passed an obscure alleyway he'd frequented as a kid. At the entrance was a cheaply fabricated storefront that was obviously put up on a limited budget. The place had once been a drugstore with a candy and ice cream parlor, a favorite haunt for local kids. Adjacent to it was a large laundromat; years ago, it had been a movie house for blacks. Micah didn't say anything to Harper or Bradley. Only he could relate to the memories. Young people couldn't begin to grasp the way things used to be, especially young Bradley. Harper could possibly relate to the pain of racial discord, but there was no discussion. Micah asked if they could go to the hotel. He was tired.

The hotel was newly developed and located in an upscale area. Micah recalled the area once being farmland and was amazed at all the development. He found it refreshing to see new infrastructure after passing through the run-down areas. After checking in and depositing their bags in the rooms, they had a quiet dinner in the hotel restaurant and went to bed early. Micah had had enough of the sordid TV channels the night before, and he left the TV switched off. He felt a little ashamed that he wasn't enjoying the trip as much as he had always anticipated. The others had been so kind in helping out. He fell asleep troubled.

CHAPTER THREE

On Thursday morning, the trio ate breakfast and set out for another drive down memory lane. This time, Micah asked them to head to South Orchid Street. Bradley plotted the location into his phone, and the tour commenced.

"What's on South Orchid Street?" Bradley asked.

"The fourth or fifth house on the left, can't remember for sure. That's where my wife grew up. We spent many hours on the front porch. I was always aware her father had me in his sights, watching over his daughter. The old rascal later became my father-in-law." Micah chuckled. The van turned onto Orchid and went south. Micah saw the house. "There it is: 565." Sadly, the house was in disrepair, and the old porch had either rotted off or been removed. Micah stared and visualized the former porch with Dottie sitting on the steps, waiting for him. Harper slowed the van to a crawl and gave Micah plenty of time to look at the old dwelling.

"Do you want me to stop so you can get out and look around?"

"No, it's OK. I've seen enough." He couldn't keep the disappointment out of his voice.

Bradley made a suggestion. "Let's go check out your homeplace. Give me the address; I'll put it into my phone."

"We don't need all that artificial junk for direction. I can find it from here. Just go to the end of Orchid and turn left onto Bridge. Keep heading west for about four miles. Then we will turn right onto Cemetery Road, and it's about two miles down the road." Bradley looked skeptical at the old-school directions, but Harper drove on, and Micah was pleased to see that he hadn't been wrong. A brief ride got them to 9000 Cemetery Road.

Micah wasn't sure what he'd expected to see, but the reality saddened him. The urban decay was glaring. The majority of the homes in the area were abandoned and boarded up. A couple had occupants, but it was apparent that no one cared about the places.

"My daddy worked six days a week and helped teach and preach on most Sundays. As busy as he was, the house and all the outside areas were always immaculate. My mother kept the inside spotless, and she was always on guard that us kids kept it that way too. Boys, I began cutting that grass when I was only five and continued up to the day I left for the army. Cut it some more when I returned, right up to the time when Dottie and I left for Detroit and gave up that old shack we rented back on Turner Street. It burned down shortly after we left. Rumor had it that it was torched by the owner." His companions were impressed with his recall.

He looked down at his hands. "How could anybody let it get this bad? The houses along this whole road look just as pitiful. Let's go back to the hotel. I'm sorry for putting you two fellows through this trip down here. I should have known better, that it wouldn't be like it was in the past."

"Nonsense, Mr. Johnson," said Harper. "It's been a fun trip, and we will make it even more enjoyable."

"Thank you, Pastor." Micah felt tired. They hung around the hotel until early evening.

*   *   *

Harper took them through a fast food place and got some hamburgers, then parked the van. He and Bradley ate, but Micah ignored his cheeseburger. Harper was concerned about the old man. He'd hardly eaten anything since they'd left Ohio. Now he was leaning against the window, staring at a park across the street.

"Look that group playing basketball," Micah said. Harper had noticed them earlier but hadn't mentioned it. There were seven young men playing on the south end of the well-maintained park. "Let's go check it out, maybe join them?" Micah gave a quick glance at Bradley. "Are you up for some scrimmage, Bradley? How about you, Harper? I'm good for at least five minutes, but that's it. No one likes a showoff."

Harper was pleased that Micah seemed to be perking up. Bradley laughed and said, "Why not? I can show them all my moves." Harper started the van, crossed the street, and parked in front of the men shooting hoops. Their session was informal and appeared to be a warmup before any real game began. It all came to a standstill when the van from Northside Bible Church pulled into the space directly behind the north goal.

The three climbed out of the van, and Harper wondered what the basketball players were thinking. *One old black man, one young black dude, and a white kid in a wheelchair. Quite a grouping.*

Harper guessed the guys on the court were all about eighteen or nineteen. One of the taller men approached him.

"What's going on, guys? Never heard of Northside Bible Church." He looked back at his buddies as if signaling them all to be cool. "What brings you all over here?" Harper didn't detect any hostility, but he knew about turf challenges and took the lead.

"I'm Harper Wolfe. I am a pastor from Toledo, Ohio. This gentleman is Micah Johnson, and this is Bradley Kincaid. We made a trip down here for Mr. Johnson's benefit. Meridian is his hometown, and…well…he hasn't been here for many years, so we agreed to bring him down for a visit."

The young men didn't take their eyes off Harper. He spoke to their leader, the tall one in front of him. "What's your name?" Harper extended his hand to the young man, who saw the intended handshake but didn't raise his hand.

"I'm Griff Johnson. Them back there are Issac, Tyson, Hernandez, Bigelow, Little Ray, and Gleason. Where you from, Harper? I once heard of a Harper Wolfe that played ball at Tuskegee. They called him the Running Lobo. That wouldn't be you, would it?" He laughed as he dribbled a basketball in-between and around his legs as if to showcase his ball-handling skills. "You never answered me. Are you the Lobo?"

"Yeah, that's me."

"I knew it, I knew it! You are the Lobo. Show us what you got, man. We can form two teams and see who wins." Harper looked over at Micah and Bradley, and they both nodded an OK. Harper had a sports bag in the van with his court shoes. *Good thing I didn't unload the bag at the hotel*, he told himself.

* * *

As Harper turned toward the van to get his shoes, Bradley saw a young black man in a wheelchair coming toward him. As he approached, Bradley realized that he was a double amputee, probably close to Harper's age. The stranger came right up to Bradley's wheelchair and introduced himself. "I am Jenkins Johnson."

"I am Bradley Kincaid."

"Have you noticed that you're the only white person on this side of town?"

"I have noticed that, but I'm no threat to anyone." He tapped his wheelchair armrest.

"I guess you're with that church van parked over there," Jenkins said, pointing back to the parking lot. "What happened to you?"

Bradley knew the inference behind the question. "I got hit by a car while riding my bike four years ago. Paraplegic damage in my lower body. Medicine is making advancements though; maybe someday they'll be able to correct it." A soon as he made the comment, he felt a pang of guilt. This man had no legs, and no medical advancement would restore them. "What about you?"

"Marine Corps, Afghanistan. Our vehicle took a hit from an IED. Killed four of my buddies and rolled our Humvee. I survived, and here I am." He quickly changed the talk. "You any good at basketball?" He picked up two basketballs and began heading toward another court away from the others. Bradley followed him.

"Actually, I'm a geek. No athletic skill whatsoever."

"Well, maybe we change that." Jenkins tossed a ball to Bradley. "What are you doing here in Meridian?"

"We are taking the older gentleman over there on a homecoming trip. We'll be here for a couple of days and then head back."

It wasn't clear whether Jenkins had heard him or not. He was fixated on the basketball. "Let's get on out there and shoot. You got a ball, so do something." Jenkins then went toward the goal and flipped a layup through the hoop. "Now, you do it." Bradley got even closer than his opponent. He too flipped the ball up and made his first goal from a wheelchair.

"There you go, tech dude. You got some potential." Both of them moved to the north goal, flipping the balls back and forth. Ten feet from the goal, Jenkins hollered for Bradley to shoot. He did and missed, but Jenkins rebounded and passed him the ball again with the same admonition: "Shoot!" Bradley scored again.

"Not bad...for a geek. Do it again." Jenkins then flipped the ball back to him, and Bradley landed it, moved a little closer to the basket, and slapped it up in the form of a layup.

"You got the moves, now pay attention." Jenkins moved back about thirty feet from the goal and swished it. After that shot, Bradley chased the ball and moved toward Jenkins, passing the ball back to him. Jenkins shot and got the same result. *Swish.*

"Not bad...for a jarhead," Bradley said.

Jenkins was smiling. "OK, now, fast break!" he shouted out to Bradley. He had a general idea of the play and moved to the basket, caught the bounce pass, and lobbed up another layup. Surprisingly, it went in. Jenkins laughed as Bradley roamed under the basket, trying to conjure up some swagger, but he didn't have the moves down.

* * *

One hundred feet away, on the south court, the other game was getting started. Sides were chosen and purposely stacked against Harper. He was teamed with the underperformers, but the former college phenom knew how to play it cool and start slow, no showboat antics. He took the inbounds pass from his unknown teammate and moved down the court, passing the ball off to another teammate. Their names became familiar as they played on and everyone clamored for the ball.

Harper kept his game slow. He hedged on the first shot and passed to Tyson, who missed, but Harper got the rebound and tapped it in. Griff brought the ball back down the court, did a hoopla grandstand shot that missed, and the rebound went to Harper. He passed to Tyson, and then a half-court heave to a fast-breaking Harper, who sank a twenty-footer swoosh. Harper was still holding back on his game.

He then got an opportunity to steal the ball from Griff, sidestepped the other three, and made a behind-the-back reverse layup. His skills were no longer hidden. He picked up the tempo and slowly took control of the game with three thirty-footer shots breaking the nets in succession. In the back of his mind, he knew that in pickup games like this cheap fouls could happen, and he was ready for some uncalled-for antics from the group, but nothing of the kind occurred. They weren't great athletes, but they had sportsmanship. In fact, Griff laughed and encouraged Harper to pick up the pace. He did.

After thirty minutes of fast play, a water timeout was called. Griff had brought a cooler full of water, soft drinks, and beer, which he willingly shared. Sipping on a cold bottle of water, Harper observed Micah dozing under a tree and Bradley playing with another man in a wheelchair on the north court. He decided to let Micah rest and suggested they move over to the other court and watch the other contest.

Griff informed him that the other guy was his older brother, Jenkins, and gave some background on the injuries he sustained in Afghanistan during his stint with the Marines. Harper had heard of such terrible injuries, but this was his first closeup encounter with a wounded warrior. Nightly news broadcasts were one thing, but this was all too real.

Jenkins and Bradley also called a water break. The cooler had been transported over to their court, and both of them were handed a bottle of water. Strangely, the cans of beer had been ignored by everyone. Bradley was introduced to all the others, and then they all sat down in a circle on the park grass and started chatting as if they'd all known one another for years.

Harper kept glancing over at Micah resting under the tree. A couple of minutes later, he decided to take him back to the hotel. He stood up and thanked his new friends for the workout. Harper was a pastor at heart as well as by vocation, and he never missed an opportunity, so he asked if everyone would join him in a closing prayer. No one replied, which he took as a good thing, and he said a quick prayer. Some of the young men looked up at the sky, and others looked down at their feet. Harper closed and then heard Jenkins speak up.

"Preacher, our mother could use some prayer."

"I would be honored to pray for her. Is there a special request?"

"She just needs some encouragement," Griff said.

"Momma is battling health issues and…addictions. She could use some good one-on-one, face-to-face talk from a preacher like you."

"Would you like me to visit her? We'll be here for a couple of days."

The brothers looked at one another, and then Jenkins said, "We would like for you to see her tonight. We live about fifteen minutes from here."

Harper hesitated. He was sweaty from the basketball game and not exactly presentable for a visit.

"Don't worry about your appearance; we've all had a little deodorant letdown."

Harper looked over at Bradley, who just shrugged his shoulders. "I am OK with it if you are."

"Let me check with Mr. Johnson." The whole group migrated to the tree where Micah lay sleeping. Harper leaned down and gently tapped him on the shoulder. There was no response. Harper tapped him again.

"Mr. Johnson? Wake up, it's time to get going." Micah stirred after Harper continued tapping on his shoulder. He looked surprised at all the faces looking down at him and didn't seem sure of where he was.

"Oh, I guess I dozed off. Is it time to go? Harper, give me a hand and help these old bones get on their feet." Harper reached down and helped him up.

"Mr. Johnson—"

"I have asked you quite a few times to just call me Micah."

"Yes, sir. Since my mother isn't around to hear me and correct me, I will call you Micah."

Micah liked his smile.

Jenkins spoke up and said, "Mr. Johnson, we are asking Pastor Harper to come and see our mom for a brief visit. She could use a preacher-type call."

"Sure, young man. Where does she live?"

"Over on South Peach street, just past Brook Boulevard." Harper caught a look from Micah and knew that they were headed to a questionable part of town.

"Whereabouts on Peach Street?" Micah asked.

"Down almost to Carter Street. 858 South Peach Street."

"I know where it is."

Back in the van, Micah said that their destination was close to the part of town where Rondo's wife, Sabrina, had once lived. Harper regretted his promise and was apprehensive about meeting strangers in this unfamiliar setting.

Bradley said, "Keep cool, man. I got your back, and Micah is our backup." The remark drew a weak smile from Harper, but he suggested they pray before going any further.

The late evening traffic was sparse, and they made good time. Micah was still quiet, watching with sad eyes as the familiar streets unfolded before him. South Peach Street was lined with cars. Harper thought that parking the van could be difficult, but Griff motioned them into the driveway of 858 South Peach Street.

Harper liked the front of this house; it stood out from the others with its neatly mown lawn, flowerbeds, and landscaping. He got out to help Bradley exit the car and noticed a couple of neighbors peeking out from behind their curtains. Micah opted to stay in the van. He said that too many people converging on the poor woman wouldn't be good. Harper saw he looked exceedingly tired. He whispered to him that it would be a very short visit.

Griff went in front of them and tapped on the door. "Hey, it's us. Unlock the door." They heard various deadbolts being pulled back. A scruffy old woman greeted them, and Jenkins introduced her as their grandma. The grandmother hugged Griff and stepped aside as Jenkins came in with his wheelchair, followed by Bradley and Harper. As the visitors walked through the door, they were hit with the stale odor of cigarettes and medicine. Fresh air was scarce around here, and their sweaty clothes wouldn't bother anyone.

"Grandma, these are friends we met tonight over at the park. This man is Harper; he's a preacher, and he wanted to come over and pray with Momma. That's Bradley."

Harper greeted her, but he felt awkward, almost like an intruder in this small house. "I hope we are not causing any inconvenience. Griff and Jenkins asked us to come over to meet their mother and pray with her. I take it that she is your daughter."

Grandma eyed them up and down. "Mercy, no, it's OK. She does need some prayer, and me too, while you're at it. You boys are welcome to stay as long as you want." She introduced herself. "I am Sabrina Johnson, and my daughter's name is Samantha." She kept glancing at Bradley in his wheelchair but didn't ask any questions.

Harper gave Bradley a look and saw that he had picked up on the names also. This visit was not a coincidence. Bradley spoke first.

"Miss Johnson, do you have a Micah Johnson in your family? Perhaps your father-in-law?"

Sabrina Johnson stiffened. "Yes, my husband's father was named Micah Johnson. Why would you ask me such a question? Who are you two, anyway?"

Harper felt a lump in his throat. *This can't be happening. Is this what they call a "divine appointment"?* "Ma'am, Micah Johnson is outside sitting in our van."

Sabrina fell back against the kitchen counter, and Griff moved to keep her from collapsing. She waved him away and took a deep breath, collecting herself, then said, "I can't believe it. All these years, I figured he was dead and gone." Then she told her side of the story. She claimed that there had always been conflict between her and her husband and his parents; her in-laws were always interfering, "pushing religion on us and judging us."

Bradley said, "Dottie has been dead for a few years, but Micah is alive and doing well. Jenkins and Griff met him earlier this evening."

Harper excused himself and went outside to get Micah. The tired old man had opened the van door for ventilation and heard Harper coming toward him.

"Everything OK?" he asked.

"You need to come into the house with me. It's very important; please don't ask any questions until we get inside." Looking dazed, Micah slowly stepped down from the van, carefully looking down at the driveway beneath his feet. He watched his steps on the dimly lit pavement but walked as briskly as he could with Harper supporting him.

They reached the open front door and entered the small foyer. Micah steadied himself and then looked up, surveyed all the faces around him. He focused on one.

"Sabrina?" His voice was a quavering whisper.

The woman stood still for a long minute before breathing, "Oh, dear Lord, it is you." All hostility had vanished, and a humbled old lady put out her arms around her father-in-law. Both were crying within seconds. The wounds of the past might not have healed completely, but they weren't festering any longer. Sabrina called out to her daughter.

"Samantha, please come in here." There was no response. "Samantha, come in here right now." They heard a door open down the hall, and another bedraggled woman made her appearance. She didn't seem pleased with this interruption.

"Momma, what do you want?"

"Girl, get over here and see your grandpa."

Samantha looked up and saw Micah. Her look changed from annoyance to surprise to fear and then something like shame.

"My little Sammy." Micah stiffly walked over to her and wrapped her in his arms. Now all three of them were sobbing, and they moved toward the living room, taking a seat on an old couch. They sat there, just holding hands. Sammy motioned for her two sons to come over and meet their great-grandfather. Harper and Bradley stood there and watched. They knew that they were privileged to be part of a special moment. This was a homecoming indeed.

The family talked softly together, and the past continued to be ignored. The yesterdays were banished. Micah was no doubt concerned about Rondo and Sissy, but he never asked, and the women never mentioned them. Harper was thrilled that, at last, Micah seemed to have found some closure from the trip. He leaned against the wall next to Bradley.

Finally, a little after midnight, Harper suggested that it was time for them to leave. They decided to meet again tomorrow. He went over and helped Micah off the couch, and as he stood up, Micah said, "Let's all go out to Cemetery Road tomorrow and take family photos. I want some to bring back to Ohio with me." He turned to Griff and hugged him, then went over to Jenkins and looked down at him in his wheelchair. "You did the Johnson name good, real good." He stepped back and gave a wobbly salute. Jenkins returned the gesture.

Bradley had gotten Sabrina's contact information, and they agreed to meet out on Cemetery Road at noon. Harper closed the eventful night—or early morning—with another prayer.

The Northside van then left the driveway and headed back to the hotel. Micah was a little shaky and unsteady on his feet, but his face was glowing. When they got back to their rooms, he reminded the other two that they needed a shower. They all decided to sleep in, and if they missed the continental breakfast, they would find a restaurant that served biscuits and gravy.

CHAPTER FOUR

Harper slept in the next morning, waking up long after the continental breakfast was cleared away. He went downstairs to the dining area and found Micah sipping coffee from a small plastic cup. He didn't seem to be enjoying it. Bradley joined them a few minutes later and said, "Come on, Micah. Let's go get you some real coffee."

They went down the street to a locally owned breakfast place. Micah didn't even open a menu, preferring to sip the freshly brewed coffee instead. Afterward, they drove around the city again, arriving at the house on Cemetery Road just before eleven o'clock. They took time to look around.

Weeds and scattered trash were partially blocking the driveway, but there was a navigable path. The past owners, or possibly trespassers, had cleared some of it. Harper assisted Bradley with his wheelchair and also held on to Micah. They reached the front porch, and Harper and Micah went up the steps. Micah looked into the windows and it was clear that he wanted to go inside.

Harper went around the back of the house, hoping to find an unlocked window. He didn't approve of trespassing, but he convinced himself that his intentions were good. The second window he tried was unlocked. *OK, Lord, you know I am not a vandal. I'm on a mission for the good of Micah Johnson.* He opened the window and climbed in, sidestepping the clutter to walk to the front door. He had to force it open, and the noise startled the other two waiting outside.

"Good morning! Please come in."

Micah walked inside, and Harper joined Bradley in the front yard while he toured the downstairs and carefully went upstairs. Micah walked through every room twice, his footsteps thumping on the bare wood floors. He never spoke a word as he carefully came back down the steps from upstairs and out onto the front porch. He stepped over to the west end of the porch and pointed upward to a couple of hooks protruding from the ceiling.

"We had an old oak swing here once, and it was occupied every evening and every morning. I sat there once and told Dottie about the future I would give her. We had many good times out here in the breeze, just the two of us." He stopped and smiled. "And her father wasn't around, or I never spotted him."

Harper helped Micah sit down on the front steps. It was good to see the old man smiling again. Then Harper walked around to look around some more at the back of the property. A pile of scrap caught his attention. As he got closer, he doubted his eyes. Was that an old swing partially buried in the heap?

Closer inspection confirmed that it was an old swing tangled in the trash and weeds. Harper knew it couldn't be the relic that Micah had recalled, but it was a swing possibly left behind by the last tenants. Remarkably, it still had the chains attached to it.

He grabbed hold of the swing and began to pull it free from the brush. It gave him some resistance, so he stepped closer and pulled even harder. The jostling annoyed a snake that slithered past him and quickly went out of sight in a nearby clump of bushes. Harper contemplated rededicating his life to Jesus after the scare, but then renewed his efforts to untangle the swing. He got it free with no more snake intrusions and began to drag it to the front of the house. By the time he reached the front yard, he saw Micah and Bradley had moved to the other side of the house and were in the old garden area that Micah's mother had once carefully maintained. He tried to imagine the countless hours spent there.

Harper reached the porch and hoisted the swing up onto it. He fastened the rusty chains to the hooks in the ceiling, and the swing dangled and began to creak. It looked sturdy enough, and Harper went ahead and gave it a test drive. He kicked back and forth and was bouncing up and down for good measure when Micah came back around to the front of the house and started laughing. Once he was satisfied that it had passed all the safety requirements, Harper called out in the tone of a carnival barker, "Next!" Micah didn't hesitate. He came back up on the porch and, with Harper's assistance, sat down on the swaying swing. Bradley recorded it all on his phone.

Micah sat there in silence, gently swinging, for several minutes. His mind seemed to have gone to a different era. Watching him, Harper imagined that the old man didn't see the weeds or trash any longer but instead a well-manicured lawn, perfected by his father. He was probably listening to his mother singing one of her favorite hymns as she attended to her garden. Micah's gnarled hand patted the empty seat beside him as though Dottie were sitting there once more.

Harper joined Bradley out in the yard, and they chatted quietly while keeping a lookout for the rest of the Johnsons. As noon drew closer, Harper turned around to see Micah leaned back in the swing with his eyes closed. "I'll go get him so he's awake when they get here."

Running up the porch steps, Harper went up to the swing and touched Micah's arm. "Mr. Johnson, they should be arriving any minute now. Micah? Can you hear me? They should be here shortly." Bradley noticed the efforts to wake Micah.

"Something wrong?" Bradley called.

Harper's heart dropped, and he pressed his fingers to Micah's wrist. There was no pulse.

A life well spent was over. Micah Johnson had just moved from this life into eternity. His Meridian homecoming was only a prelude to his heavenly homecoming. His journey had ended.

"Bradley, he's gone home."

Harper called EMS, and they arrived at the same time Samantha, Sabrina, and the boys got there. They all stood by solemnly as Micah was loaded into the transport. After it departed, Harper had them form a circle and led them in prayer.

* * *

Before Bradley and Harper concluded their trip, they went back and retrieved the old swing from the porch. After all, it had been tossed on the trash pile, so neither considered their act as stealing. The swing made the trip to Ohio, and with a fresh coat of paint, it found a new life in the Kincaid's backyard. Sometimes, when the swing stirred by itself in a passing breeze, Bradley imagined that Micah was back for a visit and waiting for a good cup of coffee.

SULLIED FACTS

CHAPTER ONE

Lee Adams, the lead pastor at Maple Grove Covenant Fellowship, pulled into his parking space in front of the administration area of the church. The reserved space was a small perk, but it had its drawbacks. Whenever he parked there, it was a beacon signaling that the pastor was in. His car was recognizable, and some took its appearance as an invitation to stop in and chat. Lee was aware of this and at times avoided the spot and parked elsewhere. Today, he parked in an out-of-the-way space and went into his office. Privacy was paramount at the moment, and he needed his breathing space.

The emotion of the funeral he'd just officiated had drained him. The two-year-old daughter of Trent and Courtney Wiggins had lost her battle with leukemia. Everyone admired her parents' spiritual stamina. The couple knew days of sorrow were before them, but they trusted that God would somehow get them through it.

Both of them had asked to be excused from the carry-in dinner the church ladies provided for families after funerals. They needed time alone. Pastor Lee had graciously accepted their wish not to attend the post-funeral dinner, but he was incensed by the circumstances that necessitated the absence of his young associate pastor, Jude Charles, and Jude's wife. One grieving couple would not be there because of understandable sorrow, but another would be absent due to flagrant sin of the husband.

Lee sat in his office stewing for a while, staring into space, then decided he needed to go home and change into something more comfortable. He felt a pang on arriving at an empty house. He quickly shed the wool suit and took a refreshing shower. He searched for some more comfortable clothes, but to no avail. Elaine might have found them . . . but he stopped thinking about his wife and her recent departure. He left for the post-funeral luncheon. His thoughts were on Jude Charles. Lee began thinking back to how Jude had penetrated their fellowship in the first place.

CHAPTER TWO

Maple Grove Covenant Fellowship had an average weekly attendance of six hundred people for both services, but had plateaued for the last few years. A few months back, the leadership had decided it was time to step back and take a hard look at what they were doing and how it could be improved. They realized the church needed to direct its focus on growth. They also developed a long overdue succession plan for the lead pastor. Several long meetings later, they concluded that the church had to begin an outreach for the college and young adult demographic, and the elder board voted to bring in a younger staff pastor to help. The plan was a simple one. This new pastor would reach out to college students at the two universities in the area and partner in developing a larger youth group. In the long term, the new pastor would possibly succeed Lee when it came time for his retirement. Other staff members approved the plan.

The search team interviewed a variety of candidates and soon formed their shortlist of applicants. One name soared to the top: Jude Charles. The dean of his seminary, Dr. Henry Gooding, had been a classmate of Lee's, and the two communicated regularly. Their association benefited when Dr. Gooding commented on the merit of Jude Charles. Lee deliberately kept the endorsement from the search team. He was willing to apply the endorsement if Jude struggled through the candidate process. The recommendation wasn't required, however, as Jude blew through the interview process with flying colors.

Jude was approved by the board and the congregation. He was a personable, good-looking man. His wife was equally attractive, plus charming and hospitable. They had been married for two years prior to joining Maple Grove. The couple was generally considered to be the perfect addition to the fellowship, and they both got involved quickly. Emma found a volunteer niche in children's ministry and a joint role with Jude working with the younger members of the flock.

The congregation's enthusiasm for the young pastor ran high. Youth attendance rose consistently, and Jude even helped bring back a fundraiser that had been tabled for the last two years. The plan was to build a new addition onto the main church building and expand the youth center.

Now all those plans were dead in the water thanks to the carnality of Jude Charles.

Lee knew he had to contact Henry Gooding about his chosen one's fall from grace. He could only speculate about the dean's reaction to Jude's indiscretions. Lee had meant to talk to Dr. Gooding for some time about some issues of his own, but this problem with Jude was far more pressing. He conveniently buried his own dilemma.

Lee's jumbled thoughts now shifted back to the post-funeral lunch and the needs of Trent and Courtney Wiggins. They had become close friends with Jude and Emma Charles, and now they had been betrayed along with Lee and the rest of the congregation.

*   *   *

Lee arrived at the church. His blood sugar was low, and he was becoming edgy, but he pushed himself to get through this portion of the day. He tried to forget about Jude for a while—their meeting this afternoon would come soon enough. Before entering the fellowship hall, he tried his wife's cell one more time and got kicked over to voicemail. He ended the call without leaving a message and walked into the crowded room.

He observed Howie Wright standing near the main food table. That man avoided every fellowship activity at the church—including most Sunday attendance—but never missed any of the church meals. Lee despised that kind of behavior but refrained from confronting him. He had other more pressing concerns.

Over in a corner, Channing Jameson was chatting with Brett—a young man whose wedding Lee had just officiated two weeks before. Channing was an attractive woman, and she knew it. Men felt free to ogle her, and she shamelessly lapped up the attention. The other church ladies often discussed the fact that Channing pushed the boundaries of her marriage.

She had a patent maneuver: At an appropriate time during every church service, she would gracefully rise from her seat and exit the auditorium. Her walk—and more specifically, her short skirts and occasional cleavage—attracted the attention of the men and the disdain of the women. The whole spectacle was repeated as she returned to the auditorium and slowly made her way back up the center aisle. Naturally, the pulpit gave Lee Quincy a unique vantage point, and he got eyefuls of Mrs. Jameson.

Channing's petty antics perturbed her husband, Clark, but he kept telling himself that it was all an act, no real cause for concern. In spite of her coquettish behavior, she was a good mother to their two sons. However, Clark had begun to discern that their marriage needed help and finally approached Pastor Lee for counseling. He was baffled when Lee referred him to the new pastor, Jude Charles. Clark was convinced that Lee had sidestepped them on purpose, but never challenged it.

And here, after a couple of weeks of counseling, Channing was flirting outrageously with a newly married young man. It just went to show how Jude's hypocrisy had made his pastoral care utterly ineffective.

It was getting close to twelve o'clock. Lee walked to the front of the dining room and called for the group's attention, then he prayed for the Wiggins family. He also thanked the care team that had provided all the food. Once everyone started eating, Lee circled the room and engaged in small talk, offering excuses to cover for Jude's conspicuous absence. His explanations were met with skepticism, but he didn't care. His mind was on his own problems. He wanted to make his afternoon meeting quick. And Jude's dismissal would even be quicker.

CHAPTER THREE

At 3:55, a downhearted Jude Charles passed through the empty secretarial office and tapped on Lee Quincy's door. A gruff voice answered, and he shuffled in. Lee was facing the back wall sifting through paperwork. After Jude had stood awkwardly for a moment or two, Lee spun around in his desk chair and told him to sit down. The following silence seemed endless to Jude, and Lee's unblinking stare was intimidating.

Lee knew he had two options. One was to choose his words carefully. The other was to blast the man in front of him. The burning anger in his gut pushed him toward the latter approach.

"Jude, I am disappointed with you. You have let me and the church down. You have stained the ministry of Christ. You have trashed your marriage, and in all likelihood destroyed the marriage of your adulterous partner. Everything I have built here is now in jeopardy. Even your petty contributions to this church are also affected."

Jude glanced up briefly and then let his head drop back down. Lee was just hitting his stride and gaining more momentum. He knew diversion was good.

"Your integrity is sullied and polluted." He raised his voice. "Look at me when I am talking to you!" Jude looked up. "When I asked you to help out and counsel Clark and Channing Jameson, I never thought you would fall for her. Couldn't you see through her flirtatious behavior? Your lust has ambushed their marriage and wounded both of them spiritually."

At this point, Jude spoke up. "Pastor Lee, Channing Jameson is not the woman in question here. I had two sessions with her and Clark in my office with the door wide open. Those are the only times we've ever spoken."

Lee was stunned. "You had no involvement with Channing Jameson?"

"None at all."

"Then who is the person you are implicated with?" His tone was incriminating.

"You don't know her. She's someone from my undergrad days. A girl I met my sophomore year in college. We dated for six months but broke it off. I got more involved in my studies, and later met Emma; then we got engaged and married, and I never even thought of the other woman again."

"How did this woman find you?"

"Through social media. She wanted to reconnect, and we casually conversed for a while, just catching up. When she learned I was a pastor, she began telling me that she and her husband were having problems. I offered to pray for them. Later, she asked if I could meet with her and her husband over dinner to discuss their marital problems. At first, I hedged, but gave in. I thought I could help them. It was agreed that the four of us would meet the following week; I insisted that Emma come too."

"Your lady friend agreed to this?"

"She did. It all seemed innocuous at the time. I wanted them to meet Emma and show them the qualities of a godly wife. My wife truly has those qualities."

Lee sucked in his breath at the blatant hypocrisy. *Honoring a Godly wife by having a tryst with another woman. Disgusting.*

"I left my office that evening and went home to get Emma. She had been feeling sick all afternoon and wasn't able to go with me. I should have canceled the dinner at that point, but I didn't."

Lee was getting impatient with all the narrative and wanted to fast-forward to the infidelities. He kept glaring at Jude to create more pressure, and the look had its intended effect. Jude shifted in his chair and sank back even lower in the seat.

"When I got to Marlowe's, I met Christi—that's her name—at the hostess counter. She was alone. When I learned her husband wasn't coming to join us, I got a bad feeling about the whole thing. Christi blew it off with an excuse about him working late. Of course, she inquired where my wife was, and seemed very pleased to learn that she wouldn't be there either.

"I kept my distance and looked around to see if I knew anyone else there, but saw no one I recognized. I felt awkward being alone with her, even though we were in a crowded restaurant."

Lee admired Jude's recall in telling the story. *He's got it well-rehearsed.*

"After we were seated, our server asked if we wanted to order drinks. Christi ordered a margarita and teased me for getting iced tea. She informed me she would get the tab and said it was a great chance to aid a humble pastor and get some much-needed brownie points with God."

Lee Quincy couldn't restrain himself any longer. "Did you two get a room after the meal?"

Jude bristled at the question. "Whoa, what are you saying?" Lee didn't respond, but Jude didn't let up. He resorted to common vernacular. "Dude, I am waiting for an answer. What have you heard and who was your source? I have a right to know."

Lee Quincy had plummeted from interrogator to defendant. He felt the weight of his overbearing presumption in coercing Jude to come clean. Excerpts from some of his own sermons echoed in the back of his mind. How many times had he taught on the merits of compassion and reaching out to share another's burden? He let up the pressure—slightly.

"OK, tell me what took place between you and Christi. And don't call me 'dude.'"

Jude winced at this comment. He saw Lee's posturing as nothing but pride. The old pastor wasn't going to apologize. Jude went back to recounting his story with renewed confidence—maybe he wasn't the only guilty one in the room.

"She had four drinks as we ate. She rambled about the fun college days and her current ascent up the corporate ladder with the help of admiring male colleagues. I soon had enough of all her crosstalk and decided to end the evening. I shook her hand and thanked her for the meal. I was relieved to get out of there and get to my car. But as got into my car, she was getting in the passenger's side door. She had followed me out of the restaurant. I was freaking out, and she was becoming hysterical. It all happened so quickly. She began removing her clothing, and at the same time, I was frantically trying to cover her up and get her calmed down. All the activity and noise brought attention to us. Unfortunately, I later found out that someone spotted me with Christi."

"Luckily, Christi began to settle down. I stepped out of the car, and after she was somewhat dressed, she got out, and I escorted her to her vehicle. She could have done a better job of arranging her clothes. It must have looked pretty damning. I left her and went inside Marlowe's, got two cups of coffee, and took them back out to her car. She'd hastily redressed, but she was crying and shaking and could hardly drink her coffee.

"The coffee helped—that and the alcohol wearing off. I started explaining my commitment to Emma and to Christ. Christi kept crying and apologizing and asked me to pray for her and her husband. We sat there for another forty-five minutes or so, car doors open and interior lights on, and prayed. God turned the whole episode into a time of grace. Too bad no informant saw us praying. We parted, and I went home to an empty house. I later found out that a phone call had preceded my arrival. The unknown caller had conveniently disclosed all the sordid details to my wife. They must have gone way overboard describing the partially naked woman with me in my car. Lee, Emma is two months pregnant. She was already sick and emotional, and that call really upset her. She packed a bag and left me a note explaining she was going to her parent's house. She warned me not to contact her.

"I sat there in our family room and tried to pray. It all was racing through my head. Here I am, a happy expectant father, I try to help a friend out, and my wife leaves me. How did all this happen? I got two phone calls from her mother and sister. I was expecting an update on my wife, but they shredded me. I tried to explain, but they weren't listening to any of it. They hung up on me. I didn't sleep that night." Jude noticed Lee Quincy had developed a forlorn look. "Lee, are you OK?"

"I am miserable," Lee told him. He tilted back in his chair and looked at Jude with dull, expressionless eyes. It was disclosure time.

"Jude, I have been directing some terrible animosity at you. You have borne the brunt of my own failures. I need to take ownership of my own indiscretions. I am going to confide in you as my associate pastor, and hopefully, as a friend."

Jude sat up on the edge of his chair. Lee began.

"I had an affair with a lady in the church about six months ago."

"Don't tell me it was Channing Jameson?" Jude quickly asked him.

Lee gave a strange smile. "You are very perceptive, but it wasn't her. Another lady beat her out in my licentious pursuits, but I had the same thoughts regarding Mrs. Jameson. All of this has shackled me ever since. I was under the asinine delusion that I could confess my adultery to God and that would be adequate. I tried to disciple myself and concluded that I could move on with the pretense of regret and a resolution not to go there again. My pride told me that I was clean because I'd ended the relationship and told God about it, but I was miserable. Finally, last week, I revealed the facts to Elaine. She was shattered and immediately left to go stay with her sister. We haven't talked since. Incidentally, my adultery stemmed from a counseling meeting with the lady."

Jude looked down at his shoes. "I gather that's why you had me talk to Clark and Channing? You didn't trust yourself? Was Channing still in your thoughts?"

"Yes, she always got my attention." Lee buried his face in his hands. "Jude, you have a tremendous future ahead of you, serving God. Never forget that unconfessed sin can smother you and render you useless."

Both were quiet for several minutes, then Jude spoke up. "You know the next step, don't you?"

"I do. It's time to meet with the elders." They prayed, and then both left the room.

Outside in the parking lot, Lee was surprised to see his wife had parked next to his car. She looked up at him.

"Lee, we need to talk." He nodded in agreement and followed her home.

* * *

The next day, the church's elder board was called to an emergency meeting. Lee made a full confession of his adultery and agreed to disclose it to the congregation that Sunday. He also submitted to the board's recommendation that he take a leave of absence for an undetermined length of time. Jude Charles would serve as lead pastor in the interim.

Lee left the meeting early, but not before asking Jude a question. "With your permission, I would like to contact Emma and explain the situation with Christi."

"I would appreciate that. She really respects you."

Lee didn't comment. He was reminded that he had a long way to go before he ever again deserved anyone's respect. The road to restoration would be anything but easy. He went home to his wife to begin the process of hopefully healing their marriage, and Jude Charles closed out the meeting. He saw Clark and Channing Jameson were in the front row holding hands. They approached Jude after the meeting and asked to speak with him.

HOMESTEAD

CHAPTER ONE

Reggie Baylor sat on his porch swing and watched the light of the setting sun sprawl over the Blueridge Mountains. He had enjoyed the same view countless times. Each season of the year hosted a different landscape, and Reggie liked them all.

He thought about his granddaughter Rachel, who would be arriving in the morning. She was the youngest of his six grandchildren, and she could be the most challenging. Rachel asked a lot of questions and expected Grandpa to supply the answers. Reggie had learned there was no way to placate her other than providing the feedback she wanted. At times it could be amusing as he attempted to trip her up with nonsense replies. Sometimes it worked, and other times it fell flat. Rachel was bright and perceptive. She could be a tomboy when she wanted, but she also loved dress-up and tea parties and painting her nails. She believed that everything would look better in pink, but no matter how she tried to convince her grandpa of the fact, he stuck to his less flamboyant color preferences.

*   *   *

The Baylor homestead was still comprised of the original three hundred acres purchased by Reggie's great grandfather after the Civil War. Family traditions revealed the various attempts of Jacob Gabriel Baylor to obtain the property. His first attempt was traditional, through a bank. He was declined on the spot. Jacob then undertook some nefarious methods to produce the needed capital, but the dealings in contraband whiskey sales, horse-trading, gambling, and possibly rustling livestock never produced the intended results.

The date—October 1, 1866—was recorded in the family Bible of Noah and Sara Baylor. That was the day their son, Jacob, finally gave up his hedonistic pursuits and began to walk with the Lord. Another notation memorialized his baptism in Foggy Creek. Everyone present saw Jacob emerge from the creek water and commit his ways to Christ. He symbolically drove a stake in the ground and promised never to take his life behind the stake. Rather, he would always move beyond the stake. Not everyone grasped the meaning, but the dramatic gesture brought a chorus of praise and hallelujahs. His skeptical friends didn't buy into the theatrics and were certain that he would join them later at the Golden Lady Saloon. Their wait was in vain.

After the baptism, Jacob Baylor climbed into the wagon next to his parents. As he gained his seat, his mother handed him a package wrapped in old paper. Even with the paper wrapping, Jacob recognized it as the Bible offered to him by his parents when he'd left for the Civil War. He had rejected it back then, but his mother was now offering it again. This time, the hardened twenty-three-year-old veteran didn't refuse. He smiled as he removed the paper.

"Looks like it's still new and needs to be broken in." Sara looked heavenward, her eyes expressing her thanks to God.

Jacob had gained a new perspective on life, but he still had a desire to own the land of his dreams—the Bowman property. On the way home, the three of them discussed the asking price of $5,000.

CHAPTER TWO

Martin Goulding owned the Johnstown Land Company, an enterprise he'd founded after returning from the Mexican War of 1846. The war had impacted his operation, but he faithfully reopened the business. Martin honed his skills as a banker and land investor, but his biggest asset was his judgment of character.

Martin was acquainted with the Baylor family and was present at Jacob's baptism. He was aware of the young man's interest to acquire the Bowman property. After some deliberation, he decided to move ahead with Jacob. Martin knew of some new regulations on lending that would soon be implemented. He moved ahead and designed a creative financing plan that would be beneficial for both parties. After its completion, he summoned Sammy the Runner, who was always hanging around near his office.

Samuel Elijah Bowerstock was ten years old, had a lot of energy, and was known by the community. Sammy's father had been killed in action at Gettysburg, leaving his widowed mother, Ruth, to care for Sammy and his two younger siblings. She began doing laundry and housekeeping, and Sammy did chores for all their neighbors. He was energetic and often ran everywhere he went. Martin Goulding wisely harnessed the boy's energy. Sammy was dependable and eager to please. He learned to deliver messages and return with the replies. He understood that promptness was critical.

* * *

Sunday afternoons would find Jacob Baylor up on a hill looking out at the Bowman property. He imagined owning the farm and saw himself making it productive. It was his quiet time. One Sunday afternoon, as he viewed the land below him, his solitude was interrupted.

"Good afternoon, Jacob Baylor."

He was startled by the voice and reached for his pistol, but then he stopped himself. He knew a sweet sound like that could bring no harm. He turned and saw Anna Marshall slowly walking toward him.

"Good afternoon to you, Miss Anna. What brings you up here?"

"Just walking and having some quiet time, thinking about things. I enjoy looking down from up here. It's a special place for me. I have seen you up here a lot, but I never wanted to disturb you."

Jacob stood up. "I am pleased that you made an exception today and did interrupt me." He winked at her. They both laughed and sat down on the ground.

"I was at Foggy Creek when you got baptized. You surprised a lot of people." Anna smiled at him.

"Yes, ma'am, that was a special day." They talked all afternoon and well into the evening.

"It's getting dark, Miss Anna. Maybe I should see you home."

"I would like that, Mr. Jacob." They smiled at their formality. Both were hoping the formal atmosphere would transform into a more intimate friendship.

Jacob escorted her home and thanked her for a pleasant time. She returned the compliment. Jacob didn't sleep that night, but it was a good restlessness. In addition to the Bowman property, a new thought was on his mind—Anna Marshall. His thoughts began to compromise each other. Jacob knew that if he intended to court Anna, he would be in a more favorable position if he had more than himself to offer her. There were challenges, and he began asking for solutions.

CHAPTER THREE

Martin Goulding had rigged an old locomotive bell outside his office. He would let it clang briefly to summon Sammy the Runner, and Sammy knew to respond quickly. On Monday morning at nine o'clock, Martin pulled the lanyard on the bell, letting it ring once. Sammy heard the clang and ran over to the Johnstown Land office.

Martin greeted him. "Good morning, Sammy. I want you to deliver a message to Jacob Baylor. I want Mr. Baylor to come and see me at my office. Jacob, not his father."

"Yes, sir. Just ask Mr. Jacob to see you? At what time?"

"Before lunch, if possible. Come right back with his reply."

"Want me to write it down?"

"No, just keep it in your head. Now get moving along, and take my canteen. It's going to be hot today." Martin ruffled his hair affectionately, and his messenger began his run to the Baylor home.

Sammy felt a sense of importance toting the old army canteen. It was heavy and cumbersome, but it added some swagger as he trotted off to the Baylor place.

He kept an eye out for some flat stones as he trotted along the road. Sammy was fascinated by the biblical account of David and Goliath. The story came from First Samuel—the Old Testament book that was the inspiration for his name. David's battle with Goliath was etched in the boy's mind. He liked to repeat David's feat of gathering up flat stones, keeping them in preparation for any giants he might encounter during his message runs. Fortunately, no giants ever challenged him. Sammy would end up taking quick breaks from his running to skip his supply of stones across Foggy Creek or harmlessly throw them at chattering crows in the treetops.

By the time he reached the Baylor homestead, Sammy had depleted all of his stone ammunition and begun thinking on the homemade dessert that Mrs. Sara always kept around. When he knocked on the door, she told him that the men were out in the woods near the south pasture clearing trees. Sammy could smell freshly baked berry pie, but he stuck to his mission and left to find Jacob.

After Jacob heard the message, he reached down and patted the young messenger on the head. He respected the son of his fellow comrade who had been killed in action.

"Any chance you worked up some hunger running all the way out here?" Sammy's smile was confirmation enough. "I bet my mom has some fresh pie. We can head back to the house after I talk to my father."

Jacob approached his father as Noah stopped to wipe his brow.

"Dad, Martin Goulding wants to see me before lunch. Can you get by without me for a few hours?" Both were aware of the tasks before them, but a meeting with an important man like Martin Goulding took precedence over chores.

Jacob followed Sammy back to the house. The young messenger was treated to two pieces of pie, and then he headed back to Martin's office. Force of habit had him stopping along the road to gather up five more smooth stones. Whether he would encounter giants or crows, he was prepared. Jacob saddled his horse and rode off to Goulding's office.

CHAPTER FOUR

Martin was standing outside, randomly gazing around at the activity in the street, when Jacob rode up.

"You want to see me, Mr. Goulding?" he said as he dismounted.

"I do, come on in." Jacob kicked the dust off his boots, slapped the dirt from his clothes as best he could, and walked inside with Martin. "Have a seat. Do you want some water?"

"No, sir."

"I will get straight to the matter at hand." Jacob winced slightly. He had no clue why Martin had called him to his office, but he was concerned that something from his past was about to catch up with him. He was prepared for the worst.

"I can help you obtain the Bowman property."

This time, Jacob's reaction was more relaxed, but it didn't last long.

"I am aware of your previous attempts to get ownership of the land."

"Yes, sir, I recall them as well. But that's all in the past."

"Good. Are you able to supply any down payment?"

"I can put some money down." Jacob paused. "I don't mind telling you, but most of my savings has been applied to making restitution to folks. Kind of straightening out some wrong dealings."

Martin understood and didn't pursue the matter. He began his proposal. "Jacob, I bought the Bowman property yesterday. The documents are being put together now. It's an investment for me. I am a businessman, and there is always the need to make a profit. From a deeper perspective, I want to be accountable for the assets I have."

"I follow you, but how does all this involve me?"

"I am offering the property to you. Here's my proposal. The purchase price will be $4,750. I will need a down payment of $400, payments to be made the first of each month in the amount of $20 for a period of fifteen years, and a final payment will come due at the end of the fifteenth year to pay off the balance. Interest on the balance will be five percent."

Jacob saw the fairness of the proposal. It was a business arrangement for Martin and an opportunity for him.

"Before you answer, I have one more stipulation. I retain the timber rights to the property, particularly the fifty acres in the northwest portion of the land. We will stake that portion out. I have some plans to resurrect Levi Schloss's sawmill and will need the timber." There was a brief lull. "One more consideration. The down payment can be generated over the first year along with the payments at no interest. What are your thoughts?"

"Mr. Goulding, you could put together a better deal with someone else. As you said, you are a businessman and need to make a profit. Why work with me?"

"I want to help you succeed."

Jacob looked him in the eye, and they shook hands. The paperwork was later formalized, but the substance of the agreement was in the handshake. Each man trusted the other's word.

CHAPTER FIVE

The following spring, two marriages were consecrated. Jacob Baylor and Anna Marshall were the first couple. One month later, to the surprise of most of the community, Martin Goulding married Ruth Bowerstock. Jacob and Anna were blessed with six children. Martin and Ruth added a daughter to their existing brood.

Martin was now a family man, and he slowed down from his hectic pace to relish his role as a father. Sammy and his siblings learned life lessons from their stepfather. All of them learned sound business principles.

The Baylor farm grew, and the whole family practiced the skills of their trade: ringing and cutting hogs, herding cattle, and harvesting crops. The original small cabin on the property was soon outgrown, and Jacob, with the help of his father and neighbors, began the construction of a brick home. A formal entryway led into a large front room, a kitchen in the rear, and a formal dining room. The upstairs had an open area and five bedrooms.

A large wraparound porch showcased the front of the home. It's ambiance always attracted folks to sit and talk. Everyone found it interesting that there was always a cool breeze present, even on the hottest days.

Other buildings were constructed on the Baylor farm. The family built a large barn that became the focal point of the homestead, a timber, brick, and stone structure situated about one hundred yards from the main house. The building was nicknamed "Gathering Barn" by the family since it served a double function as a farm barn and a gathering place for community social functions. Many weddings and funerals were held there.

The years following the depression of the 1930s found the barn slipping into decay. The old granite foundation began to crumble, and concrete blocks were integrated with the rock foundation. Eventually, the blocks replaced a significant portion of the foundation. The gray, symmetrical blocks clashed with the natural stone, which didn't cause any concern except for one person—Reggie's granddaughter, Rachel. She was appalled at the dull color of the concrete blocks. She thought the blocks needed "flair," but that wasn't a word that held much weight with Reggie.

CHAPTER SIX

As soon as Rachel was dropped off at the Baylor farm, Reggie moved into their usual routine. The first step was to go into the barn and fire up his vintage John Deere 1939 Model A. His father had purchased it used after returning home from the war in 1945. It was a general-purpose tractor, slant dash, with the optional electric start—a premium addition. It was a size that Reggie could operate as a boy, and he'd logged many hours in that tractor seat.

Reggie's sons and grandsons also spent time on the John Deere. When they were little, they would sit in his lap as they circled the back field, eventually dozing off, held firmly in Reggie's grip. Each would be handed off to his wife for nap time on the front porch. Rachel was the exception. No matter how many laps they made around the fields, she remained awake and constantly chatting. It could bug Reggie at times, but he patiently answered her questions.

Today, she asked, "Grandpa, why do we have to back the tractor up the ramp and not just drive it straight into the barn?"

"Well, little Missy, the tricycle design of the tractor creates a long frame forward that is too heavy and could cause the tractor to flip backward at the angle of the approach ramp."

Rachel squinted her eyes and made the face that told her grandpa that she was in deep-thinking mode. "So, you're telling me it's top-heavy."

Reggie laughed. "Yes. And a driver has to pay attention and not be distracted by a chattering passenger in his lap. Once, your great-great-grandpa was pulling a wagon into the barn and the wagon flipped over. He and the horses tumbled all the way to Foggy Creek and floated downstream for two days but came home washed and clean. Also, they interrupted the baptizing that was going on at the time. This made the preacher mad, and he complained to the town fathers. He made them pass a law that all wagons needed to be backed into barns. Then the geniuses that succeeded them made the law apply to tractors. Now you don't want me to get arrested for breaking the law, do you?"

Rachel stayed ahead of him. "Whatever, Grandpa." This was her classic retort to Reggie's sarcastic replies. "You know, those old gray blocks under the barn look bad. Kind of sickly, like they need to be painted."

"Painted? Foundation blocks don't get a coat of paint. They fade and blend in with everything else. There are more important chores and little time to do them. I don't have time for painting concrete blocks."

"They would look much better if they were painted."

"Really? And what color would my six-year-old decorating whiz suggest?"

"Grandpa, I am seven. And I suggest the color should be pink."

Reggie laughed at her response. "Pink! Nothing on a farm is painted pink or should ever be painted pink. Can you imagine me going into Mr. Sanders' paint store and asking him to mix up a couple of gallons of pink paint?"

"It will take more than a couple of gallons to do it right," she told him.

"Maybe a few gallons of periwinkle would help with the project."

"No periwinkle, just pink. It has to be all pink to give it the right look." Both were smiling by this time.

"Perhaps, after this masterpiece is completed, we could picnic in front of it with finger bowls, napkins, and doilies. We could have tea and pink lemonade," Reggie told her.

"Whatever, Grandpa."

"Let's head to the house and get a snack." Reggie turned the tractor toward the barn, passing in front of the gray block wall, and made a semicircle in front of the approach ramp. He held onto his passenger and backed the John Deere into the cavernous recess of the top floor. He then shut it down, waiting for the customary backfire from the exhaust. Rachel knew it was coming and covered her ears. They both dismounted and headed for the house.

Grandpa made his customary peanut butter and jelly mini sandwiches. Later, they sat on the porch swing. Seven-year-old girls finally wear out, and old grandpas are close behind. The toot of the car horn coming up the lane woke them. Rachel was picked up, and Reggie decided to go for a walk around the property.

He walked behind the barn and looked at the gray block foundation. *Pink,* he thought. *In Rachel's words, "Whatever."* He then meandered over to a grove of trees and looked at a cluster of headstones. Jacob and Anna Baylor. Noah and Sara Baylor. Whitney and Sally Baylor. Josiah and Esther Baylor. They were all there, along with many others. He glanced over to the south end of the family cemetery at the five Goulding family markers, placed at the edge of the original timber tract Martin had contracted with Jacob in the land deal. Reggie sat down on a stone bench that had been there for at least 125 years. He gave the graves one more glance and then returned to the front porch of the house.

Reggie watched the sun go down and dozed off. Later, he went upstairs to his bedroom, sat down on the bed, and looked at the picture of his wife on the dresser. She had passed when Rachel was only six months old. The two of them would have been a pair. Maybe Helen could have answered some of Rachel's silly talk about painting barn foundations pink. He mused over his chores for the next day and then added one more task to the list.

*　*　*

The next morning, Reggie's son Mark called his dad for their regular after-breakfast chat. He tried both the cell and house phones, but his father didn't pick up either of them. He called back an hour later and got the same results. Initially, he wasn't concerned. More than likely, the cell phone was lying on the counter and not in his dad's pocket. It probably wasn't charged either. *Dad must be doing chores or scoping out the property on the tractor.* He finally decided to drive out, find his dad, and once again remind him to carry his cell phone.

Mark walked across the creaky front porch into the old farmhouse. As expected, the cell phone was on the countertop, and he threw his hands into the air. The north doors of the barn were open, so he thought his dad must be out there. He called out but didn't get any reply. Concern was setting in. He went to the west end of the barn and called out again—nothing. He picked up his pace, and at the corner of the southwest end, he saw his father's truck.

"Dad, I have been looking all over this place for you. Why can't you keep your phone on you?" He never got the next sentence out. He saw his father laying on the ground behind the truck. The shock numbed him. He fumbled for his phone and made a call for EMS. He knelt down by his father, lifted him up and drew him close.

When the squad arrived, they checked his vitals, and Reggie was pronounced dead. The final report attributed his death to cardiac arrest.

*　*　*

The final day of viewing was at Gathering Barn, and Reggie was later buried in the church cemetery next to his wife. The church hosted a dinner at the Baylor homestead after the service. Family and friends joined together in food and fellowship. Some occupied the large family room, but most of the group preferred the wraparound porch.

As the activities were winding down, Reggie's two sons and their wives gathered out back, close to the barn, and Mark began recounting the circumstances of their father's death.

"It was so strange."

"What was strange?" asked his brother Bobby.

"I found Dad laying on the ground surrounded by six gallons of pink paint, and there were six more in the bed of his truck. Also, he had a gallon of paint labeled 'periwinkle.'"

"What project would require that much pink paint?" Bobby asked.

"It gets even stranger. There was a box of Mom's old dishes and some lacy looking placemats in the front seat of his truck. He must have been planning something. I took the box back to the house."

Muriel spoke up. "If it's the box I saw, it contained some of your mother's antique finger bowls. And the lacy things you mentioned are called doilies." She shook her head. "You're right, it's bizarre."

"That mystery has gone to the grave with him."

Rachel was nearby and overheard the entire conversation. "I know what Grandpa had planned." The precocious seven-year-old shared the whole story of the pink paint and the block foundation. "Anyone want to have a painting party this afternoon?"

That evening, a partially painted block wall glowed pink as the sun went down in the western sky over the Baylor family homestead. The family had gathered on the front porch and were watching Rachel sift through the box of finger bowls and doilies. The granddaughter had a picnic on her mind.

CHARLIE'S ROOM

CHAPTER ONE

On the fateful Sunday morning, at nine o'clock sharp, Charlie Ames was at his usual Sunday school post. The room he taught in was unique: It was named after him. Years ago, the sign indicating "Room 7" had been replaced with a bronze plaque symbolizing the venerable volunteer teacher: "Charlie's Room."

Charlie had persevered in his teaching duties for over six decades and somehow stayed abreast of ever-evolving technology. Flannelgraph boards had been replaced by cassette tapes, which had yielded to VHS tapes. Then shiny CDs and DVDs made their appearance. Currently, audiovisual controlled by a laptop was the choice. Charlie had the foresight to surround himself with tech-savvy young people who knew which buttons to push to keep the lesson plans moving.

But this Sunday, his key helpers had failed to show up. His only aide was a naïve new volunteer, Sara Rosen. Charlie and Sara watched as the room began to fill up with loud, excited children—and it kept filling. They were reaching capacity, and Charlie knew they needed help. He felt as though he were being compressed from all sides of the room at once.

"Sara, I need you to run up to the sound booth and have them post on the big screens in the sanctuary that we need helpers. Have them do it before the service starts. Then, hurry back here."

Sara wanted to please Mr. Ames and hastily left the room, charging down the hallway. However, after a few hectic steps, she realized that she didn't know where the sound booth was located. She quickly got lost in the maze of hallways, and Charlie was alone with an increasingly rowdy crowd of kids.

He felt hot and sweaty, constantly tugging at his collar as he tried to collect his thoughts and focus on the morning lesson. The room was getting louder. He was getting hotter.

"Hey, who threw that?" "Look out, I'm coming after you!" A six-year-old girl stood on top of a table and started shrieking.

Charlie had reached his tipping point.

"I want all of you #### kids to shut the #### up and find a seat on the floor."

His outburst carried over into the adjoining rooms and out into the crowded hallways.

Dorothy O'Brien had just entered the room with her young son, and Charlie's eruption brought her to a dead stop in the doorway. After several seconds of frozen silence, she walked to the middle of the quiet classroom.

"Is there a problem in here?" she said in a shrill voice. She saw Charlie standing awkwardly at the back of the room. "Mr. Ames, please explain yourself." The whole classroom was now focused on Charlie. He looked around at their shocked faces. He felt lost.

"I'm going home." He spoke softly, as if talking to himself, his words slightly slurred. He went through the crowded doorway and out into the parking lot searching for his car, unaware that it was in the same spot he had he occupied for years. Charlie finally found his vehicle and left for home.

*   *   *

The crowd outside Charlie's classroom was buzzing.

"He swore at the children."

"I heard him threaten them."

"I hope he didn't touch any of them."

"That man puts the 'old' in 'old-school.' He should have been booted years ago, and now he's finally lost it."

Tim Coates, the church's lead pastor, came into the room, and a few of the belligerents walked away. Tim looked around the crowd. He didn't challenge any of the accusations, but he was concerned for Charlie.

"Where is Charlie?"

"He took off right away," Dorothy told him.

"I can see that he's not here. Does anyone know where he may have gone?"

"Pastor Coates, I saw him wandering in the parking lot, apparently looking for his car," said a person from the back of the room. "He looked out of it."

The chatter of speculation grew louder. Tim asked one of his associate pastors to contact Charlie, then he went into the sanctuary as the songs were ending. He began his message, but his concern for Charlie was dogging him. The matter had to be addressed, and hopefully not in a full congregational meeting. The elders later demanded that meeting.

CHAPTER TWO

In early 1952, Charlie Ames was medically discharged from the army and returned home. He had been wounded in both legs at the Battle of Bloody Ridge, a major confrontation on the hillsides of Korea just north of the Thirty-eighth Parallel.

He and Anne Fellows were married six weeks later. After a brief honeymoon, they returned home to Morris Hill, and Charlie acquired ownership of Bishop's Hardware and Sporting Goods store located in the quiet downtown area. The transfer of the store to Charlie Ames was straightforward. The price was agreed upon and documents drawn up and signed, but the real deal-binder was a handshake. Charlie and Ann also settled into a three-bedroom Cape Cod home on Elm Street. Anne initially considered the home too big. What would they ever do with three bedrooms?

Charlie's parents were blessed late in life with a second child. At the time of his marriage, Charlie had a five-year-old brother, Nicodemus. Shortly after Charlie began running the store, his parents took off for a month-long vacation out West, and Nic remained with Charlie and Anne. Nic was all for it and looked forward to having his own bedroom in his brother's new home. Charlie was plunging into the activities of a business owner, and Anne helped and was also immersed with settling into a new home.

Four days after his parents' departure, Charlie received a shattering phone call. His mother and father had been killed in a head-on collision with a drunk driver just east of Boulder, Colorado. The veteran, newlywed, and business owner realized that he and Anne were now permanent guardians to his little brother. He never asked, "Why me?" but continued in faith on the pathway he felt that God had placed before them. Months later, He and Anne had decided to pursue a teaching ministry for children at their church. On his first day, he waited in Room 7 for the five- and six-year-old kids to be dropped off. He was a little nervous but confident. Charlie whimsically reminded himself that, after all, he had led a combat unit. What could possibly go wrong? He looked at his wife and at his first student, Nic. "It's time."

At nine o'clock, they began trickling in. The roster that morning reached ten. Not even a full squad in *the army*, Charlie thought. The military (and the army, in particular) operates on the principle that any situation may be handled by breaking it down "by the numbers." It's a simple process of communication, and Charlie applied the principles to his class of ten.

"Good morning class, I am Mr. Ames, or Mr. Charlie if you prefer. This morning we will have our Bible lesson, verse memorization, craft time, and snacks, followed by some playtime. After which, your parents will pick you up, and you will continue with your day. And don't forget your take-home sheets."

The military never tested their "by the numbers" procedure on elementary-age Sunday school students. Charlie had barely introduced himself and the schedule before several of the children broke ranks and assaulted the cache of toys. Others started swishing the air with pencils and chasing one another with scissors, all the while expressing how hungry they were. One was cowering in the corner.

Charlie called for mandatory prayer time—hands folded, heads bowed, and no one at all looking around. It worked well in the short-term, but just one distracted child can affect others. Charlie preempted that with the reminder that they were here to learn about God's word, and there was control in the midst of the chaos.

Charlie's blueprint for teaching varied slightly over the years, but it served him well for the next sixty-five years in his classroom.

CHAPTER THREE

In the spring of 1967 Nicodemus Ames graduated from college with a business degree. He would often chide his older brother for his lack of accounting experience and inventory control. Charlie brushed it all aside, but he was pleased with Nic's fledgling business acumen. Nic had plans to settle in Morris Hill and possibly get a job at the International Harvester plant in Springfield. He also planned on going back to school for an MBA program. One roadblock was in his way—his student 2-S military deferment expired.

Nic received his degree, and nine days later he reported to Ft. Dix, New Jersey, for basic training and advanced infantry training. After completion, he volunteered for Officer Candidate School, Ft. Benning, Georgia. The training course lasted for twenty-six weeks. OC class 17–68. Nic now knew firsthand where Charlie's by the numbers teaching technique had its origin. The army hadn't changed.

Nic got a two-week leave after his commissioning. The time at home was relaxing, but the whole family was aware of the uncertainty of the next two years. Charlie avoided military talk and focused on his brother one day getting out of the army and returning home to join him in business pursuits.

After the leave, Nic was assigned to the jungle warfare school in the Canal Zone of Panama. There was no mystery about his next deployment. He arrived in South Vietnam and was assigned to the 101 Airborne as a platoon infantry officer. His first duty was during phase three of the Tet Offensive that had begun in January of that year. Nic was only in country for thirty-six days. He was killed by an ambush during a team recon surveillance of his base camp area. His body arrived back in Morris Hill for burial with full military honors.

Second Lieutenant Nicodemus Ames was buried next to his parents. The turnout for his funeral was huge. After the burial, as Charlie stood by the grave, he looked up to see the color guard approaching him with the burial flag. He was silent. Deep resentment raged within him.

Now that his brother was dead, thoughts he'd never considered before filled his mind.

These kids serve and put their lives in peril for a murky political policy for a country thousands of miles away. Politicians score big, military personnel gain rank, and others reap financial profits from the wars. Now *my* brother is dead as a result of some policy-perpetuating wonks who never wore a military uniform.

Killed for what? A symbolic gesture of halting the spread of communism. The worst of them live on, and young men die.

Charlie felt the pain of his wounded legs coming back again to torment him. Anne reached out and comforted him with an embrace. He felt a slight tap on his other shoulder and turned to see Janie Roberts standing behind him. He put his arm around her and pulled her to him. The three of them held each other beside Nic's grave.

It was never official, but a lot of folks suspected that Nic and Janie would be married after Nic's discharge. One local businessman confirmed the rumor. Jerry Horner, the owner of Horner's Jewelers, waited for an appropriate moment to talk with Charlie and Anne after Janie moved away to talk with some friends

"Charlie, before your brother left for Vietnam, he made a down payment on an engagement ring and regularly sent me payments. He was going to send the final one this month. Anyway, I want you to have it. I guess it was intended for the Roberts girl."

"What's the balance due?"

Jerry handed him the ring, secured in a handmade wooden box and wrapped in brown paper. "There's nothing due. I consider it paid in full." He knew Jerry was tight and never left any money on the table. He made it a point to have lunch with his fellow businessman very soon. Charlie then placed the ring box in his coat pocket. He would wait for the appropriate time to discuss it with Janie.

* * *

Tim Coates accepted the lead pastor's role at the church in the fall of 2000. He and his wife, Hannah, quickly formed a bond with Charlie and Anne Ames. The new pastor liked the dedication of the couple and their humility. He knew their teaching commitment was unique. Both families connected. Not only did the two Coates kids find a hangout opportunity at Charlie's store, but they also gravitated to the Ames home and their refrigerator that was overstocked with treats.

In the spring of 2010, Anne Ames woke up on Sunday morning feeling extremely tired. She told Charlie that she wouldn't be attending church, but she would be fine. A cup of tea and some rest would get her back on track. Charlie kissed his wife goodbye and headed over to the church.

Neither was aware of the seriousness of Anne's condition. She had developed a blood clot in her right lung that dislodged and quickly produced a heart attack. She died almost instantly. She was buried four days later, next to her parents and one plot over from Nic. The adjacent burial plot was reserved for her husband. Charlie stared blankly at it.

Charlie went numb with grief. He seldom left the house and avoided the store. The community felt concern for him, and his friends rallied around him.

Meals were provided, lawn maintenance performed, and visits made to the home. Tim and Hannah Coates gave Charlie special attention. He was given a sabbatical from his teaching duties but surprised everyone when he returned after a week. Charlie knew an outlet for his grief was to stay involved with his kids.

CHAPTER FOUR

The Monday morning after Charlie's profane rant in the classroom, Tim Coates was in his office. Normally Monday was his day off and gave him a chance to get refreshed, but he was preparing an email blast to the congregation. It was a reminder of the meeting that evening asking them to please attend. He was relieved that, so far, none of Charlie's episode had made its way to social media. Amazing, he thought.

A few seconds later, he was back up on his feet and walking down the hall to Charlie's Room. As he got closer, he noticed that the lights were on inside. His first thought was that Charlie must be in there, and they would have a chance to talk. He moved closer to the room entrance.

Tim's elation turned sour when he saw that the commemorative plaque by the door was missing. It had been unbolted and pried from the wall. What lowlife would steal a plaque? Maybe, he thought, it was retaliation for Charlie's behavior. He decided to contact Charlie. Tim had deliberately given Charlie some time to be alone, a cooling-off period. Now it was time to reach out to him.

Tim stopped by his house to pick up Hannah. They would go over to Charlie's together.

*   *   *

Charlie Ames sat in a slumped position at his kitchen table. He needed Anne to be with him. Her comfort would help alleviate this mess he'd created. Charlie had ignored all phone calls. There was no need to talk to anyone. A little later, the doorbell rang. He remained in his chair. The unlocked front door then opened.

"Charlie? It's Tim. Hannah is with me, can we come in?"

"I'm in the kitchen," he softly called out.

Tim and Hannah proceeded into the unlit foyer. They went back to the kitchen and found Charlie looking straight ahead at the refrigerator, his face expressionless. The usual warm demeanor was not there. Tim walked over to the chair and placed his hand on Charlie's shoulder.

"Charlie, we love you."

Charlie looked up at them. "I hope those kids will forgive me." Tim didn't say anything. He knew the difference between listening and speaking. This was a time to listen.

"I just can't believe what I said. My mother used to remind me that what's in the well will come up in the bucket. Wells need to be purged and cleaned. My well is toxic." He looked up at the couple that he cherished. I really would like to be alone."

Tim respected the request. "We understand. Please remember we are here for you." He and Hannah quietly slipped out, saying nothing as they drove home. Neither was aware that today was Anne's birthday, but the date was fixed in Charlie's mind. He remained slouched in the kitchen chair for two hours after Tim and Hannah left. He had not eaten all day and was weak. He kept staring at the refrigerator.

* * *

Tim's emails had accomplished their goal; that evening, the sanctuary was full. Some congregants knew of the incident in Charlie's Room, but not of the missing plaque. Others were intrigued by the urgency of the meeting and entertained themselves discussing what it might be about. Tim looked out at the crowd noted the presence of non-regulars and even some strangers seated in front of the platform. He was aware that Charlie Ames was absent.

Tim went up on the platform, opened in prayer, and the meeting was on. He shared the details of the occurrence on Sunday morning and the follow-up visit with Charlie, and then he began sharing some advice.

"I can't condone the incident. It was inappropriate, but Charlie Ames has a contrite heart and regrets his actions. His years of faithfulness to his family, his community, and this church need to be held in respect. All of us must reflect on our lives and then ask ourselves, are we hiding anything? Charlie's meltdown is out in the open, but are any of us harboring a heart that dishonors God?"

He then opened the floor for questions and comments. Nothing like the scent of a scandal to elicit dialogue. There were some constructive comments as well as some nonsense quips. Tim was thankful that, in general, there was a spirit of sensitivity for Charlie Ames. Before closing the meeting, he brought up the missing plaque.

"Whoever removed the plaque from Charlie Ames's room, I simply ask that it be returned to me. No questions asked."

* * *

After the meeting, Tim decided to visit Charlie. He wanted to reassure him of the church's solidarity with him. Hopefully, he wasn't aware that his commemorative tablet had been taken away.

He saw lights on in the Ames home and was pleased that Charlie was probably still up. He stopped in the driveway, prayerfully made his way to the front door, and rang the bell. As he waited for a response, he continued getting his thoughts together. Tim rang the bell again. No reply. He then knocked on the door while trying the handle. The door popped open.

He called out. "Charlie? It's pastor Tim. OK if I come in? Charlie!" he spoke a little louder. Then he heard the soft volume of the TV in the family room. He walked inside, and the glow from the TV cast enough light for Tim to see Charlie tilted back in his recliner, his head hanging forward in an awkward manner. He tapped the slumbering man on the shoulder. There was no response. He felt for a pulse but knew it was in vain.

Tim pulled out his cell and summoned the squad. He pulled over a small chair and waited for them to arrive. Once there, they performed a check for vitals and pronounced him dead. One attendant commented that he must have passed hours before.

Tim remained at the Ames' home for some time, quietly thinking about Charlie. He was freed from all his burdens now—the Korean Conflict, the loss of Anne and Nic, and the silly, pathetic incident in the church. Tim secretly hoped that the callous jerk who took the plaque would be conscience-stricken over Charlie's passing and consumed in guilt.

Charlie's funeral was huge, considered by many as the largest in Morris Hill history. The military color guard made another visit to the local graveyard.

CHAPTER FIVE

Years before, Tim had been named as the executor of Charlie's estate. A purely ceremonial title, he assumed, as Charlie had lived an incredibly frugal life and there would be little to disperse. But there were certain legal formalities to follow.

A few days after the funeral, Tim had a meeting with Joseph Stilleti. Joe was a respectable attorney and a member of Tim's church; he was the attorney for the estate and had worked with Charlie for years. When he entered the lobby of Stilleti & Company Law Firm, Tim accepted a cup of coffee from the receptionist and followed her down the corridor to a small conference room. As soon as he settled into a seat and took a sip of the coffee, Joe joined him.

"Good morning, Pastor Tim. There's a lot to discuss." The attorney began placing files on the conference table. "Let me cover the details in broad strokes, and then we can go over some of the finer points. By the way, my work on the estate is pro bono. I thought the executor might want to know that." He smiled. "I really liked Charlie and Anne."

"Joe, that's very generous of you to donate your services." Joe moved on.

"Now, the bulk of the estate and assets are bequeathed to the church." Tim sat up in his chair. "These include both personal and business holdings. Besides that, Charlie left the entire inventory of the hardware store, free and clear, to John Putnam. John has the option to remain in the location on a leased basis." Tim was aware that John had worked with Charlie for years, and he wasn't surprised at the arrangement. "Any questions regarding that?"

"None."

"Good. Charlie established an LLC that not only owns his location, and adjacent storefronts, two down on both sides of his store. The LLC also includes some of the cash payments received from the sale of land south of town, occupied by the new mall and the other businesses out there. Charlie foresaw the development of that area and quietly started buying up the land.

"I will cut to the first analysis of the estate. It's approaching roughly five million dollars in value."

Tim felt like screaming, "*Say what!*" but he managed to control himself.

Joe gave him a friendly look. "Charlie's brother, Nic, and I were close friends, and we spent a lot of time at Charlie's store. As we got older, Nic often playfully criticized his big brother on his lack of business sense. In retrospect, Charlie didn't do such a bad job after all."

"Joe, one thing is bothering me. The gift to the church is wonderful, but I'm concerned that there might be a conflict of interest being the executor of Charlie's estate as well as the pastor of the church he left his millions to. Is that a concern? Should I be worried?"

"Legally, no. But you know how people can talk. I'll handle everything and keep you in the clear. Nothing to worry about. You will be fully sanitized."

"That's a relief."

"Another portion of the estate involves a woman named Jane Patterson, maiden name Roberts."

"Who is she?" Tim asked.

Joe elaborated. "She grew up here in Morris Hill, and she and Nic were pretty tight. They intended to get married after his tour in the army. No formal engagement, but it was rumored that he'd bought her a ring. After Nic was killed in Nam, she relocated to Springfield. She maintained contact with Charlie and Anne. Now she's a widow living in Brooksville, Florida. Her disbursement is half a million." Tim was shocked by the amount, but it was none of his business. The executor made no comment. Joe continued to give the details in his succinct style. The executor listened intently.

They reviewed the remainder of the estate, and Tim was more grateful than ever for Joe's integrity. There was a lot of money involved.

Tim had a four o'clock appointment back at the church, but he wanted to stop by Charlie's house and check things out. It seemed like the sort of thing an executor would do.

After arriving at the house, he sat in the car and stared straight ahead at the familiar front porch. He swallowed hard, realizing that he'd half-expected Charlie to come out and greet him. As he walked in the front door, a quick glance assured him that all was well. He cut the visit short and went to his office for his appointment. He would come back later and inspect everything a little closer.

*   *   *

Tim and his staff had developed a new summer intern program for prospective ministry students. The interns would be involved in the local church and shadow the pastors in their daily routines. It was designed to help them make an informed decision about becoming pastors. Tim was impressed with the four o'clock candidate, a young man headed to Liberty University. At least he looked good on paper.

He arrived back at his office ahead of schedule. He was tempted to plop down in his office chair, prop his feet up, and let his mind go blank, but the receptionist buzzed to let him know that his prospective intern had arrived.

"Nathan Whittier arrived early, and since you weren't in, he decided to take a tour of our facilities. He is a very nice young man. Oh, here he is now. And it's only 3:59!"

"Thank you, Carla. Have him come on in."

"Pastor Coates, I am Nathan Whittier." A cheerful, tanned young man held out his hand, and Tim shook it. He was impressed with the firm grip. "Please have a seat." Tim liked him from the outset. He had a mild tone but exhibited quiet confidence. After the normal pleasantries, Tim changed the conversation and asked about his home in Florida, jokingly asking how a church up north could lure him away from the Sunshine State.

"I was actually born in this area, over in Springfield. My mother relocated to Middletown, and I attended Middletown Christian School. Mom then moved to Florida to be near my grandmother. We all live in the Brooksville area now."

Tim asked about Nathan's father, but he instantly regretted it.

"I never knew my father. He left my mother before I was born. Mom did a good job as a single parent, and Grandma Janie was there for me anytime I needed her."

Something clicked in Tim's mind. *Brooksville, Florida...Grandma Janie...* He gave into his hunch.

"Nathan, any chance that your grandmother's maiden name was Roberts?"

Nathan looked dazed. "Yes, it is. How did you know that?"

"I have some insight, but it's too involved to discuss now. We can discuss it next time we meet." Nathan caught the drift of the conversation.

"Does this mean that I get a second interview?"

"No," Tim replied.

Nathan felt his bubble burst.

"A second interview isn't necessary. I would like you to join our intern program."

Nathan relaxed and grinned. "I accept." They stood and shook hands.

"Welcome aboard."

Tim suggested that they take a walk around the facility. Along the way, he pointed out some ministry areas, including the cubicle Nathan would be using during the program. They paused in front of Charlie's Room. Tim gave some background on the room's namesake.

Nathan said, "I remember Grandma talking about a Mr. Ames and his love for the children's ministry. I had no idea that it was this church! Funny she didn't mention it to me."

"Perhaps she wanted you to find out on your own. Maybe that was her way of keeping the interview process neutral." Tim then tapped his hand on the wall where the plaque had hung. The holes from the missing bolts were obvious.

"There was once a commemorative emblem attached here honoring Mr. Ames. Someone removed it just before he died."

"Why would anyone take a commemorative plaque? Certainly, there's no value. Was it vandalism?"

"Sad to say, it appears that way, or possibly someone's warped sense of justice." Nathan noticed some frustration in Tim's voice and dropped the subject.

"I think you've made an excellent choice of college," Tim told him.

"Thank you. Of course, it takes a lot of money, but Grandma has reassured me many times that, no matter what, God will provide." Tim thought of Charlie's estate and his provision for Jane. There was definitely more than enough for tuition at Liberty.

Tim concluded the meeting and asked Nathan to join him and Hannah for supper at their home. There was no hesitancy on Nathan's part—a home-cooked meal would be welcome.

The pastor excused himself in order to move on with his day. He walked Nathan to the front and offered to pick him up at his motel that evening, then he watched as Nathan left the doorway and made his way to his car. The old car reminded him of the vehicles he'd had while in college and seminary.

Now it was time for the executor to go back to Charlie's and inspect the home.

CHAPTER SIX

Tim walked through each room of the house to make sure everything was in order. As he looked around, he dreaded the thought of packing all of it up for sale or donation. Last of all, he went out to the garage and maneuvered through the clutter that had accumulated there.

One side of the garage had about a dozen boxes precariously stacked. The lower boxes were caving in from the weight of the upper ones. Tim began to restack them to avoid the impending collapse. The first box he picked up was water damaged and disintegrating. The bottom fell out, and there was a loud bang as several objects hit the floor. Two glass jars broke, and their accumulated nails and screws scattered over the garage floor. Tim focused on the broken glass and stooped down to pick up the bigger pieces.

As he gathered up the glass, he noticed what must have made the banging noise: a brass plaque lying face down. Tim couldn't believe it. He knew what it was. He reached down and flipped the brass rectangle over. It was Charlie's plaque. He stared at it for a moment, and then it all became clear to him. There was no theft or vandalism. Charlie had gone back to the church in his shame and exasperation and removed the tablet bearing his name. Tim was thankful that Charlie hadn't thrown it away. He picked up the plaque and saw the bolts laying at his feet.

Tim finished his original task of restacking the boxes, saying out loud, "Charlie, Charlie. All of that was so unnecessary," but smiling all the while. He closed the garage door, went back into the house, and exited through the front door. He phoned Hannah, confirming their dinner guest for the evening, and then whimsically said, "Mystery solved."

"What do you mean?" she asked him, and then she answered her own question. "You found the plaque."

"Yes, ma'am, I have it with me."

* * *

At dinner that evening, Tim's two daughters were impressed by Nathan. The one exceptionally taken with him was Johanna, their oldest. She had been considering Liberty as a possible college choice, and after meeting Nathan, she had no more doubts.

Tim went in to work early the next morning for a special meeting with Nathan. He went into his office, removed a package from the top of his desk, and met the new intern in the hall. "Let's take another stroll." They went down the corridor to Charlie's Room, and Tim stopped directly in front of the doorway. He asked for Nathan's assistance. The package was unwrapped, and the plaque was placed on the wall, aligned with the original bolt holes. They stepped back and viewed their handiwork.

"Nathan, there are many ways to serve in church ministry. Have you ever considered working with the children?" Nathan was noncommittal. Perhaps part of his internship could be in children's ministry.

* * *

The Ames estate was eventually settled. The church voted to take some of the proceeds and build a much-needed addition to the facility. The Charlie and Anne Ames Family Center was dedicated a year later. Jane Roberts Patterson was in attendance. She was pleased to finally meet the Coates family, especially Nathan's new friend at Liberty, Johanna.

After the dedication ceremony, Jane returned to her home in Brooksville. After unpacking her bags, she went to her bedroom dresser. Reaching into the bottom of the middle drawer, she pulled out a small wooden ring box. It still had the original wrapping from the day Jerry Horner had given the ring to Charlie at Nic's funeral. She had unwrapped the little box many times and carefully rewrapped it. Each time she found the ring more striking than before.

She repeated the unwrapping again and pulled the ring from the jeweler's box. She had never worn the ring, only admired it. Her family didn't know that it existed. But she thought the time to reveal it was getting close. The astute grandmother knew that her grandson had become fond of a certain classmate, and if her hunch was correct, the ring would look very nice on Johanna Coates's finger.

CORPORATE
COBRA STRIKE

CHAPTER ONE

November 1985

Nick Weldon's flight was about to land at Chicago O'Hare. He leaned forward in his window seat and looked at the familiar landscape below him. The first leg of his business trip was about to end. He heard the landing gear engage and closed his eyes tight as the plane swooped down toward the tarmac. This had been Nick's ritual ever since his Freedom Bird had brought him back to the USA from the Central Highlands of South Vietnam fifteen years before, ending his tour in the army.

Now he focused on the second phase of his trip. He would secure the premium rental car for his boss, Simon Allen, and deliver it to the hotel. The final step would be to endure the week's flurry of meetings.

The 1985 fiscal year wasn't over yet, but the focus at Buckio Brands had shifted to the upcoming new year—especially the stacked budgets for middle management and those under it. The quotas always flowed downhill. That was the system, and there were no options. Make your numbers, and life is good. Miss the numbers, and fury prevails. It was a simple battle plan.

Nick Weldon languished in middle management but desired to move upward. He would be fully vested the next year, and that inspired him. It would be nice to have his benefits locked in. A little breathing room would be refreshing for him and the family. All he had to do was run this week's gauntlet and pace himself through December.

He arrived at the Marriott and parked the rental car that his boss had requested. When he checked in, the desk clerk informed him he had a message from Simon Allen. Nick was to meet him in Room 200, review the agenda, and plan on a face-to-face meeting with him on Thursday evening. Nick knew the meeting would be his annual review. He'd had an excellent year and was looking forward to his hard-earned reward, and perhaps a little praise.

Nick was beginning to feel the effects of his four-thirty wake up. Coffee would help. As he entered the meeting room, he noticed Simon talking on a phone next to the coffee urns.

"Good morning, Nick. Steve, please hold on for a second." Simon cradled the phone receiver on his shoulder and extended his hand for a handshake. "Let's have our Thursday meeting over supper. We should be done by eight thirty, in case you have to alter your flight reservations."

A dinner meal along with the review. Something big was up—scoreboard stuff, possibly a promotion and a raise. Maybe it all would start turning around.

"Steve says hi." Simon was conversing with Steve Palmer, group vice president of their division.

"Likewise," Nick said, standing a little straighter as he poured his coffee. *This week could bring a lot of good changes.* He began pondering the possibility of relocating to the home office in New Jersey. That would be an obstacle for his wife, Amber, but he felt confident that she would appreciate how important the extra income and job security would be for the whole family.

CHAPTER TWO

Monday's meeting lasted all day long, coming to a close at five thirty. Everyone took a quick break for phone calls and then prepared to head down the block to Cornell's Steakhouse. Nick knew how these gatherings always went. Bar time was mandatory while everyone waited for the group's table to be prepared. Once at the table, everyone would order a couple of more rounds, then dinner, then more drinks, and then the party would move to a seedier location.

Unlike his coworkers, Nick abstained from alcohol, and he was mocked for his abstinence. He fended it off with good humor. Every now and then, someone would say he could at least order one drink to make the others feel more comfortable. He should participate in the late-night festivities and "hang out with the boys." Nick respectfully disagreed, although he knew it made him a thorn in the side to his peers. He had no bar bills to pad his expense account, and that tended to make everyone else look bad. But he had his convictions, and he stood by them.

Nick tried to be discreet as he checked his watch. This day had become very long. His colleagues from the southwest and western states had come in the night before and slept in that morning, nursing their hangovers. Everyone seemed pumped and ready to take on downtown Chicago. Nick was content in going back to the hotel.

As soon as he crossed the threshold of the room, he remembered that he'd be sharing with Lenny Duncan again, and he cringed inside. Lenny was one of the top men to bring in the numbers, and he stood on a high pedestal in the company. He was married, but Lenny preferred to be a free spirit while away from home—and he had no qualms about bringing women up to his hotel room. In fact, he expected peer attention for his romantic prowess.

Nick vividly recalled last year's invasion. Shortly after midnight, Lenny and two questionable women had begun shaking Nick's bed and telling him to wake up and join the party. He bluntly told them to beat it, grabbed his wallet and watch from the nightstand, and tucked them under the covers. He'd hunkered down under the covers himself and tried to focus on sleep. The next morning, he had been awakened by a frantic Lenny searching for his wallet. His cash and credit cards were gone. Lenny had a good time, but his friends, Peaches and Sugar, had a better time. Word leaked out about that little episode, but Lenny was never reprimanded. He got the proverbial "corporate pass" and the incident was buried.

Thankfully, Monday night passed without incident, and Tuesday's meeting was kept on track and ended on time. Once again, the group headed out for bar time and another meal at an upscale place. Nick joined them for dinner, but he bailed around ten thirty, enduring a chorus of jeers on his way out. After he got back to his room, he called home to check on his wife and their three kids. He'd prepared Amber for Thursday's meeting, warning her that big changes could be coming, and she sounded proud of him.

Wednesday, the routine continued. At eight o'clock that morning, Nick looked at the haggard faces around the meeting room. It was evident his colleagues were paying the price for their long nights. Nevertheless, that evening, there was more of the same. He again excused himself from the socialization at ten thirty and retreated to the hotel. *One more day,* he reminded himself, *and then I'll be home.*

Nick rose early Thursday morning, packed his bags, left them with the concierge, and checked out. He went up to Room 200 early for a cup of coffee. The room was quiet, and he savored the solitude. He finished his coffee and walked over to the urn for a refill. The hotel's china cups and saucers were nice, but he preferred paper cups. No obnoxious rattling. He knew it was a throwback to his jungle days when silence was a matter of life and death.

Balancing the cup on the saucer, he walked out of the room and toward the second-floor railing. He glanced down at the spacious lobby and observed the morning's activity.

Something caught his eye.

Simon and Lenny were greeting Sid Kittle at the front desk. Sid Kittle—the hatchet man from human resources. His purpose was to eliminate employees— or, in technical terms, "outsource them." It was well known that he reveled in his terminator role. He bore the title of "Sid the Snake," a nickname he despised but many found appropriate for him.

The second cup of coffee began to sour in Nick's stomach. *Not good for Kittle to be popping up on the last day of the meetings. Someone is going down. Why is Lenny part of the reception for Snake?* Nick stepped back from the railing, inadvertently rattling the china cup and saucer. The noise carried. The trio at the front desk stopped talking, and he saw Sid look up at him.

Nick slipped over to a nearby seating area and dropped into a chair next to a gas fireplace. *Who is the victim?* His first guess was Jerry Sable from Orlando. It was common knowledge his numbers were soft. *Poor Jerry,* he thought. *Nice guy, but you have to make your numbers.* He looked at his watch. 7:55 a.m. He raced back into the room, and the last day of meetings began.

Some of the guys were already seated. Simon was at the front preparing his spiel, but Sid the Snake was not in the room. Jerry Sable was up front, apparently unaware of his imminent demise. Lenny was next to him, looking bright and chipper with a smirk on his face. At the morning break, Simon confirmed his dinner with Nick that evening. Nick had to restrain himself to not inquire about the Snake's presence. It was not his concern. He wondered if Snake had a family. If so, could they possibly love him?

The week's meeting culminated with a surprise agenda: an hour-long demonstration of a fax machine. Corporate America had been much the same for generations, but technological advancements were beginning to shake things up. Fax machines were just coming into vogue, although they baffled practically everyone except the underpaid secretaries who operated them. Everyone present at the meeting was directed to purchase one, but the cost was not in the current budget. It was discreetly implied that they should purchase the machine and bury the cost in their expense accounts. Nick shifted in his seat and kept glancing at his watch.

The adjournment came at four o'clock, quick goodbyes were exchanged, and all were off to O'Hare. All but Nick and Simon. At Simon's request, they would eat at the Marriott for convenience. Nick looked forward to his assessment but couldn't help thinking about Jerry Sable. It was too bad.

CHAPTER THREE

Simon ordered a steak and his usual scotch. Nick was feeling unsettled and opted for a light salad. Simon drained the first scotch and reordered, then he reached into his briefcase and pulled out a thick file. He thumbed through the papers for several long minutes, sipping his drink while Nick fiddled with his napkin. At last, Simon closed the file and ordered his third scotch. Then the assault began.

"Nick, the group president has concluded that you are underperforming as regional manager of the Midwest Division. Your performance figures are sluggish. Much more could be generated from that division. Also, your personnel are complaining that you don't communicate effectively, and they feel mismanaged and left floundering. I have to agree with all of this."

Nick was stunned. He felt like the victim of a cobra strike—breathless. The fangs were in him before he knew what was happening. "I don't understand. This is contrary to my numbers, my reports, all my feedback." No matter what he said in defense, he knew he was done.

Sid Kittle, a.k.a. "the Snake," was approaching them. Staring at the man's impassive face, Nick's recalled a random fact he'd learned about cobras the last time they'd taken the kids to the zoo: one bite can inject enough venom to take down an elephant. Just like that. Sid joined them at their table as the entrees were served. Simon, without hesitation, was chewing and speaking at the same time.

"Weldon, the problem is, you are not a team player. You take any opportunity to excuse yourself early from our social events. You make the others feel uneasy when you don't share a drink with them. You appear to be too good for the other team players. Doesn't help team morale."

After all these years, Simon was referring to him by his last name. It was condescending. "Are you telling me that goals and budgets are secondary, and it's more important to be a party animal and gain social status?" Nick asked. He had nothing to lose at this point.

"Certainly, your numbers are critical, but so is the camaraderie of the company. And *you* are antisocial." The liquor was now interfering with Simon's speech. Nick knew his boss had gotten a head start on the booze prior to supper. Simon kept cutting into his steak and chewing obnoxiously. Kittle, the patient snake, remained silent as if awaiting his cue to close the deal.

"Weldon, there is one more thing that affects our decision."

"What could that possibly be?" Nick asked in a cool, indifferent manner.

"The incident in Indianapolis with Kelly Jackson during the Bell Fortune Trade Show last year."

Nick's instinct was to throw the fourth scotch in Simon's face, but he restrained himself. Up until this moment, he'd believed that matter was completely private, known only to himself and Kelly. That was the arrangement they'd made in order to protect her and her job. Nick had given her an exemption at the time and considered the matter closed. Now it was evident she'd had an agenda.

Simon was staring at him with glassy eyes, chewing louder than ever. He was obviously expecting a reaction. Nick struggled to compose himself.

"That 'incident' involved nothing more than me going to her room to pick her up for a reception and her answering the door, dressed only in a towel, and inviting me in. You know me—I'm purely *antisocial*. I turned my head and told her to get dressed, and I walked away. She later approached me and apologized profusely. The apology was accepted, and that was the end of it. Our relationship has always been professional."

Simon finally reached for the idle scotch that had almost been dumped on him and took a double sip. "That's not how she tells it. You came into the room and pulled the towel off her and proceeded to flip her with it, and then grabbed her and began fondling her—"

Nick stood up and looked down on Simon and Sid. "OK, you two. You can view me as antisocial. You can conjure up fuzzy, back-of-the-envelope math on my sales numbers, and you can question my people skills," he raised his voice, "but don't *ever* impugn my integrity, especially my marital integrity. Are we done here?" In his mind, he knew that Kelly was part of this setup.

"Not quite." Sid the Snake had spoken at last. "Please sit back down, Mr. Weldon. We have some papers for you to sign in order to close your severance package. This won't take long."

Simon echoed the Snake's remark, "It won't take long." He finished off his scotch and motioned for the waiter to bring another.

Kittle began the paperwork. Nick had to agree not to sue or challenge Buckio Brands regarding his separation from the company. Nick knew he was getting whacked, but was aware of the axiom, "If they want to get you, they will." He had no illusions about fighting the company in court. They would out-lawyer him and drag it out indefinitely. *Take the package,* he told himself.

"Unfortunately, you are not vested. You are still six months shy of the required time with the company," Sid said. Nick imagined Sid's office with a chart that tracked personnel closing in on vesting benefits, little red flags telling him when to cut them. "We are extending to you six months of severance compensation. We will retain you and your family on our health insurance for ninety days, at which time you can arrange your own coverage. You must forfeit your company vehicle immediately. A representative will pick it up tomorrow at your residence. Please have it ready and remove all personal items. Do you have any questions?"

"None at all. You're very thorough. It's all so copacetic." Nick saw the Snake peering at him with his typical supercilious manner. *What an appropriate nickname.*

"If there are no questions, please sign here, and the other pages highlighted with an X." Nick provided the signatures and dropped the pen on the table. Sid said, "My job is done here. I will excuse myself and let you and Mr. Allen continue your meal. Good luck to you, Mr. Weldon." The Snake offered to shake hands, but Nick rejected the gesture, and the oily little man departed.

"You haven't even touched your meal," Simon said.

"Sorry, I have no appetite. I'm out of here." Nick headed to the concierge's desk for his luggage. He took a couple of steps toward the door but then pivoted and returned to the table. Simon looked up expectantly, the fire in his eyes inviting confrontation, but Nick scooped up his paperwork and left without another word.

*   *   *

Nick checked in for his flight and called his wife from a payphone. He had decided to be upfront with the news.

"Hey, it's me."

"Hi. Is your flight on time?"

"Right on schedule."

"How was the meeting with Simon?" Amber asked.

"Not good at all."

"What happened?"

"They let me go. I got canned."

Amber was silent. For a moment, Nick feared the worst, but then he heard, "Nick, God will see us through this."

Now it was his turn to be silent. Her comment was timely. "Thanks, I needed to hear that. See you later tonight."

CHAPTER FOUR

Nick boarded his plane, sat back, and closed his eyes. He thought about a statistic he'd once heard about how losing a job was high on the trauma scale, close to the loss of a loved one. No argument from him. He thought of his wife's words of wisdom, and he found some solace in the fact that he was now free to do whatever he wanted with his career. Remarkably, he dozed off. The next thing he knew, the plane was touching down. The trip was over.

The next morning, Nick was playfully roused from sleep by his three girls. All of them wanted to see Daddy before they left for school. The events of the night before didn't affect his demeanor with his children. He gave them the usual attention of a father who had returned home from a long trip and missed his family. Amber took the kids to school, and Nick drank his morning coffee. Then he went to the garage and cleaned out his company car. He backed it out into the street, left the keys in the ignition, and put a note on the dashboard giving the company permission to retrieve the car and indicated that they should not bother him. By ten that morning, the car was gone.

It was now time to update and send out his resume. Nick knew his best chance would be with his former competitors. He would be contacting them, but he was concerned that his termination might have branded him as toxic. Not to mention that the Kelly incident could go against him big-time if word got out.

* * *

After four weeks of job searching, Nick began to feel a sense of panic. The fact that he had months of severance compensation didn't change the reality that he had exhausted all of his contacts. Two recruiting agencies had simply walked away from him. It was as though a black cloud loomed over him.

One morning, he received a call from an old friend, Chris John. Chris was a sales rep for a business machine conglomerate, and his territory included Indiana, Kentucky, and Ohio. In the past, he and Nick had tried to get together, but their schedules always conflicted. Now, Nick had all the time in the world. They agreed to meet at noon for a quick bite—Chris was a busy man.

After their mediocre fast food meal, Chris began his typical rant about his job: the stress he faced with his sales quotas, volume gained simply by virtue of having the lowest price, etc. It was a dog-eat-dog world. "I made it through one more quarter. I had two accounts go under and lost a bid for a school system that I had last year, but the figures weren't adjusted. I got to eat those numbers."

"I know the system," Nick said. "Those cats in the home offices need to get out into the field and learn the facts of the street."

"They never will. My boss and his supervisor have gone to sixteen Super Bowls in a row, all based on other's performances. I haven't been to a Super Bowl. It's tough for me to even get to my kid's games. I'm whipped each day, and I crash on the weekends." He paused. "How's your job search going?"

"Not good. There seems to be a big sign on my forehead saying, 'Don't hire me.'"

"Yeah, you got bean balled big-time. Any retribution I can dish out? I can make a couple of calls, get somebody roughed up, maybe break a leg or two." Nick chuckled; it felt good to laugh about it. Chris then changed direction. "Why not start your own operation?"

"Amber and I have discussed it."

"That's your downfall. Talk and more talk. Give up the talk and pull the trigger. How many times have you reminded me that God is always there to help?"

"So, you are leaning toward God now?"

"I'm getting there, but this isn't about me. The longer you are out of the job market, the more tainted you become. Hey, do you know Sol Pinsky?"

"No, why?"

"He contacts us looking for closeouts and surplus stuff. He even takes damaged products and customer returns. He starts with the bigshots, and it all filters down to me. Every time I have to inform him that we can't sell to his company because of our dealer network. He would blow the lid off any retail price points. He's got some outlet stores, does a lot of wholesale, and sends truckloads overseas.

"You want me to send him my resume?"

"Man, think outside the box. Maybe he's got some goods you can resell. He loves to flip inventories. Every time I talk to him, I learn something. If nothing else, you will gain just by meeting him. Here's a tidbit I heard over the weekend—there's a guy down in Miami sitting on three thousand pairs of athletic shoes. He's asking two bucks a pair, take all." Chris wrote Sol's contact number down and gave it to Nick.

"Interesting. It may be a long shot, but I'll check it out."

"Wasn't David a long shot against the giant? I wonder what the point spread was? The experts all picked the giant, but the underdog won. The long shot came through."

Nick smiled. "You've read your Bible. I'm impressed. I've always liked the story of David and Goliath. God had a game plan for David, and he played it out by following God."

Chris checked his watch. "Well, buddy, I got to be in Cleveland, two more calls, and then home by tonight." They slapped each other on the shoulder, and Chris headed for a payphone.

When Nick got back home, their phone was ringing. *Opportunity or a debt collector?* He picked up the phone and paused before speaking.

"Hello?"

"Nick Weldon, please." He didn't recognize the voice.

"This is Nick."

"Hi, Nick. This is Sol Pinsky. I got your name from Chris John. He asked me to give you a call. Do you have a couple of seconds?"

"Yes, sir, I do." If he only knew the free time that was accumulating.

"I know this is sudden, but can you stop by my office, possibly this afternoon? I have an opening at 4:40. Are you available?"

"Yes, I can make it." Nick hoped he didn't appear overeager.

"Excellent. See you at 4:40. Do you know where our offices are on Durant Street?"

"I do." Nick had only a vague idea of the location, but he wanted to impress his caller.

"Very good. Dress informal. I live in jeans and T-shirts, with sandals. See you at 4:40, thank you."

"Thank you." He wondered if the casual dress code could be a trick or ploy of some kind. He decided he would follow Sol's suggestion—he had nothing to lose. He left a note for Amber and left for his appointment.

CHAPTER FIVE

Nick parked his car and sat, looking out at the expanse before him. Sol Pinsky's offices were dwarfed by the adjoining warehouse on the south end of the property. Nick counted sixteen trailers backed into the loading docks. A lot of boxes either coming or going.

As he walked into the reception area, dressed as instructed in a T-shirt and jeans, he saw six men in suits and ties waiting in the lobby. Nick noticed their patronizing looks, but he was indifferent. He walked up to the receptionist and identified himself.

She responded in a perky voice that was overheard by those waiting in the lobby. "Mr. Pinsky is expecting you. Please go on back. Down the hall, turn left, the first office on the right. It's 4:37—get moving." She winked at him. The lobby patrons glanced at their watches and shuffled their briefcases with their feet. The waiting game. Nick knew that drill. They all picked up on the fact that he was meeting with Sol Pinsky.

Nick found Sol's office, and the door was ajar. He tapped on it and heard the invitation to come in. He entered and was taken aback by the condition of the office: a dozen stacks of files, piled at least fifteen high, littered the desk. The credenza was buried under even more files. Sol stood up and came out from the desk to introduce himself.

As forewarned, he was in jeans and a faded T-shirt. Nick guessed his age as early sixties, but he looked remarkably fit. Even in sandals, he was at least six feet tall. Nick was surprised by his voice: pleasant, but with a sense of purpose.

"Thanks for stopping by on such short notice. Please have a seat." Sol picked up a couple of files from one of the faded leather guest chairs in front of the desk. "Chris speaks well of you. He says you are job transitioning." Nick took the seat, wondering if Sol Pinsky was going to offer him a job.

Sol cut to the chase. "Nick, I don't want to mislead you and give any expectation of employment here at our group. The key career positions are taken by family, and I don't foresee any of them leaving." He chuckled. "At times, I *wish* they would go elsewhere, but my wife would lure them back. Now, I will be blunt. I'm very good at what I do, I have been blessed with talents, but one of my strongest gifts is my judgment of character. Chris gave me some details of your release from Buckio Brands. Hopefully, he didn't violate any confidence."

"I don't know how much Chris provided, but we go back a long way."

"He was candid. He said you got bushwhacked. I know how those corporate clowns think and how they accomplish their missions. When it comes to people, if they want to get you, they will." Nick smiled at the last remark.

"I have a suggestion for you."

"What's that?"

"Eliminate all the job transitioning and focus on your own enterprise." Nick was waiting for a multilevel marketing proposition. "There's always a pitfall in starting another job. A couple of years into it, you get eliminated again. You are now older, and your age and skills have less demand. Age discrimination is unlawful, but it exists. Do you mind if I continue?"

"No, sir, please do."

"I have been successful in spite of countless mistakes. I profited from them and enjoyed every minute of them, and I'm willing to share my blunders with you." Nick realized this was real-world business acumen coming from this man he had just met. No textbook could replace any of it.

"Let me make a proposal to you."

Sol's intercom rang and a female voice said, "Are you in your office?"

"I am."

"I have to leave for a meeting. I'll meet you at home around eight thirty."

"Before you leave, please come in here. There's someone here I would like for you to meet," Sol asked.

"Just briefly."

"Nick, my wife is coming in. I would like for you two to meet." At this point, Nick was sure they were going to double-team him on the multilevel marketing pitch.

A woman dressed in tasteful business attire walked into the office, looking sharp and professional. "Nick Weldon, meet my wife, Greta." They shook hands, and Greta looked for a place to sit among all the files assaulting her husband's office.

"Please excuse my husband for the way he processes paperwork. Only he can forge a trail through this maze. What brings you here, Nick?" Before he could reply, Sol spoke up.

"I asked him to stop by. We are considering doing some business. It's a matter of working out the details."

"Maybe he can liquidate some of the household products that are approaching forty-five days," Greta said.

"Precisely what I had in mind."

Nick breathed a sigh of relief. Maybe the MLM possibility was off the table, and he wouldn't be badgering friends and family with pleas to buy his product.

"Watch this old pirate, Nick. He's as slippery as they come, but I am stuck with him." She gave a look that expressed admiration for her husband. Greta then excused herself. "Oh, and don't let him talk you into going through our dumpsters looking for discarded products. See you later." Both of them stood up as she departed, and then Sol got back to the business at hand.

"Let me ask you something. What do you know about flea markets?"

"Nothing at all. My wife goes to them occasionally."

"Does she come home with anything?"

"A few things." Nick watched as two stacks of files began to give in to gravity and inch toward each other. Sol saw it too and tweaked them.

"Some of the vendors at the major flea markets make serious money. Their biggest challenge is to remain solvent and reinvest in inventory, not blow cash in a stupid manner. It's vital to have the right item priced right. We have a saying that applies to anyone in my type of business."

"What's that?"

"There are two staples that people will always need: food and toilet paper. The person who sells those items competitively will always enjoy cash flow." Nick was hooked by the sage advice of the man in front of him. He forgot about Greta's dumpster comment. "Excuse me, do you want something to drink: coffee, water, or pop? There's water and pop in the small fridge over there." Nick looked over in the corner and saw the small refrigerator peeking out from under another stack of files. "Go ahead and help yourself. Grab a diet cola for me, if you would." Nick got up and retrieved two cans of diet cola. He was careful about opening and closing the door. Those files were precariously stacked on top of the small fridge. He handed Sol his drink and reclaimed his seat. The diet cola was the first one since his meeting with Simon. This setting was far more pleasant.

"Greta mentioned some product we have approaching the forty-five-day inventory level. My database tells me there are four skids of name-brand trash bags in three sizes, some household cleaning products in spray bottles, paper goods, and industrial cleaners. Not exactly food and toilet paper, but they are solid sellers. These bags and cleaning products are all that's left of three trailer loads. Static inventory at this point. If you are interested, I will sell them to you, below my cost since I made my points on the front end. Thirty-day terms, but one thing to understand—you are purchasing them, and I don't want any returns. You will own them, and you need to turn them." Sol reached down into a lower desk drawer and pulled out a squirt gun. After he slammed it on his desk, he said, "I always expect to be paid!" Nick wondered if there was more to the gesture; was it a joke or an object lesson? "Are you in?"

"What's your timeline on this? How long do I have to make a decision?" Nick asked.

"Twenty-four hours. That's how this business works. The good opportunities have a short duration and are grabbed up. Move quickly but wisely. Call me tomorrow." Nick stood up and thanked Sol for his time. "Nick, talk it over with your wife, OK?"

He drove home thinking about his meeting and the possibility of distancing himself from the predatory world of corporate America. That was a comforting idea.

CHAPTER SIX

Nick's wife greeted him as he came in from the garage. "Hey, hon. Where have you been?"

"A business meeting."

Amber raised an eyebrow. "Dressed like that?"

"Yep. Never felt more comfortable."

"Umm, are you OK?"

"I'm great! Where are the kids?"

"They're at the park for another hour."

"Good, I need to talk to you." He took her by the hand out to their sunporch and sat her down on the old metal glider that had once belonged to Amber's parents. Nick had rescued it from the scrapheap when they had downsized. He had proposed to her as they sat in it years ago. He started to tell her about the meeting with Sol Pinsky but was interrupted by the phone ringing.

"Mr. Weldon?" the caller asked.

"Speaking."

"Mr. Weldon, this is Robert Varney. I am calling on behalf of Northside Christian Academy. Your tuition payment for last month is delinquent. I am asking if we can bring your account current. Are you able to drop off a check tomorrow morning?"

Nick felt his stomach drop and got a bitter taste in his mouth. He thought of all the years his three kids had attended, and they'd never missed a payment. Shouldn't that record speak for itself? He tried to remember that this man was only doing his job. "Mr. Varney, If you can give me one more week, I will make it all current. Please look at our payment history. We have never been in arrears. One more week, and I'll have it all cleaned up." There was a pause from both parties.

"Mr. Weldon, I can certainly give you one more week. Is everything OK in your household? I ask because you do have an excellent payment history."

"Everything is going to be fine with us, Mr. Varney. Thank you."

"Glad to be of help. I deal with a lot of families; thank you for your integrity. I will see you next week. Maybe we can have a cup of coffee together. Good evening."

Amber asked, "What was that all about?"

"I will tell you in a minute. But first, I had a meeting with Sol Pinsky this afternoon."

"Who is Sol Pinsky? Did he offer you a position?"

"No, he didn't offer me a job, but he offered a lot more—a chance to develop my own business."

"Slow down and tell me what's going on. And please don't tell me this is some multilevel marketing gimmick."

"Nope. This is self-employment, pure and simple."

"Well, if that's the case, maybe you should consider it. Get off the path of elusive corporate dead ends." Nick recognized some of the same logic that Sol Pinsky had spoken earlier. Amber sounded like a Sol protegee. "Besides, you know the old saying: 'If you are going to work for a jerk, why not start your own business?'"

"Where did you get all this insight on being an entrepreneur?"

"I have been praying. I would rather see you start out on your own and fail than be ambushed again by some impersonal business entity and left wounded by another cobra strike. So, tell me about your plan."

Nick took a few moments to react. *This is so amazing,* he thought. "Sol is willing to float me some products on thirty-day terms. I sell them, and he gets paid back."

"OK, Mr. Sales Magnate. Where's your outlet for this merchandise, and your target market? And how do you know he's not going to foist some bad stuff on you and hold your feet to the fire for payment?"

Nick grinned. "Granted, I just met him, but I sense that he has integrity. I haven't said that about too many people lately. And this is the first opening I've had during this whole ordeal. Do you think I should go after it?"

"I support you. Nick Weldon, Businessman…I like the sound of that. What's the next step?"

"Flea markets," Nick told her. "Sol said the right flea market would be the place to begin. Right product, priced fairly, blow it out. Manage the cash flow and reinvest it in solvent goods."

"Listen to you. You sound like you know what you're doing."

"Well, maybe I'm talented after all." He put his arm around her. "I have to get back to Sol by tomorrow. He set a deadline. According to him, that's how this business works."

They continued to swing on the glider, talking quietly and enjoying the evening air. Their three daughters returned home and, seeing their parents out on the sunporch, they quietly went upstairs. Amber soon joined them, but Nick remained on the glider. He still felt some anxiety over the future—especially making that tuition payment before the week was out—but he was convinced he could make it work. The memory of Buckio Brands—Simon, Lenny, Kelly, Sid the Snake, and the thankless servitude of the corporate world—was beginning to fade away.

CHAPTER SEVEN

The next morning, Nick confirmed to Sol that he was all in, and they agreed to meet at 1:15 p.m. Nick was beginning to understand that the odd meeting times were representative of how tight Sol's schedule was. He felt privileged to be part of the busy man's agenda.

Nick was impressed with all the activity in the warehouse; forklifts and picker carts were working in precision and each worker gave a friendly wave to the head man as Sol gave Nick the grand tour. After arriving at the extreme south end of the facility, Sol stopped in front of a row of pallets holding trash bags, paper towels, plates, cups, and other paper items.

"This is what I wanted to show you. I will sell you these goods below my cost. Trust me, I bought them right—pennies on the dollar."

Nick listened to Sol explaining cost factor as he walked around the mixture of pallets. One pallet caught his attention. "Can you make me a deal on this toilet paper?" Nick asked him. Sol quickly responded.

"Especially for you. I had it pulled from regular stock to give you some incentive. Here's my proposal. There are sixteen skids here, and you can have them for $250 each, take all. You will own them and pay me in thirty days or less. You have the potential to triple and even quadruple your money. This mix is perfect for flea markets."

Nick continued to walk among the skids, mentally making notes. He wasn't sure about the value, but he trusted Sol. "Let's do it." They shook hands. No paperwork was necessary; each knew the terms. Sol agreed to let Nick use one of his fifteen-foot box trucks for transporting the goods. The cost was $30 per day and $0.11 per mile. Nick had to provide his own insurance coverage.

Sol then gave him another piece of advice. "There is a major market up in Cleveland called Beacon Street Traders. Ever heard of it?"

"No, I haven't."

"It's always on Friday, rain or shine. Vendor spaces are on a first-come basis, or they can be prepaid and occupied the night before. All other spots are available at four thirty Friday morning."

"I'll contact them. Be ready to load me up this Thursday."

Sol gave him a hearty backslap. "Come back here Thursday morning at 7:20 and we'll get you loaded up. There is something you should be aware of: Some of the vendors and customers up there are not charm school graduates. They can be a little coarse and direct. Just be firm in dealing with them and use cash only."

Nick got the point. "Thank you for all your encouragement. I'm indebted to you."

"There is no debt between friends"—Sol smiled at him—"except open invoices. See you Thursday. Use our fax line for any documents. Those machines are taking over!" Nick remembered the rollout with his former company.

He went home with the thought of reselling the goods. He consoled himself with the thought, *I guess if I'm stupid enough to buy it, there has to be someone else equally stupid to buy from me.*

* * *

The fledgling businessman made contact with Beacon Street Traders. They promised him a prime location if he could prepay with a credit card. Nick obliged them but cringed at adding to his card balance. They asked for a fax number, and Nick provided the Pinsky Company's number. The fax arrived with all the details—ten pages full. Nick picked them up at Sol's. They asked for a follow-up call, and Nick complied.

The owner, Reno Carlotta, advised him to arrive late Thursday evening and set up. The aisles could become congested after midnight, and navigation was a problem. Quiet time was ignored. He remarked that vendors could get a little edgy, and confrontation was unlikely, but hey, things happen. Nick recalled Sol's comments about the charm school and asked about sleeping overnight in his spot. Reno didn't comment but only chuckled. Nick didn't catch the chuckle from Reno. He was hoping that Sol's truck was cozy.

Later that day, Nick was offered two job interviews. He passed on both. He'd made a commitment to Sol and himself. Beacon Street was his plan. He was all in.

Thursday morning came, and Nick was at Pinsky Companies at 7:20 sharp. He was provided with an unmarked truck to keep the company name from any spectators at Beacon Street. Discretion was key for Sol. Nick climbed in the truck, tooled around the parking lot, and backed into Dock Seven where his goods awaited him. Once loaded, he was advised to get a durable padlock. Finally, the bay door was closed and secured, and he was ready to roll.

One of the dock crew came over and offered his version of a joke. "Hey, man, get up there and come back empty. Sell out empty, and don't get robbed empty." Nick took it all casually and smiled. He started the truck and pulled out of the bay. The feel of the truck had changed completely with the heavy load, and he moved forward, carrying the weight of his new commitment.

He made it to Cleveland in two hours and found his destination in the Flats area in another twenty minutes. Before entering the market, he stopped and bought a large padlock to secure the cargo door.

The Flats area where Beacon was located was an assortment of old ware-houses and neglected properties. Beacon Street was the exception. Some of the area had seen better times, but Reno Carlotta kept his island of commerce well maintained. Security was tight during business hours, but after hours, a different standard prevailed.

CHAPTER EIGHT

Nick stopped at the main gate and went into the office to get his paperwork. The clerk informed him that he had a good spot: Row 19, Space 555. He returned to the truck and began driving the aisles of the huge outdoor market. Nick was amazed at the vastness of the place. He tried to imagine it filling up with customers.

He found his space and, as he negotiated the box truck into the spot, he was thankful that both spaces next to 555 were still empty. The office had advised him not to set up before 4:30 a.m., citing security reasons. There was exclusive selling among dealers between 4:30 and 6:30, prior to the public arriving.

Nick got out of the truck and began exploring. Restrooms were nearby with a snack bar in the next row. He was impressed at the activity of the vendors. Many were unloading their vehicles, setting up tables, and laying out their merchandise. Nick thought that was odd, remembering the office's security warning. It occurred to him that perhaps these dealers kept watch over their little empires with a shotgun or a club. That prospect gnawed at him.

He went to the snack bar and got a sandwich and chips. He nibbled as he continued checking out the market. Returning to his space, he went through the reading material Amber had sent with him: his Bible, yesterday's paper, and a scribbled note that said, "Come back empty!"

After ten o'clock, the bustle died down. It was the inferred quiet time at Beacon Street Market. Nick walked over to a row of payphones and called home. After ending the call, he returned to the truck and got acquainted with his sleeping quarters. He tilted the seat back as far as it would go and dozed off.

*   *   *

After a few hours of sleep, he was jolted awake by a loud noise. The sound was a flurry of fists banging on both the driver's and passenger's side windows of the truck. Initially, he thought the truck was on fire and someone was alerting him, but then he heard shouts laced with vulgar profanity and the box truck started rocking back and forth. His military training kicked in, and he remembered to remain calm and assess the situation. He opened the door and jumped out of the van.

There were five men surrounding the truck, and they quickly encircled him. Nick did his best to keep his voice even. "What is going on?"

"What's going on is that you're in our ######## spot," the shortest of the group shouted in his face. Though this guy was the most vocal, Nick sensed he wasn't the leader.

"There must be some mistake. I have a paid receipt from the office." Nick started to reach inside the truck for it, but the big-mouthed little guy started up again.

"Keep your ###### hands where I can see them." He pulled up the waist of his soiled T-shirt to expose the handle of a gun.

"I am just reaching for my receipt. I want to show you that I am in the correct location."

"You must be ##### stupid. We don't want to see no #### receipt. We want you out of our ####### spot. Can you ###### understand that, genius?" The belligerent man was now was on his tiptoes screaming directly in Nick's face. This guy was all mouth—Nick could easily take him down, but he was outnumbered.

"OK, guys, I don't want any trouble. You want me to move my truck out of this spot. Is that it?" He was looking directly down on his diminutive antagonist.

"Yeah, dude, you got it. I knew you were a ###### genius." At that moment, the biggest guy in the pack stepped forward and pulled the little one back at least five steps.

"Toad, let me handle this," he said.

Toad, Nick thought. *How appropriate.*

The big guy took control. "Look, man, here's the deal. This space, 555, is our lucky spot. We always do really well here. We want you to move your truck off this spot. That's all."

Nick welcomed the lack of profanity. "Hey, fellas, it's three o'clock in the morning. Where am I supposed to relocate?"

Toad retraced his steps and got back in Nick's face. "We don't ###### care where you go, just get your funky ### off this spot." Even before he finished his words, the big guy nodded to two of the others. They picked Toad up by the shoulders and carried him back to his original position. The little man mumbled a threat but was ignored.

"I see your dilemma," the man told Nick. He extended a hand, and the movement flashed a handgun at his waist. "My name is Cloud," he said. He took Nick's hand in his enormous grip.

"Like a black cloud that follows people and brings trouble." As soon as he'd said it, Nick offered an apology. He realized it could be an affront to the black man still grasping his hand. "I'm sorry, I didn't mean it to sound that way." Toad attempted to shout again, but his mouth was covered by one of the men holding him back. Cloud flashed a smile that made Nick wonder if Fort Knox was missing some of their gold reserves.

"Man, maybe you are a genius after all. That's exactly the message I send." He was molding Nick's fingers into a tight ball but mercifully relented before breaking any fingers. "I like you. You're gutsy. Here's what I can do for you." Cloud seemed to think he owned the Beacon Street Market. "I'll move you right here." He took three steps over into Space 554. "Just put your rig over here. This way, we can be neighbors."

Nick selected his words carefully. "I'm sure that 554 is taken and someone will be claiming it."

Just then, Toad broke loose and stalked over, but remained silent. Cloud gave him a look that indicated he could speak.

"You see, Genius, that ##### Space 554 belongs to brother Love. He's had it for some time but won't be needing it tomorrow. He's not doing so well."

The way he said it made Nick curious about Love's condition. "Oh? Is he sick?"

"He's #####-up with a gunshot wound, but the guy who shot him got what was coming to him." Cloud motioned for the pair of thugs to escort Toad five steps backward again and cover his mouth.

"Love is prepaid on his spot for the entire season. He hasn't been here for a month now. We'll fit you in there. It will be nice having a genius next to us. Now get in your truck and back into Love's spot." He flashed a smile.

Nick assessed the situation and quickly climbed into the truck. He was tempted to keep on going and not look back, but then he saw the group lining up on the edge of Love's spot, directing him with flashlights. *This is absolutely ludicrous*, he told himself, but he backed the truck into 554. He heard a tap on the back of the truck indicating he was in perfectly. The group then disappeared, and the night air became tranquil again. It became clear to Nick that this was all about control. He seriously thought he would never see them again. A couple of minutes later, he heard the rumblings of a truck lacking a muffler coming down Row 19. It swerved into Space 555. *So much for quiet time.*

Toad guided the truck into the space with a flashlight. The spot was secured, and the intruders drove off in another vehicle. Nick remained awake for the rest of the night.

4:30 a.m. came quickly. It was time to set up, but first he decided to go to the market office. He couldn't ignore what had happened last night, and he hoped the management wouldn't either. He reached the office and addressed the young lady behind a desk.

"Excuse me."

"Yes, how can I help you?"

"I'm Nick Weldon, and I was registered for Space 555. However, at three o'clock this morning, I was forced to leave that space and move. The whole episode was shaky, to say the least." As he spoke, he noticed a large dog behind the lady's desk. It appeared to be a Rottweiler-Doberman mix with possible wolverine bloodlines. The massive dog growled at Nick with a look that said he was not bluffing.

The lady whispered to the 150-pound sentry, "Angel, it's OK; lay down." Angel obeyed. *Angel?* Nick thought. *Maybe Death Angel.* He didn't take his eyes off the dog.

"I know what happened and who confronted you. I'm surprised that 555 was rented to you, but that's another story. Where is your truck now?"

"Yeah, I was surprised too. The night visitors directed me to 554."

"Ah, Rafael Love's spot. He's occupied it for years. Some of his pals like to be near him in 555. But Cloud and his entourage never pre-pay. They settle up on Friday morning. Frankly, they can be a nuisance. I can have them removed from the market."

Nick was about to mention that they were much more than a nuisance (*How about a direct threat to society?*), but he backed off. He was tired, and after today, he wouldn't see them or Beacon Street Market again. He started out the door.

The lady spoke again. "Raphael Love is in the hospital, and it's unlikely that he'll be using 554, so go ahead and keep that space." He ignored her but definitely heard Angel growling. *Too bad that beast wasn't around last night; he would have been useful.*

* * *

Returning to 554, Nick saw his acquaintances of the night before. Toad looked up and waved at him, as if it was good to see him. *If anyone ever collected characters, Toad would be a keeper.* Nick then unlocked the truck, rolled up the door, and started preparing his wares. His neighbors in 555 were watching his every move.

Nick had just begun setting up when he was rushed by other dealers seeking wholesale pricing. He knew his costs and quoted his packed prices. The cash-flow thrilled him and offset the lack of sleep—he was on a roll. After the selling flurry, Nick looked at the rear of the truck and realized he had put a significant dent in its contents. He whispered a quiet prayer of thanks.

The market opened about twenty minutes later. Ten gates opened simultaneously, and the influx began; Nick was caught off guard by the incoming crowd. Some knew what they wanted and targeted those dealers while others began combing in search of bargains. Sales were brisk up to noon and then tapered off. Customers headed for the snack bars, and a dealer auction began at noon. Select dealers consigned a portion of their merchandise to the auction, hoping to make quick cash the easy way. Typically, they lost money.

The selling in the market resumed around one thirty and remained steady until three o'clock. Even though Beacon Street was open until five, shoppers started heading for the exit gates around three. A few of the vendors slowly began packing up in order to leave promptly at five. Rookie Nick was the exception. He guessed he had blown out at least seventy-five percent of his load, but he was hungry for more. He wanted to go home empty.

Cloud and his group had been observing Nick all day; he had been looking their way as well. He could see they had a plethora of items: cheap costume jewelry, outdated food product, and a mixture of clothing in all the wrong sizes and styles. They also had a huge inventory of cassette tapes from obscure artists that created no demand. Nick knew they needed a new mix of goods.

At half past three, Cloud approached his neighbor in 554.

"Hey, Genius, you wanna sell the rest of your stuff cheap?"

"I'll give you a take-all price."

"I'm listening." Cloud's golden grin reflected the late afternoon sun.

Nick looked at the rest of his inventory and came up with a price. He had mastered his cost on each item and knew where he had to be in his quotes. He decided to play it tough and threw everything he had from his military back-ground to his corporate training into the pitch. "Everything here—you can have it for $721 cash." He knew the odd number would throw Cloud off-balance. "However, any of this you buy today, you can't resell at this market. I'm coming back with more of the same, and it's my prerogative to continue selling these goods. I can get you more at the same deal level if you agree." Nick had changed his mind about being at Beacon Street. He was coming back. "If you agree, it's all yours for $721."

Cloud was quick on his feet, and a good businessman. He agreed to Nick's demands and countered at $629. He could play tough too.

Nick laughed. "$774 and I am all done."

Cloud grinned even bigger. "You're whacking me. Let's do $700 right now. Toad, go fetch my money." Toad returned and handed Cloud a thick white envelope stuffed with cash. Cloud pulled out seven one-hundred-dollar bills and stuffed them in Nick's front pocket. Nick accepted the payment.

"Do you want a receipt?" Nick asked him.

Cloud laughed. "Sure, make it for $7,000. I need a little boost in my tax sit-uation. Helps my cost of goods." Then he ordered Toad to put his cash envelope back in the van. Nick glanced up and noticed Toad burying it in the cassette tapes. *Good move. No one will be digging in that box.* Nick watched as Cloud's crew loaded up their van with their wares, shoving the old goods deeper into their truck in order to accommodate the new stuff they'd bought from him.

As for Nick, he would be going home empty.

CHAPTER NINE

Nick decided to hit the snack bar again before he left. He came back with his order to find that Cloud and his cronies had cleared out, but they'd left a lot of trash in their space.

It was rush hour, and traffic outside the market would be a bear. Nick decided to cool it in his space. He finished his hot dogs and looked again over at 555, strewn with garbage. *Might as well do my good deed for the day.* He began to pick up after Cloud and his crew, tossing beer cans and wrappers in a nearby trashcan. As he bent over to retrieve a wad of soiled napkins, he froze. Cloud's cash envelope was buried in the pile. He quickly picked it up and looked all around. He got in his truck, paused, then opened the envelope.

The amount of cash slammed him. There were at least eight packets of one-hundred-dollar bills. He guessed each packet must contain a thousand dollars. He was holding $8,000 or more. He certainly couldn't keep it, but he felt uneasy about immediately turning it into the office. He knew nothing about the integrity of anyone there. *Eight grand—people are killed for a lot less.* He climbed into the truck and tucked the money under his seat next to his proceeds for the day. His dilemma intensified, and he nervously prayed for guidance.

*   *   *

Cloud's group stopped at a convenience store two blocks from Beacon Street Market. Cloud was going to treat them all to a hot dog and drink for their hard day's work. After parking the van, Cloud told Toad to get his envelope. Toad reached behind the seat and rifled through the cassette box. He came up empty. Toad was panic-stricken and feared the consequences he knew would be forthcoming. *How did that packet fall out of the van?* He jumped from the driver's seat and went to the sliding door and shoved it open, now frantically searching. He was sweating.

Cloud bellowed, "Toad! Where is my ##### cash?"

Toad shrugged his shoulders and hung his head. "It must have fallen out at the market." Cloud ordered him back in the van and squealed out of the parking lot, leaving their companions to run behind them.

Cloud and Toad pulled up to the gate of the market, but it was closed to inbound traffic. The guard informed them they could enter on foot. They raced to 555. Toad was usually not the fastest of the group, but when he feared bodily harm, he could sprint with the best of them. Cloud was close behind. The others had now joined Cloud and Toad where they stood staring at the empty spot. Even their trash was gone. 555 was clean. Cloud screamed at everyone to dump all the trashcans and pick through them for the envelope. Toad wanted to climb in one of the cans and close the lid. He knew the missing cash could result in him coming up missing.

*   *   *

Nick was still in his truck when he heard the commotion. He knew the reason for the hysteria.

"Cloud, come over here, I have what you're looking for." Nick waved the cash envelope out the window. Toad sprinted toward Nick. He started to grab the money packet, but Nick hesitated, reminding him that it belonged to Cloud.

"Man, you just saved my life. Is it all there?"

"All of it." Cloud was slow in coming over to Nick. Nick saw that the big man looked weary. He knew full well that honesty was a virtue missing in Cloud's domain. Nick handed over the envelope, and Cloud ran his fingers over every bill before looking up. Suddenly, he wrapped his arms around Nick.

"Thank you, Genius. By the way, what is your name?"

"Nick Weldon. What is your name?" Cloud looked at him for a minute, hesitating, then said, "Very few know this. It's Sherman Lamar Apple. But only my grandmother calls me by my name."

The reprieved Toad had morphed from a state of fright to a state of hilarity. "Sherman—man, I never knew that!" Cloud moved toward him, and Toad retreated like a scared pup. "Easy now, big Sherm."

Cloud's menacing look transformed into a grin, and he gave a short laugh. There was a sense of relief amongst the whole group.

"OK, Toad. 'Fess up time—what name did they lay on you? Tell me before I squeeze it from you."

Toad stood up as tall as he could and blurted out his name. "Abner Arthur Anderson."

Cloud couldn't restrain himself. "Man, your initials are A.A.A., just like little flashlight batteries. Somebody saw into your future when they named you. Triple A. I love it." Toad was seething but wisely remained quiet.

"Nick Weldon, thanks for being straight on this money." Cloud clapped him on the back and nearly knocked the wind out of him. "You got class. Man, Love could use some talk from you. He's at St. Luke along with those other poor dudes in intensive care. Stop by and see him. But it's your—what did you call it? Yeah, your *prerogative* to contact him." This time, Sherman a.k.a. Cloud gave him a gentle handshake. Then they all disappeared. Cloud had his money.

Nick knew it was time for him to move on. He went to a payphone, called Amber, and then got in the truck and headed south. A lot had transpired in the previous twenty-four hours. When he got back home, the family greeted him as if he had been gone for days. Pizzas were ordered. When the girls had gone to their rooms, Nick and Amber went out to the sunporch and sat on the glider. Nick informed her of all the details of the trip, especially the experience with Cloud.

He was feeling the effects of his sleepless night, but a deep concern was brewing inside him: concern for Raphael Love. A man suffering a gunshot wound and confined to ICU in a hospital in Cleveland—that image was fixed in his mind.

* * *

Saturday was another work day for Sol Pinsky. He was in the warehouse when Nick returned the truck that morning. Nick shared some of the details of the trip, including the sales success, but passed on the episode with Cloud. That could wait for a later meeting. Sol went about his business in the warehouse, and Nick tagged behind. Sol's advice kept flowing: insurance, business registration, legal recommendations, a business plan, and more. Nick was grateful to be the mentee and expressed it to the mentor.

He left Sol around noon. Returning to his house, he continued to grapple with the thought of Raphael in St. Luke's ICU. Nick had seen numerous wounds in the army, and he knew most were extremely painful. He would follow up on Sol's advice about creating a business plan on Tuesday, but he decided to spend Monday morning visiting Raphael Love.

CHAPTER TEN

Early Monday morning, Nick arrived at the sprawling Cleveland hospital facility. The downtown location meant this hospital saw more than its fair share of wound trauma victims. Gunshot wounds were at the top of the scale. The ER remained busy.

Nick asked about Raphael Love and was directed to Room 107. As he proceeded down the long halls, he eyed the double rooms and their occupants. Some were sleeping, and others were seeking attention from the nursing staff. None of it looked pleasant.

He found the ICU and followed the room numbers to 107. He prayed before walking through the door. Fast asleep in the midst of the medical devices that encircled him was Raphael Love. Nick stood still for a few minutes, observing the complete stranger. He was a big man, close in size to Cloud, but possibly older. Then a nurse appeared.

"Good morning. You here to see Mr. Love?"

"I am."

"That's nice. He don't get many folks dropping by. He could use some encouragement. I'm about to wake him. Is he expecting you?"

"We've never met."

The nurse gave him a sharp look. "You a police officer?"

"No, I just stopped by to pray with him."

"Must be a pastor then."

"No, not a pastor. We have some mutual friends, and they asked me to stop by."

"That's decent of you. He's going to need a lot of support. Mr. Love can be challenging. Like I said, he doesn't get many visitors. Just his grandmother and a couple of shady rascals that pop up unexpectedly. Makes me want to call security every time I see them. What they need is to be rapped upside the head with a bedpan."

Who else but Cloud and Toad? Nick thought.

"He's got to wake up to take his medicine, so go ahead and tap him on the shoulder. He's in no shape to fight back. Well, go on."

Nick tapped as instructed.

Raphael Love woke up bleary-eyed and tried to focus on the man standing before him. "You a police officer?"

"No, Cloud asked me to stop by."

At the mention of that name, the nurse narrowed her eyes. "I knew it."

Nick quickly qualified his relationship with Cloud and Toad and the rest of the gang. He spoke to both the nurse and Love.

"I just met them last Friday at Beacon Street. I learned that you were here, and I wanted to stop by and pray with you."

"I don't want to hear from no preacher."

Nick smiled at the man lying before him. "I'm not a preacher, just a believer in Jesus Christ. I wanted to share the gospel of salvation with you."

"Well, Mister Gospel Peddler, as you can see, I ain't doing so well, so why don't you just get on out of here and leave me alone."

Nick didn't respond; he was observing the nurse, who appeared to be busy but was listening intently. She smiled over at him and flashed a thumbs-up. That encouraged Nick to stand his ground and he extended his hand to the bedridden Love. "Nick Weldon. Pleased to meet you."

Love shook his hand. "I guess you ain't about to leave. Sit down for a minute."

Nick found a visitor's chair crammed into the corner of the small ICU room. He pondered his words and then began. "I saw a lot of gunshot wounds in Vietnam, and I know the pain can be excruciating."

Love perked up at the comment. "You were in Nam? Who you with over there?"

"173 Airborne, up in Central Highlands, Pleiku, Ankeh, and every firebase in the area. We were Westmoreland's favorites—everywhere he went, we went. Sounds like you were there?"

"Yeah, down in the Delta, 9th infantry. Came home in June of '68. Hell, I even got shot over there; sniper got me in the ass. It sure didn't hurt as much as this one does. I got a Purple Heart for that one. This one gave me nothing but pain, a lot of questions from the police, and maybe some jail time."

Nick smiled. "God knows your situation."

"You starting to sound like my grandmother."

"She must care for you very much."

"Yeah, she does. Only family I ever had. Never knew my parents. My mom died from drugs shortly after I was born. Never met my father. Grandmother and Grandpa Louie raised me up. He died right after I got back to the world." Nick recognized the reference to getting out of the hellhole of Nam and back to the USA. He quickly reflected on his Freedom Bird flight and landing at Fort Ord, California.

"Love, that sniper could have taken you out. You were lucky he was a poor shot and only got you in the butt. God was—and still is—watching over you. I don't care to know any of the details of your current wound, but please realize that God loves you and wants to know you personally."

Love looked up at Nick and something clouded his eyes. "You know, man, I didn't fear death in the army or the streets, but this place...." He began to drop the macho façade. "Man, you are just like my grandmother. I've heard this so many times from her. You and her would hit it off real big."

Nick knew that Love was deflecting the issue. "One of two things happens when we die. The saved are united with Christ in heaven, and the unrepentant person is separated from Christ. Both have eternal consequences." Nick reached out and touched Love's hand. "Would you like to pray now and receive Christ, and have all your sins forgiven?"

Love flinched, but didn't withdraw his hand. He glanced over at the nurse, who was looking upward and saying something under her breath. Nick saw the man's eyes dart around as if taking in the bleak scene and all the medical paraphernalia attached to him. The room became still. Tears welled in Love's eyes, and Nick saw the combat veteran and victim of the streets develop a look of fear.

He said in a hoarse whisper, "I need Jesus."

The two men prayed together, and a new name was written in the Lamb's Book of Life. After the solemn moment, Nick and Love chatted for a short time. When Nick could see that Love was tired and in pain, he excused himself and promised to come back soon. Love pulled him down and gave him a hug. In the hallway, Nick got another hug from the attending nurse.

"Man, you need to explain that gospel to those other two—Cloud and Toad! Would you mind giving me your phone number? I'm Beatrice Fuller, and here's my station phone number. If anything happens…well…." Nick suspected the nurse wanted to keep him updated on Love's condition, even though he wasn't family, so he nodded and slipped his number to her on a scrap of paper. He looked back at Love and saw he had dozed off. He thanked Nurse Fuller for her compassion and then gave his brother-in-arms a parting salute.

The trip home had Nick burning with thoughts. Primarily, he was looking forward to Love's recovery and hanging with him at Beacon Street. Maybe they could double up on Cloud and the others with the gospel.

He got home feeling tired, as though he'd just run a marathon. Amber was understanding and sent him out to the glider without a word, quickly joining him with a warm plate of food. Nick had just begun to share his day with her when the phone rang. Amber answered.

"Hello, Weldon residence. Yes, certainly, I will get him." She placed her hand over the receiver and called out, "Honey, it's for you. It's a Nurse Fuller from St. Luke's. She wants to speak with you."

Nick was surprised but jumped up immediately and went to the phone. "Hi. I didn't expect to hear from you this quickly."

"Mr. Weldon, Raphael Love passed away at 3:38 this afternoon. I chose not to share his condition this morning, but we knew he was declining. I'm sure you know this call violates quite a few policies, so please keep it confidential, but I had to say thank you for being there for him."

Nick cleared his throat. "Regardless of the medical conditions that claimed him, let's just say God called him home."

"You got that right, young man. You take care of yourself."

"Yes, ma'am, and thank you for the call."

Amber had remained on the line. She had tears in her eyes. "That is so sad," she whispered as she joined Nick on the sunporch. "I hope you didn't mind me listening in."

"Not at all." He pulled her close. *Only God could have orchestrated all of this.* Raphael Love would be having supper in heaven. Nick called the number that he had for Cloud. The unfamiliar voice that answered the call sounded defensive and started asking questions. Nick told him the Genius needed to talk to Cloud and left his number. Cloud called back in two minutes, and Nick broke the news about his friend.

They talked more at Beacon Street on Friday, and Cloud told Nick about Love's funeral arrangements. The funeral was set for Sunday afternoon at Mt. Victory Church in Cleveland, Bishop Terrence Comer officiating. The burial would be at All Saints Cemetery followed by lunch back at the church. All were invited. Nick contacted the VA in Cleveland and notified them of the Purple Heart recipient's death. They agreed to check his veteran status and provide a flag and a color guard for the service.

CHAPTER ELEVEN

Terrence Comer was a wise and experienced pastor. He didn't talk as if everyone got to heaven simply by dying. He knew God's Word and the one pathway to heaven, and he wasn't about to compromise the truth. He never knew Raphael Love personally, but at the man's funeral he talked of heaven and the place Jesus has prepared for those who believe in Him. Bishop Comer concluded his remarks and asked for members of the congregation to share memories and anecdotes from Raphael's life.

There were a few comments about how cool Love was and his respect on the street. His military record was obvious due to the presence of the color guard. Then the footnotes on Love's life ended, and it was quiet. Extremely quiet. Bishop Comer continued looking out at the crowd—especially at Lydia Love, Raphael's grandmother, and the ladies around her. The old woman's grief was spilling over.

Then Nick Weldon, the stranger in the back pew, stood up and introduced himself. "I want all of you to know that Raphael Love is now with Jesus." His boldness pumped life into the room. "I had the privilege of sharing the good news of Jesus Christ with him just hours before he passed. He prayed with me. I was there, and I saw and heard it happen. He's looking down on us right now, no doubt about it. Nothing can ever separate him from the arms of Jesus."

All eyes were now pinned on the man orating from the last pew. The silence was broken by Raphael's grandmother: "Thank You, Jesus." Others followed with praises.

Bishop Comer pointed at Nick and called out, "This young man is not ashamed of the gospel of Jesus Christ!" More praises filled the air. The mood of uncertainty had become a joyous celebration of life. The piano at the side of the platform came alive with a hand-clapping hymn.

The grandmother at the front walked down the aisle to meet Nick. Lydia Love grabbed him and embraced him. Miss Lydia, as all called her, asked Nick to ride to the gravesite with her in the procession car.

Love was buried military honors and the flag presented to Miss Lydia. It was a somber moment but offset by rejoicing.

The group then returned to Mt. Victory Church. Miss Lydia escorted Nick into the kitchen area. She was affectionately hanging onto the young man. "You need to stay and have some food. Put some meat on those bones," she told him. The man who had been wined and dined at countless corporate functions was smothered in homemade potluck dishes. Nick was Miss Lydia's special guest, and he was ushered to the head of the line. He politely declined and deferred to the ladies. Miss Lydia went before him and described the dishes on the long table: ribs, chicken, greens, sweet and mashed potatoes, and assorted desserts. Nearly everyone at the lunch was part of Miss Lydia's church fellowship—none of the folks or their recipes were strangers to her. Lydia took Nick's plate and heaped the food on it, and then told him to come back for seconds.

Nick sat between Lydia and Bishop Comer. The previous strangers had formed a warm bond. Nick kept looking around at the humble interior of the church. He was humbled by those doing so much with so little.

The gathering was over in the late afternoon. Miss Lydia insisted that Nick take food home to his family. If they looked like him, they needed some more meat on their bones too. All this was coming from a lady five feet tall and weighing in at ninety pounds, but full of the Holy Spirit.

As Nick left, a dozen promises were made to "stay in touch" and "please come back soon." Nick intended to keep those promises. He stopped at the first rest area and phoned Amber. He would be back soon, bringing supper home with him. Nick got home and presented the food to his family, and the second time around was as tasty as the first. Nothing was left over, and the girls were asking for more ribs and biscuits for days afterward.

*   *   *

As the weeks passed, Nick became a fixture at beacon street. He always arrived early on Thursdays and met with Cloud, Toad, and others in the group. Bishop Comer occasionally joined them, and a Bible study developed among the group. The change in the men baffled everyone who had previously known them.

Eventually, after a lot of vetting, training and supervision, Cloud and Toad got involved in the Thursday evening children's ministry at Mt. Victory. Their audience was a large group of young children bussed in on church vehicles from a wide radius. Cloud and Toad had a unique influence on the kids, who were drawn by Cloud's big golden smile and the playfulness of Toad, who was just a little bigger than them.

One Thursday evening, Nick was asked by a child if he could read him a Bible story. Nick took the young man over to a corner where Cloud and Toad were reading to a group of other kids.

"Let's go join Mr. Sherman and Mr. Abner and their group over in the corner," Nick said.

"I don't see a Mr. Sherman or Mr. Abner, but I do see Mr. Cloud and Mr. Toad."

Nick laughed at the innocent remark. Cloud looked over at them and patted the floor, indicating the child could sit next to him. Nick and his young friend joined the circle.

Nick was appreciative of his new flexibility and the chance to give back to others. It was an option that had never existed in his former corporate quagmire. He cherished the mentorship of Sol Pinsky and the development of his own business. He enjoyed the friendship of Cloud and the pack, the blessings of his family, and the new fax machine Amber got him for his birthday. He rejoiced in Raphael Love's homecoming and the meals at Miss Lydia's house.

Nick often thought of all those corporate workers out there slaving away at budgets, stabbing each other in the back, numbing their realities with booze, and living in constant uncertainty. The next time he met with his friend Chris John, he discovered that Chris's boss hadn't qualified for the annual Super Bowl trip. Chris's numbers were not high enough. He got his cobra strike, but Nick knew the cure. Maybe Chris and Sol Pinsky could do business together after all.

POP-UP CLOSURE

CHAPTER ONE

Harvey Webber was startled by the ringing of the doorbell. He reached for the remote to put an idiotic TV program out of its misery and then tried heaving himself out of his recliner. He braced his skinny arms and pushed, but he fell back gasping. After two more tries and another ring from the doorbell, he grumbled and huffed and grabbed the walker next to him, pulled himself up, and ambled toward the door.

The bell rang again, and he shouted, "Hold on!" When he reached the front door, he pulled back the curtain and looked out at the doorstep. His wrinkled face split into a wide grin at the sight of his boon companion, Leo Kessler waving at him. Harvey began the complicated process of opening the front door. Two deadbolts unlocked, door lock opened, safety chain released—all of it had been installed by Leo, the man patiently waiting to be let in.

Once the door was open, Harvey breathed the fresh air. It felt good after the stuffy living room. "Leo! Come on in." The middle-aged Leo turned and headed back to his truck. "Where you going?" Harvey had known his friend long enough to recognize when Leo had something up his sleeve. Leo reached into the front seat of the truck and pulled out a small bundle wrapped in a blue blanket. "What you got, Leo?" Leo squeezed past his friend and went into the house. He proceeded to the couch next to Harvey's recliner and sat down with the bundle in his lap.

"Come over here, Harvey. I've got something for you."

By this point, Harvey was eaten up with curiosity. Leo began unwrapping the mystery item.

Out of the blanket wriggled a black and brown pup.

Harvey bent down to touch the warm puppy. It began licking Harvey's hand and nudging him with its cold nose. He remembered the last dog he'd owned—fifteen years ago—and smiled at the memories. "It's cute, but there's no way Francine is going to let you keep it. Anyway, you already have a dog."

"Yes, we do, and Francine doesn't want another. Brie found this little guy under a bush in Vinson Park, cold and wet. Evidently, he'd spent the night there. It's a miracle the coyotes didn't find him and enjoy the snack. Yes, sir, he's very fortunate to be still here." Leo gave him a sly glance. "Look at him, Harvey. He needs a warm, caring home."

"Humph. He will be ideal for Brie. Or that animal shelter over on Mound Street. They won't have any difficulty in placing him."

"Well, Francine and I were sort of hoping that you would be willing to give him a new home. What do you think, Harvey?"

The subject of their conversation had curled up behind a throw pillow and was fast asleep, his fuzzy stomach rising steadily up and down.

"Leo, you are priceless. I can hardly move from one room to another. I got to catch my breath and rest after changing sitting positions from the chair to the sofa. Can't even get out of my recliner without that pain-in-the-butt walker." Harvey began breathing a little deeper, raising his bushy eyebrows while squinting at Leo. Leo had anticipated these theatrics. He knew his friend well.

Harvey Webber, now in his eighties, was a retired structural engineer. He had been the one to inspire Leo to pursue his degree in mechanical engineering. During his summer breaks, Leo had worked for the same firm as Leo and benefited from the mentoring. They had been through a lot together.

"Now, you just pick that pup up and take him on out of here."

Leo finally divulged his motive. "Francine and I are concerned for you and your lack of physical activity. If you just got out of the house more often and took some short walks, it would be a vast improvement."

"It's not that easy, and you know it."

"It would be easier if you actually used your walker."

"Now, don't you go beating that dead horse." Harvey balked at the indignity of clinging to a walker. He would rather wander around the house, leaning on successive pieces of furniture, or go outside with the thing after dark when the streets were deserted.

The puppy whimpered in his sleep and made a tiny yipping noise. Harvey sighed and sat down on the couch beside Leo. "Ah, let him sleep. He looks worn out. You can pick him up later. He'll be hungry by then, and you can take him on home and feed him."

Leo reached into his jacket pocket and pulled out a pouch of puppy food. "Well, if he wakes up, you can feed him this in the meantime." Harvey knew he was being set up; worse yet, he was being coerced. He reluctantly gave in and said goodbye to Leo.

"I will be back." A smiling Leo went out of the door.

Harvey sat on the opposite end of the couch and gazed at the ball of fur laying on his back, giving off a tiny snore. After a few minutes passed, the canine intruder rolled over, stretched, and then pounced on the cushion next to Harvey. The bony little dog snuggled up next to Harvey's leg and dozed off again. Harvey poked the sleeping pup and reached into his sweater pocket to pull out the food packet that Leo had left. He crumbled up some of the doggy chow and placed it in front of the dog's nose. The reaction was swift. The tiny morsels were quickly eaten, and the hungry pup began sniffing Harvey's sweater pocket, seeking some more of the chow. Harvey produced it, and it was gulped down. The pup licked Harvey's hand and playfully bounced in front of him.

Harvey had been dog-free for years, but he knew what the next step was. He cradled the puppy in his arms, grabbed the deplorable walker, and headed for the backyard. Once outside, he placed the pup in the grass and watched him sniff around before doing his business. Immediately, Harvey had an urge and realized it was now his turn to hit the bathroom. He called, and the little dog followed him back into the house, all the way to the bathroom where he whimpered at the closed door. After Harvey finally re-emerged, he looked down at the puppy's blinking brown eyes. This was no time for bonding.

Suddenly, a noise came from the backyard. The pup perked up his ears and tried to growl ferociously, though it sounded more like a whine. Harvey knew the noise was nothing but reached down and patted his five-pound bodyguard.

They both returned to the couch. It was nearly time for the big game Harvey had been waiting for, but he paid no attention to the TV. He sat at one end of the couch and tapped the cushion for the dog to join him. The pup responded and circled up in his potential master's lap. He was asleep in about ten seconds, and Harvey wasn't far behind. They both snoozed until the ringing phone woke them up.

"Hey, Harvey, it's Leo. Do you want me to come over and get the puppy?"

"Not now. This little guy is tuckered out. Maybe you can retrieve him in the morning."

"I can arrange that. Incidentally, I left more of the puppy chow on your front porch. You better get it before some critter comes up there and helps himself. Your new little friend may freak out."

"I will, I will." Harvey hung up and went out to the porch, returning with the puppy food. He congratulated himself that he had made it without the aid of his walker or the furniture.

Harvey made himself dinner, fed the dog, and then they went back outside for the pup's call of nature. After a long time playing on the couch, Harvey picked his companion up and went to the laundry room. He found an old towel and placed it in a cardboard box. The exhausted pup now had his own resting place.

Harvey lay on his bed with many thoughts bouncing together in his mind. One, in particular, gnawed at him. Perhaps it was time to name the pup, but since he had no intention of keeping it, it would be better not to bond. Never name something unless you want to get attached to it.

Leo came over the next morning, tapped on the door, and walked on in. He expected Harvey to be in front of the TV, but found him out in the backyard, under a patio umbrella, fanning the sleeping puppy with a piece of newspaper. Harvey put his fingers to his mouth, indicating silence. Then all three of them heard a loud slamming of a vehicle door out front and a loud knock on the front door. The dog shot up and ran, barking, to the house.

"Are you expecting anyone this morning?" Leo asked him.

"No one today or any other day." Leo crossed the yard to go into the house with Harvey following behind. Leo opened the front door and saw two young men standing there. He noticed their truck parked behind them; it had Colorado plates.

"Hi, fellas. How can I help you?"

"We're looking for Mr. Harvey Webber," the taller of the two said. Before Leo could answer, Harvey had come up behind him.

"I am Harvey Webber. Who are you two?"

Both of the strangers smiled at the old man standing in the doorway. The shorter one spoke.

"I am Levi Webber, and this is my brother, Eli Webber. We are your grandsons."

CHAPTER TWO

It had only been a year since Harvey lost his wife, Bertie. The loss was compounded by the previous years of friction and bitterness they'd experienced with their only child, Jamie. She had split from her parents during her senior year in college and remained out of touch for twenty years. Before she left, clashes with her parents were frequent, and Jamie eventually fled with a campus rebel, Primo Ventura. The parents heard rumors that they were living an unconventional lifestyle with other society dropouts in a Colorado commune. Harvey and his daughter had the same obstinate traits, and he refused to communicate with her, so rumors were all he heard.

Harvey later learned that the ideological Primo had left Jamie and wandered back home to hole up with his parents. At last report, he was working the night shift at an all-night grocery chain, stocking shelves while contemplating ways to change society. Harvey despised the man, and he had no interest in the hearsay that Jamie had been pregnant with his child when he left her. Jamie was a disgrace. She deserved all the fallout from her fast and loose behavior.

The only time he had contacted his daughter was to send Bertie's funeral invitation to her last known address, and he'd never gotten a response.

Leo helped Harvey sit down on one of the porch chairs and invited the surprise visitors to join them. He saw the wary look on Harvey's face and hoped that this would be a brief encounter, never going farther than this porch.

Harvey grunted, "Boys, what are your names again?"

"I am Levi Harvey Webber, and this is Eli James Webber. Our mother is Jamie Webber, your daughter. Mom, in her own unique reasoning, gave us the Webber name instead of our fathers' names." Harvey perked up and sat straight in his chair. He could hardly believe that his daughter had named a child after him, and even more surprised that the young man looked decent and spoke politely. Leo was looking at the two young men, deliberately trying to find fault with them.

Levi, apparently the older one, was olive-skinned with an athletic build. Eli had about two inches in height on his brother and was on the skinny side with floppy brown hair that fell into his eyes. Both had blue eyes and charming smiles. Leo sat back and pegged them right away as the kind of boys his daughter, Brie, called "chick magnets."

"Well, boys, tell me about yourselves."

Eli spoke up. "Well, like I just mentioned, we have different fathers, but Mom never married." That remark set Harvey to slouching again. His opinion of Jamie—never very high—was lowering by the moment. She had removed herself from her parents, had two children out of wedlock, blown off her mother's funeral—but for some reason, he wanted to hear about his daughter. Perhaps he wanted to get the worst over with.

"Where is your mother now?"

The boys exchanged glances, and then Levi spoke. "We all live in Woodland Park, Colorado, which is about twenty miles west of Colorado Springs." This information meant nothing to Leo or Harvey, neither of whom had been to Colorado. "She runs a very successful practice, but she caps the growth. Her focus is on working with the underprivileged."

"Her practice? Is she an attorney?" Harvey asked.

"No, she's a doctor. A general practitioner. Occasionally, she does some pediatric stuff. Mom also visits homeless shelters and runs a free clinic in the area."

Harvey Webber exhaled slowly, mulling this information over. His daughter, a doctor. "How did she manage to fund all that education?"

"She worked hard, earned excellent grades, and applied for grants and scholarships, all while raising us. She's phenomenal." He paused. "Grandpa, Eli and I don't know all the details about you and Mom's relationship, and frankly, we don't want to know. All I can say is that she has been a selfless mother to both of us. The best mom we could ask for. We respect her."

Harvey shook his head and stared at the floor of the porch. He couldn't square this image of a selfless, generous, beloved woman with the girl he remembered as his rebellious daughter. These kids had no idea what their mother was really like. They were probably freewheelers, living hand-to-mouth while bumming the ski slopes and aimlessly wandering mountain trails. They respected her because she was their money source as they backpacked through life.

He smiled and decided to prove his point. "Have you two attempted any college training?"

Levi said, "I will be a senior at the Colorado School of Mines, earning a degree in applied mathematics and statistics."

Harvey gave Leo a look and then turned to Eli. "What about you? Going in for a liberal arts degree?" Harvey sensed that he had just hit the nail on the head.

"No, sir. I will be a sophomore this fall in a chemical and biological engineering program at the same school."

Harvey was stunned. Both of Jamie's sons were pursuing degrees that required intensive study and discipline. He was struggling with that revelation. Oddly, he had a feeling that he wanted to see his daughter. He had pushed his resentment aside. He couldn't believe his thoughts, but he was yearning to see Jamie. Reality told him that Colorado might as well be lightyears away.

Jamie's location there was a just a blot on a map. Then his grandsons put it all on the line.

"Grandpa, we are here on a mission," Levi said.

"Well, I am pleased that you came. Hopefully, you can stay for a while, and we can get acquainted."

It was Eli's turn. "It's more than that. We came here with a special request from Mom. She wants you to return with us to Colorado. She really wants to see you."

Leo had been silent but now asked a question. "Why didn't she accompany you boys on this trip?"

"I know this sounds vague, but the timing isn't right for her to take a trip right now. That's all I can say."

Harvey gave a dry chuckle. "So, if I travel all the way out there, she will conveniently find time to visit with me."

"Harvey," Leo said, "these young men have come quite a distance to meet with you. You need to respect the fact that Jamie can't get away. Take it all at face value. I think you should make the trip. Your quarrel with Jamie has gone on far too long. Forget all the antagonism." Leo got up and stood before Harvey. "Do it, OK?"

Harvey sat stroking the pup curled up in his lap. Levi and Eli waited respectfully, but they were sitting on the edge of their seats.

"OK, let's do it," Harvey said. "But only if Leo join us, and if I can bring my new friend here." The puppy squirmed and yipped.

"We are cool with that," Eli said. Now the focus was on Leo. He had come over that morning to visit his friend and possibly find a new home for a puppy. Now he was faced with a 1,500-mile trip with two strangers, an elderly man, and a dog. His analytical mind was processing the pros and cons. He capitulated.

"I'm in."

They spent the rest of the afternoon sharing family stories and discussing the trip.

CHAPTER THREE

Francine's phone rang, and she saw it was a call from Leo.

"Hello, honey. What's keeping you at Harvey's so long?"

"I know this way too short notice, but Harvey has two unexpected guests. How about the three of them join us for dinner this evening?"

Francine didn't hesitate. "Should I use paper plates or china? Who are these impromptu guests of Harvey's?"

"I can't explain it all now; I'll leave that to the guests themselves. It appears that we're hearing from Jamie again after all these years."

"Leo, what are you talking about?"

"Later, dear. I love you. Got to go."

Francine rolled her eyes and went to get the china plates from the cabinet. She muttered to herself that a china plate would be more effective for whopping her husband than a paper plate.

The mystery guests arrived and were greeted at the door by Leo's daughter, Brie. She was a perky young woman with short-cropped blonde hair and a full course load at Lackawanna College in nearby Scranton. She greeted the visitors with more enthusiasm than Harvey had ever seen her show whenever he'd turned up on his own, and she kept glancing over at his grandsons, Eli in particular. Eli caught it all. *This girl is cute and interesting.*

The meal was well-received, and Levi and Eli especially appreciated the home-cooked dinner. At dessert time, Francine took Harvey aside.

"I know how pop-up visitors can be a challenge, and sometimes there's prep work that needs to be done. Let me come over and help you get the rooms ready for the boys, OK?"

Harvey appreciated her desire to help and thanked her.

* * *

The Webber home was a modest ranch-style house with a master bedroom, guest bedroom, and Jamie's old bedroom. Only the master bedroom was ever slept in. The guest room hadn't been used in years, and Jamie's room had been mentally shut up since she left home.

Francine and Brie readied the house, putting fresh sheets on the beds and opening the windows for ventilation. Francine noticed the dog bowls in the kitchen and assumed that the pup had found a home.

Eli was given the guest bedroom, and Levi got his mother's room. When Harvey showed them Jamie's room, they were surprised at the array of family pictures. The boys were fascinated by the pictures of the grandmother they'd never known. They didn't notice that Harvey teared up as he looked at the pictures. He seldom came into that room, and then only to air it out. He never lingered. The room held too many memories and always set him to thinking about the way things used to be.

When they'd finished the tour, Eli and Brie went out to the front porch together and talked for a long time while the others discussed trip plans.

Leo and Francine took charge right away. Both had analytical minds—he was the engineer and she the attorney—and both thrived on data.

Francine said, "Here's how I see it. Two young men, who are supposedly safe drivers," she winked at Levi, "are embarking on a trip with an elderly man, my husband—who thinks he's Daniel Boone—and a puppy, all the way to Colorado. What could possibly go wrong?"

Leo grinned. "It will all be OK. Oh, and something else. Harvey and I will need sleeping bags."

"A sleeping bag for a hotel room?" Francine knew what was coming next.

"We will be spending some, or possibly all, of the nights under the moonlight."

Although not ski bums, Levi and Eli were outdoors guys. They seldom stayed in hotels, opting for the fresh air accommodations of nature. They'd asked Harvey and Leo if they were opposed to camping on the way to Colorado, and Leo had enthusiastically accepted the challenge. Harvey was skeptical.

Francine had all the answers. "Make sure you get a bag with a three-season rating and a pad. And maybe get something to keep the bears away. I want my husband to come home in one piece."

Leo chuckled at his wife. *Where does she get this stuff?*

The next day, they all visited Jack's Outdoor Emporium, and conveniently, there was a sale. Francine's advice on sleeping bags was confirmed by the experts. Leo enjoyed seeing Harvey getting involved in the trip preparation, but he was concerned about the impending face-to-face meeting between father and daughter. Harvey still had a lot of fire in his tank.

The next day, they put the final touches on the trip to Woodland Park, Colorado. Normally, the boys would crunch through the twenty-five-hour trip in one long ride, rotating driving chores. This time, they had passengers to consider. They also had doubts about the staying-power of Harvey and Leo's resolve to sleep rough.

Finally, it was time to head west. That morning, Harvey began taking a closer look at the truck that was taking him out west.

"What model of truck is this?"

"Toyota Tundra. It's ten years old, has a lot of miles on it, but it's solid. Levi and I do all the maintenance, so it's done right." Harvey admired Eli's knowledgeable description and respected his grandsons' confidence and implied mechanical abilities. He began loading bags into the truck with some help from Levi. He looked up and saw Leo's car. "Here comes Mr. Kessler."

Leo, Francine, and Brie got out of the car. Eli immediately went over to greet Brie. Leo gave his gear to Levi for loading but kept his daughter in sight. The group chatted briefly, then Levi checked the time and announced that the moment had come. He got behind the wheel, Eli joined him in the front seat, and Harvey and Leo settled into the back seat of the crew cab truck. Eli waved goodbye as they drove off, but the wave was intended only for Brie. She got the message and waved back. Francine detected the waving and smiled as they went into Harvey's house to make sure it was closed up properly.

*   *   *

The four men reached St. Louis ahead of schedule. The eight hours on the road passed quickly for them. Each had his own unique thoughts. Levi was considering their overnight lodging, Eli was thinking about Brie, Leo was concerned about Harvey, and Harvey was apprehensive about seeing Jamie.

Levi spoke first. "There are a lot of decent motels in this area, but I know of a nice state park about a hundred miles west of here. Who's up for spending the night outdoors?" Leo was all for it, and although Harvey had never camped a night in his life, he opted to side with the majority.

They checked into the park's main office and received their campsite assignment. Harvey looked at the all upscale RVs as they drove deeper into the state park campground, admiring the shiny rigs. They certainly gave a new perspective on roughing it in the great outdoors. The luxury RVs gradually gave way to truck campers and then homemade campers cobbled together from school buses and delivery trucks. Soon, tents appeared, scattered among the trees.

The Tundra ascended a hill to their site: 254 A. Eli pulled in front of the spot and Harvey powered his window down. "Honey, I'm home!" Only Leo recognized the quote from an old TV sitcom. The boys looked at each other, and the pup indicated he wanted out of the truck.

They were sitting atop a knoll surrounded by the large pine trees, and they had a view of the western sky. Beyond was a picturesque valley extending even further westward. They were out of view of the other campsites and had the place to themselves. They began setting up camp.

Levi and Harvey drove back down the trail toward the park's general store to purchase food for the evening. Again, they went past those imposing RVs.

Harvey said, "They look plush, but not for real campers like us. I wonder how may sleeping bags they carry with them?" His grandson was beginning to appreciate his grandpa's dry humor. He was, without a doubt, his mother's father.

They reached the store and bought some steaks, beef patties, charcoal briquettes, canned goods, breakfast items, and dog treats—all at premium prices; it was a seller's market. Harvey didn't flinch at the exorbitant prices and picked up the tab. They drove back to their site.

A park ranger stopped by and gave them the usual talk on rules and cleanup. He also recommended the dog be leashed due to predators. He said the local wildlife could be stealthy and quick to snatch their prey. Harvey heard the remark and reached down and picked the puppy up, cradling him in his arms. He still had no name for the dog, but they were forming a bond.

The ranger encouraged them to enjoy their stay and moved on to the next site. He was impressed with the courtesy of the two young men. They weren't typical of the wild college crowd he usually encountered. He was convinced that the two had benefited from good parental influences.

Eli started the grill. Soon the steaks and hamburgers were sizzling. Harvey took the lead in giving thanks and praying for continued traveling mercies; no one commented. As they ate, they enjoyed the glorious sunset. Levi and Eli reminded the others that it would get much better as they headed west. It was obvious they were hooked on the mountains, and they missed them.

The campsite had a fire ring, and they put it to use. The four camp chairs from Jack's Outdoor Emporium were perfect. Harvey took the lead in the conversation. He mentioned some of his obstacles in structural engineering and the bureaucracy levels that had confronted him at every step in the planning and construction. Harvey overdramatized most of it, but the student engineers took heed.

Harvey also spoke about his wife, their grandmother, Bertie, sharing some of his favorite memories. Conspicuously absent was any mention of their mother. They were aware of the tension and didn't want to get entangled in it.

Levi then got up, went to the truck, and pulled out a cot for Harvey. "Grandpa, this is for you." Harvey gave it a hard look, and Levi quickly realized his blunder.

"Do we all get one of these?"

Levi smiled and wisely put the cot back in the truck. Jamie had forewarned him of Harvey's pride and obstinance, and he recognized the same strong personality in his grandfather that he knew all too well in his mother. Still waters run deep. The cot never reappeared.

The sleeping bags and pads were placed around the fire ring. Harvey and Leo were soon asleep, but the boys and the pup stayed awake for a while, the little dog cocking his head back and forth as he heard unfamiliar night sounds.

Harvey had heeded the ranger's advice and put him on a leash tethered to his wrist. The pup finally snuggled closer to his master.

Levi texted his mother with a trip update. She texted her own personal update back. Eli glanced over at his brother's phone, and they read her message together. It disturbed them, and both had a troubled night.

CHAPTER FOUR

Three of them were up at dawn, watching the sunrise as it bumped heads with the retreating darkness of the night. Harvey remained asleep while Leo prepared a fire, and the aroma of coffee and bacon soon permeated the air. Eli unleashed the pup, who momentarily growled, but then scampered over to the smell of sizzling bacon. The breakfast scents cut through the early morning air and reached the sleeping Harvey.

He got up and fed his dog some puppy chow, then Leo handed him a fresh cup of coffee. Harvey grasped the large handle in one hand and wrapped the other around the mug. The warmth felt good, and the first sip of coffee felt even better.

Harvey shook his head. "I just spent the night on the ground, hundreds of miles from home, and headed even farther west. Look at that beautiful sunrise." He didn't mention his angst at the upcoming meeting with Jamie. He'd cross that bridge—and, if necessary, destroy it—when he came to it.

Levi's phone vibrated. He saw it was his mother calling and walked away from the group. Eli got up and followed him.

"Mom is up early. Something wrong?" Eli asked.

"She wants us to arrive late tomorrow morning instead of this evening." They both knew the reason behind the delay and were troubled by the request. They walked back to the fire. Neither of them made mention of the pending change in their arrival plans. They began the process of breaking up the camp and repacking. Levi was mulling over their options when the ranger they had met last night came over to see them.

"Good morning, fellows. Everyone sleep well?" He eyed Harvey.

"Of course. Nothing like sleeping out under the stars," Harvey told him. The ranger liked the old man's spunk. He was happy the old man had survived the night.

Levi asked the ranger if he could talk to him in private.

"What can I do for you?"

"Sir, we have had a quick change of plans and will be spending another night on the road. Grandpa is enjoying this trip, and I would like to take him to Fancy Gap to spend a night there." The ranger knew that Fancy Gap was one of the most desirable parks in the west. It was booked out months in advance, but he liked this group of campers. They were the opposite of the characters he normally had to deal with. He decided to help them out.

"I have a little influence at that park; they owe me a couple of favors. At times, they hold some spots back for special situations. Give me your cell number, and I'll see what I can do."

"Thank you, sir." Levi shook his hand.

As they drove out of the park, Eli informed Harvey and Leo of the change in their itinerary.

"Mom called this morning and is backed up with her schedule. She wants us to arrive mid-morning tomorrow."

Harvey couldn't help himself. "We travel 1,700 miles to get there, and now she can't fit us into her schedule? I think I'll call this whole thing off and have you two drop Leo and me off at a bus depot or an airport. We can find our way back home."

Leo intervened. "Get that inane thought about turning back out of your head. It's not going to happen. Give Jamie the benefit of the doubt. Most physicians are busy, and she is probably juggling her workload to accommodate you."

Levi's cell received the text confirming their reservations for Fancy Gap and prayed a silent prayer of thanks. "There is some good news." Harvey was still fuming.

Leo said, "Share the good news; maybe that will calm your grandpa down."

"That ranger from the camp just texted me and confirmed that he got us into Fancy Gap Park. It will be very different compared to last night. The campground is higher up in the mountains, and we should have clear skies to see the full moon." He glanced in the rearview mirror at Harvey. He was scowling. Full moon or thunderstorm, he didn't care. This trip was a big mistake.

They arrived at Fancy Gap by late afternoon. Their spot was confirmed at the gate, and the ranger was cordial enough to share some insights. "You are reserved for our Cougar Crag location. It's our prime spot and is normally booked all year. You have it for one night, and I know you will want to return. Incidentally, which of you is Mr. Harvey Webber?" Harvey opened his window.

"I am Harvey."

"Ranger Fisk tells me you are a real outdoorsman." Harvey was flattered by the comment, and his mood started shifting to a better outlook.

"Well, I do like to rough it," the veteran of one night in the elements told him.

"It's a good thing, sir." He turned to Eli. "Young man, you may need your four-wheel drive to get to the top. If that fails, Mr. Webber can always get out and push." He winked at the beaming Harvey and handed them their pass and a map. Harvey was beginning to show a slight change in character.

They soon turned onto a narrow mountain trail. The men felt a sense of camaraderie with their fellow campers as they passed them. Levi spotted a vintage Land Cruiser pulled over at a scenic overlook and honked at the group around it. They all waved back and gave a thumbs-up as the Tundra trudged up the steep slope. When their tires slipped, Levi shifted to four-wheel drive, and the Tundra took control. Both boys smiled as their truck dug in. Eli turned and glanced at the back seat passengers, who were shaking their heads. Their confidence wasn't as keen as the front seat occupants, and they were holding on.

The vista that opened before them would be locked in their minds for years. They kept climbing higher and eventually saw a sign for Cougar Crag, another quarter of a mile. The boys' smiles became larger with each turn of the four-wheel drive. They were in their zone.

When they reached their destination, no one spoke. The trail ended on a highland table encompassed by rock walls on two sides. The view was directed west toward a majestic mountain range divided by a river gorge with green valleys on either side.

Harvey got out of the truck and stood staring for several minutes. He wished that Bertie could have experienced this. He forgot about the white-knuckle drive. He forgot about Jamie stalling their arrival. He knew they only had one night at this idyllic site, and he would make the most of the stay. He took a deep breath of the mountain air.

Leo started a fire, Harvey got the enameled coffee pot ready, and the boys unloaded the cooler and readied the steaks. The clean air was mixed with the tang of the cooking and brewing. Harvey and Leo paced themselves in the high altitude, but Levi and Eli were accustomed to it. The puppy dropped himself beside the cooking steaks.

Sunset came at ten minutes to nine, giving them extra time to enjoy the moment as the moon ascended into view. The entire disc radiated down on them. None of the men had a poetic flair, but they could appreciate the sublime beauty of the moment.

Leo woke early the next morning and got the bacon and sausage grilling. Harvey was awake but remained in his sleeping bag. His reunion with Jamie would happen later today. He couldn't imagine what it would be like to see her again after all these years. He got up and joined the others at the fire to get his first cup of coffee. He felt rested and had no serious pains from sleeping on the ground. No one wanted to leave Cougar Crag, but they had an agenda. *Jamie's agenda*, Harvey thought.

When they departed the park, the ranger who had greeted them was on duty. They all thanked him for securing Cougar Crag for them. He gave them his card and contact info. Should they ever want to come back, he would attempt to get them back in that spot. The boys were elated. Harvey and Leo knew this was a one-time trip but appreciated the ranger's thoughtfulness. The ranger, like his counterpart, was impressed with the two young men in the group. Other college-aged visitors could learn from them.

Eli was driving, and he took them northwest to Woodland Park. The travel time was three hours, but he took some side excursions to buy some time prior to their arrival. Harvey knew the pace had slowed down, but like a good passenger, he made no comment. He was in no hurry. He sat back and enjoyed the scenery.

They reached Woodland Park, Colorado. Harvey and Leo admired the attractive community, and the boys pointed out sites of interest. Harvey enjoyed the mini-tour, but it was overshadowed by the impending reunion.

Eli called Jamie's office and briefly conversed with a receptionist. "Good news. Mom has taken the day off and is waiting for us at the house."

Ten minutes later, they pulled into Jamie's driveway. Harvey liked the sprawling ranch design, immaculate lawn, and landscaping. The boys left the truck and went into the house, but Leo pulled Harvey aside and urged him to pray with him. Harvey was grateful; he could feel anxiety churning his stomach. The solitude and tranquility of Cougar Crag had left him. This trip had reached its climax, good or bad. They were here.

After thanking Leo for the prayer and support, Harvey picked up his dog, took a deep breath, and followed his grandsons through the front door.

CHAPTER FIVE

Levi and Eli walked into the kitchen area and greeted their mother. Harvey came behind them. As he rounded the corner and his daughter came into view, he almost collapsed. Leo supported his friend on one arm and took the pup from him with the other.

They watched as the two boys helped a thin, frail woman up from a wheel-chair and guided her to a walker. She wore a bandana on her head that covered only a few scanty hairs. Harvey immediately recognized the adverse effects of chemotherapy treatments.

"Go slowly, no rush. We have you," Levi murmured.

"I'm OK." Jamie moved toward her father, inching forward with the walker. Harvey looked on in silent disbelief.

"Hi, Dad. It's good to see you. We have a lot to catch up on." Harvey took a step forward. He couldn't believe he was looking at his daughter. He took hold of her cold hand and kissed her on the forehead. Tenderly, he guided her to a chair. After he situated Jamie, Harvey sat down next to her. Harvey couldn't tear his eyes away from her. *This can't be happening*. He had anticipated a contentious reunion, but this was devastating.

Jamie, the physician, took a medical approach. "Dad, I have bone cancer, and the metastasis is spreading rapidly. My health is declining, and the outcome is not favorable."

Harvey started to cry for the first time since Bertie's funeral. He wanted to embrace the frail woman beside him, but he was afraid of hurting her. Jamie reached over and patted her father's hand. The former wayward child told him, "I am OK with my condition. I've prayed diligently for healing, but maybe this is how it's meant to be." She paused and looked over at Leo. "Hello, Mr. Kessler." Leo was choked up and had to clear his throat.

"Hi, Dr. Jamie."

There was stillness in the room—until the puppy barked. Jamie hadn't noticed him. "Who is this little guy?" She looked back at her sons. "Did you two find it on your trip?"

"No, he's mine," said Harvey. He patted the front of the loveseat, and the dog ran over to them. He reached down and picked up his canine buddy, putting him in Jamie's lap. She began scratching his chin, smiling down on him. Her smiles had been absent for many months.

"About Mom's funeral—"

"Jamie, you don't have to explain."

"I think I do. Dad, I suffered when Mom died. I wanted to be there for you, but I still harbored some bitterness after all these years. Anyway, laying all that aside, my oncology team had just implemented a new round of chemo for me. They warned me it was not a good time to travel since my bones were becoming more fragile and susceptible to fractures.

"You don't know how I agonized about not going back to see you. I wanted to just crawl away from the treatments and make the trip, to hell with any frac-tures, but that wouldn't have gained me anything. My mobility was getting more challenging every week. I did research on all the oncology reports and probed my medical team for answers. Bottom line, I couldn't have made the trip."

She continued stroking her father's pet, and another smile appeared. There was a brief silence. Harvey cleared his throat, wiped his eyes on an old tissue he had tucked away, and asked his daughter about her diagnosis. Inside, he was hoping that he had misunderstood how serious it was. "How bad is it?"

Six months, perhaps. Realistically, maybe three months." The old man who had just heard his daughter's death sentence hung his head. He would bury his child after hardly knowing her. It wasn't supposed to happen that way. He looked at the others, gingerly touched his daughter's shoulders, and began to pray out loud for Jamie's healing and God's grace for his grandsons—that they would be equipped to continue caring for their mother.

Jamie then beckoned him to come closer and wrapped her arms around his neck. Both were crying as they hugged. Jamie summed up her strength and then sent the conversation in a new direction.

"Who's hungry? There's an excellent pizza place ten minutes away. Great food and quick delivery. I may be able to put down a couple of slices. Dad, Mr. Kessler, what's your liking?" Both shrugged their shoulders. "Levi, order three of the Sicilian extra-large with their Cobb salads and get three orders of wings." All of them knew she was overordering but said nothing.

The pizzas, salads, and wings arrived within thirty minutes, but no one had much of an appetite. Jamie gallantly tried to eat one slice but was unable to finish. The delivery went to the refrigerator.

Levi took Harvey aside. "This is difficult to say, but Mom's condition has declined even while we were gone. Both of us really appreciate you coming back with us, and we thank you." Harvey hugged his grandsons while fighting back his tears. Leo sensed he should step out for a while and let the father and daughter talk. He suggested that the boys could give him a tour of the area. They agreed and got back into the Tundra. The atmosphere in the truck was totally different from the one present during the trip to Colorado.

*　*　*

"Jamie, I should have reached out to you years ago. I'm humbled by my own dense stupidity. Many a time your mother asked me to contact you, and I always refused. I even warned her not to make any contact with you. My pride blocked God out. I had the pretense of walking with Christ, but I was blinded by my selfishness. I ask your forgiveness."

Jamie looked at her father and felt lost for words but struggled to express herself. "Daddy, you're not the only one who's stubborn or just plain ol' bull-headed. Mom was a positive influence on me, but I'm wired just like you. Strong-willed. I look back at some of my decisions and actions and realize that many were careless and idealistic.

"I regretted my behavior a long time ago, and I had to deal with the consequences. I made a vow to change, but I failed in not reaching out to you and Mom. You were in my thoughts much more than you can ever comprehend. I knew restoration was needed, but I walked away from it." Jamie shifted her position in the chair, trying to get comfortable. "Later today, we can talk about Mom." Jamie gave a slight smile. "Right now, I just want to say that I love you, and I ask your forgiveness." Harvey was in tears.

The conversation that had been delayed for twenty years had finally taken place. Jamie then made a request of her father.

"Dad, as I indicated before, my health is not good."

"Don't even go there, sweetie. There may be a breakthrough cure."

"Daddy, I'm a physician, and my medical team is honest with me. I have asked them not to mince words when it comes to my diagnosis. Again, from a medical perspective, it doesn't look good. That being said, I have a special request to make of you as my father. I love my sons. I have been so blessed that they are what they are. As you know, they have never had a father figure. I want you to fill that gap."

Her comment brought a smile from Harvey. The rebellious daughter was now asking her father to parent her sons. "Whatever you need, I am here."

"When I am gone, I would like you to stay here in Colorado for a while and give them some direction. They will need some guidance." Jamie again shifted her sitting position. "You don't know how thankful I am that they aren't following in their fathers' footsteps, but they could use some input from a wise grandfather. I know this is asking a lot, but would you be willing to, well, sort of bird-dog them for me?"

Harvey smiled at the term, one he had used often in the past.

"It would require you to move in with them, temporarily."

"I will help out in any way, but will they want to live with an old man who's practically a stranger? I might be in their way."

"During your trip out here, they were texting me and phoning me saying all kinds of nice things about you. They don't need supervision, just a presence. It may even be good for you to experience life away from Pennsylvania. Enjoy mountain life for a while."

Her comments were again hitting home with Harvey. He could only surmise that this was truly a God moment in his life, and maybe the others' lives as well. He wanted Jamie to live and share all of it with them.

"I accept." He grinned. "But my dog is part of the package. He'll have to stay too. He can help me bird-dog." Jamie forced a smile.

She scratched the puppy behind his ears. "We have never had a dog in this house, but maybe I can make an exception. Certainly can't be any more trouble than having a grumpy old man around." She gave Harvey the quirky half-smile that she'd manipulated him with many times as a young girl. It was still effective. He cherished it.

Suddenly, she leaned back and gave her father a look that concerned him. "Dad, I'm tired and need to get some rest. Give me about thirty minutes of quiet time." Harvey helped her up, and she shuffled down the hallway. Before she entered her room, she turned her head and said, "Make yourself at home. Plenty of sports channels on the TV."

He had no interest in watching any TV programs.

Jamie closed the door behind her and Harvey remained standing outside it, listening to make sure she made it to her bed. Then he walked down the hall toward the sunroom but stopped on the way to peek into a bedroom whose door was ajar.

CHAPTER SIX

It was a trip back in time. Placed around the bedroom were pictures of himself and Bertie throughout the years, some of them quite recent.

He then spotted a familiar quilt on the bed. Bertie had made it for their daughter when she was a toddler. He began to recall the memories intertwined with it. It had served as a play tent canopy to protect them from the T-Rex and other predators that roamed her bedroom. Jamie would cuddle in his arms as they waited for the monsters to leave. At other times, Jamie would play schoolteacher and have her friends sit attentively on the quilt spread on the floor.

How did she get this? She hadn't taken the quilt with her to college, he was sure. In fact, he could have sworn it had remained in her bedroom up until a few years ago. He kept looking around the room and recognized several things that Jamie couldn't have had before she left home.

He realized that Bertie must have gotten these things to her. She had to have done it on the sly since he was so adamant that they should have no contact with Jamie. He never noticed any of these things missing from their home. Now he remembered how Levi and Eli had played their role while viewing the pictures back at his home. They had seen them all before.

Harvey sat down on the bed and put his head in his hands. He had been the rebellious one, not his daughter, and he finally realized it. He began praying for Jamie.

When he finished and stood up, he steadied himself on the nightstand by the bed. It was then he saw her children's Bible resting there. He opened it up and looked at all the notes written in it. He saw the inscription from six-year-old Jamie: "I Love Jesus and my mommy and daddy." The memory hit him. He sat back down on the bed, and then he heard the front door open and realized the others were back. Harvey wiped the tears from his eyes and hurried to intercept them, letting them know Jamie was resting and to keep it down. He was the man of the house now.

The leftovers were reclaimed from the refrigerator, and they all went out to the sunroom to eat. There was some small talk about their tour of the area, and then Harvey intervened.

"Your mother and I discussed her condition. Please bear with me, because all of this is difficult." Harvey took a deep breath. "In the event she doesn't make it, she has asked me to stay on here with you boys. She's convinced my presence may be helpful."

Eli spoke with an air of responsibility. "Both of us are aware of the realities. There will be a ton of stuff to cope with. Your help would be appreciated."

"I am willing to stay as long as required, but I don't want to interfere in your lives."

"Grandpa, you call the plays."

Harvey looked at his friend sitting across from them.

"Leo, you may be returning to Old Forge alone."

"I thought of that, but I know Jamie needs you here."

"Grandpa, how long has Mom been napping?" Levi asked.

"Close to thirty minutes."

"I am going to wake her. If she naps too much during the day, she has difficulty falling asleep at night."

Levi walked down the hall, tapped on her door, and peeked in on his mother. He quietly walked to the bed and gave her an adoring look. She looked so relaxed that he hesitated to wake her, but he knew her preference for short naps. He gently tapped her shoulder. "Mom, do you feel like getting up?" Jamie didn't respond. "Mom? Mom?" She was lying very still. He called his brother.

"Eli, Mom's lost consciousness. Call EMS."

Eli reacted instantly, making the programmed call as he ran to his mother's room. They both stood beside the bed. Their mother was lying motionless with her eyes closed. Leo came over and attempted to feel for a pulse but found none. Harvey stood in the doorway, bracing himself for the worst.

The EMS team arrived, went down the hallway, and gently removed Harvey from the doorway. They asked everyone to stand aside and started their procedures. It all was in vain. Jamie was gone. Her sons remained in the room while Leo helped Harvey out to the living room where they sat on the sofa.

"Harvey, I am so sorry."

He looked at Leo with a faint smile. "Aren't those boys of hers, something else? What a legacy she has left me." Harvey had his back to the hallway and didn't see the gurney carrying Jamie to the transport. Eli came behind them, carrying the dog.

"Look who was hiding out under Mom's bed." Harvey took the pup from and began rubbing his back.

Levi and Eli left for the hospital and were informed that her heart had given out. They confirmed it was common in cases like hers, and unpreventable.

Later, they had a family meeting. The conversation was scattered. Harvey began talking about the quilt in the back bedroom. He told Jamie's sons about how Bertie had handsewn it from scraps of her own childhood dresses. He described the hours he had spent with his daughter in that special tent, and how they'd spread it on the lawn to stargaze. They reminisced until Harvey could hardly keep his eyes open. He requested the bedroom with the quilt and fell asleep wrapped in its familiar folds.

The next day, Leo got a flight from Colorado Springs and returned home. He and Francine drove back out in a few days after packing up a long list of items from Harvey's house. Harvey remained in Colorado for a couple of months and then returned home after his grandsons returned to college. On his next birthday, he was given a plane ticket back to Woodland. He asked Leo, Francine, and Brie to accompany him.

While in Colorado, they spent two nights at Cougar Crag. On the first evening, the steaks were prepared and grilled over the fire pit. The meal was enhanced by Leo's fire-brewed coffee. The fellowship was good, and it was quite late before the group retired to their sleeping spots.

Harvey was eager to sleep under the stars again. He prepared his sleeping bag and crawled into it. The pup, now a grown dog named Cougar, slept at his side. Harvey lay awake for a long while, gazing upward into the starlit sky enhanced by a brilliant full moon. Memories of Bertie and Jamie washed over him as he fell asleep.

Made in the USA
Lexington, KY
29 October 2019